PENGUIN CLASSICS

PENGUIN POETS IN TRANSLATION
GENERAL EDITOR: CHRISTOPHER RICKS

THE PSALMS IN ENGLISH

DONALD DAVIE, a Fellow of the British Academy and for forty years a poet and translator, was educated in Barnsley and at Cambridge University. His academic career continued through various English, Irish and American universities, where he taught literary history and verse-writing. He chiefly concerned himself with poetry in English from the eighteenth and twentieth centuries, though he also wrote on Slavic literature. He served with the Royal Navy during the Second World War in Russia and India. He was an Honorary Fellow of St Catharine's College, Cambridge, and of Trinity College, Dublin. He also edited *The New Oxford Book of Christian Verse*. Donald Davie died in September 1995.

THE PSALMS IN ENGLISH

Edited by DONALD DAVIE

PENGUIN BOOKS

PENGUIN BOOKS

Published by the Penguin Group
Penguin Books Ltd, 27 Wrights Lane, London w8 5TZ, England
Penguin Books USA Inc., 375 Hudson Street, New York, New York 10014, USA
Penguin Books Australia Ltd, Ringwood, Victoria, Australia
Penguin Books Canada Ltd, 10 Alcorn Avenue, Toronto, Ontario, Canada M4V 3B2
Penguin Books (NZ) Ltd, 182–190 Wairau Road, Auckland 10, New Zealand

Penguin Books Ltd, Registered Offices: Harmondsworth, Middlesex, England

This edition first published 1996
10 9 8 7 6 5 4 3 2 1

This edition copyright © the Estate of Donald Davie, 1996
All rights reserved

The moral right of the editor has been asserted

Set in 10/12.5 pt Bembo Monotype
Typeset by Datix International Limited, Bungay, Suffolk
Printed in England by Clays Ltd, St Ives plc

And David underneath a tree
Sought when a shepherd Salems springs

Where moss did unto cushions spring
Forming a seat of velvet hue
A small unnoticed trifling thing
To all but heavens daily dew
And Davids crown hath passed away
Yet poesy breaths his shepherd-skill
His palace lost – and to this day
The little moss is blooming still

John Clare, 1832

CONTENTS

PREFACE

This is an anthology of the Psalms in English translation since the Reformation. To avoid monotony, it also takes in certain poems which through the centuries have meditated on David the Psalmist as an alternative model to the ancient Greek figure of Orpheus, and on ancient Hebrew poetry as an alternative model to ancient Greek. The alternative is real; and whereas attempts to reconcile the Greek and the Hebrew inheritances have been made, and encouragingly still are, the tension between them cannot be argued away. It is not a matter of choosing between the happily amoral and the moralistic: the ancient Greek poems are insistently moral, though according to a code that we find it hard to define; and the ancient Hebrew poems appeal to a moral code nearer to us in our historical experience, yet for just that reason more passionately repudiated by many.

There is no way now to off-load the ideological cargo that this body of ancient poetry has been made to carry. Any attempt to reconstruct the society of ancient Israel, or to imagine the office of these poems in that society, runs at once – if we consult the best authorities – into a labyrinth of dubiety, conjecture and supposition. There is no 'real' or pristine Psalter that we can hope to hack our way back to. This body of poems lives only in the fact of its transmission over centuries. The record of that transmission – a record of which this anthology sketches only a couple of chapters – constitutes nearly as much substance as these poems can ever have. Accordingly there is no way to respond to them except by way of the responses that they have elicited over the centuries. Responses in English that we can document from, for instance, the seventeenth and eighteenth centuries reveal not passages in the history of these cryptic texts, but part of their *meaning*. Certainly twentieth-century

translators and commentators have not made those earlier endeav-
ours obsolete.

In addition to the list of Contents drawn up in the usual way,
giving translators and imitators in their chronological order, I have
devised a Table of Psalms in Translation, taking the psalms one by
one and listing the acceptable versions that have been made of each
of them. This invites a different kind of reading from that prompted
by the Contents page, and one that I hope readers will undertake, if
not on a first reading then on a second. Where no version is listed
against a psalm, it may be supposed that I have found none that will
hold its own against the Authorized or 'King James' version (1611),
or else the Book of Common Prayer. And I confess that even when
one or many alternative versions are supplied, I have liked to think
that the reader has to hand one or other of these canonical texts.
Here and there I have jogged his or her elbow by supplying, within
brackets and out of chronological order, the 'King James' version
for instance. If after checking back to these the reader feels some
bewilderment, the bewilderment is salutary and corresponds to the
facts of the case. The psalms are not clear and straightforward; and
no one, whether fundamentalist Christian or dogmatic atheist,
should persuade us that they are.

I claim to have observed chronological order. But this is easier
said than done, as every anthologist discovers. Not every item can
be dated, and in most cases the date of composition differs from that
of first publication. Where certain compositions are not printed
until long after the author's death – G. M. Hopkins is a well-known
example, Sir John Denham is another – the difference is very great
and can lead to misconceptions. To guard against this I have, in
these and less obvious cases (for instance Kipling as against Isaac
Rosenberg), departed in my arrangement from strict chronological
order based on the birth-dates of the translators. Some translators
live a long time, others (Kirke White, John Oldham) die young;
and this too is a difference that strictly chronological order must be
eased to take account of. I crave the reader's indulgence in such
cases, pleading that in every such instance I have a reason for
placing a psalm-version where I do. Ideally, the date that matters is

the date when such or such a version, being available and taken note of, feeds into the tradition. For a tradition is what we are concerned with, and trying to document.

Rather late in the game I was persuaded to put a date at the end of each psalm-version that I print. This is valuable in so far as it enables the attentive reader to determine whether the version comes early or late in a poet's career, and accordingly with what other version by another hand it is contemporary. But, for reasons just given, these datings are often approximate; they have not, and shouldn't be supposed to have, scholarly authority.

Finally, whereas the Table of Psalms in Translation (p. 385) is meant to prompt or provoke cross-reference from one version to another, I have allowed myself in my Notes to draw attention to a few such cross-references that strike me as particularly illuminating.

Of the many people who have helped me with this venture, I should like to name Gordon Jackson and David L. Frost; C. H. Sisson, CH, for the loan of rare and valuable books; Jacque Voegeli of Vanderbilt University, Tennessee, and the Reverend Harold Brumbaugh of Nicasio, California; Dr R. M. Davie, and Clive Wilmer. My greatest obligation is as always to my wife.

The abbreviations I have used are few, and I hope transparent:

AV	The Authorized or 'King James' version of the Bible
BCP	The Book of Common Prayer in the Church of England
DNB	*Dictionary of National Biography*
NOAB	The New Oxford Annotated Bible, Revised Standard Version, edited by Herbert G. May and Bruce M. Metzger. New York, Oxford University Press, 1977
OED	*Oxford English Dictionary.*

DONALD DAVIE

ACKNOWLEDGEMENTS

Grateful thanks are due to Ruth Clemo for permission to reprint 'Growing in Grace' (Psalm 81) by Jack Clemo from *New Oxford Book of Christian Verse* (1981), ed. Donald Davie; to Allen Curnow and Penguin Books (NZ) Ltd for 'Not in Narrow Seas' (Psalm 122) from *Selected Poems* (1982); to Carcanet Press Ltd for 'The Thirty-ninth Psalm, Adapted' by Donald Davie from *To Scorch or Freeze* (1988); to David Frost and Harper Collins Publishers Ltd for translations of Psalms from *The Liturgical Psalter* (1977); to Jeremy Hooker for 'At the Statue of Isaac Watts' from *Solent Shore* (Carcanet, 1978); to Gordon Jackson for his translations of the Psalms; to Faber and Faber Ltd and the Ezra Pound Literary Property Trust, and New Directions Publishing Corporation for 'Canto 29' and 'Canto 83' by Ezra Pound from *The Cantos of Ezra Pound*. Copyright © 1934, 1948 by Ezra Pound; to Carl Rakosi for 'Exercises in Scriptural Writing' from *Collected Poems* (1986); to Chatto & Windus Ltd for 'Ode to David's Harp' by Isaac Rosenberg from *Collected Poems of Isaac Rosenberg*, ed. Gordon Bottomley and Denys Harding (1949); to Carcanet Press Ltd for 'The Earth Rising' and 'Psalm 137' by Clive Wilmer from *Of Earthly Paradise* (1992).

Extracts from the Book of Common Prayer and the Authorized Version of the Bible (The King James Bible), the rights in which are vested in the Crown, are reproduced by permission of the Crown's Patentee, Cambridge University Press.

INTRODUCTION

1 David the Psalmist

The psalms as they appear in the Old Testament comprise poems composed over a period of at least 500 years. It's possible that some psalms, or elements in them, hark back to the ninth and tenth centuries B.C. At the other historical extreme the anthology as we have it was certainly fixed by the second century B.C., when the Septuagint, the translation of the Bible into Greek, reproduced the same order and chapter divisions as have come down to us. The anthology is now thought to be a splicing together (not always expert) of at least four earlier collections. Fortunately those earlier collections seem to have been incorporated in order of their ancientness, so that by and large the first psalms we encounter are the most 'primitive', and the more highly numbered pieces are more sophisticated.

On this showing we have in the Book of Psalms a graph of how one ancient community moved from a Boeotian to an Athenian, or proto-Athenian, cast of mind. These terms I take over from Les Murray writing in 1978 (reprinted in *The Paperbark Tree*, Manchester, 1992); and they must be handled with care since Murray, because of the sort of Australian he is or conceives himself to be, rather consistently tips the scales in favour of the Boeotian, or Theban, against Athens. Thus he can say that 'conflict and resolution take the place, in a crowded urban milieu, of the Boeotian interest in celebration and commemoration, modes that perennially appear in spacious, dignified cultures'. We must certainly resist the rhetorical arm-twisting worked on us by words like 'spacious' and 'dignified'. Yet the distinction is real and valuable: a culture focussed on celebration is undoubtedly very different from a culture based on argument or, as the late William Empson had it, 'argufying'. The author of Psalm 139 is obviously much nearer to 'argufying' than is the author of Psalm 51. As Les Murray says elsewhere ('A Folk Inferno', 1988), 'Unlike poetries of formula and definition, the celebratory doesn't pretend to understand the world ... and so leaves it open and expansive, with unforeclosed potentials.' Most of the psalms, perhaps all of them, answer to this definition.

Does this make nonsense of the rubric, 'Psalms of David'? Not at all. The Hebrew word that we translate 'of' in that expression can as well mean 'in the manner of', or even 'conceived as from the mouth of'. But let not the ascription of the psalms to David be dismissed as ecclesiastical fabrication, so much mumbo-jumbo. David is certainly as much a composite author as, so recent opinion tells us, Homer. But David, as king and poet (also musician, also dancer, also army-commander and adulterer), has an emblematic significance beyond that of Homer, powerful as is the emblem of Homer's blindness. It was – the historical evidence points in no other direction – the fiction of David as author of the psalms that ensured for these compositions a formal integrity that persisted through many centuries. The author of Psalm 139, 'Athenian' though he may have been, obeyed the rules set down by his Boeotian ancestor. So far from authorizing (as some Anglophone poets have foolishly supposed) a 'free-form' poetics, the psalms represent a strict form preserved and observed through hundreds of years. The Psalter as a whole is remarkably, even indignantly, conservative – in form and content alike.

David, King of Israel, is much less of a legendary personage than we may suppose if we haven't looked at recently uncovered archaeological and literary evidence. Using such evidence, it is possible to construct a plausible and unillusioned narrative of how David, originally one of a *corps d'élite* assembled by Saul, the first Israelite king, was able, by cultivating influence with Saul's principal enemy, the Philistines, to supplant Saul; how the Philistines in turn were hoodwinked by David into thinking him an agent securely in their service whereas he was cultivating contacts in Judaea; how the

Philistines woke up too late to the fact that one they thought their vassal had created an independent kingdom for himself under their noses. When they put it to the test they were defeated in a crucial battle. Thus an entirely new situation was created. Only a few years previously, 'Israel' had consisted of a few loosely organized tribes under foreign domination; there was now an Israelite empire stretching from the border of Egypt to the Euphrates. Its creator, David, was to rule it for forty years (c. 1000–961). David, that is to say, achieved his heroic status by a double betrayal: first, of his first patron, Saul; then of his second patrons, the Philistines. But that is the stuff of which heroes and empire-builders are made, in modern and ancient times alike.

However, once he had achieved power, David no longer ran true to type. The vanquished Philistines were not put to the sword but, disarmed, remained independent in their homeland. More importantly the Canaanites, at one time in possession of all the territories that the nomadic Israelites overran, had subsequently in their city-states suffered from both Israelite and Philistine onslaughts; David in power, recognizing the value of their urban skills, employed them as administrators ('scribes'), and favoured them so far as to tolerate their peculiar religious observances even in Jerusalem. This was remarkable, since it was essential to David's authority to have Jerusalem (rather than ancient sacred sites like Hebron or Shiloh) the focus of the religion of Yahweh, and the place where was kept the pre-eminently sacred object, the Ark of the Covenant. Nevertheless, what looks like magnanimity towards the Canaanites may have been only political shrewdness. But then there is the best attested of David's poems, as recorded in the first chapter of the Second Book of Samuel:

> The beauty of Israel is slain upon thy high places: how are the mighty fallen!

> Tell it not in Gath, publish it not in the streets of Askelon: lest the daughters of the Philistines rejoice, lest the daughters of the uncircumcised triumph.

Ye mountains of Gilboa, let there be no dew, neither let there be rain upon you, nor fields of offerings: for there the shield of the mighty is vilely cast away, the shield of Saul, as though he had not been anointed with oil.

From the blood of the slain, from the fat of the mighty, the bow of Jonathan turned not back, and the sword of Saul returned not empty.

Saul and Jonathan were lovely and pleasant in their lives, and in their death they were not divided: they were swifter than eagles, they were stronger than lions.

Ye daughters of Israel, weep over Saul, who clothed you in scarlet with other delights; who put on ornaments of gold upon your apparel.

How are the mighty fallen in the midst of the battle! O Jonathan, thou wast slain in thine high places.

I am distressed for thee, my brother Jonathan: very pleasant hast thou been unto me: thy love to me was wonderful, passing the love of women.

How are the mighty fallen, and the weapons of war perished!

Doubtless Saul and his son Jonathan, though they were killed by the Philistines, would have had to be eliminated anyway if David was to accomplish what there is little doubt he saw as his destiny. And yet, whatever the anachronism, it's impossible to see the sentiment of these extraordinary verses as anything but *chivalrous*.

Moreover, the same gulf between public necessity and private affection shows up, as something David was agonizingly aware of, in the matter of his rebellious son Absalom, whose life political necessity demanded, though David to the end pleaded that he be spared; and (rather differently) in the matter of his passion for Bathsheba, whose husband Uriah the Hittite he therefore arranged to have killed in battle – a sin by Israelite as well as Christian standards, for which David was required to make, and did make, public confession and atonement. His human relations – with Joab, his veteran commander who in the end dispatched Absalom, or with Shimei, the impenitent Saulite who heaped David with reproaches yet was spared – take the stress of this unresolvable conflict between the public realm and the private. In the other poem by David that the Book of Samuel records, naming him in passing as 'the sweet psalmist of Israel', there is in the *AV* what I take to be an acknowledgement of the taint of Uriah's murder:

> The Spirit of the Lord spake by me, and his word was in my tongue.

> The God of Israel said, the Rock of Israel spake to me. He that ruleth over men must be just, ruling in the fear of God.

> And he shall be as the light of the morning, when the sun riseth, even a morning without clouds: as the tender grass springing out of the earth by clear shining after rain.

> Although my house be not so with God: yet he hath made with me an everlasting covenant, ordered in all things, and sure: for this is all my salvation, and all my desire, although he make it not to grow.

> But the sons of Belial shall be all of them as thorns thrust away, because they cannot be taken with hands:

> But the man that shall touch them must be fenced with iron and the staff of a spear: and they shall be utterly burned with fire in the same place.

But *NOAB* has eliminated the crucial clause, 'Although my house be not so with God'; and another which seems to depend on it, 'although he make it not to grow'. In this way the modern translators, following whatever scholarly scruple, have flattened the poem into a commonplace.

However that may be, these instances are among those which present David to us as indeed an extraordinary individual, sufficiently vivid in his individuality for us to resist those authorities who would have it that, whenever David seems to speak in the psalms, we must always understand by it 'as if David'. Undoubtedly many of the psalms depend on such an 'as if'; but it is hazardous to suppose that all of them do. Yet this is implied, if not declared outright, by many influential commentators of the last hundred years. And it is easy to see why. Those scholars had seized on the undeniably illuminating investigations – for instance by Sir James Frazer in *The Golden Bough* – of 'the cultic' as a defining feature of some civilizations, and an important element in all civilizations, including our own. For Frazer showed how common, if not irre-placeable, in the practice of a cult was and is impersonation, 'standing for' – as when a chosen person, at once victim and hero, 'stands in for' the vegetation god who must be ritually sacrificed and dismembered at the growing season so as to ensure that, reborn (perhaps in another guise), he shall guarantee fruition and harvest. There is an obvious match between this pattern and certain crucial ceremonies of the ancient Israelites, as indeed of modern Christians (in the Eucharist, for instance). Such matchings gave ammunition to unbelievers, even as believers like T. S. Eliot strove to accommodate them.

What is at issue here is the alleged uniqueness of the ancient Jewish experience – something that the psalms both take for granted and continually reiterate, which Christians too are required to subscribe to. And in certain ways modern scholarship supports their contention. Notably, the ancient Israelite understanding of kingship is out of line with that of other peoples of the ancient Middle East. Moreover, as regards 'fertility rituals', it was the Canaanites who had been agriculturists long before the Israelites overran them; the latter had been, on the contrary, and in their own sense of themselves long remained, nomadic sheep-herders. Perhaps most momentously, whereas the gods of other peoples were discredited when calamity came on the peoples they had been trusted to protect, Yahweh was the more exalted when the Northern Kingdom collapsed before the Assyrians in 726 B.C., and the Southern Kingdom to the Babylonians in 587. These calamities were interpreted by the Israelites as just punishments for their failure to keep the covenant that their god had made with them, and they with him; their prophets had told them that this would happen if they didn't keep their side of the bargain, and so the calamities that came upon them were further and perhaps conclusive proof that their god was just, and would keep his promises. Such an understanding of covenant, between a god and his chosen people, does indeed seem to have been peculiar to the Israelites. This oddity, this 'chosen-ness', is overlooked whenever David is presented as just one more instance in the category 'priest-king'.

Particularly to the point, in this connection, are the fourteen psalms which have headings linking them to events in David's career as we know it from the two books of Samuel. To be sure, these may be regarded as editorial glosses introduced long after David was dead and gone. But in the case, for instance, of the long and bafflingly specific headnote to Psalm 60 (given in *AV*, but not *BCP*), we can only suppose that, if indeed this is a gloss by an editor, that editor was an antiquarian pedant. In fact the headnote or long title, backed up in the body of the psalm by a litany of obscure and ill-assorted place-names, suggests rather a genuine though doubtless mutilated testimony from Davidic times. And on the other hand, if indeed we have to deal with an intrusive editor, his antiquarianism is itself significant: it supports the notion that among the ancient Israelites we are concerned with an intellectual elite whose motives were, however crudely, historiographic rather than mythopoeic. David for them was historical, not a cultic necessity. Psalm 63 with its headnote is a clear example of how a poem can be drained of meaning, once David is seen as other than a historical person operating among quite specific historical contingencies of time and place. In short, when we engage with the psalms the name 'David' cannot always be set inside quotation-marks.

Outside quotation-marks David is in many ways fearsome; and the fearsomeness must be acknowledged. We can never again, though some pretend otherwise, extol the psalms as Richard Hooker did under Elizabeth I:

What is there necessary for man to know which the psalms are not notable to teach? They are to beginners an easy and familiar introduction, a mighty augmentation of all virtue and knowledge in such as are entered before, a strong confirmation to the most perfect among others. Heroical magnanimity, exquisite justice, grave moderation, exact wisdom, repentance unfeigned, unwearied patience, the mysteries of God, the sufferings of Christ, the terrors of wrath, the comforts of grace, the works of Providence over this world, and the promised joys of that world which is to come, all good necessarily to be either known or done or had, this one celestial fountain yieldeth.

Among several things that stand between us and Hooker's sublimely eloquent naivety (for so it must seem to us), there is what the poet Eleanor Wilner points to when she speaks of 'the historical horrors attendant on heroizing male rage'. This is, she says 'a cultural habit which is intrinsic to both source books of the Western tradition. The anger of Achilles. The wrath of God. And the darker the deed, the brighter the fiction it has generated, the worst atrocities requiring nothing less than divine sanction.'* At this point it seems she goes wrong; for in our century neither the Stalinist nor the Hitlerite atrocities, surely not the least among the historical horrors she exhorts us to contemplate, pretended to divine sanction (but to 'science' or else a Hegelian philosophy of history). And she is wrong more momentously when she treats the anger of Achilles and the wrath of God as on a par. For Achilles is a man, whereas God is ... well, a god; that is to say, a Being who by definition eludes such man-based criteria as adequate motivation. What can it mean for a god to have motives? The ancient Greeks, by ascribing motives to their gods, thereby demoted them to the status of men and women. Yahweh was never so demoted. Hooker, who as we have seen listed 'the terrors of wrath' among 'good necessarily to be either known or done or had', elsewhere in *The Laws of Ecclesiastical Polity* (Book VI, Chapter V, 4) takes care to guard against a misunderstanding like Eleanor Wilner's:

* 'Sujata Bhatt in conversation with Eleanor Wilner', *PN Review*, 90 (1993), pp. 34–40.

Anger and mercy are in us passions; but in him not so. 'God', saith St Basil, 'is no ways passionate, but because the punishments which his judgments do inflict are, like effects of indignation, severe and grievous to such as suffer them, therefore we term the revenge which he taketh upon sinners, anger: and the withdrawing of his plagues, mercy.' 'His wrath', saith St Augustine, 'is not as ours, the trouble of a mind disturbed and disquieted with things amiss, but a calm, unpassionate, and just assignation of dreadful punishment to be their portion which have disobeyed; his mercy a free determination of all felicity and happiness unto men, except their sins remain as a bar between it and them.'

Hooker's appeal to St Basil and St Augustine isn't a feeble resting on hoary authority; they, like him, take seriously the consequences of making an absolute distinction between the divine and the human. 'Wrath', in the expression 'wrath of God', is not, and *logically cannot be*, an intensive form of the word 'anger', in the expression 'anger of Achilles'.

However, it is idle to pretend that the author of Psalm 78 held this distinction steadily in mind, or that it was in the mind of his first and subsequent hearers. In that psalm and in many others God's wrath is so perfunctorily distinguished from the anger of his human agents – David, Ahab, why not Sennacherib? Why not Nebuchadnezzar? – that we have to concede Eleanor Wilner's charge, that 'heroizing male rage' lies against these ancient poems only a little less heavily than against the *Iliad*. Speaking in the immediate aftermath of Operation Desert Storm ('the deaths of tens of thousands of children from a ruined electrical and water system . . . a land left burning, a poisoned gulf . . .') she says, passionately and persuasively:

Now if there is anything poetry is about, it is about assuring continuity while preventing repetition. Remember the quotation they so often repeated in school – 'those who don't know history are condemned to repeat it'. But maybe the opposite is true. Maybe it is precisely the history we know that we are condemned to repeat. And that, I guess, is why I think it is necessary to go back to the founding fictions of Western culture to alter them, to take them out of the deep freeze of received truth and put them back into time's continuum in order to imagine another history.*

But imagining another history was precisely what the authors of the New Testament did when they conceived the Son of David as Jesus, he who said, 'Turn the other cheek.' This alternative history, it may be thought, has turned out no less woeful than the history it sought to supplant; in Christian terms, mankind has muffed its second chance as certainly as it muffed its first – we have broken the second covenant as our forefathers broke the first. But the many who sought to Christianize the psalms even as they paraphrased them are not to be set down as ignoramuses or hypocrites, in either case falsifiers. Hooker and after him such as Isaac Watts were trying to 'imagine another history'; and we do no service at all if we insist on reinstating the original barbaric history behind and beneath their Christianizings. In that alternative history human rage – as it may be, David's – will be less admired, less 'heroized', than in the first history. But 'the wrath of God' will be as essential to the revised reading of history as it was to the unrevised.

2 Translating the Bible

Of all the translators in this anthology none will be so influential in the foreseeable future as David L. Frost. This is because his versions of the 150 psalms are bound up with The Alternative Service Book (1980; reprinted 1984), having previously appeared in *An Australian Prayer Book* (1977). Other churches, for instance the Church of Ireland, have announced their intention to follow suit. Though the Alternative Service Book is still vigorously resisted in many quarters and at different levels (see *No Alternative. The Prayer Book Contro-versy*, edited by David Martin and Peter Mullen, Oxford, 1981), its victory over *BCP* seems already assured, backed as it is by the

* ibid.

Church of England Synod and a majority of the clergy. Accordingly we can see a time when Coverdale's versions in the Book of Common Prayer will be consulted only by connoisseurs and historians, superseded for churchgoers and thereafter for most others by the versions of Professor Frost. Inevitably therefore, for those like myself who deplore the Alternative Service Book, Frost is declared guilty by association. But this is not fair to him. Though his *Liturgical Psalter* (as it is called, when published independently of the Prayer Books) was by no means a one-man effort, yet it came into being by a very different process from the Alternative Service Book. In particular the eight Hebraists who supported and advised Frost agreed with him that they must 'avoid the flatness of what has been described as "committee English"' – a danger that, through fifteen years of work on the Prayer Book, the Church of England Liturgical Commission seems to have been quite unconcerned about. The difference shows; and the English of *The Liturgical Psalter* is consistently more sensitive and more sensible than the 'committee English' of what precedes it in the Alternative Service Book – largely, we may suppose, because the responsibility for that English rested in the end with one man, Frost.

David Frost explained and defended his translations in 1980 in his Morpeth Lectures for the Diocese and University of Newcastle, New South Wales.* Much of the time Frost is sensible and instructive, notably when he appeals to that pioneering classic of translation theory in English, John Dryden's preface to his version of Ovid's *Epistles*. Dryden there distinguishes three paths open to any translator: *metaphrase*, *paraphrase* and *imitation*. And Frost comments, justly enough: 'The success in our century of imitations like Ezra Pound's "Wayfarer" from the Anglo-Saxon ... has tended to make us forget that Dryden himself preferred the middle way of *paraphrase*' – which is, we are to understand, the way that Frost himself has chosen. But in *paraphrase*, Dryden says, the words of an author 'are not so strictly followed as his sense, and that too is amplified, but not altered'. This, as has often been remarked, allows the paraphrast

* *Making the Liturgical Psalter* (Grove Books, Bramcote, Notts., 1981).

considerable freedom, so much so that Pound's 'Wayfarer' may as well be considered paraphrase as imitation. Moreover Dryden's definition supposes that the *sense* of the author to be translated is never in doubt. And Frost himself points out that the sense of the psalmists is by no means so clear as that:

With ancient Hebrew we find ourselves in the situation we might be in if we were expected to translate the works of Shakespeare, when no other writing in the English language had survived. Words, phrases, constructions, idioms, references to events or customs cannot be certainly interpreted, because they occur nowhere else in the Bible. Even worse, we cannot always be sure that the written text is accurate, for though it was carefully copied, at first only the consonants were written down, and the vowels were added centuries later, having in the interval been handed down from scribe to scribe, each of whom coached his successor in his recollection of what vowels went with what consonants.

Add to this that 'biblical Hebrew has no clear way of distinguishing past, present or future action through the verb', and we may conclude that the texts to be translated were not such that paraphrase, in the sense that Dryden gave to it, was an option. We may be grateful that, by supposing they were paraphrasts, Frost and his colleagues spared us sprightly or cocky modernizings. But in Dryden's sense of the matter they were not, because they could not be, paraphrasing. Their aims were engagingly and reverently modest; but the nature of the texts they were dealing with must have obliged them to be, from time to time, immodest in practice.

It's not hard to find places where they have done this; a ready instance is their elimination of 'shield' from the close of Psalm 47. But such radical revisions are masked by the steady equability that David Frost imposes on *The Liturgical Psalter* as a whole. Frost is well aware of this, and eager to defend it. 'The translator', he says, 'must maintain an appropriate level of diction.' And again, 'a recurrent fault in modern translations of the Bible is their inability to sustain an appropriate level of language . . .' But where does this 'must' come from? Who except David Frost decided that 'an appropriate level of diction', or 'an appropriate level of language', is called for? (Diction isn't the same as language, but let that pass.) And 'appropriate' begs every question in sight. Appropriate to what? To Sunday morning sung Eucharist in a rural parish church in England? But why should *that* occasion be made the standard for all others? And if we check back to the Hebrew originals, it seems we have to deal with poems composed many centuries apart, by individuals no less separated by temperament as well as time: poems serving, or adapted to serve, quite different ritual or non-ritual occasions. It is in the highest degree unlikely that the diction of such poems, originating as they do in such dissimilar historical circumstances, should be of the same 'level'. If this is so, then a radical readjustment of the level of diction between one psalm and the next, so far from reflecting discredit on the translator, should be thought to count unto him for virtue. David Frost's arbitrary requirement of 'an appropriate level' rules all such more adventurous versions out of court; though in English Renaissance verse, like the Countess of Pembroke's or Donne's, a lurch or switch from formal to colloquial English seems often to signal an intensifying of concern. Moreover, since many of the psalms are now thought to be composites, we may expect to find such changing of levels inside a given psalm, not just between one psalm and the next.

But these objections from literary history are in any case secondary. We need only appeal to our own experience to recognize that such equability as Frost asks for and effects is, in the event, soporific. His undemanding but agreeable rhythms lull us too comfortably. One need not be any sort of militant evangelical to think that on the contrary what we need is to be stirred *awake*. This is as true of thoroughly secular poetry as of religious. David Frost (he is explicit about it) comes down on the side of decorum. But in the case of Ezra Pound and of poets influenced by him, including the young T. S. Eliot, the basic stratagem this century has been calculated *in*decorum. This is a continually wasting asset, since it depends on an awareness by the reader of the decorums that have been flouted: an awareness that, as the years pass, can be depended on less and less.

However much they are thus 'of their period' and will in time be dated, more venturesome versions – like Gordon Jackson's – at their best shock us into attentiveness, as Frost's don't, and by his own account don't aim to. Thus the difference between their versions and his is not the difference between Dryden's 'imitation' and his 'paraphrase'; it rests on a different understanding of history, and hence of what we stand most in need of.

What is striking of course, and lamentable in the perspective of this anthology, is that Frost's *Liturgical Psalter* has never been considered as what it is: for good or ill, a *literary* exploit. Translating the psalms is now thought to be a sub-literary activity, properly to be considered only in the very rarefied and marginal context of ecclesiastical politics. Miles Coverdale has been supplanted after four hundred years. The overthrow has gone unremarked by the literary community, and the name of Coverdale's supplanter is hardly known.

We are not called upon to beat our breasts. For this is not a specifically modern catastrophe, but rather the culmination of something that has been gathering head for two hundred years. As I assembled items for this anthology I was astonished to find how unequivocal the historical record is: through four centuries there is hardly a poet of even modest ambition who does not feel the need to try his hand at paraphrasing some part of Scripture, most often the psalms; but Robert Burns, hardly the most pious of our poets, is the last in this line; thereafter the task is delegated to worthy persons who make few or no pretensions to being poets in (as we oddly say) their own right. Some of these Victorian translators were indeed worthy; and I hope their representation in these pages will prove their worth. But Wordsworth and Coleridge and Southey, Tennyson and Browning and Arnold, Elizabeth Barrett and Christina Rossetti – they have yielded me nothing at all. (I have clutched gratefully at one poem by John Clare, two by Thomas Hardy – exceptions to the sorry rule.) This quite sudden development has nothing to do with any falling away from the Faith; for Christina Rossetti was nothing if not devout, and all the other Victorians I have named worried about Christian faith, often at length and strenuously – though not in a form that could claim a place in this anthology, however I might bend the rules. Moreover, I have failed to find any correlation with developments in socio-economic history. And so I am forced to find the root cause nowhere but in ideology – and in an ideology generated inside literature, not imposed on it from outside. In short, it was the Romantic Movement that put paid to the long endeavour that I have tried to illustrate from the sixteenth through the eighteenth centuries. Self-expression, individualism and originality – these three principles of Romanticism, variously understood and variously combined, produced a climate of ideas in which it could seem beneath the poet's dignity for him to subject his 'genius' to anything so servile as the rendering of an ancient canonical text. Poets were creatures too splendidly and severally irreplaceable for them to bend their necks to such a yoke; that notion, still rife among us, has created the two-tier literary hierarchy in which any poet, however self-regarding, is thought essentially superior to any translator, however scrupulous and inventive. The present century has seen resolute attempts to turn this tide back, and to recover more ancient principles reaching back not just to the Renaissance but as far as Aristotle. The tide, however, continues to run – as the lack of attention given to Frost's *Liturgical Psalter* eloquently shows.

This explains why I have been unable to represent, as fully as I had hoped and intended, English-speaking literatures outside the British Isles. Those literatures found a voice mostly in Romantic or post-Romantic times; and accordingly their writings suffer from the Romantic assumption that the translation of ancient texts was a task too servile for the true poet to stoop to. Moreover, English and Scottish emigrants to, for instance, New Zealand would tend to use through many generations the English or Scottish texts, supposed canonical, that the first pioneers had brought with them. On the other hand I cannot explain why women poets, with the solitary and of course momentous exception of the Countess of Pembroke, fail to appear in these pages. I can assure anyone who cares that it is not for the want of looking.

3 *The Psalms as Poems*

If I were to represent Miles Coverdale (1488–1568) by only one of his psalm-versions, it might be Psalm 51:

> 1. Have mercy upon me, O God, after thy great goodness: according to the multitude of thy mercies do away my offences.
>
> 2. Wash me throughly from my wickedness: and cleanse me from my sin.
>
> 3. For I acknowledge my faults: and my sin is ever before me.
>
> 4. Against thee only have I sinned, and done this evil in thy sight: that thou mightest be justified, and clear when thou art judged.
>
> 5. Behold, I was shapen in wickedness: and in sin hath my mother conceived me.
>
> 6. But lo, thou requirest truth in the inward parts: and shalt make me to understand wisdom secretly.
>
> 7. Thou shalt purge me with hyssop, and I shall be clean: thou shalt wash me, and I shall be whiter than snow.
>
> 8. Thou shalt make me hear of joy and gladness: that the bones which thou hast broken may rejoice.
>
> 9. Turn thy face from my sins: and put out all my misdeeds.
>
> 10. Make me a clean heart, O God: and renew a right spirit within me.
>
> 11. Cast me not away from thy presence: and take not thy holy Spirit from me.
>
> 12. O give me the comfort of thy help again: and stablish me with thy free Spirit.
>
> 13. Then shall I teach thy ways unto the wicked: and sinners shall be converted unto thee.
>
> 14. Deliver me from blood-guiltiness, O God, thou that art the God of my health: and my tongue shall sing of thy righteousness.
>
> 15. Thou shalt open my lips, O Lord: and my mouth shall shew thy praise.
>
> 16. For thou desirest no sacrifice, else would I give it thee: but thou delightest not in burnt-offerings.
>
> 17. The sacrifice of God is a troubled spirit: a broken and contrite heart, O God, shalt thou not despise.

18. O be favourable and gracious unto Sion: build thou the walls of Jerusalem.

19. Then shalt thou be pleased with the sacrifice of righteousness, with the burnt-offerings and oblations: then shall they offer young bullocks upon thine altar.

Subsequent translators have cleared up some seeming mistakes by Coverdale. On the other hand, in the ante-penultimate verse the three epithets, 'troubled', 'broken' and 'contrite', are replicated in no other version that I have consulted (Wyatt's, Arthur Golding's, the *AV*'s, the Sidney Psalter's, Watts's, Christopher Smart's). A multiplication of epithets is seldom a sign of poetic virtue; rather, the reverse. And Coverdale's threesome − 'troubled', 'broken', 'contrite' − enjoys an adventitious advantage for some readers in that it figures in *BCP* in the Collect for Ash-Wednesday, to be read every day in Lent. However, to a mind chiefly concerned with poetry, 'contrite' (used also in this place by Wyatt and the *AV*) has a peculiar power. The *OED* shows it used in a devotional context 200 years before Coverdale by Rolle of Hampole (1340), by Langland (1377) and Wyclif (*c*. 1380); but *OED* lists also a thoroughly secular sense which, though obsolete and rare, survived long enough to be noticed in Johnson's *Dictionary* (1755): 'Bruised, crushed; worn or broken by rubbing'. Thus 'contrite', when used by Coverdale in juxtaposition with 'broken' (its near but not exact synonym), has the force of − I give the hackneyed example − Shakespeare's harnessing of 'incarnadine' with (implicitly) 'redden'. The Latinate and the Germanic components of English collide and nearly overlap, but never exactly. It is a glory peculiar to English; and it would be foolish to look for anything comparable in the Hebrew original. In the case of this psalm, 'heart-broken' has been rubbed so smooth by over-use that Isaac Watts's version −

A broken heart, my God, my King,
Is all the sacrifice I bring;
The God of grace will ne'er despise
A broken heart for sacrifice

– comes over as insipid and mawkish, in a way that Watts can't altogether be blamed for. Thanks to 'contrite' along with 'broken', the sixteenth-century text can be relished in the twentieth century as the eighteenth-century text can't be. So much for any notion that, as centuries go by, we get better at interpreting Holy Scripture, or any other ancient literature.

But what are we to make, as regards the original, of the reversal at the end by which God, having just been congratulated on taking no pleasure in burnt-offerings, in the last verse is offered just such offerings ('young bullocks')? If this were a modern or modernist Anglo-American poem, we might read into this a sardonic, perhaps nihilistic, irony; if it were a Christian poem, we might suppose that we were meant to allegorize, to decode 'young bullocks' as meaning 'contrite hearts'. But of course this piece of writing is neither modern nor Christian. The *NOAB* takes care of the difficulty by describing the last two verses (confidently, though on grounds that are not disclosed) as 'a later addition, designed to modify the anti-sacrificial spirit of the preceding verses and to adapt the poem to liturgical use'. Which is fine, except that it leaves us with what isn't a poem at all, since it doesn't hang together.

A lot of the psalms are like this: mutilated torsos, or unnatural conjunctions of disparate and irreconcilable elements. (The extreme example is probably Psalm 68.) Though we call Psalm 51 a poem to indicate the genre that it belongs to, in doing so we dishonour the term 'poem', which must signify something that coheres. Shall we say that Psalm 51 is certainly poetry, but it is not a poem? Before we say this, we need to remember that there are other sorts of 'hanging together' than those we recognize as either 'modern' or 'Christian'. Some readers, not necessarily devotees of D. H. Lawrence or Ted Hughes, might argue that Psalm 51 *does* hang together after all since even those of a contrite heart must seal their compact with God *in blood*. This would be to appeal to a sort of 'hanging together' which is ancient indeed and widespread, which survives (so some say) in the Christian Eucharist; but it still doesn't explain, nor by itself can it justify, how Psalm 51 contradicts itself.

Of course once the Christian translator, unlike Coverdale, conceived himself at liberty – if not indeed in duty bound – to Christianize his pre-Christian original, the possibility arose of his making a poem out of what seemed to be only a disjointed though intermittently splendid piece of poetry. The first of such Christianizers in English seems to have been Sir Thomas Wyatt, writing in perhaps 1536. And it's interesting to see how he deals with the last verses of Psalm 51:

> But thou delyghtes not in no such glose
> Off owtward dede, as men dreme and devyse,
> The sacryfise that the lord lykyth most
> Is spryte contrite. Low hert in humble wyse
> Thou dost accept, O god, for plesant host.
> Make Syon, Lord, accordyng to thy will
> Inward Syon, the Syon of the ghost:
> Off hertes Hierusalem strengh the walles still.
> Then shalt thou take for good these uttward dedes,
> As sacryfice thy plesure to fullfyll
> Off the alone thus all our good procedes.

As we foresaw would be the case, Wyatt gets round the difficulty of self-contradiction by allegorizing. But his allegorizing is so thorough that a better word for it is internalizing: Zion itself or Jerusalem – the citadel and metropolis of the Jews – becomes, as Wyatt handles the matter, entirely notional; as the sacrifice isn't *really* a sacrifice, so the city isn't *really* a city. These transformations, of the actual into the notional, became over the centuries characteristic of Protestantism: the overt meaning of a word or a name must always be undermined so as to produce a covert meaning which is then designated 'spiritual'.

It is too easy to label this manoeuvre dishonest or disingenuous. It may or may not have been that in the first place, but as through the generations one after another devoted or even saintly person bent his back to the task, the endeavour took on a dignity that its questionable origin did not promise: the allegorizing and internalizing of Scripture became, not merely the staple fare of Protestant pulpits, but a mode of thought for which many thousands suffered and died. An anthology of the psalms in English translation and adaptation has to remember that suffering and dying.

Though Wyatt had the chance to make a poem out of a disjointed piece of poetry, it cannot be thought that he succeeded. Apart from anything else, at least one modern commentator (G. A. F. Knight, The Psalms, in *The Daily Study Bible*, Volume I, Edinburgh, 1982) finds not just the last two but the last *five* verses of this psalm a later addition to a poem that properly (originally) ended with verse 14. And in any case when Wyatt made this version he was still far short of the achievements, in a very different mode, that would compel us to describe him as a great poet.

Psalm 51, though it is certainly poetry, seems not to be, as it has been handed down to us, a poem. How much does that matter? Sadly for many of us, including fervent believers and worshippers, it matters not at all. But according to a different scale of values it matters crucially; and that scale, labelled 'aesthetic', is not irreligious. On the contrary it takes seriously what orthodox and heterodox alike, much to their disadvantage, shrug off as optional. What is at issue is the composing, by human means, of a unity and harmony that shall mirror what the Divine has pre-ordained. The difference between a piece of poetry and a poem reaches as far as that.

If the Hebrew text of Psalm 51 is so corrupt, at all events so disputable, perhaps the English versions made from it should be ruled out of consideration? But the case is not so simple. The Christianizing of these pre-Christian texts was not solely the work of Christian translators who took liberties that Coverdale denied himself. Much more potent has been Christian liturgy. For instance the Psalmist is quite categorical in verse 4: 'Against thee only have I sinned . . .' Cranmer's Book of Common Prayer falls into line:

> We acknowledge and bewail our manifold sins and wickedness,
> Which we, from time to time, most grievously have committed
> By thought, word, and deed, Against thy Divine Majesty . . .

But the Alternative Service Book offers three 'alternative confessions', of which two cleave to Coverdale's and the Hebrew understanding, whereas the third, given pride of place, insinuates something quite different: 'Almighty God, our heavenly Father, we have sinned against you *and against our fellow men*' (my italics). Is what Psalm 51 calls 'sin' to be understood as an offence committed by man peculiarly against God, or as bad behaviour generally? It would surely be quite wrong to think this a narrowly theological question; it is from our point of view immediately a poetic question, since it concerns what Psalm 51 is urgently *about*. If 'sin' means only 'behaving badly', then the psalm can look like self-indulgent breast-beating; for we all behave badly much of the time, as we all know. Only if 'sin' is conceived of as an offence against God, not (except incidentally) against human beings, can the urgency and elevation of the ancient piece be understood and tolerated. Those for whom 'God' is a meaningless expression must take the consequences; for them Psalm 51 is, and cannot help but be, trivial, an antiquarian curio. And it is frivolous to pretend that the existence or non-existence of God, whether conceived in Judaic or Christian or even Islamic terms, is a matter of no moment in our reading of this psalm. That is aestheticism in the worst sense. Either the poem, mutilated as it is, addresses matters of ultimate import to human life, or else it doesn't. No one can pretend that that question doesn't matter – *poetically*.

A psalm that is as truly a poem, an integrated composition, as Psalm 51 clearly isn't, is Psalm 139. Not surprisingly it is, for just this reason among others, thought to be of late date. W. O. E. Oesterley (*The Psalms*, 1939; reprinted 1959) declared firmly: 'Doubts as to unity of authorship may be disregarded.' This psalm too I give in Coverdale's version:

> 1. O Lord, thou hast searched me out, and known me: thou knowest my down-sitting, and mine up-rising; thou understandest my thoughts long before.
>
> 2. Thou art about my path, and about my bed: and spiest out all my ways.
>
> 3. For lo, there is not a word in my tongue: but thou, O Lord, knowest it altogether.
>
> 4. Thou hast fashioned me behind and before: and laid thine hand upon me.

5. Such knowledge is too wonderful and excellent for me: I cannot attain unto it.

6. Whither shall I go then from thy Spirit: or whither shall I go then from thy presence?

7. If I climb up into heaven, thou art there: if I go down to hell, thou art there also.

8. If I take the wings of the morning: and remain in the uttermost parts of the sea;

9. Even there also shall thy hand lead me: and thy right hand shall hold me.

10. If I say, Peradventure the darkness shall cover me: then shall my night be turned to day.

11. Yea, the darkness is no darkness with thee, but the night is as clear as the day: the darkness and light to thee are both alike.

12. For my reins are thine: thou hast covered me in my mother's womb.

13. I will give thanks unto thee, for I am fearfully and wonderfully made: marvellous are thy works, and that my soul knoweth right well.

14. My bones are not hid from thee: though I be made secretly, and fashioned beneath in the earth.

15. Thine eyes did see my substance, yet being imperfect: and in thy book were all my members written;

16. Which day by day were fashioned: when as yet there was none of them.

17. How dear are thy counsels unto me, O God: O how great is the sum of them!

18. If I tell them, they are more in number than the sand: when I wake up I am present with thee.

19. Wilt thou not slay the wicked, O God: depart from me, ye blood-thirsty men.

20. For they speak unrighteously against thee: and thine enemies take thy Name in vain.

21. Do not I hate them, O Lord, that hate thee: and am not I grieved with those that rise up against thee?

22. Yea, I hate them right sore: even as though they were mine enemies.

23. Try me, O God, and seek the ground of my heart: prove me, and examine my thoughts.

24. Look well if there be any way of wickedness in me: and lead me in the way everlasting.

If, as we are assured, this is the deliberated composition of one distinguished person, then it should stand up to the sort of modern scrutiny sometimes called 'close reading'. And so it does if, as isn't always the case, the scrutiny pays proper attention to genre and period. But it is the vice of close reading that it tends to home in on local felicities or local snags without attending to the structure of the whole. If on the contrary we attend to structure, we must in the first place get clear in our minds the formal conventions which govern the verse of the psalms, and ancient Hebrew verse in general.

One great advantage of Coverdale's versions, at least as printed in *BCP*, is that they bring out the most basic of these conventions. This Coverdale does by punctuating each verse with a heavy colon at or near the mid-point. Despite appearances, these are not colons according to English usage whether of the twentieth or the sixteenth century; they mark the break between the two 'members' which, tilted one against the other, constitute the verse-line as the ancient Hebrews understood it. If this should seem obvious, it is chastening to note that it went largely unremarked and unexplained until 1753. In that year Bishop Robert Lowth published his lectures on Hebrew poetry, entitled *De Sacra Poesi Hebraeorum Praelectiones Academicae*. It is one of the triumphs of English literary scholarship, and should be honoured more than it is, especially since the greatest English poet of the age, Christopher Smart, who had attended Lowth's lectures, at once set about seeing whether this Hebrew notion of the verse-line couldn't be acclimatized in English. (The outcome was Smart's *Rejoice in the Lamb*, which – fragmentary and incomplete as it undoubtedly is – is still treated as a demented free-for-all, rather than what it is, an audacious experiment in poetic form.) What Lowth observed was that 'every line of Hebrew poetry is divided into at least two parts, of which the second frequently repeats the thought of the first'. Note that the word is 'frequently', not 'invariably'; and also that the repeat of a thought very often comes with greater emphasis and intensity. Thus, whereas Lowth's principle – *parallelism of verse-members* – stands unchallenged after two and a half centuries as a perception of how the ancient Hebrew verse-line is structured, yet 'the greatest stumbling block in approaching biblical poetry has been the misconception that parallelism implies synonymity, saying the same thing twice in different words'. This warning is Robert Alter's, who goes on to point out that 'good poetry at all times is an intellectually robust activity to which such laziness is alien, that poets understand more subtly than linguists that there are no true synonyms, and that the ancient Hebrew poets are constantly advancing their meanings where the casual ear catches mere repetition'.* Thus, in verse 2 of Psalm 139, 'and spiest out all my ways', is at one level, and *only* one level, a repeat of 'Thou art about my path, and about my bed'; but the repetition encompasses so much more than the original statement that it represents a momentous advance.

Lowth recognized three kinds of parallelism: synonymous, antithetic, and *synthetic*. This last, exemplified in a verse from Psalm 2, 'Yet have I set my King: upon my holy hill of Sion', employs no parallelism at all beyond the fact that the second member of the line has the same number of significant Hebrew words as the first member. In Lowth himself at times, and much more abundantly in those who have for the most part disastrously tried to refine his distinctions, the declared parallelism turns out to be no more than this: three portentous Hebrew words in the first member, balanced by three such words in the second. (True, if such words always received a heavy stress in speech, we have a sort of rhythmical parallelism, and 'rhythm' and 'stress' are terms that have been thrown about rashly by certain commentators; but the truth is that we are too ignorant of the phonetics of biblical Hebrew to be at all confident about this, or about *sounded* parallelism in general.) A sensibility trained on poetry in English can't tolerate, nor should it,

* R. Alter and F. Kermode, *The Literary Guides to the Bible* (Cambridge, Mass., 1987).

an alleged equivalence so merely quantitative: rightly or wrongly we ask, for the relation between two members of a verse-line, something of the nature of 'for instance' or 'moreover' or 'although'. Accordingly even in Coverdale the two members of the verse-line cannot lie together so equably and unarguably as they do in the Hebrew.

Equally we find ourselves asking that at least sometimes a verse-line, so far from merely succeeding the one before, should *follow* it, logically. This happens in Coverdale's Psalm 139 at verses 8 and 9, which go together in the logical pattern, 'If so ... then so ...'; and again at verse 15 and 16, where verse 16, dependent from 'Which', is logically as well as grammatically a subordinate clause. Semicolons rather than full-stops at the ends of verses 8 and 15 should make these two exceptions leap to the eye. The poem, we may therefore say, is structured around two disturbances near to its centre: parallelism is the convention established from the first and returned to before the end, but in between come the two cases where, though formally parallelism is still observed, the observance is indeed no more than formal – the thought and feeling burst that bond, seeking out and covertly finding a larger syntactical unit so as to express themselves fully. This is the drama of the poem: 'drama' and 'structure' being, as often in talking of poems, interchangeable terms.

Of the two 'disturbances' it is the first, I dare say, that has entered most fully into English-speakers' awareness:

> If I take the wings of the morning: and remain in the uttermost parts of the sea;

> Even there also shall thy hand lead me: and thy right hand shall hold me.

Oesterley explains 'wings of the morning': 'here he [the Psalmist] uses a picture taken from Greek mythology; Eos, the Greek goddess of the dawn, had white wings, and flew from the Eastern Ocean, illuminating the sky with red glory'. It is an explanation that we could have done without, and may exert ourselves to forget. For the phrase in English, and (we may reasonably suspect) in the Hebrew, is in no way 'a picture'. Particularly unwanted are the

colours: that white, that red. (Strawberries and cream!) We are not
looking at a picture, but are ourselves involved in the thrust up and
away, as if we should take off at dawn from a Canadian airfield and
head north-west. We may be grateful to the ancient poet for not
evoking the Greek goddess, if indeed she was in his mind at all,
except very allusively; for that is what allows us to participate. As
happens in poetry more often than is commonly acknowledged, it
is the *generality* of the poet's presentation (not vagueness, for vague
it isn't) which charges his locution with energy that we can share,
across centuries of change in technology and much else.

The other 'disturbance' has not entered into our consciousness at
all so deeply or so widely, though as we shall see it sparked off what
may be the most fuliginous irruption of invention in the entire
record of English metrical psalters:

> Thine eyes did see my substance, yet being imperfect: and in thy
> book were all my members written;

> Which day by day were fashioned: when as yet there was none of
> them.

Here again I'm afraid W. O. E. Oesterley offers us a gloss that is
meant to be helpful, but isn't: 'the psalmist gives expression to an
old-world and widespread belief that, prior to its entry into the
womb, the human body has been *skilfully wrought in the depths of the
earth*. This belief in the pre-existence of the body may have come to
the Jews from Zoroastrianism . . .; though very different from the
belief in the pre-existence of the soul, this latter is but a refined
form of the other.' Surely we don't need Zoroastrians to cause us to
wonder that every baby (except for some misbegotten whose
condition we lament and cannot explain) is born with five toes on
each foot, four fingers and a thumb on each hand. Where in
Creation is the template which is thus replicated in virtually every
human birth? If not in the mind and intention of God, then
somewhere else – but where? These are not childish or primitive
questions; they must confront and baffle obstetricians and embry-
ologists along with the rest of us. From this point of view the

pre-existence of the human body is an observable fact, as the pre-existence of a human soul certainly isn't; and it is this insoluble mystery that these verses of Psalm 139 worry at.

If we wonder that Oesterley makes such heavy weather of them, the answer lies I suspect in the habit that he shares with other commentators of extolling Psalm 139, and others they particularly admire, as 'deeply personal'. We may ask ourselves why such or such a baby has or will have hazel eyes rather than blue eyes; why this baby will be prone to freckles, whereas the next baby won't; why this baby will grow into a chess master, whereas the next baby won't. But all such questions – intriguing as they are, and doubtless in time answerable after a fashion – depend upon taking the 'I' of the Psalmist to mean 'I' as peculiar unrepeatable individual; not 'I' as representative human being. Such individualism is, as many have noticed, peculiar to a historically determinable phase in the chronicle of Western man; the Psalmist, all the psalmists, belong to a phase of history before such individualism was conceived of, and thus when they say 'I' they mostly mean 'I, as representative man', not 'I, as unique individual'. It's from that standpoint – of 'generality' – that the Psalmist's probing of the mysteries of embryology has still, and must continue to have, meaning.

This was grasped, magnificently, in what is surely the most splendid Englishing (by the Countess of Pembroke) of these verses from Psalm 139:

> Each inmost piece in me is thine:
>   While yet I in my mother dwelt,
>   All that me clad
>   From thee I had.
>   Thou in my frame hast strangely dealt;
> Needs in my praise thy works must shine,
>   So inly them my thoughts have felt.
>
> Thou, how my back was beam-wise laid
>   And raft'ring of my ribs, dost know;
>   Know'st ev'ry point
>   Of bone and joint,

> How to this whole these parts did grow,
> In brave embroid'ry fair array'd
> Though wrought in shop both dark and low.
>
> Nay, fashionless, ere form I took,
> Thy all-and-more beholding eye
> My shapeless shape
> Could not escape;
> All these, time-framed successively
> Ere one had being, in the book
> Of thy foresight enroll'd did lie.

It goes without saying that, in such a rehandling, the structure of the Hebrew verse-line is quite lost sight of. But consider what we are offered in recompense!

Psalm 139 is, among the psalms, one that the irreligious can easily respond to. 'For I am fearfully and wonderfully made' – where could Humanism go for a better motto? This psalm says nothing of sin. It names 'hell'; but this is a traditional and seemingly unavoidable mistranslation that may as well be scotched here and now – the Hebrew *sheol* implies nothing of punishment, nor indeed of judgement. *Sheol* is the place of the undifferentiated dead, a place imaged sometimes as a field, sometimes as a pit. Late medieval treatments of 'The Harrowing of Hell', conceived as recording what Christ did on Easter Saturday, therefore have to be revised:

> He descended into –
> Not into Hell but
> Into the field of the dead
> Where he roughs them up like a tractor
> Dragging its tray of links.

That mistranslation dealt with (and it's notable that this is the one place in the psalms where God is thought to take care of the dead as well as the living), there is nothing in this poem to prevent the irreligious from translating, perhaps not fully conscious of what they are doing, 'God' into 'Nature' or 'the Cosmos'. Some who have made that translation no doubt experience the poem as elevating and comforting; and their experience is not to be gainsaid. What is missing from it is what Robert Alter defines as the element common to all the psalms: 'the heavily charged field of relationship between man and God'. A relationship between man and the Cosmos can hardly be 'heavily charged' in the way that Robert Alter intends: recrimination, reproach, striking of unequal bargains, reconciliation (partial or entire) – these belong exclusively to a relation between persons. Man does not stand towards the Cosmos in any such relation.

4 The Case for Metrical Psalms

The metrical psalm is one of the principal genres of English Renaissance poetry. This cannot be denied, given what we know of the volume and frequency of the printings of, pre-eminently, the so-called 'Old Version' of Sternhold and Hopkins (originally 1551). Yet, even as we acknowledge this, it disconcerts us and we huddle it away as best we can; for the plain fact is that, by the standards not just of our own day but of virtually every generation since the Old Version first appeared, the versifications of Sternhold and Hopkins seem to be, and have been acknowledged to be, *wretched*. In fact the virtual unanimity on this score is something valuable; for it vindicates the conviction, now continually assailed, that there is in the judging of poetry a standard simply technical and stylistic, unaffected by ideology, by class- or gender-warfare, by considerations of socio-political history. The versions of the psalms by Sternhold and Hopkins were – there is no doubt of it – cherished by thousands of English people who lived through the lifetimes of Sidney and Herbert, of Vaughan and Milton and Dryden, who preferred to those masters, in so far as they knew of them, the far from masterly compositions that they droned, Sunday by Sunday, in their parish churches. The common people of England preferred the worse to the better long before the Industrial Revolution happened.

On the history of the metrical psalm in the sixteenth and seventeenth centuries, I know nothing better than Coburn Freer's *Music for a King* (Baltimore and London, 1974). This has for sub-title 'George Herbert's Style and the Metrical Psalms'. And this is invaluable for positing, what Freer's scrupulous readings undoubtedly bear out, that *The Temple* of George Herbert defines one point where the writing of metrical psalms feeds into what we can all agree is the mainstream of English poetry. No one can think he or she has come to terms with Herbert's poetry, without taking note of the contribution to that poetry of the metrical psalters. However, because Coburn Freer has (I suspect) populist sympathies, he focusses on those humble versions, chiefly Sternhold's and Hopkins's, that Herbert can be shown to have known about. What gets less attention is the fact that from the first, already in Elizabethan times, there were 'elitist' versions of the Psalter in at least notional competition with the popular versions. The most notable instance is the so-called Sidney Psalter which, unpublished in the translators' lifetimes, has ever since played hide-and-seek in our libraries. The one and only reliable modern printing (edited by Rathmell, New York, 1963) has for years been out of print. When in 1981 I edited *The New Oxford Book of Christian Verse*, I tried to stem the tide of oblivion by printing five of the Countess of Pembroke's psalmversions, proposing for good measure that on the evidence of these compositions the Countess was 'the first woman-poet of genius in the history of English poetry'. This was designedly a gift to feminist literary criticism. But the gift was spurned: women no more than men were prepared to recognize a poet whose great achievement was in versifying the psalms. Accordingly, when in Coburn Freer's account we find the Countess's versions rather consistently damned by faint praise when compared with her brother's, Philip Sidney's, we have a case perhaps of male chauvinism but also of something more interesting. Between Psalm 43, the last of Philip Sidney's versions, and Psalm 44, the first by his sister, we cross a cultural divide. If both sets of versions are 'elitist', the elite that Sidney addressed is much farther from our comprehension than what the Countess had in mind. The clue is in the French precedent that both brother and sister were aware of: Clément Marot, in his *Trente Pseulmes de David* (1542). We have a reliable account of how in the

circles around the Dauphin, later Henri II (he came to the throne in
1547), courtiers 'adopted their special psalms, just as they adopted
their special arms, mottoes or liveries'; how their choice of psalm
often alluded deliberately to their amorous or conjugal predica-
ments; how Henri himself set to music Marot's *sanctes chansonettes*
(Marot's own description of his psalm-versions), and sang them to
accompaniment on the viol or the lute. It is hard to envisage a
milieu more remote from all that we English-speakers associate
with psalm-singing. Coburn Freer wittily describes these French
persons as 'fugitives from *Love's Labour's Lost*'. Yet he ventures that
'something of the atmosphere of Marot's psalms seems to be caught
in the Sidney psalms and *The Temple*, something to do with the
idea of devotion as a joyful game'. And he reminds us that Sidney
in his *Apologie for Poetrie* says that the Psalter 'must be used, by
whosoever will follow S. James his counsell, in singing Psalmes
when they are merry'.

Freer insists, however, that this element of the *fête galante*, of
'joyful religious play', though it persists or recurs in Herbert, is not
to be found in the Countess of Pembroke. And we may readily
concur. The circle that the Countess wrote in and wrote for is
altogether more grave and learned; a long way from the Dauphin
carolling Psalm 42 ('Like as the hart desireth the water-brooks')
when, with Diane de Poitiers at his side, he hunted the stag in the
forest of Fontainebleau. And yet there is a sort of playfulness which
persists into the Countess of Pembroke, and even into those, the
more ambitious, among her successors as versifiers of the psalms. If
we look again at the three intricate stanzas that the Countess makes
of verses from Psalm 139, we discover that the translator indeed
elaborates on her original, but not in the sense that she *ornaments* it.
The details that she discovers – for instance, 'raft'ring of my ribs' –
are not extraneous, but implicit in the original once one ponders
what that original is saying. To ponder, to *relive*, the experience of
the ancient Hebrew – that is what is going on. To say that the
translation incorporates interpretation or commentary is true, but it
is even truer that it incorporates exhortation and meditation, in fact
exhortation *to* meditation. Ponder, it says: this is what the ancient

poet is saying, if only you'll attend to him. It is a work, *the* work, of devotion. The Countess's poem is a work of literary art, but only in the second place; in the first place it is a work of devotion. To think that its devotional dimension detracts from its status as art is to devalue everything, including art. For this is what art is, when it is more than a social *divertissement*; it is pondering, weighing. In this respect the Countess is not at all remote from us, not in the least 'quaint'. She is only telling us what we must be telling ourselves whenever we go to worship: 'Think what it is that you are saying!' And from this point of view the sportiveness that links by alliteration 'raft'ring' with 'ribs' is as much an aid to devotion as an accomplishment of verse-writing.

Another of Mary Herbert's ways of being sportive shows up in the title-page that she either composed or authorized: 'The Psalmes of David translated into divers & sundry kindes of verse, more rare & excellent for the method & varietie than ever yet hath bene don in English . . .' What the Countess boasts of as 'rare and excellent' is above all the variety of her verse-forms – a boast thoroughly borne out, for she hardly ever used the same stanza pattern twice. And that variety did not merely come about 'organically'; plainly it was imposed by deliberate design. The manuscripts show the Countess to have been indeed methodical and laborious – to the point where Coburn Freer gets annoyed with her as an inveterate tinkerer who could not leave well alone.

This brings us to what may be the most challenging question that can be posed on metrical Psalters. If Coverdale and King James's translators have given us Psalters that generations have recognized (though inertly of late) as very beautiful and moving, what is the point of trying to improve on them? This is part of the arsenal of traditionalists in every generation, when they oppose modernizing of Scripture generally. And my heart is with them when they respond in this way to protests, often enough from the clergy, that 'this Olde Englysshe isn't meaningful to our young people'. However, their objection in so far as it bears on the psalms can be answered in several ways. We can say that as a classic of ancient literature, the psalms ought to be, like the *Iliad* or the *Aeneid*, translated afresh in every generation, simply to prove how inexhaustibly relevant they are; and this is what vindicates, for instance, the always resourceful and sometimes brilliant translations into eighteenth-century idiom by Watts and Smart. Secondly, though we may concede for the sake of argument that no one versified psalm as a whole is as good, as *poetic*, as the non-versified version in *AV* or *BCP*, yet time and again one verse or part of a verse provokes the best versifiers to astonishing felicities. But there is a third consideration which returns us immediately to the Countess of Pembroke. When we say that she boasts of her expertise and versatility, we miss the point. What looks like vaunting is really apprehensive humility. The poems that she makes out of the psalms are gifts that she lays on the altar; and she is at pains to show that her gifts are as 'costly' as those that the Magi brought to the Christ-child in Bethlehem. Their brilliance, their variety, their dexterity are pressed on our attention to persuade us that anything less would fail to meet the awe-inducing occasion. To say it again, the entire enterprise is a work of devotion; it glorifies God by heaping up before Him all the glories that it can muster. The versifier has one gift, that of versifying: and that gift, the only one he or she has, is laid before the Throne. This is a motive that, one may suppose and hope, impels certain poets in this as in previous centuries.

5 The Psalms and Music

Percy A. Scholes, in *The Oxford Companion to Music* (10th edition, revised, 1970), calls the Book of Psalms 'the oldest and the greatest book of songs now in use anywhere in the world'. And the word 'songs' must give us pause. Scholes suggests that in the beginnings of every race, and certainly among the Jews, all poems were chanted; that is to say, for the Psalmists the arts of poetry and music were so closely akin that they can hardly be distinguished. David, when he is called 'the sweet singer of Israel', is being extolled as musician certainly no less than as poet. Though in the English-speaking tradition there are figures like John Dowland and Thomas

Campion of whom as much must be said, these are for us exceptional cases which we have rather great difficulty in accommodating, not just in our histories but in our personal experience of their composi- tions. The same difficulty arises with the Psalmists, to the extent that a venture like this one, treating the psalms as poems, can be thought to be wrong from the start. The psalms were never conceived as, nor composed as, self-sufficient verbal artefacts; to regard them so is to skew the investigation from the start.

This objection can be answered only as one answers the objection that many of our translators are Christianizing pre-Christian texts. The psalms survive to us through many centuries of Christian handling as well as through many pre-Christian centuries. In the course of the Christian centuries there emerged the notion of a poem as self-sufficient, as something spoken rather than sung, independent therefore of whatever musical accompaniment might be found for it. And this is not a recent development: Philip Sidney's psalm-versions might at a pinch be sung; his sister's version of Psalm 139 surely can't be. The Gentiles found a way of integrating and harmonizing the psalms, different from the Jewish way.

All the same, the tension between 'song' and 'speech' remains. It may be thought an inevitable consequence of Les Murray's distinc- tion between Boeotian (Theban) and Attic (Athenian), but this won't quite do. Neither Dowland nor Campion seems Boeotian in the sense that Murray intends; nor do, in the present century, such song-writing poets as Ivor Gurney, A. E. Housman, W. H. Auden. (Burns in his songs may be genuinely Boeotian in Murray's sense – which may account for the general conviction that Robert Burns is unique and irreplaceable.) The name of Auden deserves to be dwelt on; for he wrote poems that are songs, as well as poems that are nothing of the kind. And he reflected acutely on the crucial differ- ences between writing poems for musical setting and writing for the speaking voice. He says, for instance, 'since music, generally speaking, can express only one thing at a time, it is ill adapted to verses which express mixed or ambiguous feelings, and prefers poems which either express one emotional state or successively contrast two states'.* This explains why, as we read the psalms, and certainly if we try to translate them, we are repeatedly brought up short by what seem to be very abrupt transitions from one state of feeling to another at odds with it. Often what the Psalmist says to God is backed up against what God replies; and the 'emotional state' implied by the first utterance is therefore wholly at odds with what is implied by the second. What is baffling, time and again, is to determine in such cases where Man stops speaking and God starts to retort. Translators use devices like inverted commas and indentations to fix such moments of take-over by one voice from another; but it will be seen that they seldom agree just where the take-over occurs. This means that 'abrupt transitions' will hardly meet the case. Properly speaking, there are no transitions at all, only collisions. Such psalms, as Auden says, 'successively contrast two states', and they suppress all clues about how the first state leads into, or provokes, the second. Another way of putting this is to say that, whereas many of the most impassioned psalms represent a dialogue between God and His people, the Psalmists seem quite uninterested in making drama out of this; their focus is so intently on *song* that they eschew drama no less than argument. There may originally have been musical means (for instance, a change of key) for signalling where God speaks; but there are no such indications in the verbal text.

Auden's observation can take us further. In 1955, when with Chester Kallman and Noah Greenberg Auden published his anthology of lute songs, madrigals and rounds, Anglo-American literary criticism had not yet plunged into the morass of ideological lobbies and French fads which has since disgraced it. In the years before that, at the hands of such as William Empson and John Crowe Ransom, criticism of poetry had made startling advances by showing how often poetry was able to express what Auden calls 'mixed or ambiguous feelings'. Those advances were made at the cost of not knowing how to deal with songs, a sort of poem which does not traffic in such feelings since the singing voice cannot deal with

---

* W. H. Auden and C. Kallman, *An Anthology of Elizabethan Lute Songs, Madrigals and Rounds* (New York, 1955).

them. So highly esteemed was Empson's kind of criticism that at that time, and even today, ambiguity and semantic complexity are what knowledgeable readers first look for in poems that they want to admire. As we have seen, the psalms like other bodies of song can only disappoint such readers. Whenever we think that we find such complexities in the psalms, we can be sure that we are wrong. For this is not that sort of poetry. Coming to it with those expectations, we shall inevitably find it flat and thin. The archaism of Coverdale and the Authorized Version hides this from sight, somewhat; but the flatness and thinness show up inescapably when we look at later translators and imitators who have tried to produce versions for singing. The clearest instances of this are those poets, like Isaac Watts and James Montgomery, who adapt or boil down the psalms into congregational hymns. Sometimes 'thin' and 'flat' are indeed the appropriate epithets. They damn for instance Montgomery's 'Lord, for ever at thy side' (1819), based on Psalm 131 – though even in that case the threadbare verses, when married to a stately tune by Orlando Gibbons,* can disconcertingly provide a satisfying devotional experience. The richness of the music in such a case ekes out the poverty of the words; there are other cases where a distinction in the wording has to make up for being set to a commonplace melody – the marriage of the two arts is seldom a happy or an equal union. On the other hand, what seems to be threadbare in the diction may come about simply by the poet's leaving a space for the musician to elaborate in. There can be no doubt, however, that no one will be so disappointed by Watts's psalm-versions as those who, seeing the lines in cold print on the page, supply from memory the tune to which, as choristers in an enthusiastic choir, or simply as churchgoers, they have been used to singing them. To them it must seem that they are scanning the libretti to vanished operas. (And the comparison is not extravagant: if, as Percy Scholes assures us, 'Under King David, out of 38,000 Levites, 4,000 were appointed as musicians', the rendering of the psalms in the Temple can hardly have been, in scale, less than operatic.) Watts's wording, however,

---

* As in No. 451 of *The Hymnal of the Protestant Episcopal Church in the U.S.A.*

if we look at it in isolation allowing for the conventions of his age, is seldom less than distinguished, though undoubtedly and quite deliberately *frugal*.

The two modern translators whom I have chosen to represent at some length show very clearly the difference between versions for singing and versions for saying. David Frost's title – *The Liturgical Psalter* – advertises quite firmly that his versions are for singing; Gordon Jackson's on the other hand, if I may trust my ear, are just as unequivocally for saying. Thus Frost and Jackson are not in competition, since they address quite different needs and different audiences; our preference for one over the other depends on extra-literary considerations as to which mode of translating is more needful, which audience it is more needful to reach. Now, when debased and commercialized versions of song command a vast audience (as in 'Top of the Pops'), it may be thought that our weight should be thrown in fairness on versions for speaking.

But there are places where the Hebrew is so obscure that it will lend itself to singing no more than to speaking. After all, a song is still an utterance; and we cannot allow ourselves to utter incoherent nonsense. But that is what we are committed to if we follow either *BCP* or *AV* through some verses from Psalm 141:

> O let not mine heart be inclined to any evil thing: let me not be occupied in ungodly works with the men that work wickedness, lest I eat of such things as please them.

> Let the righteous rather smite me friendly: and reprove me.

> But let not their precious balms break my head: yea, I will pray yet against their wickedness.

> Let their judges be overthrown in stony places: that they may hear my words, for they are sweet.

> Our bones lie scattered before the pit: like as when one breaketh and heweth wood upon the earth.

> But mine eyes look unto thee, O Lord God: in thee is my trust, O cast not out my soul.

Thus Coverdale in *BCP*. And the incoherence is evident: who are 'they'? If they are 'the righteous', why should the Psalmist vow to 'pray yet against their wickedness'? And when the mysterious 'they' come a cropper, why exhort them to attend to the Psalmist's words, 'for they are sweet'? To whom are they 'sweet'? To those whose judges have been overthrown? To God, whose edict perhaps decreed their overthrowing? Or only to the Psalmist and his like-minded friends? Does 'sweet' mean 'comforting', or something more general and far-reaching, or else indeed something narrower and more technical? These are not the only questions that can be put to this passage, but they are quite enough to be going on with.

When state-of-the-art Hebraists go to work on such a passage, they answer our questions briskly, as in *NOAB*:

> Incline not my heart to any evil,
> to busy myself with wicked deeds
> in company with men who work iniquity;
> and let me not eat of their Dainties!
>
> Let a good man strike or rebuke me in kindness,
> but let the oil of the wicked never anoint my head;
>
> for my prayer is continually against their wicked deeds.
> When they are given over to those who shall condemn them,
> then they shall learn that the word of the Lord is true.
> As a rock which one cleaves and shatters on the land,
> so shall their bones be strewn at the mouth of Sheol.
>
> But my eyes are toward thee, O Lord God;
> in thee I seek refuge, leave me not defenseless!

This answers all our questions – but at what a cost! Coverdale's incoherence opened up issues that *NOAB* buries; for instance, the state of mind in which one acknowledges as just and well-meant the straight 'talking-to' by a friend, towards whom one nevertheless thereafter feels sore and vindictive. And it is certainly more logical, but is it therefore more moving or more true to have the bones strewn at the mouth of Sheol the bones of the enemies rather than the bones of the Psalmist and his friends? The *NOAB* clears up by ironing out: and what we have in the end is certainly something ironed-out, flat and dead.

The Hebraists who looked over the shoulder of David Frost clearly were pushing him in the same direction as *NOAB*. And he goes along with them, except at one point where he breaks ranks:

> Let not my heart incline to evil speech,
> > to join in wickedness with wrongdoers:
> Let me not taste the pleasures of their table.

> But let the righteous man chastise me:
> and the faithful man rebuke me.

> Let not the oil of the wicked anoint my head:
> for I pray to you still against their wickedness.

> They shall be cast down
> > by that Mighty One who is their judge:
> and how pleasing shall my words be to them then!

> As when a farmer breaks the ground:
> so shall their bones lie scattered at the mouth of Sheol.

> But my eyes look to you, O Lord my God:
> to you I come for refuge, do not pour out my life.

'And how pleasing shall my words be to them then!' is a brilliant and daring solution of the problem set by 'they may hear my words, for they are sweet' – a problem blandly bypassed by *NOAB*, which substitutes 'true' for 'sweet', and makes the word of the Psalmist the word of the Lord. The gleeful vindictiveness of Frost's 'how pleasing shall my words be to them then!' succinctly preserves the resentment of the individual corrected (however justly) towards those who have corrected him – an emotion certainly allowed for by Coverdale, which the *NOAB* translators have done away with. But we cannot fail to note that this is possible only because the author of *The Liturgical Psalter* has at this point diverged from a translation for singing into a translation for saying. It's impossible to imagine how the taunting sarcasm could be conveyed by a singing voice; the inflection required could be supplied only by a speaker. This is a good example of how a version for singing and a version for speaking, though in principle and in the abstract they are quite distinct, in practice take in each other's washing. The Hebraists, supposing that they act in a surgically cleansed area from which distinctions between song and speech are excluded, rule out any possibility of adjudicating between them.

But in the end it is *song* that must get the emphasis. A title like *The Printed Voice of Victorian Poetry* has nothing to say to this poetry:

> Speech murmurs, and is always
> forked, but this is song.
> Nothing in this is talked.

And nothing in our poetry or in any other of our forms of discourse equips us for dealing with this, except very imperfectly.

GEORGE JOYE (d. 1553)

Psalm 1

Blessed is that man which walketh not in the counsel of the ungodly: and standeth not in the way of sinners/and sitteth not in the seat of the pestilent scorners.

But hath all his pleasure in the law of the lord; and upon it his mind is occupied/both day and night.

Such a man shall be like a tree planted by the riverside: which will give forth her fruits in due time/and her leaves shall not wither: for whatsoever he shall do shall prosper.

But so shall not the ungodly: for they shall be like dust which is dispersed with the wind.

Wherefore these ungodly shall not stand in the judgement: neither these sinners may abide in the company of the rightwise

For the lord approveth the way of the rightwise: but the way of sinners shall perish.(1530)

Joye's Psalter was printed in Antwerp in 1530, the day before William Tyndale's English Pentateuch, to which it appears to have been an unsolicited supplement. It was promptly denounced by the ecclesiastical authorities as heretical. Coverdale can be seen to have known of Joye's Psalter when he composed his own Psalter for the Bible of 1535. Joye's use of the archaic form 'rightwise' gives a different inflection to the word 'righteous', which has taken on unwelcome associations through later centuries. 'Righteous' rings differently when we hear it as analogous to a modern usage like 'streetwise'.

SIR THOMAS WYATT (1503?–1542)

Psalm 102

Lord, hear my pray'r, and let my cry pass
   Unto the Lord without impediment.
   Do not from me turn thy merciful face,
Unto myself leaving my government.
   In time of trouble and adversity
   Incline to me thine ear and thine intent;
And when I call, help my necessity:
   Readily grant th' effect of my desire.
   These bold demands do please thy majesty,
10 And eke my case such haste doth well require.
   For like as smoke my days been passed away.
   My bones dried up as furnace with the fire,
My heart, my mind is withered up like hay
   Because I have forgot to take my bread,
   My bread of life, the word of truth, I say:
And for my plaintful sighès, and my dread,
   My bones, my strength, my very force of mind
   Cleaved to the flesh and from the sprite were fled,
As desperate thy mercy for to find.
20   So made I me the solaine pelican,
   And like the owl that fleeth by proper kind

Light of the day and hath her self beta'en
  To ruin life out of all company.
  With waker care that with this woe began,
Like the sparrow was I solitary,
  That sits alone under the house's eaves.
  This while my foes conspired continually,
And did provoke the harm of my disease
  Wherefore like ashes my bread did me savour,
30   Of thy just word the taste might not me please.
Wherefore my drink I tempered with liqueur
  Of weeping tears that from mine eyes do rain:
  Because I know the wrath of thy furor
Provok'd by right had of my pride disdain;
  For thou didst lift me up to throw me down,
  To teach me how to know my self again.
Whereby I know that helpless I should drown,
  My days like shadow decline and I do dry;
  And thee forever eternity doth crown;
40 World without end doth last thy memory.
  For this frailtee that yoketh all mankind,
  Thou shalt awake and rue this misery,
Rue on Zion, Zion that as I find
  Is the people that live under thy law;
  For now is time, the time at hand assign'd,
The time so long that doth thy servants draw
  In great desire to see that pleasant day,
  Day of redeeming Zion from sin's awe:
For they have ruth to see in such decay
50   In dust and stones this wretched Zion low'r.
  Then the gentiles shall dread thy name alway;
All earthly kings thy glory shall honour,
  Then when that grace thy Zion thus redeemeth,
  When thus thou hast declar'd thy mighty pow'r.
The Lord his servants' wishes so esteemeth
  That he him turneth unto the poors' request.
  To our descent this to be written seemeth,

Of all comforts as consolation best;
    And they that then shall be regenerate
60   Shall praise the Lord therefore both most and least.
For he hath look'd from the height of his estate,
    The Lord from heaven in earth hath looked on us,
    To hear the moan of them that are algate
In foul bondage: to loose and to discuss
    The sons of death from out their deadly bond,
    To give thereby occasion gracious
In this Zion his holy name to stand
    And in Jerusalem his laudès lasting aye:
    When in one church the people of the land
70 And realms been gather'd to serve to laud, to pray
    The Lord alone so just and merciful.
    But to this assembly running in the way
My strength faileth to reach it at the full.
    He hath abridg'd my days; they may not dure,
    To see that term, that term so wonderful.
Although I have with hearty will and Cure
    Prayed to the Lord: 'Take me not, Lord, away
    In middès of my years, though thine ever sure
Remain eterne, whom time can not decay.
80   Thou wrought'st the earth, thy hands th' heavens did
            make;
    They shall perish and thou shalt last alway,
And all things Age shall wear and overtake
    Like cloth; and thou shalt change them like apparel,
    Turn and translate and they in worth it take.
But thou thy self the self remainest well
    That thou wast erst, and shall thy years extend.
    Then since to this there may no thing rebel,
The greatest comfort that I can pretend

---

64 *Discuss* has the obsolete meaning 'dispel'.
76 *Cure*: care.

>   Is that the children of thy servants dear
> ·90   That in thy word are got shall without end
>   Before thy face be stablish'd all in fear.'   (1536?)

This psalm is thought to have been disrupted by the editorial intrusion of a middle section (vv. 12–22). But this is posited on supposing incompatible the sentiments of a sick individual (vv. 1–11, 23–9) with his sentiments about the sickness of his community ('Zion'). It is not at all certain that to Wyatt, suffering under Henry VIII, this distinction between the personal and the communal would have been clear. For tradition has it that Wyatt's quarrel with his king was at once private (over possession of the person of Anne Boleyn) and public. There thus arises the possibility that what may have been disparate elements in the Hebrew were welded into unity by the conditions of a Tudor court.

   I have amended the spelling of the text in *Collected Poems of Sir Thomas Wyatt*, ed. Kenneth Muir (1949), but some obscurities remain. The metre can be eased in places by giving a 'Romance' pronunciation, e.g. by treating 'gracious' (l. 66) as a trisyllable; but again, roughness persists.

HENRY HOWARD, EARL OF SURREY (1517?–1547)

Psalm 88

> Oh Lord, upon whose will dependeth my welfare,
> To call upon thy holy name since day nor night I spare,
>   Grant that the just request of this repentant mind
> So pierce thine ears that in thy sight some favour it may find.
>   My soul is fraughted full with grief of follies past;
> My restless body doth consume and death approacheth fast,
>   Like them whose fatal thread thy hand hath cut in twain,

Of whom there is no further bruit, which in their graves
    remain.
  Oh Lord, thou hast cast me headlong to please my foe,
10 Into a pit all bottomless, where as I plain my woe.
   . The burden of thy wrath it doth me sore oppress,
And sundry storms thou hast me sent of terror and distress.
    The faithful friends are fled and banished from my sight,
And such as I have held full dear have set my friendship light.
    My duraunce doth persuade of freedom such despair
That, by the tears that bane my breast, mine eyesight doth
    appaire.
    Yet did I never cease thine aid for to desire,
With humble heart and stretchèd hands for to appease thy
    ire.
    Wherefore dost thou forbear, in the defence of thine,
20 To shew such tokens of thy power, in sight of Adam's line,
    Whereby each feeble heart with faith might so be fed
That in the mouth of thy elect thy mercies might be spread?
    The flesh that feedeth worms can not thy love declare,
Nor such set forth thy faith as dwell in the land of despair.
    In blind endurèd hearts, light of thy lively name
Can not appear, as can not judge the brightness of the same.
    Nor blasted may thy name be by the mouth of those
Whom death hath shut in silence, so as they may not disclose.
    The lively voice of them that in thy word delight
30 Must be the trump that must resound the glory of thy might.
    Wherefore I shall not cease, in chief of my distress,
To call on thee till that the sleep my wearied limbs oppress.
    And in the morning eke, when that the sleep is fled,
With floods of salt repentant tears to wash my restless bed.
    Within this care-full mind, burdened with care and grief,
Why dost thou not appear, Oh Lord, that shouldst be his
    relief?

---

16 *appaire*: deteriorate.

My wretched state behold, who death shall straight assail;
Of one from youth afflicted still, that never did but wail.
The dread, lo, of thine ire hath trod me under feet;
40   The scourges of thine angry hand hath made death seem full
            sweet.
Like to the roaring waves the sunken ship surround,
Great heaps of care did swallow me and I no succour found.
For they whom no mischance could from my love divide
Are forcèd, for my greater grief, from me their face to
            hide.   (1546)

The text is from *Henry Howard, Earl of Surrey. Poems*, ed. Emrys
Jones (Oxford, 1964).

MILES COVERDALE (1488–1568)

Psalm 42

1. Like as the hart desireth the water-brooks: so longeth my soul after thee, O God.

2. My soul is athirst for God, yea, even for the living God: when shall I come to appear before the presence of God?

3. My tears have been my meat day and night: while they daily say unto me, Where is now thy God?

4. Now when I think thereupon, I pour out my heart by myself: for I went with the multitude, and brought them forth into the house of God;

5. In the voice of praise and thanksgiving: among such as keep holy-day.

6. Why art thou so full of heaviness, O my soul: and why art thou so disquieted within me?

7. Put thy trust in God: for I will yet give him thanks for the help of his countenance.

8. My God, my soul is vexed within me: therefore will I remember thee concerning the land of Jordan, and the little hill of Hermon.

9. One deep calleth another, because of the noise of the water-pipes: all thy waves and storms are gone over me.

10. The Lord hath granted his loving-kindness in the day-time: and in the night-season did I sing of him, and made my prayer unto the God of my life.

11. I will say unto the God of my strength, Why hast thou forgotten me: why go I thus heavily, while the enemy oppresseth me?

12. My bones are smitten asunder as with a sword: while mine enemies that trouble me cast me in the teeth;

13. Namely, while they say daily unto me: Where is now thy God?

14. Why art thou so vexed, O my soul: and why art thou so disquieted within me?

15. O put thy trust in God: for I will yet thank him, which is the help of my countenance, and my God. (1535)

Psalm 60

1. O God, thou hast cast us out, and scattered us abroad: thou hast also been displeased; O turn unto us again.

2. Thou hast moved the land, and divided it: heal the sores thereof, for it shaketh.

3. Thou hast shewed thy people heavy things: thou hast given us a drink of deadly wine.

4. Thou hast given a token for such as fear thee: that they may triumph because of the truth.

5. Therefore were thy beloved delivered: help me with thy right hand, and hear me.

6. God hath spoken in his holiness, I will rejoice, and divide Sichem: and mete out the valley of Succoth.

7. Gilead is mine, and Manasses is mine: Ephraim also is the

strength of my head; Judah is my law-giver;

8. Moab is my wash-pot; over Edom will I cast out my shoe: Philistia, be thou glad of me.

9. Who will lead me into the strong city: who will bring me into Edom?

10. Hast thou not cast us out, O God: wilt not thou, O God, go out with our hosts?

11. O be thou our help in trouble: for vain is the help of man.

12. Through God will we do great acts: for it is he that shall tread down our enemies.   (1535)

It is barely credible that such gibberish (for so it necessarily appears to most of us) should be required to be said or sung at Evening Prayer, according to *BCP*, on Day 11 of the Church calendar. For what is Sichem to us, or Succoth, or Gilead, Moab, or Edom? It is not even clear what these place-names, severally or together, would mean to the audience for which the psalm was originally intended, since that audience changed over perhaps a thousand years. The canonical headnote or title only aggravates the specificity, and therefore the obscurity: 'David's Michtam, to teach, when he fought against the Syrians of Mesopotamia, and against the Syrians of Soba, and that Joab returning home had slain the Edomites in the King's Dale about twelve thousand' (Arthur Golding's version). One may suppose that for Jews, even ancient Jews, the psalm may have been, as it necessarily is for Christians, a sort of mantra. And of course if a mantra, a sacred text used as an incantation, is an aid to devotion for Hindus, why should it not serve in the same way for Jews and Christians? But this is an argument to be used only in desperation.

Psalm 77

1. I will cry unto God with my voice: even unto God will I cry with my voice, and he shall hearken unto me.

2. In the time of my trouble I sought the Lord: my sore ran

and ceased not in the night-season; my soul refused comfort.

3. When I am in heaviness, I will think upon God: when my heart is vexed, I will complain.

4. Thou holdest mine eyes waking: I am so feeble, that I cannot speak.

5. I have considered the days of old: and the years that are past.

6. I call to remembrance my song: and in the night I commune with mine own heart, and search out my spirits.

7. Will the Lord absent himself for ever: and will he be no more intreated?

8. Is his mercy clean gone for ever: and is his promise come utterly to an end for evermore?

9. Hath God forgotten to be gracious: and will he shut up his loving-kindness in displeasure?

10. And I said, It is mine own infirmity: but I will remember the years of the right hand of the most Highest.

11. I will remember the works of the Lord: and call to mind thy wonders of old time.

12. I will think also of all thy works: and my talking shall be of thy doings.

13. Thy way, O God, is holy: who is so great a God as our God?

14. Thou art the God that doeth wonders: and hast declared thy power among the people.

15. Thou hast mightily delivered thy people: even the sons of Jacob and Joseph.

16. The waters saw thee, O God, the waters saw thee, and were afraid: the depths also were troubled.

17. The clouds poured out water, the air thundered: and thine arrows went abroad.

18. The voice of thy thunder was heard round about: the lightnings shone upon the ground; the earth was moved and shook withal.

19. Thy way is in the sea, and thy paths in the great waters: and thy footsteps are not known.

20. Thou leddest thy people like sheep: by the hand of Moses and Aaron.   (1535)

Psalm 102

1. Hear my prayer, O Lord: and let my crying come unto thee.

2. Hide not thy face from me in the time of my trouble: incline thine ear unto me when I call; O hear me, and that right soon.

3. For my days are consumed away like smoke: and my bones are burnt up as it were a fire-brand.

4. My heart is smitten down, and withered like grass: so that I forget to eat my bread.

5. For the voice of my groaning: my bones will scarce cleave to my flesh.

6. I am become like a pelican in the wilderness: and like an owl that is in the desert.

7. I have watched, and am even as it were a sparrow: that sitteth alone upon the house-top.

8. Mine enemies revile me all the day long: and they that are mad upon me are sworn together against me.

9. For I have eaten ashes as it were bread: and mingled my drink with weeping;

10. And that because of thine indignation and wrath: for thou hast taken me up, and cast me down.

11. My days are gone like a shadow: and I am withered like grass.

12. But thou, O lord, shalt endure for ever: and thy remembrance throughout all generations.

13. Thou shalt arise, and have mercy upon Sion: for it is time that thou have mercy upon her, yea, the time is come.

14. And why? thy servants think upon her stones: and it pitieth them to see her in the dust.

15. The heathen shall fear thy Name, O Lord: and all the kings of the earth thy Majesty;

16. When the Lord shall build up Sion: and when his glory shall appear;

17. When he turneth him unto the prayer of the poor destitute: and despiseth not their desire.

18. This shall be written for those that come after: and the people which shall be born shall praise the Lord.

19. For he hath looked down from his sanctuary: out of the heaven did the Lord behold the earth;

20. That he might hear the mournings of such as are in captivity: and deliver the children appointed unto death;

21. That they may declare the Name of the Lord in Sion: and his worship at Jerusalem;

22. When the people are gathered together: and the kingdoms also, to serve the Lord.

23. He brought down my strength in my journey: and shortened my days.

24. But I said, O my God, take me not away in the midst of mine age: as for thy years, they endure throughout all generations.

25. Thou, Lord, in the beginning hast laid the foundation of the earth: and the heavens are the work of thy hands.

26. They shall perish, but thou shalt endure: they all shall wax old as doth a garment;

27. And as a vesture shalt thou change them, and they shall be changed: but thou art the same, and thy years shall not fail.

28. The children of thy servants shall continue: and their seed shall stand fast in thy sight.   (1535)

Psalm 114

1. When Israel came out of Egypt: and the house of Jacob from among the strange people,

2. Judah was his sanctuary and Israel his dominion.

3. The sea saw that, and fled: Jordan was driven back.

4. The mountains skipped like rams: and the little hills like young sheep.

5. What aileth thee, O thou sea, that thou fleddest: and thou Jordan, that thou wast driven back?

6. Ye mountains, that ye skipped like rams: and ye little hills, like young sheep?

7. Tremble, thou earth, at the presence of the Lord: at the presence of the God of Jacob;

8. Who turned the hard rock into a standing water: and the flint-stone into a springing well. (1535)

Psalm 118

1. O give thanks unto the Lord, for he is gracious: because his mercy endureth for ever.

2. Let Israel now confess that he is gracious: and that his mercy endureth for ever.

3. Let the house of Aaron now confess: that his mercy endureth for ever.

4. Yea, let them now that fear the Lord confess: that his mercy endureth for ever.

5. I called upon the Lord in trouble: and the Lord heard me at large.

6. The Lord is on my side: I will not fear what man doeth unto me.

7. The Lord taketh my part with them that help me: therefore shall I see my desire upon mine enemies.

8. It is better to trust in the Lord: than to put any confidence in man.

9. It is better to trust in the Lord: than to put any confidence in princes.

10. All nations compassed me round about: but in the Name of the Lord will I destroy them.

11. They kept me in on every side, they kept me in, I say, on every side: but in the Name of the Lord will I destroy them.

12. They came about me like bees, and are extinct even as the fire among the thorns: for in the Name of the Lord I will destroy them.

13. Thou hast thrust sore at me, that I might fall: but the Lord was my help.

14. The Lord is my strength, and my song: and is become my salvation.

15. The voice of joy and health is in the dwellings of the righteous; the right hand of the Lord bringeth mighty things to pass.

16. The right hand of the Lord hath the pre-eminence: the right hand of the Lord bringeth mighty things to pass.

17. I shall not die, but live: and declare the works of the Lord.

18. The Lord hath chastened and corrected me: but he hath not given me over unto death.

19. Open me the gates of righteousness: that I may go into them and give thanks unto the Lord.

20. This is the gate of the Lord: the righteous shall enter into it.

21. I will thank thee, for thou hast heard me: and art become my salvation.

22. The same stone which the builders refused: is become the head-stone in the corner.

23. This is the Lord's doing: and it is marvellous in our eyes.

24. This is the day which the Lord hath made: we will rejoice and be glad in it.

25. Help me now, O Lord: O Lord, send us now prosperity.

26. Blessed be he that cometh in the Name of the Lord: we have wished you good luck, ye that are of the house of the Lord.

27. God is the Lord who hath shewed us light: bind the sacrifice with cords, yea, even unto the horns of the altar.

28. Thou art my God, and I will thank thee: thou art my God, and I will praise thee.

29. O give thanks unto the Lord, for he is gracious: and his mercy endureth for ever. (1535)

Psalm 124

1. If the Lord himself had not been on our side, now may Israel say: if the Lord himself had not been on our side, when men rose up against us;

2. They had swallowed us up quick: when they were so wrathfully displeased at us.

3. Yea, the waters had drowned us: and the stream had gone over our soul.

4. The deep waters of the proud: had gone even over our soul.

5. But praised be the Lord: who hath not given us over for a prey unto their teeth.

6. Our soul is escaped even as a bird out of the snare of the fowler: the snare is broken, and we are delivered.

7. Our help standeth in the Name of the Lord: who hath made heaven and earth. (1535)

Coverdale's 'had' in vv. 2, 3 and 4 is a subjunctive, accordingly rendered by the modern translator Frost as 'would have'. But of course though this is nowadays more usual, Coverdale's subjunctive 'had' is a usage not yet obsolete. Retaining it gives a splendid exultant speed through the sentence, something which the ancient poet makes the most of by reiterating – for emphasis, but also to start his sentence slowly – the conditional clause in v. 1. Such creative use of syntax is rare in the psalms, for reasons glanced at in the Introduction. Accordingly the poem is thought to be late (post-exilic); more importantly, it leaps off the page for the speaking voice like nothing else in the Psalter. Compare versions of it by Anon., and by Gordon Jackson.

Psalm 135

1. O praise the Lord, laud ye the Name of the Lord: praise it, O ye servants of the Lord;

2. Ye that stand in the house of the Lord: in the courts of the house of our God.

3. O praise the Lord, for the Lord is gracious; O sing praises unto his Name, for it is lovely.

4. For why? the Lord hath chosen Jacob unto himself: and Israel for his own possession.

5. For I know that the Lord is great: and that our Lord is above all gods.

6. Whatsoever the Lord pleased, that did he in heaven and in earth: and in the sea, and in all deep places.

7. He bringeth forth the clouds from the ends of the world: and sendeth forth lightnings with the rain, bringing the winds out of his treasures.

8. He smote the first-born of Egypt: both of man and beast.

9. He hath sent tokens and wonders into the midst of thee, O thou land of Egypt: upon Pharaoh, and all his servants.

10. He smote divers nations: and slew mighty kings;

11. Sehon king of the Amorites, and Og the king of Basan: and all the kingdoms of Canaan;

12. And gave their land to be an heritage: even an heritage unto Israel his people.

13. Thy Name, O Lord, endureth for ever: so doth thy memorial, O Lord, from one generation to another.

14. For the Lord will avenge his people: and be gracious unto his servants.

15. As for the images of the heathen, they are but silver and gold: the work of men's hands.

16. They have mouths, and speak not: eyes have they, but they see not.

17. They have ears, and yet they hear not: neither is there any breath in their mouths.

18. They that make them are like unto them: and so are all they that put their trust in them.

19. Praise the Lord, ye house of Israel: praise the Lord, ye house of Aaron.

20. Praise the Lord, ye house of Levi: ye that fear the Lord, praise the Lord.

21. Praised be the Lord out of Sion: who dwelleth at Jerusalem.   (1535)

THOMAS STERNHOLD (d. 1549)

Sternhold was a pioneer, if only in getting his metrical versions out of manuscript and into print. As often happens in literary history, his pioneering is counted unto him for virtue or as compensating for what even his apologists recognize as 'stylistic ineptitudes'. In fact the exasperation that in the next century Sternhold aroused in John Donne and Henry King was thoroughly deserved. His versions were written in rhyming fourteeners disguised in the printing as alternating tetrameters and trimeters. The modern reader can learn to relish that obsolete measure, the fourteener, in for instance Golding's translation of Ovid's *Metamorphoses*; but recasting Sternhold's false quatrains as true fourteeners does not rescue him; the metre remains jog-trot. His Psalm 23 is unrepresentative, a happy exception.

Psalm 23

My shepherd is the living Lord,
    nothing therefore I need;
In pastures fair with waters calm
    he sets me forth to feed.
He did convert and glad my soul,

and brought my mind in frame,
To walk in paths of righteousness,
    for his most holy Name.

Yea, though I walk in vale of death,
10   yet will I fear none ill:
Thy rod, thy staff doth comfort me,
    and thou art with me still.
And in the presence of my foes
    my table thou shalt spread:
Thou shalt, O Lord, fill full my cup,
    and eke anoint my head.

Through all my life thy favour is
    so frankly shew'd to me,
That in thy house for evermore
20   my dwelling-place shall be.   (1565)

WILLIAM WHITTINGHAM
(1524?–1579)

In 1555 Whittingham fled the Marian persecution to Geneva, where he married Calvin's sister and succeeded Knox as pastor of the English congregation. He had much to do with the translation of the Geneva Bible, and out of his expertise as a Hebraist revised Sternhold's translations and the first seven by Hopkins. Returning to England on Elizabeth's accession, Whittingham was made Dean of Durham in 1563, and from Durham was in touch with John Knox across the border. Certainly an uncompromising Puritan, he is accused of having destroyed in Durham the image of St Cuthbert. In view of his Genevan connections it is not surprising that Whittingham favours French Calvinist conventions in verse and music, as against the Lutheran German precedents followed by Coverdale and his successors.

Psalm 51

O Lord, consider my distress,
   and now with speed some pity take;
My sins deface, my faults redress,
   good Lord, for thy great mercies' sake.
Wash me, O Lord, and make me clean
   from this unjust and sinful act,
And purify yet once again
   my heinous crime and bloody fact.

Remorse and sorrow do constrain
10   me to acknowledge mine excess;
My sin alas doth still remain
   before my face without release.
For thee alone I have offended,
   committing evil in thy sight;
And if I were therefore condemnèd,
   yet were thy judgments just and right.

It is too manifest alas
   that first I was conceiv'd in sin;
Yea, of my mother so born was,
20   and yet vile wretch remain therein.
Also behold, Lord, thou dost love
   the inward truth of a pure heart;
Therefore thy wisdom from above
   thou hast reveal'd me to convert.

If thou with hyssop purge this blot,
   I shall be cleaner than the glass;
And if thou wash away my spot,
   the snow in whiteness shall I pass.

Therefore, O Lord, such joy me send
    that inwardly I may find grace,
And that my strength may now amend
    which thou hast 'ssuag'd for my trespass.

Turn back thy face and frowning ire,
    for I have felt enough thy hand;
And purge my sins I thee desire,
    which do in number pass the sand.
Make new my heart within my breast,
    and frame it to thy holy will;
Thy constant Spirit in me let rest,
    which may these raging enemies kill.

The second part

Cast me not, Lord, out from thy face,
    but speedily my torments end;
Take not from me thy Spirit of grace,
    which may from dangers me defend.
Restore me to those joys again
    which I was wont in thee to find;
And let me thy free Spirit retain,
    which unto thee may stir my mind.

Thus when I shall thy mercies know,
    I shall instruct others therein;
And men that are likewise brought low
    by mine example shall flee sin.
O God, that of my health art Lord,
    forgive me this my bloody vice;
My heart and tongue shall then accord
    to sing thy mercies and justice.

Touch thou my lips, my tongue untie,
  O Lord, which art the only key;
And then my mouth shall testify
60   thy wondrous works and praise alway.
And as for outward sacrifice,
  I would have offered many a one;
But thou esteem'st them of no price,
  and therein pleasure tak'st thou none.

The heavy heart, the mind opprest,
  O Lord, thou never dost reject;
And, to speak truth, it is the best,
  and of all sacrifice th'effect.
Lord, unto Sion turn thy face,
70   pour out thy mercies on thy hill,
And on Jerusalem thy grace
  build up the walls, and love it still.

Thou shalt accept then our off'rings
  of peace and righteousness, I say;
Yea calves and many other things
  upon thine altar will we lay.   (1556)

Consult the Introduction for the problems set by this psalm, and for how Coverdale and Wyatt tried to deal with them. This is the first in the Old Version to employ 'long measure'; and is surely less congested than Wyatt's.

WILLIAM KETHE (d. 1608?)

William Kethe, apparently a Scot who in the time of the Marian persecutions found refuge in Geneva, ended his life as a rector in Dorset. Unable to ascertain for him a date either of birth or death, we have to recognize in him the sort of immortality that resides in his having his verses sung every Sunday across the English-speaking world.

Psalm 100

All people that on earth do dwell,
   Sing to the Lord with cheerful voice:
Him serve with mirth, his praise forth tell,
   Come ye before him, and rejoice.

The Lord, ye know, is God indeed;
   Without our aid he did us make;
We are his folk, he doth us feed,
   And for his sheep he doth us take.

Oh enter then his gates with praise,
10   Approach with joy his courts unto;
Praise, laud, and bless his name always,
   For it is seemly so to do.

For why, the Lord our God is good;
   His mercy is for ever sure;
His truth at all times firmly stood,
   And shall from age to age endure.   (1561)

Psalm 104

My soul, praise the Lord,
   speak good of his Name.
O Lord our great God,
   how dost thou appear,

So passing in glory
   that great is thy fame?
Honour and Majesty
   in thee shine most clear.

With light, as a robe,
10   thou hast thee beclad,
Whereby all the earth
   thy greatness may see;
The heavens in such sort
   thou also hast spread,
That it to a curtain
   comparèd may be.

His chamber-beams lie
   in the clouds full sure,
Which as his chariots
20   are made him to bear;
And there with much swiftness
   his course doth endure,
Upon the wings riding
   of winds in the air.

He maketh his spirits
   as heralds to go;
And lightnings to serve
   we see also prest.
His will to accomplish
30   they run to and fro,
To save or consume things
   as seemeth him best.

---

7 H. Leigh Bennett, in Julian's *Dictionary of Hymnology*, points out that 'Honour and Majesty' can be made metrical if we accord to the two abstractions the pronunciation of their French (i.e. Genevan) cognates.

He groundeth the earth
   so firmly and fast,
That it once to move
   none shall have such power.
The deep a fair covering
   for it made thou hast;
Which by his own nature
40   the hills would devour.

But at thy rebuke
   the waters do flee;
And so give due place
   thy word to obey.
At thy word of thunder
   so fearful they be,
That in their great raging
   they haste soon away.

The mountains full high
50   they then up ascend;
If thou do but speak,
   thy word they fulfil.
So likewise the valleys
   most quickly descend;
Where thou them appointest
   remain they do still.

Their bounds thou hast set
   how far they shall run,
So that in their rage
60   not that pass they can.
For God hath appointed
   they shall not return
The earth to destroy more,
   which made was for man.

The second part

He sendeth the springs
　　to strong streams or lakes,
Which run do full swift
　　among the huge hills;
Where both the wild asses
70　　their thirst oft-times slakes,
And beasts of the mountains
　　thereof drink their fills.

By these pleasant springs
　　of fountains full fair,
The fowls of the air
　　abide shall and dwell;
Who movèd by nature
　　to hop here and there,
Among the green branches
80　　their songs shall excel.

The mountains to moist
　　the clouds he doth use;
The earth with his works
　　is wholly replete,
So as the brute cattle
　　he doth not refuse,
But grass doth provide them
　　and herb for man's meat.

Yea, bread, wine, and oil
90　　he made for man's sake,
His face to refresh,
　　and heart to make strong.
The cedars of Liban
　　this great Lord did make;
Which trees he doth nourish
　　that grow up so long.

In these may birds build
  and make there their nests;
In fir-trees the storks
100   remain and abide.
The high hills are succours
  for wild goats to rest;
And eke the rock stony
  for conies to hide.

The moon then is set
  her seasons to run;
The days from the nights
  thereby to discern.
And by the descending
110   also of the sun,
The cold from heat alway
  thereby we do learn.

When darkness doth come
  by God's will and power,
Then creep forth do all
  the beasts of the wood.
The lions range roaring
  their prey to devour;
But yet it is thou, Lord,
120   which givest them food.

As soon as the sun
  is up, they retire.
To couch in their dens
  then are they full fain;
That man to his work may,
  as right doth require,
Till night come and call him
  to take rest again.

The third part

How sundry, O Lord,
130   are all thy works found!
With wisdom full great
    they are indeed wrought;
So that the whole world
    of thy praise doth sound,
And as for thy riches
    they pass all men's thought.

So is the great sea,
    which large is and broad,
Where things that creep swarm,
140   and beasts of each sort.
There both mighty ships sail,
    and some lie at road;
The whale huge and monstrous
    there also doth sport.

All things on thee wait,
    thou dost them relieve;
And thou in due time
    full well dost them feed.
Now when it doth please thee
150   the same for to give,
They gather full gladly
    those things which they need.

Thou openest thy hand,
    and they find such grace,
That they with good things
    are fillèd we see.
But sore are they troubled
    if thou turn thy face;
For if thou their breath take,
160   vile dust then they be.

Again, when thy Spirit
   from thee doth proceed
All things to appoint,
   and what shall ensue,
Then are they created
   as thou hast decreed,
And dost by thy goodness
   the dry earth renew.

The praise of the Lord
170   for ever shall last,
Who may in his works
   by right well rejoice.
His look can the earth make
   to tremble full fast,
And likewise the mountains
   to smoke at his voice.

To this Lord and God
   sing will I always;
So long as I live,
180   my God praise will I.
Then am I most certain
   my words shall him please;
I will rejoice in him,
   to him will I cry.

The sinners, O Lord,
   consume in thine ire;
And eke the perverse
   them root out with shame.
But as for my soul now,
190   let it still desire,
And say with the faithful,
   'Praise ye the Lord's name.'

(1562)

This is the psalm that produced Robert Grant's 'O worship the King' (see *post*). Those modern readers who find this version moving, despite its quaintnesses, may fix upon the sparseness of its rhyming, so unobtrusive that at first reading we may think it not rhymed at all. But Victorian readers, for example H. Leigh Bennett in Julian's *Dictionary of Hymnology*, who didn't share our feelings about rhyme, esteemed Kethe's version no less.

From Psalm 107

Let men therefore before the Lord
    confess his kindness then;
And shew the wonders that he doth
    before the sons of men.
And let them offer sacrifice
    with thanks, and also fear;
And speak of all his wondrous works
    with glad and joyful cheer.

Such as in ships and brittle barks
10   into the seas descend,
Their merchandise through fearful floods
    to compass and to end;
Those men are forcèd to behold
    the Lord's works what they be,
And in the dangerous deep, the same
    most marvellous they see.

For at his word the stormy wind
    ariseth in a rage,
And stirreth up the surges so
20   as naught can them assuage.
Then are they lifted up so high
    the clouds they seem to gain,
And plunging down the depth until
    their souls consume with pain.

And like a drunkard, to and fro
   now here now there they reel,
As men with fear of wit bereft
   or had of sense no feel.
Then did they cry in their distress
30   unto the Lord for aid;
Who did remove their troublous state,
   according as they pray'd.

For with his word the Lord doth make
   the sturdy storms to cease;
So that the great waves from their rage
   are brought to rest and peace.
Then are men glad when rest is come
   which they so much did crave;
And are by him in haven brought,
40   which they so fain would have.   (1562)

Psalm 122

I did in heart rejoice
To hear the people's voice,
   In offering so willingly:
For let us up, say they,
And in the Lord's house pray.
   Thus spake the folk full lovingly.

Our feet that wandered wide
Shall in thy gates abide,
   O thou Jerusalem full fair,
10 Which art so seemly set
Much like a city neat,
   The like whereof is not elsewhere.

The tribes with one accord,
The tribes of God the Lord,
   Are thither bent their way to take.
So God before did tell
That there his Israel
   Their prayers should together make.

For there are thrones erect,
20 And that for this respect,
   To set forth justice orderly;
Which thrones' right to maintain
To David's house pertain,
   His folk to judge accordingly.

To pray let us not cease
For Jerusalem's peace,
   Thy friends God prosper mightily;
Peace be thy walls about,
And prosper thee throughout
30   Thy palaces continually.

I wish thy prosperous state
   For my poor brethren's sake
That comfort hath by means of thee.
God's house doth me allure
Thy wealth for to procure
   So much always as lies in me.   (1562)

GEORGE GASCOIGNE (1534–1577)

George Gascoigne, educated at Cambridge, was MP for Bedford in
the 1550s. Patronized by the Earl of Leicester, he was a soldier in
the Netherlands from 1572 to 1574. See C. T. Prouty, *George*

Gascoigne: Elizabethan Courtier, Soldier and Poet (New York, 1942); also Yvor Winters's appreciation of Gascoigne's style, in *Forms of Discovery* (Denver, 1967), pp. 15–19.

Psalm 130 *De Profundis*

From depth of dole wherein my soul doth dwell,
From heavy heart which harbours in my breast,
From troubled sprite which seldom taketh rest,
From hope of heaven, from dread of darksome hell,
O gracious God, to thee I cry and yell:
My God, my Lord, my lovely Lord alone,
To thee I call, to thee I make my moan.
And thou, good God, vouchsafe in gree to take
    This woeful plaint
10   Wherein I faint:
Oh, hear me then, for thy great mercy's sake!

Oh, bend thine ears attentively to hear,
Oh, turn thine eyes – behold me how I wail;
Oh, hearken, Lord, give ear for mine avail;
Oh, mark in mind the burthens that I bear!
See how I sink in sorrows everywhere;
Behold and see what dolors I endure;
Give ear and mark what plaints I put in ure:
Bend willing ear, and pity therewithall
20   My wailing voice
    Which hath no choice
But evermore upon thy name to call.

If thou, good Lord, shouldst take thy rod in hand,
If thou regard what sins are daily done,
If thou take hold where we our works begone,
If thou decree in judgment for to stand,
And be extreme to see our 'scuses scann'd, –

If thou take note of everything amiss,
And write in rolls how frail our nature is,
30 O glorious God! O King! O Prince of power!
   What mortal wight
   May then have light
To feel thy frown, if thou hast list to lour?

But thou art good, and hast of mercy store;
Thou not delight'st to see a sinner fall;
Thou heark'nest first before we come to call;
Thine ears are set wide open evermore;
Before we knock, thou comest to the door:
Thou art more prest to hear a sinner cry
40 Than he is quick to climb to thee on high.
Thy mighty name be praisèd then alway:
   Let faith and fear
   True witness bear
How fast they stand which on thy mercy stay.

I look for thee, my lovely Lord, therefore;
For thee I wait, for thee I tarry still:
Mine eyes do long to gaze on thee my fill;
For thee I watch, for thee I pry and pore:
My soul for thee attendeth evermore;
50 My soul doth thirst to take of thee a taste;
My soul desires with thee for to be plac'd;
And to thy word, which can no man deceive, –
   Mine only trust,
   My love and lust, –
In confidence continually shall cleave.

Before the break or dawning of the day,
Before the light be seen in lofty skies,
Before the sun appear in pleasant wise,
Before the watch – before the watch, I say,
60 Before the ward that waits therefore alway,

My soul, my sense, my secret thought, my sprite,
My will, my wish, my joy, and my delight,
Unto the Lord that sits in heaven on high,
   With hasty wing
   From me doth fling,
And striveth still unto the Lord to fly.

O Israel, O household of the Lord,
O Abraham's brats, O brood of blessed seed –
O chosen sheep, that love the Lord indeed –
70 O hungry hearts, feed still upon his word,
And put your trust in him with one accord!
For he hath mercy evermore at hand;
His fountains flow, his springs do never stand;
And plenteously he loveth to redeem
   Such sinners all
   As on him call,
And faithfully his mercies most esteem.

He will redeem our deadly, drooping state;
He will bring home the sheep that go astray;
80 He will help them that hope in him alway;
He will appease our discord and debate;
He will soon save, though we repent us late.
He will be ours, if we continue his;
He will bring bale to joy and perfect bliss;
He will redeem the flock of his elect
   From all that is,
   Or was, amiss
Since Abraham's heirs did first his laws reject.   (1563?)

ARTHUR GOLDING (1536?–1605?)

Arthur Golding is known to readers of Ezra Pound as a greatly applauded verse-translator of Ovid's *Metamorphoses*. Golding's other publications reveal him, surprisingly, as a polemicist in the Calvinist interest. His *Psalms of David & Others*, translated from Calvin's Latin, appeared first in 1571 as part of his version of Calvin's *Commentaries on the Psalms*; they were extracted from that context and, edited by R. G. Barnes, appeared separately in San Francisco in 1977.

Though I reproduce the spacious printing of the San Francisco version, this should not delude the reader into thinking that Golding is versifying; his is a prose version, like Coverdale's, with which he can hold his own.

Psalm 12

1. Save me O Lord, for the merciful is waxed scant,
   and the faithful are wasted away
   from among the children of men.

2. Every man talketh deceit with his fellow,
   with the lips of flattery in their heart
   and in their heart do they speak.

3. Let the Lord cut out all the lips of flattery,
   and the tongue that speaketh great things

4. Which have said,
   With our tongues will we be strengthened:
   our lips are in our own power: who is our Lord?

5. For the spoiling of the needy,
   for the deep sighing of the poor,
   will I now rise up, saith the Lord:
   I will set him in safety whom he snareth.

6. The words of the Lord are pure words:
   silver cast in a principal cup of the earth, tried seven times.

7. Thou O Lord shalt keep them,
   thou shalt preserve him from this generation for ever.

8. The ungodly walk about on every side,
   when they are exalted,
   they are a reproach to the children of men.   (1571)

In this very ancient (pre-exilic) psalm those who oppress the needy
are above all talkers, darkeners of counsel: those who sophisticate
with novelties the truths that the humble hold by. We might say it
is a poem against the avant-garde, or the 'chattering classes'.

Psalm 18

1. And he said, I will love thee O Lord my strength.

2. The Lord is my rock, my fortress, and my deliverer:
   my God, my strength, I will trust in him:
   my shield, the horn of my welfare, and my refuge.

3. I will call upon the praised Lord,
   and I shall be saved from mine enemies.

4. The cords of death had compassed me about,
   the watershots of wickedness had made me afraid.

5. The cords of the grave had compassed me about,
   the snares of death had overtaken me.

6. In my distress I called upon the Lord,
   and I cried unto my God:
   and he hath heard my voice out of his Temple,
   and my cry before him came unto his ears.

7. Then the Earth moved itself and quaked,
and the foundations of the Mountains shook
and stirred themselves, because he was wroth.

8. There went up a smoke into his nostrils,
and the fire consumed which went out of his Mouth:
Coals were kindled at it.

9. And he bowed the Heavens and came down:
and there was darkness under his feet.

10. And he rode upon Cherub, and flew:
and was carried upon the wings of the wind.

11. He made darkness his secret place,
round about him was his tent,
darksomeness of water and the clouds of Heaven.

12. At the brightness of his presence his clouds passed away:
hailstones and coals of fire.

13. And he sent out his arrows, and scattered them:
and he multiplied lightnings, and astonished them.

14. And the headsprings of the waters were seen,
and the foundations of the round world were discovered
at thy rebuking, O Lord,
at the blast of the breath of thy nostrils.

15. He sent down from aloft, and took me up:
he led me out of many waters.

16. He delivered me from my strong enemy,
and from mine adversary:
because they were too strong for me.

17. They had prevented me in the day of my trouble:
    and the Lord was my stay.

18. And he brought me forth at large:
    he delivered me because he had a favor unto me.

19. The Lord hath rewarded me after my righteousness,
    according to the cleanness of my hands
    hath he recompensed me.

20. Because I have kept the ways of the Lord,
    and have not wickedly shrunk from my God.

21. Because all his judgments are before me
    and I have not cast his commandments from me.

22. And I have been found with him,
    and have kept my self from mine own wickedness.

23. And the Lord hath rewarded me
    according to my righteousness,
    and according to the cleanness
    of my hands before his eyes.

24. With the meek thou wilt deal meekly,
    and with the sound thou wilt deal soundly.

25. With the pure thou wilt be pure,
    and with the froward thou wilt deal frowardly.

26. For thou wilt save the folk that be brought low,
    and cast down the eyes of the proud.

27. For thou shalt light my candle O Lord:
    my God shall lighten my darkness.

28. For in thee shall I break through the wedge of a battle,
    and in my God shall I leap over a wall.

29. The way of God is perfect,
    the word of the Lord is tried in the fire,
    he is a shield to all that trust in him.

30. For who is God but the Lord?
    and who is strong but our God?

31. It is God that hath girded me with strength,
    and hath made my way perfect.

32. Making my feet like Hinds' feet,
    and it is he that hath set me upon my high places.

33. Teaching my hands to fight:
    and mine arms shall break a bow of steel.

34. And thou hast given me the shield of safeguard,
    and thy right hand hath shored me up,
    and thy mercifulness hath increased me.

35. Thou hast enlarged my paces under me:
    and mine ankles have not staggered.

36. I will pursue mine enemies, and overtake them:
    and I will not return till I have consumed them.

37. I have smitten them, and they could not rise:
    they are fallen under my feet.

38. And thou hast girded me with strength unto battle:
    thou hast bowed down mine enemies under me.

39. And thou hast given me the neck of mine enemies:
    and thou hast destroyed those that hate me.

40. They shall cry out, and there shall be none to save them:
    even unto the Lord, but he shall not answer them.

41. And I shall grind them as small
    as the dust before the wind:
    as the mire in the streets shall I tread them under foot.

42. Thou shalt deliver me from the strivings of the people:
    thou shalt make me the head of the Heathen.
    A people whom I have not known, shall serve me.

43. As soon as they hear, they shall obey me:
    the children of the strangers shall lie unto me.

44. The children of the strangers shall shrink away,
    and tremble in their privy chambers.

45. Let the Lord live, and blessed be my strength,
    and the God of my welfare be exalted.

46. It is God that giveth me power to avenge me,
    and subdueth the people under me.

47. My deliverer from mine enemies,
    thou hast set me up even from them
    that have risen up against me:
    thou hast rid me from the cruel man.

48. Therefore will I praise thee, O Lord, among the Nations,
    and sing unto thy name.

49. He worketh mightily the welfare of his King,
    and performeth mercy to David his anointed,
    and to his seed for ever.

(1571)

Though there have been later accretions, this psalm (which appears also at 2 Samuel 22) is 'certainly one of the most ancient in the Psalter' (Oesterley). If any psalm reaches back to King David's period, if not indeed into David's own mouth, this may be the one. The psalm has found few translators, for the obvious reason that it can hardly be Christianized. No ingenuity in 'spiritualizing' can conceal that it is the vaunt of a victor in battles actual and bloody, though for a strenuous Christianizing of it (as 'Messianic') see Derek Kidner, *Psalms 1–72. An Introduction and Commentary* (1973).

Psalm 19

1. The skies declare the glory of God,
   and the Cope of heaven telleth forth
   the works of his hands.

2. Day unto day uttereth speech,
   and night unto night telleth forth knowledge.

3. There is no speech, nor language,
   where their voice is not heard.

4. Their writing is gone forth into the uttermost coasts of
       the world
   in them hath he set a pavilion for the Sun.

5. And he cometh forth as a bridegroom out of his chamber,
   and rejoiceth like a strong man to run his race.

6. His coming out
       is from the uttermost coast of the heavens,
       and his going about
       is upon the uttermost point of the same:
       and no man is hid from the heat of him.

7. The law of the Lord is perfect, repairing the Soul:
   the testimony of the Lord is faithful,
   instructing the little ones in wisdom.

8. The statutes of the Lord are right, and rejoice the heart:
   the commandment of the Lord is pure
   and giveth light to the eyes.

9. The fear of the Lord is clean, and endureth for ever:
   the judgments of the Lord are truth, and justified together.

10. More to be desired than gold, yea than much fine gold:
    sweeter also than honey, and the honeycomb.

11. Moreover, by them is thy servant made circumspect,
    and in keeping of them there is great reward.

12. Who can understand his faults?
    Cleanse me from my secret faults.

13. Withhold thy servants also from presumptuous sins,
       that they overmaster me not:
       then shall I be found,
          and shall be cleansed from much wickedness.

14. Let the words of my mouth and the conceits of my heart
    be acceptable in thy sight,

15. O Lord, my strength and my redeemer.   (1571)

This may be preferred to the versions in *AV* and *BCP* because of
the starkness with which it renders the disconcerting v. 12: 'Who
can understand his faults?/Cleanse me from my secret faults.' To
compare this with Addison's famous version (see *post*, 'The spacious
firmament on high') is to reveal that Addison translated less than
half the psalm, restricting himself to the first six verses, which have
been thought to come from a Babylonian hymn to a Sun-god.

Psalm 37

1. Fret not thy self because of the wicked,
   neither spite thou them that work iniquity.

2. For they shall soon be cut down like grass,
   and they shall wither as the green grass.

3. Put thy trust in the Lord and do good:
   dwell in the land and be fed faithfully.

4. Delight in the Lord,
   and he will give thee thy heart's desire.

5. Commit thy ways unto the Lord, and trust in him,
   and he will bring it to pass.

6. And he will bring forth thy righteousness as the light,
   and thy judgments as the noon day.

7. Hold thy peace unto the Lord, and tarry his leisure,
   fret not thyself at him that proceedeth prosperously in his
       way
   at the man that bringeth his wickedness to effect.

8. Cease from wrath, away with chafing,
   and be not angry, for fear lest thou sin.

9. For evildoers shall be cut up,
   but they that tarry the Lord's leisure shall inherit the land.

10. Yet a while, and the ungodly shall be quite gone:
    and thou shalt look to his place, and shalt not find him.

11. But the meek shall inherit the land,
    and shall take their pleasure in the multitude of peace.

12. The ungodly deviseth against the righteous,
    and gnasheth upon him with his teeth.

13. But the Lord shall laugh him to scorn,
    for he seeth that his day is coming.

14. The ungodly draw their swords, and bend their bow,
    to throw down the poor and needy,
    and to slay such as be of a right conversation.

15. Their sword shall enter into their own heart,
    and their bow shall be broken.

16. Better is a small thing to the righteous,
    than is the wealthiness of the ungodly great ones.

17. For the arms of the ungodly shall be broken,
    but the Lord holdeth up the righteous.

18. The Lord knoweth the days of the righteous
    and their inheritance shall be everlasting.

19. They shall not be shamed in the time of adversity,
    and in the days of famine they shall have enough.

20. But the ungodly shall perish,
    and the Lord's enemies shall be consumed
    as the preciousness of Lambs,
    in the smoke shall they be consumed.

21. The ungodly borroweth, and payeth not again:
    but the righteous is merciful and giveth.

22. For such as be blessed of God shall inherit the land,
    and such as be cursed of him shall be cut up.

23. The steps of man are directed by the Lord,
    and he loveth his ways.

24. Though he fall he shall not be bruised,
    because the Lord putteth under his hand.

25. I have been young, and now am old:
    yet saw I never the righteous forsaken,
    and his seed beg their bread.

26. He is daily merciful and lendeth,
    and his seed is unto the blessing.

27. Depart from evil and do good,
    and dwell for ever.

28. For the Lord loveth judgment,
    and forsaketh not his meek ones, they shall be kept safe
        for ever,
    and the seed of the ungodly shall be rooted out.

29. The righteous shall inherit the land,
    and dwell upon it for ever.

30. The mouth of the righteous will speak of wisdom,
    and his tongue will talk of judgment.

31. The Law of God is in his heart,
    and his feet shall not slide.

32. The wicked watcheth the righteous,
    and seeketh to slay him.

33. The Lord will not leave him in his hand,
    nor condemn him when he is judged.

34. Tarry thou the Lord's leisure and keep his way,
    and he will exalt thee, that thou mayst inherit the land:
    when the wicked men shall be cut up, thou shalt see it.

35. I have seen the wicked strong
    and spreading himself out like a green Bay.

36. And he passed away, and lo he was gone:
    and I sought his place, and he was not found.

37. Mark the perfect man, and consider the just:
    for the end of that man is peace.

38. But the transgressors shall be wiped out together,
    the end of the ungodly shall be cut off.

39. But the welfare of the righteous is of the Lord,
    he is their strength in the time of trouble.

40. And the Lord shall help them and deliver them:
    he shall deliver them from the ungodly:
    he shall preserve them because they trust in him.   (1571)

No denying it, this psalm is tiresomely repetitious. The repetitions are so insistent as to make one wonder whether at some earlier stage the piece was not blocked out as stanzas with refrains. More certainly it was, and largely still is, structured as an acrostic, each couple of verses beginning with the same letter of the Hebrew alphabet. Probably no twentieth-century taste, however sympathetic, can tolerate the expedients to which the poet is driven in meeting the demands of a form so rigid and so external. (But see *post*, Gordon Jackson's valiant approximation to a similar structure in Psalm 119.)

Psalm 45

1. My heart is boiling of a good word.
   The work that I indite shall be of the King.
   My tongue is the pen of a swift writer.

2. Thou art much fairer than the sons of men,
   grace is shed forth in thy lips,
   therefore hath God blessed thee for ever.

3. Gird thee with thy sword upon thy thigh, O thou mighty,
   in beauty and glory.

4. Good luck have thou with thy worship:
   thou ridest upon the word of truth, meekness, and
        righteousness
   and thy right hand shall teach thee terrible things.

5. Thine arrows are sharp
   to pierce into the hearts of the King's enemies,
   that Nations may fall under thee.

6. Thy throne, O God, is for ever and ever:
   the sceptre of uprightness is the sceptre of thy Kingdom.

7. Thou lovest righteousness and hatest ungodliness:
   therefore hath God even thy God anointed thee
   with the oil of gladness above thy fellows.

8. All thy garments smell of Myrrh and Aloes and Cassia
   out of the Ivory palaces from whence they made thee glad.

9. Kings' daughters were among thy honorable women:
   thy wife stood on thy right hand in gold of Ophir.

10. Hearken O daughter, and consider,
    and bow down thine ear:
    and forget thine own people and thy Father's house.

11. So shall the king have pleasure in thy beauty:
    for he is thy Lord and thou shalt worship him.

12. And the daughter of Tyre with a gift:
    the rich people shall do homage before thy face.

13. The king's Daughter is altogether glorious within,
    her raiment is of cloth of Tissue.

14. She shall be brought to the King in raiment of needle
        work:
    her maidens that are next about her
    shall be brought unto thee.

15. They shall be brought with joy and gladness,
    and they shall enter into the king's Palace.

16. Thy children shall be in stead of thy fathers,
    thou shalt make them Princes through the whole earth.

17. I will make thy name renowned throughout all
        generations:
    therefore shall the Nations magnify thee for ever
    world without end.   (1571)

This barbaric and erotic occasion, which may at one stage have
been the marriage of Ahab to the Tyrian Jezebel (between 874 and
852 B.C.) has been better caught in Golding's English than in
anyone else's. It is not surprising that Christianizing versions, like
Watts's, seem not to be dealing with the same text.

Psalm 48

1. Great is the Lord, and greatly to be praised,
   in the City of our God, and in the hill of his holiness.

2. Mount Zion at the sides of the North, fair in situation,
   is the joy of the whole earth, and the City of the great
         king.

3. God in the palaces thereof
   is known to be a defense.

4. For behold, kings are gathered together,
   and are passed by together.

5. They have seen, so have they wondered
   and trembled, and been driven headlong.

6. Fearfulness hath caught hold of them,
   and sorrow is come upon them
   as upon a woman laboring of child.

7. With an eastern wind
   shalt thou break the Ships of Tarshish.

8. As we have heard, so have we seen
   in the City of the Lord of hosts, in the City of our God:
   God shall establish it for evermore.

9. Lord we have waited for thy mercy
   in the midst of thy Temple.

10. Like as thy name is O God
    so is thy praise upon the uttermost Coasts of the earth:
    thy right hand is full of righteousness.

11. Mount Zion shall rejoice, the daughters of Judah shall
    leap for joy
    for thy judgment's sake.

12. Encompass ye Zion, and walk about it,
    and number the towers of it.

13. Mark well the walls thereof, exalt her Towers,
    that ye may make report to the generations that come
    after you.

14. For this God is our God for ever and ever:
    he shall be our guide even unto the death.   (1571)

This is thought (largely because of allusions to Isaiah 31 and 37) to
celebrate a historical event: the raising of the siege of Jerusalem by
Sennacherib's Assyrians in 701 B.C. However, the poem also incorp-
orates mythological features. Pointless to ask, for instance, from what
geographical standpoint Jerusalem ('Mount Zion') can be visualized
as 'at the sides of the North'; apocalyptic texts in Isaiah, Ezekiel and
elsewhere had declared the holy city (not yet established) as in the
far North. Similarly, no need to think Sennacherib was helped by a
naval force from Tarshish, the Phoenician colony in Spain; 'Tarshish'
meant for the Jews the location farthest away from them by water,
from which the passage was most hazardous. The mythological or
mythic dimension of the poem is scant if we take too literally the
survey of the city in the last verses as relating to an actual celebratory
circuit of the walls.

Psalm 63 *A Song of David's, when he was in the wilderness of Judah*

1. Thou O God art my God, I will seek thee early:
   my soul hath thirsted after thee,
   my flesh hath hungered after thee
   in a barren and thirsty land without waters.

2. So have I beheld thee in thy Sanctuary,
   to see thy strength and thy glory.

3. For thy loving kindness is better than life:
   my lips shall praise thee.

4. So will I praise thee in my life:
   in thy name will I lift up my hands.

5. My Soul shall be satisfied as with marrow and fatness,
   and my mouth shall praise thee with lips of joyfulness.

6. Surely, I will be mindful of thee upon my bed:
   I will think upon thee when I lie awake.

7. For thou hast been my help,
   and I shall rejoice under the shadow of thy wings.

8. My soul hath reached after thee:
   thy right hand shall hold me up.

9. And they in seeking to destroy my soul,
   shall go into the lowest parts of the earth.

10. They shall cast him down upon the edge of the sword,
    they shall be the portion of Foxes.

11. But the King shall rejoice in God:
    and whosoever sweareth by him shall be joyful:
    for the mouth of them that speak lies shall be
        stopped.   (1571)

This is one place where the canonical title, reproduced by Golding and in *AV*, but suppressed in most versions, may well be crucial. For David was 'in the wilderness of Judah' only when hard-pressed by the rebellion of his son Absalom; and so the phrase calls up all the astonishingly complex feelings aroused by the narrative in 2 Samuel – David's many stratagems for overlooking and containing Absalom's rash ambition, his attempt to protect Absalom's person when the showdown came, and his grief when this proved imposs-ible. To renew his devotion to Yahweh in these harried and torment-ing circumstances is an action on David's part much more telling than anything envisaged by Oesterley, who takes the allusion to the 2 Samuel narrative only lightly, supposing it extraneous to what is for him a *pro forma* plea out of the Babylonian exile centuries later. Oesterley's scepticism in such a case is surely excessive and disabling; 'the King' in the last verse, for instance, has poignancy and power if taken to be spoken by David of himself at a moment when his kingship seemed to hang by a thread.

Psalm 110

1. The Lord said unto my Lord, Sit thou upon my right
       hand,
   until I make thine enemies thy footstool.

2. The Lord shall send the sceptre of thy power out of Zion:
   bear thou rule in the midst of thine enemies.

3. Thy people shall come with willing oblations
   in the day of the mustering of thine army, in beauty of
       holiness
   the dew of thy youth shall come unto thee
   out of thy womb from the morning.

4. The Lord hath sworn and will not repent him:
   Thou art a priest forever according to the manner of
       Melchizedek.

5. The Lord at thy right hand
   hath broken Kings in the day of his wrath.

6. He shall judge among the heathen, he shall fill all with
       ruins,
   he shall break the head over a mighty land.

7. He shall drink of the brook in the way,
   therefore shall he lift up his head.   (1571)

Psalm 110 is very ancient, certainly pre-exilic. It is momentous in
that it proclaims the king as also high-priest. (Melchizedek is named
in that office in Genesis.) For that reason the psalm is frequently
cited in the New Testament, notably in the Epistle to the Hebrews;
and among the 'comfortable words' in the Anglican rite of the
Eucharist is an assurance that Jesus also is a 'great high-priest'.
However, as might be expected of a text so ancient, it is textually
very corrupt. Because it is only seven verses long, the psalm permits
better than any other a comparison point by point between several
versions. Such comparison must focus in particular on vv. 7 and 3.
   For v. 7, David L. Frost in *The Liturgical Psalter* gives

> He shall slake his thirst from the brook beside the way:
> therefore shall he lift up his head.

The 'therefore' makes no sense, nor does the entire verse in relation
to the preceding six. *NOAB*, accepting this, comments lamely:

'The meaning is not clear. The verse may be only a fragment.' (Oesterley in 1939 made surprising though not very agreeable sense of the Hebrew: 'He watereth the brooks with their blood; therefore he lifteth up thy head.' But apparently this emendation has not been accepted.) We are no further forward on this than 400 years ago, when both *BCP* and *AV* settled in despair for the same inscrutable nonsense that we get from David Frost and *NOAB*.

The Christologists among translators allow themselves more latitude, but try harder to make sense. The soberest among them is the Countess of Pembroke:

> If passing on these ways
> Thou taste of troubled streams;
>   Shall that eclipse thy shining rays?
> Nay, light thy glory's beams.

Isaac Watts more boldly deserts the Old Testament for the New:

> Though while he treads his glorious way
> He drinks the cup of tears and blood;
> The suff'rings of that dreadful day
> Shall but advance him near to God.

And Christopher Smart, I'm afraid, takes refuge in sonorities:

> Where the breeze sigh'd and Cedron purl'd,
> There drank the Saviour of the world,
>   Without an home or friend;
> For which his name above all names
> Is glorious, and his meekness claims
>   All honour without end.

Arthur Golding, one of the earliest translators, agrees with the latest in thinking that since the original ends with a nonsense, a *non sequitur* is all he can decently offer as a translation.

Verse 3 is a different case. *NOAB* splits the verse into two sentences:

> Your people will offer themselves freely
> on the day you lead your host
> upon the holy mountains.
> From the womb of the morning
> like dew your youth will come to you . . .

then comments morosely: 'The meaning of the second sentence can no longer be recovered with certainty.' David Frost also discovers two sentences, but strikingly different ones:

> Noble are you, from the day of your birth
> upon the holy hill:
> radiant are you, even from the womb,
> in the morning dew of your youth.

The *AV* has at least recognized the recruiting-station:

> Thy people shall be willing in the day of thy power, in the beauties of holiness from the womb of the morning: thou hast the dew of thy youth

– though *BCP* (wordy as Coverdale tends to be when flummoxed) is not at all so clear that what the people offer is their persons, or the persons of their sons, as soldiers:

> In the day of thy power shall the people offer thee free-will offerings with an holy worship: the dew of thy birth is of the womb of the morning.

Heaven knows what Coverdale thought he meant by the last sentence.

The Countess of Pembroke does better, though at the cost of more words even than Coverdale:

> But as for them that willing yield,
>   In solemn robes they glad shall go:
>   Attending thee when thou shalt show
> Triumphantly thy troops in field:

> In field as thickly set
> With warlike youthful train
>   As pearlèd plain with drops is wet,
> Of sweet Aurora's rain.

Watts simply evades the issue (that is to say, the metaphor):

> That day shall show thy power is great
> When saints shall flock with willing minds,
> And sinners crowd thy temple gate,
> Where holiness in beauty shines.

Trying again in a different metre (common measure as against long measure) Watts offers:

> What wonders shall thy gospel do!
>   Thy converts shall surpass
> The num'rous drops of morning dew,
>   And own thy sovereign grace

– which, tamely though it may fall on our ears, effectively replays the ancient barbaric narrative so as to transform David's assembling warriors into 'soldiers of Christ'. However, the image-cluster of 'morning–dew–youth' has still to be addressed. Christopher Smart, as is his wont, goes for broke:

> The day thou art install'd the King,
> From far shall pious easterns bring
>   Their off'rings of perfume;
> The benediction on thy birth
> Is as the dew-drops fresh on earth
>   From morning's pregnant womb.

This is, though splendid, unacceptable; for where do those 'pious easterns' come from, except from the New Testament? Only Golding, among the translators surveyed, decodes plausibly the image-cluster in v. 3: the youth that the king there assembles is on the one hand the youth of his kingdom, mustering to his banner; on the other hand, and by the same token, it is his own personal youth recovered. This idea, that the virility of the king was as manifest in the men he could recruit as in the sons he could father, survived from ancient Israel into seventeenth-century Europe; but alone among the translators, Arthur Golding was able to tap into it.

Psalm 114

1. When Israel went out of Egypt,
    and the house of Jacob from the strange Nation,

2. Judah was his sanctification,
    and Israel his dominion.

3. The sea saw it and fled:
    Jordan was turned back.

4. The Mountains skipped like Rams,
    and the Hills like the Lambs of sheep.

5. What ailed thee O Sea that thou fleddest?
    and thou Jordan that thou turnedst backward?

6. Ye mountains that ye leaped like Rams?
    and ye hills like the Lambs of sheep?

7. Tremble thou earth at the presence of the Lord,
    at the presence of the God of Jacob,

8. Which turned the Rocks into pools of water,
    and the Flint into a fountain of water.   (1571)

Cf. Coverdale, *ante*. This is one of a few psalms which appeal particularly to a modernist taste – meaning, a taste formed in part by admiration of poems by Pound and Eliot. In a loose but legitimate sense, its structure may be called 'imagistic'. This is particularly true of how it ends, with a deliberate terseness, on an image notably more contracted in its sphere of reference than the exuberantly cosmic images that have led up to it. Accordingly, metrical versions from the sixteenth through the twentieth century dilute the poem by 'padding'; only in the present century has such padding been seen as vicious, and only in the present century has poetry (at the hands of the masters) been required to observe the terse requirements of good prose, such as Golding's.

Psalm 132

1. Lord remember David
   with all his afflictions:

2. Who swore unto the Lord,
   and vowed to the mighty of Jacob,

3. 'If I enter into the tabernacle of my house,
   or come upon the pallet of my bed,

4. If I suffer mine eyes to sleep,
   or mine eyelids to slumber,

5. Until I have found a plot for the Lord
   and dwelling places for the mighty one of Jacob.'

6. 'Lo, we heard of it in Ephratah,
   and found it in the fields of the forest:

7. We will enter into his dwelling places,
   we will worship at his footstool.'

8. Up Lord into thy rest,
   thou and the Ark of thy strength.

9. Let thy Priests be clothed with righteousness,
   and let thy meek ones rejoice.

10. For thy servant David's sake,
    shun not the face of thine anointed.

11. The Lord hath sworn unto David in truth,
    and he will not turn away from it.
    'Of the fruit of thy womb will I set upon thy throne.

12. If thy Sons keep my league, and my covenants,
    which I shall teach them:
    their Sons also shall sit upon thy Seat for evermore.'

13. Because the Lord hath chosen Zion,
    he hath loved to dwell in it.

14. 'This is my rest forever, here will I dwell:
    for I have a love to her.

15. Blessing will I bless her victuals,
    and satisfy her poor with bread.

16. And I will clothe her Priests with welfare,
    and her meek ones shall leap for joy.

17. There will I make the horn of David to bud,
    I have prepared a candle for mine anointed.

18. I will clothe his enemies with shame:
    but upon him shall the diadem flourish.'   (1571)

SIR PHILIP SIDNEY (1554–1586)

Psalm 19

The heav'nly frame sets forth the fame
    Of him that only thunders;
The firmament so strangely bent
    Shows his hand-working wonders.

Day unto day it doth display,
    Their course doth it acknowledge;
And night to night, succeeding right,
    In darkness teach clear knowledge.

There is no speech nor language which
10   Is so of skill bereaved,
But of the skies the teaching cries
    They have heard and conceived.

There be no eyne but read the line
    From so fair book proceeding;
Their words be set in letters great
    For ev'rybody's reading.

Is not he blind that doth not find
    The tabernacle builded
There, by his grace, for sun's fair face
20   In beams of beauty gilded?

Who forth doth come, like a bridegroom
    From out his veiling places;
As glad is he as Giants be
    To run their mighty races.

His race is ev'n from ends of heav'n;
    About that vault he goeth:
There be no Realms hid from his beams,
    His heat to all he throweth.

O law of his, how perfect 'tis,
30   The very soul amending;
God's witness sure for aye doth dure,
    To simplest, wisdom lending.

God's dooms be right, and cheer the sprite;
    All his commandments being
So purely wise, as give the eyes
    Both light and force of seeing.

Of him the fear doth cleanness bear
    And so endures for ever:
His Judgments be self-verity
40   They are unrighteous never.

Then what man would so soon seek gold
    Of glitt'ring golden money?
By them is passed, in sweetest taste,
    Honey, or comb of honey.

By them is made thy servants' trade
    Most circumspectly guarded;
And who doth frame to keep the same
    Shall fully be rewarded.

Who is the man that ever can
50   His faults know and acknowledge?
O Lord, cleanse me from faults that be
    Most secret from all knowledge.

Thy servant keep, lest in him creep
    Presumptuous sin's offences;
Let them not have me for their slave,
    Nor reign upon my senses.

So shall my sprite be still upright
    In thought and conversation;
So shall I bide, well purified
60   From much abomination.

So let words sprung from my weak tongue
    And my heart's meditation,
My saving might, Lord, in thy sight
    Receive good acceptation.   (1580–86)

To compare this with Arthur Golding's version (*ante*) is to perceive
how fatally verbose is Elizabethan verse, set beside the best Eliza-
bethan prose. And yet Elizabethan verse, in the hands of the
Countess of Pembroke, can contain this proclivity, and compensate
for it. Only male chauvinism through the centuries has maintained
the pretence that Philip Sidney's contributions to the Sidney Psalter
are equal to his sister's.

MICHAEL COSOWARTH (b. 1568)

Michael Cosowarth was of Cornish extraction. Richard Carew, a
cousin, praised Cosowarth's psalm-versions in his *Survey of Cornwall*
(1602). But they have never been published.

Psalm 30

Since thou hast not, O Lord, left me to lie
A scorn to foes in my o'erwhelmèd right,
But hast exalted up my head on high,
Of thee my song shall be, and of thy might.

When I cried for thy all-relieving aid,
Thou didst restore to joy my sad distress;
When at the grave my soul for entrance stayed,
From grave thou didst return my heaviness.

O sing, therefore, due praises to the Lord;
10   You blessed saints, do you his praises sing.
Do you the holiness with thanks record,
Which doth belong to this our heavenly King.

For he no long time doth his ire prolong,
His frowning wrath within a while is dead,
When then, as if he'd done me wretch a wrong,
In 's smiling brow glad life is picturèd.

This did my whining life endure awhile,
Whilst th'earth was buried with an evening's shade;
But when the morning's light began to smile,
20   My joy did come, and all my woe did fade.

And when things flowèd to my full content,
And blind prosperity on me attended,
'Now shall these joys', quoth I, 'which God hath sent,
Now shall these lasting joys be never ended.'

'For thou, dear Lord, ev'n thou of tender love,
And of that goodness which doth dwell in thee,
As with a mountain which can never move
Stand fast about the moving state of me.'

Therewith he turned his milder face aside,
30 And all with turnèd thoughts bestead was I;
And every thought a world of woes implied,
Which strainèd forth from me this doleful cry:

'Ah, Lord! if to the ground down sunk I were,
What price is in my blood to profit thee?
If thou disrobe me of th'earth's attire I wear,
Can thy great praises then be sung by me?'

'O can the mute and the untonguèd dust,
Which in th'eternal house of death doth dwell,
Consum'd with worms and ever-eating rust, –
40 O can the dust of thy great glories tell?'

'O hear me then, O Lord! O Lord, me hear,
And send some mercies, Lord, some mercies send;
O let thy saving health betimes appear,
And give my woes unto an happy end.'

'But thou hast turned about my mourning song;
New tunes of joy have drownèd up my sadness,
And for the sack which shrouded me so long,
Thou hast clothed my soul with never-wearing
        gladness.'

                                                            (1590?)

This psalm, says Oesterley, is 'somewhat in the nature of an
autobiographical sketch', and this seems right, even allowing for
Oesterley's wish to 'personalize' whenever he can. He believes the
poem to be pre-exilic, though other commentators put it later.

MARY HERBERT, COUNTESS OF PEMBROKE (1561–1621)

Psalm 52

Tyrant, why swell'st thou thus,
   Of mischief vaunting?
Since help from God to us
   Is never wanting.

Lewd lies the tongue contrives,
   Loud lies it soundeth;
Sharper than sharpest knives
   With lies it woundeth.

Falsehood thy wit approves,
10   All truth rejected:
Thy will all vices loves,
   Virtue neglected.

Not words from cursèd thee,
   But gulfs are poured;
Gulfs wherein daily be
   Good men devoured.

Think'st thou to bear it so?
   God shall displace thee;
God shall thee overthrow,
20   Crush thee, deface thee.

The just shall fearing see
   These fearful chances,
And laughing shoot at thee
   With scornful glances.

Lo, lo, the wretched wight,
   Who, God disdaining,
His mischief made his might,
   His guard his gaining.

I as an olive tree
30   Still green shall flourish:
God's house the soil shall be
   My roots to nourish.

My trust on his true love
   Truly attending,
Shall never thence remove,
   Never see ending.

Thee will I honour still,
   Lord, for this justice;
There fix my hopes I will
40   Where thy saints' trust is.

Thy saints trust in thy name,
   Therein they joy them:
Protected by the same,
   Naught can annoy them.

(c. 1594)

The point of this psalm is sharpened, and corrected more than a little, if we supply from *AV* the canonical title: '*When Doeg the Edomite came and reported to Saul, and said to him, David is come into the house of Ahimelech*.' The brief and contemptible story of Doeg is told in 1 Samuel 22: David, in flight from Saul, prevailed on the priest Ahimelech to give him some provisions; Ahimelech was denounced to Saul, and his whole community was massacred; the informer was Doeg, who was deputed to carry out the slaughter. At 1 Samuel 22.22 David makes what reparation he can to Ahimelech's son, assuring him of his protection in future.

Thus the Countess's first word, 'Tyrant', is misleading. Doeg is a

tittle-tattle, a currier of favour, an informer. And it is this kind of
person, not the tyrannical kind, that the psalm treats less with anger
than contempt: the Doegs of the world will in the end be laughed
at – as the Countess acknowledges, though only in passing, in her
sixth quatrain.

Psalm 58

And call ye this to utter what is just,
    You that of justice hold the sov'reign throne?
And call ye this to yield, O sons of dust,
    To wrongèd brethren ev'ry man his own?
O no: it is your long malicious will
    Now to the world to make by practice known
With whose oppression you the balance fill,
    Just to yourselves, indiff'rent else to none.

But what could they, who ev'n in birth declin'd
10   From truth and light to lies and injuries?
To show the venom of their cankered mind
    The adder's image scarcely can suffice;
Nay, scarce the aspic may with them contend,
    On whom the charmer all in vain applies
His skilfullest spells, aye missing of his end
    While she self-deaf and unaffected lies.

Lord, crack their teeth! Lord, crush these lions' jaws!
    So let them sink as water in the sand;
When deadly bow their aiming fury draws,
20   Shiver the shaft ere past the shooter's hand.
So make them melt as the dishousèd snail
    Or as the embryo, whose vital band
Breaks ere it holds, and formless eyes do fail
    To see the sun, though brought to lightful land.

O let their brood, a brood of springing thorns,
  Be by untimely rooting overthrown;
Ere bushes waxed, they push with pricking horns,
  As fruits yet green are oft by tempest blown.
The good with gladness this revenge shall see,
30   And bathe his feet in blood of wicked one,
While all shall say: 'The just rewarded be,
  There is a God that carves to each his own.'   (c. 1594)

John Ruskin, who in *Rock Honeycomb* (1877) either didn't know, or
affected not to know, about the Countess of Pembroke, remarked
of the poem in this version: 'Another of the great Psalms teaching
the eternal separation between the sinner and the just man; farther
notable for its assertion of the sinner's being born such, irredeem-
ably.' Ruskin's evident relish in inferring this is far from attractive;
nor is it clear that his inference is warranted.

Psalm 74

O God, why hast thou thus
  Repuls'd, and scatter'd us?
Shall now thy wrath no limits hold,
  But ever smoke and burn
  Till it to ashes turn
The chosen folk of thy dear fold?

Ah! think with milder thought
  On them whom thou hast bought
And purchasèd from endless days!
10   Think of thy birthright lot
  Of Sion, on whose plot
Thy sacred house supported stays.

Come, Lord, O come with speed!
    This sacrilegious seed
Root quickly out, and headlong cast;
    All that thy holy place
    Did late adorn and grace,
Their hateful hands have quite defac'd.

        Their beastly trumpets roar
20   Where heavenly notes before
In praises of thy might did flow;
    Within thy temple they
    Their ensigns oft display,
The ensigns, which their conquest show.

        As men with axe on arm
        To some thick forest swarm
To lop the trees which stately stand,
    They to thy temple flock
    And, spoiling, cut and knock
30 The curious works of carving hand.

        Thy most, most holy seat
        The greedy flames do eat
And have such ruthless ruin wrought
    That all thy house is rased,
    So rased and so defac'd
That of that all remaineth nought.

        Nay, they resolvèd are
        We all alike shall fare,
All of one cruel cup shall taste.
40   For not one house doth stand
        Of God in all the land
But they by fire have laid it waste.

We see the signs no more
We wont to see before;
Nor any now with spirit divine
Amongst us more is found,
Who can to us expound
What term these dolours shall define.

How long, O God, how long
50   Wilt thou wink at the wrong
Of thy reviling, railing foe?
Shall he that hates thy name,
And hatred paints with shame,
So do, and do for ever so?

Woe us! what is the cause
Thy hand its help withdraws,
That thy right hand far from us keeps?
Ah let it once arise
To plague thine enemies
60   Which now, embosomed, idly sleeps!

Thou art my God, I know,
My King, who long ago
Didst undertake the charge of me;
And in my hard distress
Didst work me such release
That all the earth did wond'ring see.

Thou by thy might didst make
The seas in sunder break,
And dreadful dragons which before
70   In deep or swam or crawl'd,
Such mortal strokes appall'd
They floated dead to ev'ry shore.

Thou crush'd that monster's head
Whom other monsters dread,
And so his fishy flesh didst frame
To serve as pleasing food
To all the ravening brood
Who had the desert for their dame.

Thou wondrously didst cause,
80   Repealing nature's laws,
From thirsty flint a fountain flow,
And of the rivers clear
The sandy beds appear,
So dry thou mad'st their channels grow.

The day array'd in light,
The shadow-clothèd night,
Were made, and are maintain'd, by thee.
The sun, and sun-like rays,
The bounds of nights and days,
90   Thy workmanship no less they be.

To thee the earth doth owe
That earth in sea doth grow,
And sea doth earth from drowning spare;
The summer's corny crown,
The winter's frosty gown,
Nought but thy badge, thy livery are.

Thou, then, still one, the same,
Think how thy glorious name
These brain-sick men's despite has borne,
100   How abject enemies
The Lord of highest skies
With cursèd, taunting tongues have torn.

Ah! give no hawk the power
Thy turtle to devour
Which sighs to thee with mourning moans;
Nor utterly out-rase
From tables of thy grace
The flock of thy afflicted ones.

But call thy league to mind,
110   For horror all doth blind,
No light doth in the land remain;
Rape, murder, violence,
Each outrage, each offence,
Each where doth range, and rage and reign.

Enough, enough we mourn!
Let us no more return
Repuls'd with blame and shame from thee;
But succour us oppress'd
And give the troubled rest
120   That of thy praise their songs may be.

Rise, God, plead thine own case;
Forget not what disgrace
These fools on thee each day bestow;
Forget not with what cries
Thy foes against thee rise,
Which more and more to heav'n do grow.   (c. 1594)

Ruskin in *Rock Honeycomb* confessed: 'I always used to read the fifth
and sixth verses as having prophetic reference to the Cromwellian
and Reforming rage, but on now referring to Septuagint and
Vulgate, which Sidney also follows, I find nothing about famousness
or carved work: only that the enemy destroys the doors of sanctuary
. . . and throws all down, not with axes and hammers, but with axes
and the *mason's trowel*. (Restoration – and building leases – to wit.)'
Sadly comical though it is to have the ancient poet scaled down to a

commentator on Victorian church-restoration, recent scholarship supports Ruskin in thinking that the *artistry* of the Temple's fabric isn't in question. See versions of this psalm by Isaac Watts and Christopher Smart, *post*.

Psalm 115

Not us, I say, not us,
But thine own name respect, eternal Lord,
And make it glorious
To show thy mercy and confirm thy word.
Why, Lord, why should these nations say:
'Where doth your God now make his stay?'

You ask where our God is?
In heav'n enthron'd, no mark of mortal eye;
Nor hath, nor will he, miss
10 What likes his will, to will effectually.
What are your idols? we demand:
Gold, silver, works of workmen's hand.

They mouths, but speechless, have;
Eyes, sightless; ears, no news of noise can tell;
Who them their noses gave
Gave not their noses any sense of smell;
Nor hands can feel, nor feet can go,
Nor sign of sound their throats can show.

And wherein differ you
20 Who, having made them, make of them your trust?
But Israel, pursue
Thy trust in God, the target of the just.
O Aaron's house, the like do ye:
He is their aid, their target he.

    All that Jehovah fear
Trust in Jehovah, he our aid and shield.
    He us in mind doth bear,
He will to us abundant blessings yield;
Will evermore with grace and good
30 Bless Jacob's house, bless Aaron's brood.

    Bless all that bear him awe,
Both great and small. The conduits of his store
    He never dry shall draw,
But you and yours enrich still more and more.
Blest, O thrice blest, whom he hath chose,
Who first with heav'ns did earth enclose.

    Where height of highest skies
Removèd most from floor of lowly ground
    With vaulted roof doth rise,
40 Himself took up his dwelling there to found.
To mortal men he gracious gave
The lowly ground to hold and have.

    And why? His praise to show;
Which how can dead men, Lord, in any wise?
    Who down descending go
Into the place where silence lodgèd lies?
But save us. We thy praise record
Will now, and still: O praise the Lord!   (*c.* 1594)

Psalm 117

Praise him that ay
Remains the same:
All tongues display
Iehovas fame.
Sing all that share

This earthy ball:
His mercies are
Expos'd to all:
Like as the word
10   Once he doth give,
Rold in record,
Doth tyme outlive.   (*c.* 1594)

The poem is an acrostic: the initial letters of the lines read, 'Prais'
The Lord'.

Psalm 120

As to th'Eternal often in anguishes
Erst have I called, never unanswered,
Again I call, again I calling
Doubt not again to receive an answer.

Lord rid my soul from treasonous eloquence
Of filthy forgers craftily fraudulent;
And from the tongue where lodg'd resideth
Poison'd abuse, ruin of believers.

Thou that reposeth vainly thy confidence
10   In wily wronging, say, by thy forgery
What good to thee? what gain redoundeth?
What benefit from a tongue deceitful?

Though like an arrow strongly delivered
It deeply pierce, though like to a Juniper
It coals do cast which, quickly fired,
Flame very hot, very hardly quenching?

---

11 *Rold*: enrolled.

Ah God! too long here wander I banished,
Too long abiding barbarous injury;
With Kedar and with Mesech harbour'd,
20   How? in a tent, in a houseless harbour.

Too long, alas, too long have I dwelled here
With friendly peace's furious enemies;
Who when to peace I seek to call them,
Faster I find to the war they arm them.   (c. 1594)

This version is curious and effective in being unrhymed and in a dactylic, apparently quantitative, metre.

Psalm 125

As Sion standeth very firmly steadfast,
Never once shaking: so, on high, Jehovah
Who his hope buildeth, very firmly steadfast
           Ever abideth.

As Salem braveth with her hilly bulwarks
Roundly enforted: so the great Jehovah
Closeth his servants, as a hilly bulwark
           Ever abiding;

Though Tyrant's hard yoke with a heavy pressure
10 Wring the just shoulders: but a while it holdeth
Lest the best minded by too hard abusing
           Bend to abuses.

As to the well-workers, so the right believers;
Lord favour further; but a vain deceiver,
Whose wryèd footing not aright directed
           Wand'reth in error,

Lord him, abjected, set among the number
Whose doings lawless, study bent to mischief
Mischief expecteth: but upon thy chosen
20   Peace be for ever.   (*c.* 1594)

Though the Countess's sapphic stanzas are thought to be an outland-
ish curiosity in English, I find no version which so faithfully cleaves
to, and yet organizes, the Hebrew original beginning with (in the
AV), 'They that trust in the Lord shall be as mount Zion'.

Psalm 139

O Lord in me there lieth nought
    But to thy search revealèd lies:
        For when I sit
        Thou markest it;
    No less thou notest when I rise.
Yea, closest closet of my thought
    Hath open windows to thine eyes.

Thou walkest with me when I walk;
    When to my bed for rest I go,
10   I find thee there,
        And ev'rywhere;
    Not youngest thought in me doth grow,
No, not one word I cast to talk,
    But yet unuttered thou dost know.

If forth I march, thou goest before,
    If back I turn, thou com'st behind;
        So forth nor back
        Thy guard I lack,
    Nay on me too thy hand I find.
20 Well I thy wisdom may adore,
    But never reach with earthy mind.

To shun thy notice, leave thine eye,
   O whither might I take my way?
     To starry sphere?
     Thy throne is there.
   To dead men's undelightsome stay?
There is thy walk, and there to lie
   Unknown in vain I should assay.

O Sun, whom light nor flight can match,
30   Suppose thy lightful, flightful wings
     Thou lend to me,
     And I could flee
As far as thee the ev'ning brings,
Ev'n led to West he would me catch
   Nor should I lurk with western things.

Do thou thy best, O secret night,
   In sable veil to cover me,
     Thy sable veil
     Shall vainly fail;
40   With day unmask'd my night shall be,
For night is day, and darkness light,
   O father of all lights, to thee.

Each inmost piece in me is thine:
   While yet I in my mother dwelt,
     All that me clad
     From thee I had.
   Thou in my fame hast strangely dealt;
Needs in my praise thy works must shine,
   So inly them my thoughts have felt.

50   Thou, how my back was beam-wise laid
   And raft'ring of my ribs, dost know;
     Know'st ev'ry point
     Of bone and joint,

How to this whole these parts did grow,
In brave embroid'ry fair array'd
    Though wrought in shop both dark and low.

Nay, fashionless, ere form I took,
    Thy all-and-more beholding eye
        My shapeless shape
60   Could not escape;
    All these, time-framed successively
Ere one had being, in the book
    Of thy foresight enroll'd did lie.

My God, how I these studies prize
    That do thy hidden workings show!
        Whose sum is such
        No sum so much,
    Nay, summ'd as sand, they sumless grow.
I lie to sleep, from sleep I rise,
70   Yet still in thought with thee I go.

My God, if thou but one wouldst kill,
    Then straight would leave my further chase
        This cursèd brood
        Inur'd to blood
    Whose graceless taunts at thy disgrace
Have aimèd oft, and, hating still,
    Would with proud lies thy truth outface.

Hate not I them, who thee do hate?
    Thine, Lord, I will the censure be.
80   Detest I not
        The cankered knot
    Whom I against thee banded see?
O Lord, thou know'st in highest rate
    I hate them all as foes to me.

Search me, my God, and prove my heart,
   Examine me, and try my thought;
     And mark in me
     If aught there be
   That hath with cause their anger wrought.
90 If not (as not) my life's each part,
   Lord, safely guide from danger brought.   (*c.* 1594)

Psalm 147

Sing to the Lord, for what can better be
   Than of our God that we the honour sing?
With seemly pleasure what can more agree
   Than praiseful voice, and touch of tunèd string?
    For lo, the Lord again to form doth bring
       Jerusalem's long ruinated walls;
And Jacob's house, which all the earth did see
       Dispersèd erst, to union now recalls;
And now by him their broken hearts made sound,
10   And now by him their bleeding wounds are bound.

For what could not, who can the number tell
   Of stars, the torches of his heav'nly hall;
And tell so readily, he knoweth well
   How ev'ry star by proper name to call?
    What great to him, whose greatness doth not fall
       Within precincts? whose power no limits stay?
Whose knowledges all number so excel
       Not numb'ring number can their number lay?
Easy to him, to lift the lowly just;
20 Easy, to down proud wicked to the dust.

O then Jehovah's causeful honour sing,
   His, whom our God we by his goodness find!
O make harmonious mix of voice and string

To him by whom the skies with clouds are lin'd;
  By whom the rain, from clouds to drop assign'd,
    Supples the clods of summer-scorchèd fields,
Fresheth the mountains with such needful spring,
    Fuel of life to mountain cattle yields,
  From whom young ravens careless old forsake,
30   Croaking to him of alms, their diet take.

The stately shape, the force of bravest steed,
  Is far too weak to work in him delight;
No more in him can any pleasure breed
  In flying footman, foot of nimblest flight.
    Nay, which is more, his fearers in his sight
      Can well of nothing but his bounty brave;
Which, never failing, never lets them need
    Who fix'd their hopes upon his mercies have.
  O then, Jerusalem, Jehovah praise,
40   With honour due thy God, O Sion, raise.

His strength it is thy gates doth surely bar;
  His grace in thee thy children multiplies;
By him thy borders lie secure from wars,
  And finest flour thy hunger satisfies.
    Nor means he needs; for fast his pleasure flies
      Borne by his word, when aught him list to bid.
Snow's woolly locks by him wide scatter'd are,
        And hoary plains with frost, as ashes, hid;
    Gross icy gobbets from his hand he flings,
50   And blows a cold too strong for strongest things.

He bids again, and ice in water flows,
  As water erst in ice congealèd lay;
Abroad the southern wind, his melter, goes;
  The streams relenting take their wonted way.
    O much is this, but more I come to say:
      The words of life he hath to Jacob told;
Taught Israel, who by his teaching knows

> What laws in life, what rules he wills to hold.
> No nation else hath found him half so kind,
60 For to his light, what other is not blind?   (*c.* 1594)

GEORGE PEELE (1556–1596)

From *David and Fair Bethsabe*

Of Israel's sweetest singer now I sing,
His holy stile and happy victories,
Whose Muse was dipt in that inspiring dew
Arch-angels stillèd from the breath of Jove,
Decking her temples with the glorious flowers
Heavns rain'd on tops of Sion and Mount Sinai.
Upon the bosom of his ivory Lute
The Cherubins and Angels laid their breasts,
And when his consecrated fingers struck
10 The golden wires of his ravishing harp,
He gave alarum to the host of heaven
That, wing'd with lightning, brake the clouds and cast
Their christall armor at his conquering feet.
Of this sweet Poet, Jove's Musician,
And of his beauteous son I press to sing.
Then help, divine Adonai, to conduct
Upon the wings of my well-tempered verse
The hearers' minds above the towers of Heaven,
And guide them so in this thrice haughty flight,
20 Their mounting feathers scorch not with the fire
That none can temper but thy holy hand.
To thee for succour flies my feeble muse,
And at thy feet her iron Pen doth use.   (1599)

See *The Dramatic Works of George Peele*, Volume 3: *David and Bethsabe*, ed. Elmer Blistein (New Haven and London, 1970).

WILLIAM SHAKESPEARE
(1564–1616)

1. Psalm 147, v. 9

As You Like It, II.iii (Adam speaks)

But do not so. I have five hundred crowns,
The thrifty hire I sav'd under your father,
Which I did store to be my foster-nurse
When service should in my old limbs lie lame,
And unregarded age in corners thrown.
Take that; and He that doth the ravens feed,
Yea, providently caters for the sparrow
Be comfort to my age!

Cf. 'Who giveth fodder unto the cattle: and feedeth the young ravens that call upon him' (*BCP*).

2. Psalm 22, v. 12

Antony and Cleopatra, III.xiii (Antony to Cleopatra)

To let a fellow that will take rewards
And say 'God quit you!' be familiar with
My playfellow, your hand; this kingly seal
And plighter of high hearts. O! that I were
Upon the hill of Basan, to outroar
The horned herd; for I have savage cause; . . .

Cf. 'Many oxen are come about me: fat bulls of Basan close me in on every side' (*BCP*).

3. Psalm 18, v. 10

Macbeth, I.vii (Macbeth speaks)

>   Besides this Duncan
> Hath borne his faculties so meek, hath been
> So clear in his great office, that his virtues
> Will plead like angels trumpet-tongued against
> The deep damnation of his taking-off;
> And pity, like a naked new-born babe
> Striding the blast, or heaven's cherubin, hors'd
> Upon the sightless couriers of the air,
> Shall blow the horrid deed in every eye
> That tears shall drown the wind.

Cf. 'He rode upon the cherubins, and did fly: he came flying upon the wings of the wind' (*BCP*).

4. Psalm 40, v. 15

Macbeth, V.ix (Old Siward speaks)

> Had I as many sons as I have hairs,
> I would not wish them to a fairer death:
> And so, his knell is knoll'd.

Cf. '. . . my sins have taken such hold upon me that I am not able to look up: yea, they are more in number than the hairs of my head, and my heart hath failed me' (*BCP*).

According to Rivkah Zim (*English Metrical Psalms*, Cambridge, 1987), 'Siward echoes the Psalmist: Shakespeare turned "sins" into "sons" and made an English pun on "heirs".'

ABRAHAM FRAUNCE
(*fl.* 1587–1633)

Psalm 73

GOD, th'aeternal God, no doubt is good to the godly,
Giving grace to the pure, and mercy to Israel holy:
And yet, alas! my feet, my faint feet, gan to be sliding,
And I was almost gone and fall'n to a dangerous error.
For my soul did grudge, my heart consumed in anger,
And mine eyes disdained, when I saw that such men
    abounded
With wealth, health, and joy, whose minds with mischief
    abounded.
Their body stout and strong, their limbs still lively appearing,
Neither fear any pangs of death, nor feel any sickness:
10 Some still mourn, they laugh: some live unfortunate ever,
They for joy do triumph, and taste adversity never;
Which makes them with pride, with scornful pride to be
    chained,
And with blood-thirsting disdain as a robe to be cov'red.

'Tush!' say they, 'can God from the highest heavens to the
    lowest
Earth vouchsafe, think you, those prince-like eyes be
    bowing?
'Tis but a vain conceit of fools to be fondly referring
Every jesting trick and trifling toy to the Thunderer.
For lo these be the men who rule and reign with abundance;
These, and who but these? Why then, what mean I to lift up
20 Clean hands and pure heart to the heav'ns? what mean I to
    offer
Praise and thanksgiving to the Lord? what mean I to suffer
Such plagues with pestilence?' Yea, and almost had I spoken

Even as they did speak, which thought no God to be guiding.
But so should I, alas! have judged thy folk to be luckless,
Thy sons forsaken, thy saints unworthily hapless.
Thus did I think and muse, and search what might be the
    matter;
But yet I could not, alas! conceive so hidden a wonder,
Until I left myself, and all my thoughts did abandon,
And to thy sacred place, to thy sanctuary, lastly repaired.
30   There did I see, O Lord, these men's unfortunate endings;
Endings mute, and fit for their ungodly beginnings.
Then did I see how they did stand in slippery places,
Lifted aloft, that their downfalling might be the greater.
Living Lord, how soon is this their glory triumphant
Dash'd, confounded, gone, drown'd in destruction endless!
Their fame's soon outworn, their names extinct in a moment,
Like to a dream, that lives by a sleep, and dies with a
    slumber.
  – Thus my soul did grieve, my heart did languish in anguish;
So blind were mine eyes, my mind so plunged in error,
40   That no more than a beast did I know this mystery sacred.
Yet thou held'st my hand, and kepst my soul from the
    dungeon;
Thou didst guide my feet, and me with glory receivedst.
For what in heav'n or in earth shall I love, or worthily wonder,
But my most good God, my Lord and mighty Jehova?
Though my flesh oft faint, my heart's oft drowned in horror,
God never faileth, but will be my mighty protector.
Such as God forsake, and take to a slippery comfort,
Trust to a broken staff, and taste of worthy revengement.
In my God, therefore, my trust is wholly reposèd,
50   And his name will I praise, and sing his glory renownèd.

Fraunce's version of Psalm 73 first appeared in *The Countesse of
Pembrokes Emanuel* (1591), along with versions of seven other psalms,
all in English hexameters. However, I have taken the text (moderniz-
ing lightly) from the Parker Society's *Select Poetry Chiefly Devotional*

of the Reign of Queen Elizabeth (Cambridge, 1845). Edward Farr, who edited this anthology, opined that the measure which Fraunce proudly adopted is 'altogether foreign to our inflexible English language'. And he quoted with approval Fraunce's contemporary, Thomas Nashe: 'The hexameter verse I grant to be a gentleman of an ancient house – so is many an English beggar; – yet this clime of ours he cannot thrive in: our speech is too craggy for him to set his plough in; he goes twitching and hopping like a man running upon quagmires, up the hill in one syllable and down the dale in another, retaining no part of that strictly smooth gait which he vaunts himself with among the Greeks and Latins.' Yet even as Farr wrote, the English hexameter was being exhumed to startling effect by Arthur Hugh Clough. Readers who have learned to relish Clough's hexameter rhythms in *The Bothie of Tober-na-Vuolich* (1848), or in his posthumous *Amours de Voyage*, will find themselves on delightfully familiar ground with:

> 'Tis but a vain conceit of fools to be fondly referring
> Every jesting trick and trifling toy to the Thunderer.

Moreover, Fraunce stays close to his original, catching the note of 'bitter humour' that has been detected in the Hebrew. If Fraunce's version should be thought better than any other in English verse, this would be important; for Psalm 73 in the Hebrew is thoroughly integrated, strikingly original and strenuous, not in the least 'barbaric'. At least the shadowy Abraham Fraunce deserves better on this showing than to be a byword for pedantic quaintness.

Psalm 104

Living Lord, my soul shall praise thy glory triumphant,
Sing thy matchless might, and shew thine infinite honour.
Everlasting light thou putst on like as a garment
And purpled-mantled welkin thou spreadst as a curtain:
Thy parlour pillars on waters strangely be pitched,

Clouds are thy chariots, and blustring winds be thy coursers,
Immortal Spirits be thy ever-dutiful Heralds,
And consuming fires as servants daily be waiting.
   All-maintaining earth's foundations ever abideth
10   Laid by the Lord's right-hand, with seas and deeps as a
              garment
Cov'red; seas and deeps with threatning waves to the huge
              hills
Climbing; but with beck their billows speedily backward
All do recoil; with a check their course is chang'd on a
              sudden;
At thy thundring voice they quake. And so do the mountains
Mount upward with a word; and so also do the valleys
Down with a word descend, and keep their places appointed:
Their meres are fixd, their banks are mightily barred,
Their bounds known, lest that, man-feeding earth by the rage
              of
Earth-overwhelming waters might chance to be drowned.
20   Still-springing fountains distil from the rocks to the rivers,
And crystal rivers flow over along by the mountains.
There will wild asses their scorched mouths be refreshing,
And field-feeding beasts their thirst with water abating.
   There by the well-welling waters, by the silver-abounding
Brooks, fair-flying fowls on flowring banks be abiding,
There shall sweet-back'd birds their bowers in bows be
              a-building,
And to the waters' fall their warbling voice be a-tuning.
   Yea those sun-burnt hills, and mountains all to be
              scorched,
Cooling clouds do refresh, and watery dew from the heavens.
30   Earth sets forth thy works, earth-dwellers all be thy wonders:
Earth earth-dwelling beasts with flowring grass is a-feeding;
Earth earth-dwelling men with pleasant herbs is a-serving.
Earth brings heart's-joy wine, earth-dwelling men to be
              heart'ning,

Earth breeds cheering oils, earth-dwelling men to be
     smoothing,
Earth bears life's-food bread, earth-dwelling men to be
     strengthening.
  Tall trees, up-mounting Cedars, are cheerfully springing,
Cedars of Libanus, where fowls their nests be preparing;
And Storks in Fir-trees make their accustomed harbours.
  Wild goats, does, and roes do rove and range by the
     mountains,
40 And poor seely conies to the ragged rocks be repairing.
  Night-enlight'ning Moon for certain times is appointed,
And all-seeing Sun knows his due time to be setting.
Sun once so setting, dark night wraps all in a mantle
All in a black mantle: then beasts creep out from the
     dungeons,
Roaring hungry Lions their prey with greedy devouring
Claws and jaws attend, but by God's only appointment.
When Sun riseth again, their dens they quickly recover,
And there couch all day; that man may safely the daytime
His day's work apply, till day give way to the darkness.
50   O good God, wise Lord, good Lord, and only the wise
     God,
Earth sets forth thy works, earth-dwellers all be thy wonders.
So be seas also, great seas, full fraught with abundant
Swarms of creeping things, great, small: there ships be
     a-sailing,
And there lies tumbling that monstrous huge Leviathan.
All these beg their food, and all these on thee be waiting;
If that thou stretch out thine hand, they feed with abundance,
If thou turn thy face, they all are mightily troubled;
If that thou withdraw their breath they die in a moment,
And turn quickly to dust, whence they were lately derived.
60 If thy spirit breathe, their breath is newly created,

And the decayed face of th'earth is quickly revived.
   O then, glory to God, to the Lord then, glory for ever;
Who in his own great works may worthily glory for ever.
This Lord looks to the earth, and steadfast earth is
        a-trembling,
This God toucheth mounts, and mountains huge be
        a-smoking.
All my life will I laud this Lord; whilst breath is abiding
In my breast, this breath his praise shall still be a-breathing.
   Hear my words, my Lord, accept this dutiful off'ring,
That my soul in thee may evermore be rejoicing.
70   Root the malignant race, rase out their damnable offspring;
But my soul, O Lord, shall praise thy glory triumphant,
Sing thy matchless might, and shew thine infinite
        honour.   (1591)

The text is from *Miscellanies of the Fuller Worthies' Library*, Volume 3,
ed. Alexander B. Grosart (1872).

FRANCIS DAVISON
(*c.* 1575–*c.* 1619)

Psalm 13

Lord, how long, how long wilt thou
   Quite forget, and quite neglect me?
How long, with a frowning brow,
   Wilt thou from thy sight reject me?

How long shall I seek a way
   Forth this maze of thoughts perplexèd,
Where my griev'd mind, night and day,
   Is with thinking tried and vexèd?

How long shall my scornful foe
10   (On my fall his greatness placing)
Build upon my overthrow,
    And be grac'd by my disgracing?

Hear, O Lord and God, my cries;
    Mark my foe's unjust abusing;
And illuminate mine eyes,
    Heavenly beams in them infusing:

Lest my woes, too great to bear
    And too infinite to number,
Rock me soon, 'twixt hope and fear,
20   Into Death's eternal slumber;

Lest my foes their boasting make,
    'Spight of right on him we trample';
And in pride of mischief take,
    Hearten'd by my sad example.

As for me, I'll ride secure
    At thy mercies' sacred anchor,
And undaunted will endure
    Fiercest storms of wrong and rancour.

These black clouds will overflow,
30   Sun-shine shall have his returning;
And my grief-dull'd heart, I know,
    Into mirth shall change his mourning.

Therefore I'll rejoice, and sing
    Hymns to God in sacred measure,
Who to happy pass will bring
    My just hopes, at his good pleasure.   (*c.* 1602)

Davison, author of *A Poetical Rapsodie* (1602), appears on that
showing a sort of virtuoso of the poetic genres, experimenting to

the limit with Elizabethan expectations and conventions. We see that here, in his treatment of metre. 'How long shall I seek a way' and 'How long shall my scornful foe' sound in our ears initially as irregular, trimeters among tetrameters; but they are not so, as soon as we recognize that the poem is written not in iambic rising measure, but in trochaics; the piece, it turns out, is throughout in regular trochaic tetrameters. The uncertainty in our ears was without doubt deliberately induced, and is suavely resolved – if, that is, we can scan as certainly as could the readers Davison had in mind. This is a sort of sophistication common around 1600, which is lost on most modern readers. Its virtuosity falls in with the cocky assurance of the title of the collection where it first appeared (known to us only in manuscript): *Divers Selected Psalms of David, in verse, of a different composure from those used in the Church* – an enterprise in which Davison seems to have been the moving spirit. A glance at *AV* or *BCP* will show that he was just as bold and adventurous in his imagery. 'At thy mercies' sacred anchor' is, though delightful, entirely Davison's idea, not the Psalmist's. It may be thought that Davison takes too many liberties; certainly he does so, in his versions of, for instance, Psalms 73 and 132. On the other hand it's certainly refreshing to find the iambic beat disturbed so that we hear the rhythms of a speaking voice playing over and against the metre.

JOSEPH BRYAN (?)

Of Joseph Bryan nothing is known except that he seconded Francis Davison in *Divers Selected Psalms* – a Harleian manuscript in the British Museum.

Psalm 127

Except the Lord himself will deign
To build the house, the work to guide,
The builder's labour is in vain;
Like Babel's builders' haughty pride.

Nor watch, nor guard, nor sentinel
Can batteld, scourg'd, fenced towns defend,
Unless the God of Israel
Do guard and guide, and his help send.

It is not early rising up,
10   Nor going very late to bed,
Nor drinking of a strengthless cup,
Nor sweating, eating careful bread,

That aught avails. 'Tis all in vain;
Carking is naught worth approv'd;
But God gives rest, and without pain
All needful things to his belov'd.

Children, the staff and crown of age,
Is sure for to succeed their sires, –
Are the Almighty's heritage
20   Wherewith he crowns his saints' desires.

As shafts are in an archer's hand,
Who draws a stiff-bent sinewy bow;
Even so are children in thy hand,
Which up in strength and virtue grow:

Straight, shaft-like sprouts in shape and mind,
Strong but to virtue, not to vice,
Straight bent to glorious deeds by kind,
And to no brave achievements nice.

O happy sire, whose agèd wings
30   Are imped with plumes of this airount!
He need not fear the face of kings,
But eagle-like his fame shall mount.   (*c.* 1602)

Bryan's version of Psalm 127 is admirably muscular, for instance in
the sixth line the crowding together of stressed syllables. Unfortu-
nately Bryan no more than any other translator can conceal that the
psalm consists of two distinct poems, each incomplete, rudely
wedged together. The second of these – on the gladness a man may
take in his sons – is undoubtedly barbaric in feeling, yet Bryan's
verse, 'And to no brave achievements nice', deftly shows how some
Renaissance courts were still, in these matters, barbaric.

RICHARD VERSTEGAN
(*fl.* 1565–1620)

Psalm 51

Have mercy, O good God, on me,
   In greatness of thy grace:
O let thy mercies manifold
   My many faults deface.

Foul, filthy, loathsome, ugly sin
   Hath so defilèd me:
With streams of pity wash me clean,
   Else clean I cannot be.

---

30 *airount*: this word is not known to *OED*.

Too well my foul uncleansèd crimes
10   Remembrance do renew;
Too plain in anguish of my heart
      They stand before my view.

To thee alone, O Lord, to thee,
      These evils I have done,
And in thy presence; woe is me
      That e'er they were begun!

But since thou pardon promisest,
      Where heart's true ruth is shown,
Shew now thy mercies unto me,
20   To make thy justice known;

That such as do infringe thy grace
      Be made ashamed and shent,
As rife thy mercies to behold
      As sinners to repent.

With favour view my foul defects:
      In crimes I did begin;
My nature bad; my mother frail;
      Conceiv'd I was in sin.

But since thyself affectest truth,
30   And truth itself is thee,
I truly hope to have thy grace,
      From sin to set me free;

Since to the faithful thou before
      The secret science gave,
Whereby to know what thou wouldst spend
      The sinful world to save,

Whose heavenly hyssop, sacred drops,
   Shall me besprinkle so
That it my sin-defilèd soul
40   Shall wash more white than snow.

O when mine ears receive the sound
   Of such my soul's release,
How do sin-laden limbs rejoice
   At heart's true joy's increase!

From my misdeeds retire thy sight;
   View not so foul a stain;
First wipe away my spots impure,
   Then turn thy face again.

A clean and undefilèd heart,
50   O God, create in me;
Let in me, Lord, of righteousness
   A spirit infusèd be.

From that most glorious face of thine
   O cast me not away;
Thy Holy Ghost vouchsafe, O God,
   With me that it may stay.

The joy of thy salvation, Lord,
   Restore to me again;
And with the spirit of graces chief
60   Confirm it to remain,

That when at thy most gracious hand
   My suits receivèd be,
The impious I may instruct
   How they may turn to thee.

For when, O Lord, I am releas'd
   From vengeance and from blood,
How joyful I shall speak of thee,
   So gracious and so good!

The Lord wilt give me leave to speak,
70   And I thy praise will shew;
For so thy graces do require,
   Thou dost on me bestow.

If thou sin-offerings hadst desired,
   As wonted were to be,
How gladly those for all my ills
   I would have yielded thee!

But thou accepts in sacrifice
   A sorrowing soul for sin;
Despising not the heart contrite,
80   And humble mind within.

Deal graciously, O loving Lord,
   In thy free bounty will,
With Zion, thy dear spouse on earth,
   And fortify it still;

That so thou mayest thence Receive
   That sovereign sacrifice
From altar of all faithful hearts,
   Devoutly where it lies.

To thee, O Father, glory be,
90   And glory to the Son,
And glory to the Holy Ghost
   Eternally be done.   (1601)

At one time this was attributed to Elizabeth Grymestone (*née* Bernys), who died in 1603. However, it is found in Verstegan's

Odes in Imitation of the seaven penitential psalms . . . (Antwerp, 1601), which was dedicated to Roman Catholic Englishwomen. Elizabeth Grymestone, one of these in Yorkshire, copied Verstegan's sadly repetitious verses into the manuscript which became her posthumous *Miscelanea: Meditations: Memoratives* (1604). Verstegan, unlike his Protestant contemporaries, worked from the Vulgate.

JOHN DONNE (1572–1631)

Upon the Translation of the Psalms by Sir Philip Sydney, and the Countess of Pembroke his sister

Eternal God – for whom whoever dare
Seek new expressions, do the Circle square,
And thrust into strait corners of poor wit
Thee, who art cornerless and infinite –
I would but bless thy Name, not name thee now;
And thy gifts are as infinite as thou.
Fix we our praises therefore on this one,
That, as thy blessed Spirit fell upon
These Psalms' first Author in a cloven tongue
10   (For 'twas a double power by which he sung
The highest matter in the noblest form),
So thou hast cleft that spirit, to perform
That work again, and shed it, here, upon
Two, by their bloods, and by thy Spirit one;
A Brother and a Sister, made by thee
The Organ, where thou art the Harmony.
Two that make one *John Baptist*'s holy voice,
And who that Psalm, *Now let the Isles rejoice*,
Have both translated and applied it too,
20   Both told us what, and taught us how, to do.
They show us Islanders our joy, our King,
They tell us *why*, and teach us *how*, to sing.

Make this All, three Quires, heaven, earth, and spheres:
The first, Heaven, hath a song, but no man hears;
The Spheres have Music, but they have no tongue,
Their harmony is rather danc'd than sung;
But our third Quire, to which the first gives ear
(For Angels learn by what the Church does here),
This Quire hath all. The Organist is he
30 Who hath tun'd God and Man, the Organ we;
The songs are these, which heaven's high holy Muse
Whisper'd to *David*, *David* to the Jews;
And *David*'s Successors, in holy zeal,
In forms of joy and art do re-reveal
To us so sweetly and sincerely too
That I must not rejoice as I would do,
When I behold that these Psalms are become
So well attir'd abroad, so ill at home,
So well in Chambers, in thy Church so ill,
40 As I can scarce call that 'Reform'd' until
This be reform'd. Would a whole State present
A lesser gift than some one man hath sent?
And shall our Church, unto our Spouse and King
More hoarse, more harsh than any other, sing?
For *that* we pray, we praise thy name for *this*
Which by this *Moses* and this *Miriam* is
Already done. And as those Psalms we call
(Though some have other Authors) *David*'s all,
So though some have, some may, some Psalms translate,
50 We thy Sydnean Psalms shall celebrate
And, till we come th' Extemporal song to sing
(Learn'd the first hour that we see the King
Who hath translated these translators) may
These their sweet learned labours all the way
Be as our tuning, that, when hence we part,
We may fall in with them, and sing our part.   (*c.* 1622)

From John Donne, *Poems*, (1635).

GEORGE SANDYS (1578–1644)

Sandys, the son of an Archbishop of York, travelled in Palestine and the Middle East, and published an account of his travels. In the 1620s he was in Virginia, and his version of Ovid's *Metamorphoses* has been saluted as the first literary work composed on American soil.

Psalm 21

> Lord, in Thy salvatiòn,
> In the strength which Thou hast shown,
> Greatly shall the king rejoice.
> How will joy exalt his voice!
> Thou hast granted his request;
> Of his heart's desire possess'd;
> Blest with blessings manifold;
> Crown'd with sparkling gems and gold.
> Pray'd-for life Thou granted hast;
> 10   Length of days which never waste;
> By Thy safeguard glorious made;
> With high majesty array'd;
> Of resistless pow'r possess'd;
> By thy favours ever bless'd.
> Lo! his joys are infinite;
> Joy reflected from Thy sight;
> For the king in God did trust.
> Through the mercy of the just,
> He shall ever fixèd stand.
> 20   For thy hand, thy own right hand,
> Shall thy enemies destroy,
> Who would in thy ruin joy.
> When thy anger shall awake,
> Them a flaming furnace make.

God shall swallow in His ire,
And devour them all with fire.
From the earth destroy their fruit;
Never let their seed take root.
Mischievous was their intent;
30 All their thoughts against me bent;
Thoughts, which nothing could perform.
Let Thy arrows, like a storm,
Put them to inglorious flight;
On their daunted faces light.
Lord, aloft Thy triumphs raise,
While we sing Thy pow'r and praise.   (1638)

A very ancient poem, pre-exilic, to be understood as sung in the Temple by the Temple choir (though it may be a solo voice renders one or more verses in the middle). It's hard to see how it could ever assist Christian devotions.

    Sandys's trochaic tetrameters are remorselessly end-stopped.

Psalm 77

To God I cried, He heard my cries
Again, when plung'd in miseries,
Renew'd with raisèd hands and eyes.

My fester'd wounds ran all the night,
No comfort could my soul invite
To relish long outworn delight.

I call'd upon the Ever-blest,
And yet my troubles still increas'd,
Almost to death by sorrow press'd.

10 Thou keep'st my gallèd eyes awake;
  Words fail my grief; sighs only spake,
  Which from my panting bosom brake.

  Then did my memory unfold
  The wonders which Thou wrought'st of old,
  By our admiring fathers told.

  The songs which in the night I sung,
  When deeply by affliction stung,
  These thoughts thus mov'd my desperate tongue:

  'Wilt Thou for ever, Lord, forsake?
20 Nor pity on th' afflicted take?
  O shall Thy mercy never wake?'

  'Wilt Thou Thy promise falsify?
  Must I in Thy displeasure die?
  Shall grace before Thy fury fly?'

  This said, I thus my passions check'd:
  His changes on their ends reflect;
  To punish and restore th'elect.

Part II

  His great deliverance shall dwell
  In my remembrance; I will tell
30 What in our fathers' days befell.

  His counsels from our reach are set,
  Hid in his secret cabinet.
  What God like ours, so good, so great?

25-7 I do not pretend to understand the last tercet in Part I – E̠d̠.

What wonders can effect alone,
His people's great redemptiòn,
To Jacob's seed, and Joseph's, known.

The yielding floods confess Thy might,
The deeps were troubled at Thy sight,
And seas recoil'd in their affright.

40   The clouds in storms of rain descend,
The air thy hideous fragors rend,
Thy arrows dreadful flames extend.

Thy thunders roaring rake the skies,
Thy fatal light'ning swiftly flies,
Earth trembles in her agonies.

Thy ways ev'n through the billows lie,
The floods then left their channels dry,
No mortal can Thy steps descry.

Like flocks, through wilderness of sand,
50   Thou led'st us to this pleasant land,
By Moses' and by Aaron's hand.   (1638)

Psalm 77 (*The Authorized Version*)

1. I cried unto God with my voice, even unto God with my voice;
and he gave ear unto me.

2. In the day of my trouble I sought the Lord: my sore ran in the
night, and ceased not: my soul refused to be comforted.

3. I remembered God, and was troubled: I complained, and my
spirit was overwhelmed.

---

41 *Fragor*: crash.

4. Thou holdest mine eyes waking: I am so troubled that I cannot speak.

5. I have considered the days of old, the years of ancient times.

6. I call to remembrance my song in the night: I commune with mine own heart: and my spirit made diligent search.

7. Will the Lord cast off for ever? and will he be favourable no more?

8. Is his mercy clean gone for ever? doth his promise fail for ever more?

9. Hath God forgotten to be gracious? hath he in anger shut up his tender mercies?

10. And I said, This is my infirmity: but I will remember the years of the right hand of the most High.

11. I will remember the works of the Lord: surely I will remember thy wonders of old.

12. I will meditate also of all thy work, and talk of thy doings.

13. Thy way, O God, is in the sanctuary: who is so great a God as our God?

14. Thou art the God that doest wonders: thou hast declared thy strength among the people.

15. Thou hast with thine arm redeemed thy people, the sons of Jacob and Joseph.

16. The waters saw thee, O God, the waters saw thee: they were afraid: the depths also were troubled.

17. The clouds poured out water: the skies sent out a sound: thine arrows also went abroad.

18. The voice of thy thunder was in the heaven: the lightnings lightened the world: the earth trembled and shook.

19. Thy way is in the sea, and thy path in the great waters, and thy footsteps are not known.

20. Thou leddest thy people like a flock by the hand of Moses and Aaron.

Psalm 78

My people, hear my words: I will unfold
Dark oracles and wonders done of old;
By our great ancestors both heard and known,
Successively unto their children shown.
Which we will to posterity relate,
That people yet unknown may celebrate
God's pow'r, His praise and glorious acts; since He
Wills this tradition by divine decree,
Until one day shall give the world an end,
10   That all their hopes might on His help depend,
Nor ever let His noble actions sleep
In dark oblivion, but His statutes keep;
Unlike their rebel sires, a stubborn race
Who fell from God, nor sought His slighted grace.
The Ephraimites, though expert in their bows,
Though arm'd, ignobly fled before their foes;
Who vainly brake the cov'nant of their God,
Nor in the ways of His prescription trod;
Forgot His famous acts, His wonders shown
20   In Zoan, and the plains by Nile o'erflown.
He brought them through the bowels of the flood,
The parted waves like solid mountains stood;
By day with leading clouds affords a shade,
By night a flaming pyramis display'd.
Hard rocks He in the thirsty deserts clave,
And drink out of their stony entrails gave.
Ev'n from their barren sides the waters gush'd,
And down in rivers through the valleys rush'd.

Part II

Yet still they sinn'd, and meat to satisfy
30   Their lust demand, provoking the Most High,

Blaspheming thus: 'Can God our wants redress?
A table furnish in the wilderness?
Though from the cloven rocks fresh currents drill,
Can He give bread? with flesh the hungry fill?'
Thus tempted by their hourly murmurings,
He to His long retarded wrath gives wings.
Their infidelity enrag'd the Just,
That would not to His sure protection trust,
Who all the curtains of the skies withdrew
40   And made the clouds resolve into a dew;
With manna, food of angels, mortals fed,
And fill'd with plenty of celestial bread;
Then caus'd the early eastern winds to rise,
And bade the dropping south obscure the skies,
Whence show'rs of quails descend, as thick as sand
On sea-wash'd shores, or dust on sun-dried land,
Which fell among their tents. They their delights
Enjoy and feast their deadly appetites.
For lo! while they those fatal dainties chew
50   And their inordinate desires pursue,
The wrath of God surpris'd them, and cut down
The choice of all, ev'n those of most renown.
Nor by their own mishaps admonishèd,
Would they His work believe or judgments dread.
So He their spirits quench'd with daily fears,
In vanity and toil consum'd their years.

Part III

But when, by slaughter wasted, the forlorn
Return'd and sought Him in the early morn,
They then confess'd and said: 'Thou art our tow'r,
60   Our strength, alone protectest by Thy pow'r.'
Yet their sly tongues did but their souls disguise,
Full of deluding flatteries and lies.

Their faithless hearts revolted from His will,
Nor ever would His just commands fulfil.
How oft would He Whose mercy hath no bound
Their pardon sign, nor in their sins confound!
How oft did He His burning wrath assuage!
How oft divert the fury of His rage!
Consider'd them as flesh in frailty born,
70 A passing wind that never can return.
Yet still would they His sacred laws transgress,
Provok'd Him in th' unpeopled wilderness,
Confin'd the Holy One of Israel,
Against their Saviour franticly rebel,
Forgetful of His pow'r, nor ever thought
Of that great day when from long bondage brought,
His dreadful miracles to Egypt known,
And wonders in the fields of Zoan shown.
The river chang'd into a sea of blood,
80 Men faint for thirst t'avoid th'infected flood.
Huge swarms of unknown flies display their wings,
Which wound to death with their envenom'd stings.
Loath'd frogs ev'n in their palaces abound,
And with their filthy slime pollute the ground.

Part IV

Their early fruits the caterpillars spoil,
And grasshoppers devour the ploughman's toil.
Long vines with storms their dangling burdens lost,
The broad-leav'd sycamores destroy'd with frost;
Their flocks, beat down with hailstones, breathless lie,
90 Their cattle by the stroke of thunder die.
The vengeance of His wrath all forms of woes,
More plagues than could be fear'd, upon them throws,
Whom evil angels to their sins betray.
He to the torrent of His wrath gave way,

Nor would with man or sinless beasts dispense,
Shot by the arrows of His pestilence.
Slew all the flow'r of youth, their first-born sons,
There where old Nilus in seven channels runs;
But like a flock of sheep His people led,
100 Safe and secure through deserts full of dread;
Ev'n through unfathom'd deeps, which part and close
Their tumbling waves to swallow their proud foes.
Then brought them to His consecrated land,
Ev'n to His mountain purchas'd by His Hand,
Cast out the giant-like inhabitants,
And in their rooms the tribes of Israel plants.
Yet they (O most ungrateful!) falsify
Their vows and still exasp'rate the Most High,
Who in their faithless fathers' traces go,
110 And start aside like a deceitful bow.
Their altars on the tops of mountains blaze,
While they their hands to cursèd idols raise.

Part V

These objects fuel to His wrath afford,
Whose Soul revolted Israel abhorr'd.
The ancient seat of Shiloh then forsook,
Nor longer would that hated mansion brook.
His ark ev'n to captivity declin'd,
His strength and glory to the foe resign'd,
And yielded up His people to the rage
120 Of barbarous swords, nor would His wrath assuage.
Devouring flames their able youth confound,
Nor are their maids with nuptial garlands crown'd.
Their mitred priests in heat of battle fall,
No widows weeping at their funeral.
Then as a giant, folded in the charms
Of wine and sleep, starts up and cries 'To arms!'

So rous'd, His foes behind Jehovah wounds,
And with eternal infamy confounds;
Yet would in Joseph's tents no longer dwell,
130 Nor Ephraim chose, who from His cov'nant fell;
But Judah's mountain for His seat elects,
And sacred Sion, which He most affects.
There our great God His glorious temple plac'd,
Firm as the centre, never to be raz'd.
And from the bleating flocks His David chose,
When he attended on the yeaning ewes,
And rais'd him to a throne, that he might feed
His people, Israel's selected seed;
Who fed them faithfully, and all the land
140 Directed with a just and equal hand.   (1638)

This long psalm, which can never have played a part in Temple
ritual, seems to offer substantially a coherent and stirring history of
the fluctuating fortunes of ancient Israel, though no doubt as often
mythological as historical. In fact the account is tendentious and
revisionist (therefore late, as Aramaic intrusions in the language
make clear), and it is history told from the standpoint of Judea, not
Israel. The distinction is unfamiliar to the modern reader. But
'Israel', strictly speaking, denotes only those tribes which in northern
Palestine consolidated themselves into an independent kingdom
under Saul about 1025 B.C. The apogee of this Israelite independence
was a short period, from about 1000 to 926 B.C., when David and,
following him, Solomon ruled the Israelite tribes from Jerusalem.
At the death of Solomon, Jeroboam seems to have withdrawn from
the southern provinces to create the independent Northern King-
dom. There were however twelve tribes, we are told; and two of
them, Judah and Benjamin, had stayed out of the Israelite confedera-
tion to constitute the minuscule and (within limits) autonomous
kingdom of Judea. This arrangement lasted for 200 years. But
whereas in 722 B.C. the Assyrians destroyed Israel and deported
most of its inhabitants, the kingdom of Judea, though it became
tributary to Assyria, retained its nominal independence. Judea in

due course suffered its own (Babylonian) 'exile'; but it survived as a political entity as Israel did not. To do so ideologically it had to take over the Israelite hero, David, and also to magnify Jerusalem as the religious metropolis, at the expense of earlier Israelite shrines like the Ephraimite Shiloh. Psalm 78 shows how this ideological exercise involved the rewriting of history, particularly the telescoping of many eras into one or two: the Israelites are convicted of impiety and ingratitude, so that the tribe of Judah shall stand out as alone faithful, and god-fearing.

Sandys is not always grammatical, and throughout is uninspired; however, more exuberant versions (for instance by the Countess of Pembroke and by Smart) only obscure further a narrative that is in any case complicated and deceptive.

Psalm 137

As on Euphrates shady banks we lay,
And there, O Sion, to thy Ashes pay
Our funerall teares; our silent Harps, unstrung
And unregarded, on the Willowes hung.
Lo, they who had thy desolation wrought
And captiv'd Judah unto Babel brought,
Deride the teares which from our Sorrowes spring;
And say in scorn, 'A Song of Sion sing'.
Shall we prophane our Harps at their command?
10 Or holy Hymnes sing in a forraigne Land?
O Solyma! thou that art now become
A heape of stones, and to thy selfe a Tomb!
When I forget thee, my deare Mother, let
My fingers their melodious skill forget:
When I a joy disjoyn'd from thine, receive;
Then may my tongue unto my palate cleave.
Remember Edom, Lord; their cruell pride,
Who in the sack of wretched Salem cry'd:

'Downe with their Buildings, raze them to the ground,
20   Nor let one Stone be on another found.'
Thou Babylon, whose towers now touch the Skie,
Thou shortly shalt as low in ruines lie;
O happy! O thrice happy they, who shall
With equall cruelty revenge our fall!
That dash thy Childrens braines against the stones:
And without pity heare their dying grones.

From *Paraphrase on the Psalms* (1638).

GEORGE WITHER (1588–1677)

Psalm 137

As we nigh *Babel*'s River sate,
We overcharg'd with weepings were
To think on *Sion*'s poor estate;
And hung our harps on willows there.
    For they to whom we were inthralled
    On us, for songs of *Sion*, called.
Come sing, they said, a *Sion-hymn*.
Lord! can we sing thy songs in thrall?
Unless (oh dear *Jerusalem*)
10   Thee, in my mirth, prefer I shall;
    Or, if the thought of thee forgo me,
    Let hand & tongue prove useless to me.
Oh Lord, remember *Edom*'s brood,
And how, whilst thy *Jerusalem*
Unsacked and undefacèd stood,
Her spoil was hast'ned on, by them.
    For loud they cried, 'Rase it, rase it,
    And to the groundwork down deface it.'

  O daughter of proud *Babylon*,
20 Thou shalt likewise destroyèd be;
  And he will prove a blessed one
  Who shall avenge our Cause on thee;
   Ev'n he that pays thee our disgraces,
   And brains thy babes in stony places.   (1632)

This, with its grotesque inversions, is so manifestly inferior not only to Sandys's version (*ante*) but to subsequent versions that it bears out the currently accepted estimate of the prolific and argumentative Wither as a wretched journeyman at best. This psalm, because it has entered so completely into secular and popular memory – 'I'll hang my harp on a weeping willow-tree' – can serve as a register of English psalm-translation through the centuries. Wither typically is quite indifferent about the affront to Christian sensibility offered by the vengeful last verse: 'Happy shall he be, that taketh and dasheth thy little ones against the stones.'

See *The Hymns and Songs of the Church* by George Wither, The Spenser Society (1881; reprinted New York, 1967).

For a Musician

Many Musicians are more out of order than their Instruments: such as are so, may by singing this Ode, become reprovers of their own untuneable affections. They who are better tempered are hereby remembered what Music is most acceptable to GOD, and most profitable to themselves.

What helps it those
  Who skill in *Song* have found,
Well to compose
  (Of disagreeing notes)
By artful choice
  A sweetly pleasing sound,
To fit their Voice
  And their melodious throats?

What helps it them
10 That they this cunning know,
If most condemn
 The way in which they go?

What will he gain
 By touching well his lute,
Who shall disdain
 A grave advice to hear?
What from the sounds
 Of organ, fife or lute
To him redounds,
20 Who doth no sin forbear?
A mean respect,
 By tuning strings, he hath,
Who doth neglect
 A *rectifièd-path*.

Therefore, oh Lord,
 So tunèd, let me be
Unto thy word
 And thy *ten-stringèd law*
That in each part
30 I may thereto agree;
And feel my heart
 Inspir'd with loving awe.
He sings and plays
 The Songs which best thou lovest
Who does and says
 The things which thou approvest.

Teach me the *skill*
 Of him whose harp assuaged
Those passions ill

40 Which oft afflicted Saul.
Teach me the strain
 Which calmeth minds enrag'd;
And which from vain
 Affections doth recall.
So, to the Quire
 Where angels music make
I may aspire
 When I this life forsake.   (1641)

Psalm 91

Who in the Closet & the shade
Of God almighty still resides
Is, by his Highness, fearless made
And alway safe with him abides.
For I confess the Lord hath been
A Fortress, & a Rock to me;
My God alone I trusted in,
 And he my trust shall always be.

He will, no doubt, secure thee from
10 The Fowler's traps, & noisome Pest:
His wings thy shelter shall become;
Thou shalt beneath his feathers rest.
Thou for thy Shield his Truth shalt bear,
And nothing then shall thee dismay:
Not that which we at Midnight fear
 Nor any shaft that flies by day.

No secret plague offend thee shall,
Nor what in public wastes the Land,
Though at thy side a thousand fall,
20 And ten times more, at thy right hand.

But thou shalt live to mark & see
The due reward of men unjust;
For God (most high) will favour thee
 Because in him thou putst thy trust.

No mischief shall to thee betide,
Nor any plague thy house infect;
For he doth Angel-guards provide,
Which in thy ways will thee protect.
Their hands will thee uprightly lead
30 And from thy Paths all harms expel;
Thou shalt on Asps & Lions tread,
 On Lions young, on Dragons fell.

For, seeing his delight I am,
I will (saith God) be still his guard;
And, since he knows my holy Name,
To honours high he shall be rear'd.
When he doth call, an ear I'll give,
In troubles, I with him will be;
On earth he long shall honor'd live,
40 And he my saving health shall see.   (1632)

This is the psalm behind Martin Luther's famous *Ein feste Burg ist unser Gott*. Wither's bumbling and verbose opening is in sorry contrast to the direct 'attack' of Luther and the Psalmist, and also (in the next piece) Thomas Carew.

THOMAS CAREW (1594?–1640)

Carew, a self-confessed 'son of Ben' (Jonson), nevertheless wrote a fine elegy on John Donne. By thus straddling what had seemed to be a non-negotiable divide in Jacobean and Caroline poetry, Carew has earned in the present century a deserved respect.

Psalm 91

Make the great God thy Fort, and dwell
　　In him by faith, and do not care
(So shaded) for the power of hell
　　Or for the cunning Fowler's snare,
　　Or poison of th' infected air.

His plumes shall make a downy bed,
　　Where thou shalt rest: he shall display
His wings of truth over thy head
　　Which, like a shield, shall drive away
10　　The fears of night, the darts of day.

The wingèd plague that flies by night,
　　The murdering sword that kills by day,
Shall not thy peaceful sleeps affright,
　　Though on thy right and left hand they
　　A thousand and ten thousand slay.

Yet shall thine eyes behold the fall
　　Of sinners; but, because thy heart
Dwells with the Lord, not one of all
　　Those ills, nor yet the plaguey dart,
20　　Shall dare approach near where thou art.

His Angels shall direct thy legs,
　　And guard them in the stony street:
On lions' whelps and adders' eggs
　　Thy steps shall march; and if thou meet
　　With dragons, they shall kiss thy feet.

When thou art troubled, he shall hear,
   And help thee for thy love embrast
Unto his name; therefore he'll rear
   Thy honours high, and when thou hast
30   Enjoyed them long, save thee at last.   (1634?)

See *The Poems of Thomas Carew*, ed. W. Carew Hazlitt, The Roxburghe Library (1870).

GEORGE HERBERT (1593–1633)

Psalm 23

The God of love my shepherd is,
   And he that doth me feed;
While he is mine, and I am his,
   What can I want or need?

He leads me to the tender grass,
   Where I both feed and rest;
Then to the streams that gently pass:
   In both I have the best.

Or if I stray, he doth convert,
10   And bring my mind in frame;
And all this not for my desert
   But for his holy name.

Yea, in death's shady black abode
   Well may I walk, not fear;
For thou art with me, and thy rod
   To guide, thy staff to bear.

---

27 *embrast*: inflamed.

Nay, thou dost make me sit and dine
    E'en in my enemies' sight;
My head with oil, my cup with wine
20   Runs over day and night.

Surely thy sweet and wondrous love
    Shall measure all my days;
And as it never shall remove,
    So neither shall my praise.   (1633)

This, from Herbert's *Temple*, and the only accredited psalm-version
(though others have been attributed to him), has been in congrega-
tional use as a hymn since 1645. Its style differs so markedly from
that of Herbert's own sacred poems that it has plausibly been
conjectured that he contrived a special *rusticity* so as to appeal to an
unlettered congregation used to the Old Version of Sternhold and
Hopkins.

FRANCIS QUARLES (1592–1644)

Emblem IV.iii
Psalm 17.5 *Stay my steps in thy paths, that my feet do not slide*

When e'er the old exchange of profit rings
    Her silver saint's-bell of uncertain gains,
My merchant soul can stretch both legs and wings;
    How I can run, and take unwearied pains!
      The charms of profit are so strong that I,
      Who wanted legs to go, find wings to fly.

If time-beguiling pleasure but advance
    Her lustful trump, and blow her bold alarms,
Oh how my sportful soul can frisk and dance,

10   And hug that siren in her twinèd arms!
            The sprightly voice of sinew-strengthening pleasure
            Can lend my bedrid soul both legs and leisure.

If blazing honour chance to fill my veins
    With flattering warmth and flash of courtly fire,
My soul can take a pleasure in her pains;
    My lofty strutting steps disdain to tire;
        My antic knees can turn upon the hinges
        Of compliment, and screw a thousand cringes.

But when I come to thee, my God, that art
20   The royal mine of everlasting treasure,
The real honour of my better part,
    And living fountain of eternal pleasure,
        How nerveless are my limbs! How faint and slow!
        I have nor wings to fly, nor legs to go.

So when the streams of swift-foot Rhine convey
    Her upland riches to the Belgic shore,
The idle vessel slides the watery lay,
    Without the blast or tug of wind or oar;
        Her slippery keel divides the silver foam
30   With ease: so facile is the way from home!

But when the home-bound vessel turns her sails
    Against the breast of the resisting stream,
Oh then she slugs; nor sail nor oar prevails!
    The stream is sturdy, and her tide's extreme:
        Each stroke is loss, and every tug is vain;
        A boat-length's purchase is a league of pain.

---

27 *lay*: pool.

Great all in all, that art my rest, my home;
   My way is tedious, and my steps are slow:
Reach forth thy helpful hand, or bid me come;
40   I am thy child, oh teach thy child to go;
      Conjoin thy sweet commands to my desire,
      And I will venture, though I fall or tire.

Epigram

Fear not, my soul, to lose for want of cunning;
Weep not; heaven is not always got by running:
Thy thoughts are swift, although thy legs be slow;
True love will creep, not having strength to go.   (1635)

HENRY KING (1592–1669)

King, son of a Bishop of London, became Bishop of Chichester in 1642. His ecclesiastical safe passage through a tumultuous period may seem suspect. His *Exequy* (for his dead wife) has been much admired.

From *To my honoured friend Mr George Sandys*

Your Muse rekindled hath the Prophet's fire,
And Tun'd the Strings of his neglected Lyre;
Making the Note and Ditty so agree,
They now become a perfect Harmony.
   I must confess, I have long wish'd to see
The Psalms reduc'd to this conformity;
Grieving the Songs of Sion should be sung
In Phrase not diff'ring from a Barbarous Tongue,

As if, by Custom warranted, we may
10   Sing that to God we would be loath to say.
Far be it from my purpose to upbraid
Their honest meaning, who first offer made
That Book in Meter to compile, which You
Have mended in the Form, and built anew.
And it was well, considering the time,
Which hardly could distinguish Verse and Rime.
But now the Language, like the Church, hath won
More Lustre since the Reformation,
None can condemn the Wish or Labour spent
20   Good Matter in Good Words to represent.
   Yet in this jealous Age some such There be,
So without cause afraid of Novelty,
They would not (were it in their pow'r to choose)
An Old Ill Practise for a Better lose;
Men who a Rustic Plainness so affect
They think God servèd best by their Neglect,
Holding the Cause would be Profaned by it
Were they at charge of Learning or of Wit.
And therefore bluntly (what comes next) they bring
30   Coarse and unstudied Stuffs for Offering;
Which, like th' old Tabernacle's Cov'ring, are
Made up of Badgers' skins, and of Goats' hair.   (1638)

Like Donne when he addressed the Sidneys, Bishop King uses his complimentary verses to Sandys so as to gird at the deficiencies of Sternhold and Hopkins.

Psalm 130 ('paraphrased for an Antheme')

Out of the horror of the lowest Deep,
Where cares and endless fears their station keep,
To thee (O Lord) I send my woeful cry:

O hear the accents of my misery.
If Thy enquiry (Lord) should be severe,
To mark all sins which have been acted here,
Who may abide? or, when they sifted are,
Stand un-condemnèd at Thy Judgment's bar?
But there is mercy (O my God) with Thee,
10 That Thou by it may'st lov'd and fearèd be.
My Soul waits for the Lord, in Him I trust,
Whose word is faithful, and whose promise just.
On him my longing thoughts are fixt, as they
Who wait the comforts of the rising day;
Yea more than those that watch the morning light
Tir'd with the sorrows of a rest-less night.
O Israël, trust in that Gracious Lord
Who plentiful remission doth afford;
And will His people, who past pardon seem,
20 By mercies greater than their sins redeem.   (1651)

See *The Poems of Henry King*, ed. Margaret Crum (Oxford, 1965).

WILLIAM HABINGTON
(1605–1654)

Paucitatem dierum meorum nuncia mihi
Psalm 102.23 *He weakened my strength in the way: he
shortened my days*

Tell me O great All-knowing God!
    What period
Hast thou unto my days assign'd?
Like some old leafless tree, shall I
Wither away; or violently
Fall by the axe, by lightning, or the Wind?

Here, where I first drew vital breath
    Shall I meet death?
And find in the same vault a room
10 Where my forefathers' ashes sleep?
Or shall I die where none shall weep
My timeless fate, and my cold earth entomb?

Shall I 'gainst the swift *Parthians* fight
    And in their flight
Receive my death? Or shall I see
That envied peace, in which we are
Triumphant yet, disturb'd by war;
And perish by th' invading enemy?

Astrologers, who calculate
20   Uncertain fate
Affirm my scheme doth not presage
Any abridgement of my days;
And the Physician gravely says
I may enjoy a reverent length of age.

But they are jugglers, and by sleight
    Of art the sight
Of faith delude; and in their school
They only practise how to make
A mystery of each mistake,
30 And teach strange words, credulity to fool.

For thou who first didst motion give,
    Whereby things live
And Time hath being! to conceal
Future events didst think it fit
To check th' ambition of our wit,
And keep in awe the curious search of zeal.

Therefore so I prepar'd still be,
    My God, for thee,
O' th' sudden on my spirits may
40   Some killing Apoplexy seize,
Or let me by a dull disease
Or weakened by a feeble age decay.

And so I in thy favour die,
    No memory
For me a well-wrought tomb prepare,
For if my soul be 'mong the blest
Though my poor ashes want a chest,
I shall forgive the trespass of my heir.   (1640)

Non nobis Domine

Psalm 115.1 *Not unto us, O Lord, not unto us, but unto thy
name give glory, for thy mercy, and for thy truth's sake*

No marble statue, nor high
Aspiring Pyramid be rais'd
To lose its head within the sky!
What claim have I to memory?
    God, be thou only prais'd!

Thou in a moment canst defeat
The mighty conquests of the proud,
And blast the laurels of the great.
Thou canst make brightest glory set
10   O' th' sudden in a cloud.

How can the feeble works of Art
Hold out 'gainst the assault of storms?
Or how can brass to him impart
Sense of surviving fame, whose heart
    Is now resolv'd to worms?

Blind folly of triumphing pride!
Æternity why buildst thou here?
Dost thou not see the highest tide
Its humbled stream in th' Ocean hide,
20   And ne'er the same appear?

That tide which did its banks o'er-flow,
As sent abroad by th' angry sea
To level vastest buildings low
And all our Trophies overthrow,
        Ebbs like a thief away.

And thou who to preserve thy name
Leav'st statues in some conquer'd land!
How will posterity scorn fame
When th' Idol shall receive a maim,
30   And lose a foot or hand?

How wilt thou hate thy wars, when he
Who only for his hire did raise
Thy counterfeit in stone, with thee
Shall stand Competitor, and be
        Perhaps thought worthier praise?

No Laurel wreath about my brow!
To thee, my God, all praise, whose law
The conquer'd doth and conqueror bow!
For both dissolve to air, if thou
40   Thy influence but withdraw.   (1640)

Nox nocti indicat Scientiam
Psalm 19.2 *Day unto day uttereth speech, and night unto night
sheweth knowledge*

When I survey the bright
    Coelestial sphere,
So rich with jewels hung, that night
Doth like an Æthiop bride appear,

My soul her wings doth spread
    And heaven-ward flies,
Th' Almighty's Mysteries to read
In the large volumes of the skies.

For the bright firmament
10   Shoots forth no flame
So silent, but is eloquent
In speaking the Creator's name.

No unregarded star
    Contracts its light
Into so small a Character,
Remov'd far from our human sight,

But if we steadfast look,
    We shall discern
In it as in some holy book
20 How man may heavenly knowledge learn.

It tells the Conqueror
    That far-stretch'd power
Which his proud dangers traffic for
Is but the triumph of an hour;

That from the farthest North
   Some Nation may
Yet undiscovered issue forth,
And o'er his new-got conquest sway.

Some nation yet shut in
30   With hills of ice
May be let out to scourge his sin
'Till they shall equal him in vice.

And then they likewise shall
   Their ruin have,
For as yourselves your Empires fall,
And every Kingdom hath a grave.

Thus those Coelestial fires,
   Though seeming mute,
The fallacy of our desires
40 And all the pride of life confute.

For they have watch'd since first
   The World had birth;
And found sin in itself accurst,
And nothing permanent on earth.   (1640)

Et alta a longè cognoscit

Psalm 138.6 *Though the Lord be high, yet hath he respect unto
the lowly: but the proud he knoweth afar off*

To the cold humble hermitage
(Not tenanted but by discoloured age,
   Or youth enfeebled by long prayer
And tame with fasts) th' Almighty doth repair.
   But from the lofty gilded roof
Stain'd with some Pagan fiction, keeps aloof,
   Nor the gay Landlord deigns to know,

Whose buildings are like Monsters but for show.
    Ambition! whither wilt thou climb,
10 Knowing thy art the mockery of time?
    Which by examples tells the high
Rich structures, they must as their owners die;
    And while they stand, their tenants are
Detraction, flatt'ry, wantonness, and care,
    Pride, envy, arrogance, and doubt,
Surfeit, and ease still tortured by the gout.
    O rather may I patient dwell
In th' injuries of an ill-cover'd cell!
    'Gainst whose too weak defence the hail,
20 The angry winds and frequent show'rs prevail;
    Where the swift measures of the day
Shall be distinguish'd only as I pray,
    And some star's solitary light
Be the sole taper to the tedious night.
    The neighbouring fountain (not accurst
Like wine with madness) shall allay my thirst;
    And the wild fruits of Nature give
Diet enough, to let me feel I live.
    You wantons! who impoverish Seas,
30 And th' air dispeople, your proud taste to please!
    A greedy tyrant you obey
Who varies still its tribute with the day.
    What interest doth all the vain
Cunning of surfeit to your senses gain?
    Since it obscure the Spirit must
And bow the flesh to sleep, disease, or lust.
    While who, forgetting rest and far,
Watcheth the fall and rising of each star,
    Ponders how bright the orbs do move,
40 And thence how much more bright the heav'ns above
    Where on the heads of Cherubins
Th' Almighty sits disdaining our bold sins
    Who while on earth we grovelling lie
Dare, in our pride of building, tempt the sky.   (1640)

Quid gloriaris in malicia?
Psalm 52.1 *Why boastest thou thyself in mischief, O mighty*
man? the goodness of God endureth continually

Swell no more, proud man, so high!
For enthron'd where'er you sit
Rais'd by fortune, sin and wit,
In a vault thou dust must lie,
He who's lifted up by vice
Hath a neighb'ring precipice
Dazzling his distorted eye.

Shallow is that unsafe sea
Over which you spread your sail;
10   And the Bark you trust to, frail
As the Winds it must obey.
Mischief, while it prospers, brings
Favour from the smile of Kings;
Useless, soon is thrown away.

Profit, though sin it extort,
Princes even accounted good,
Courting greatness, ne'er withstood,
Since it Empire doth support.
But when death makes them repent
20   They condemn the instrument,
And are thought Religious for 't.

Pitch'd down from that height you bear,
How distracted will you lie,
When your flattering Clients fly
As your fate infectious were?
When of all th' obsequious throng
That mov'd by your eye and tongue,
None shall in the storm appear?

When that abject insolence
30 (Which submits to the more great,
And disdains the weaker state,
As misfortune were offence)
Shall at Court be judged a crime
Though in practice, and the Time
Purchase wit at your expense.

Each small tempest shakes the proud,
Whose large branches vainly sprout
'Bove the measure of the root.
But let storms speak ne'er so loud,
40 And th' astonisht day benight,
Yet the just shines in a light
Fair as noon without a cloud.   (1640)

See, for this and preceding poems by Habington, *The Poems of William Habington*, ed. Kenneth Allott (Liverpool and London, 1948).

JOHN MILTON (1608–1674)

Psalm 1

Blessed is the man who hath not walked astray
In council of the wicked, and i' the way
Of sinners hath not stood, and in the seat
Of scorners hath not sat. But in the great
Jehovah's law is ever his delight,
And in his law he studies day and night.
He shall be as a tree which planted grows
By watery streams, and in his season knows

To yield his fruit, and his leaf shall not fall,
10   And what he takes in hand shall prosper all.
Not so the wicked, but as chaff which fanned
The wind drives, so the wicked shall not stand
In judgment, or abide their trial then,
Nor sinners in the assembly of just men.
For the Lord knows the upright way of the just,
And the way of bad men to ruin must.   (1653)

Milton's versions of the First Psalm through the Eighth, written
through the second week of August 1653 and each formally different
from the others, must witness to one sustained access of poetic
power. Hence the sequence must be presented in its entirety, even
though there is, it may be thought, something wrong with Milton's
Psalm 5.

    These psalm-versions have a quite different motive from the nine
psalms (80–88) paraphrased by him five years earlier. Whereas those
of April 1648 bear on public affairs canvassed in his polemical
pamphlets of those years, the versions of 1653 come to terms with
the private affliction of his onset of blindness. Note, for instance, ll.
13–15 of Psalm 6.

Psalm 2

Why do the Gentiles tumult, and the Nations
   Muse a vain thing, the Kings of th' earth upstand
   With power, and Princes in their Congregations
Lay deep their plots together through each Land,
   Against the Lord and his Messiah dear?
   Let us break off, say they, by strength of hand
Their bonds, and cast from us, no more to wear,
   Their twisted cords. He who in Heaven doth dwell
   Shall laugh, the Lord shall scoff them, then severe
10   Speak to them in his wrath, and in his fell
   And fierce ire trouble them; but I, saith he,

Anointed have my King (though ye rebel)
On Sion my holy hill. A firm decree
   I will declare: The Lord to me hath said,
   Thou art my Son I have begotten thee
This day; ask of me, and the grant is made;
   As thy possession I on thee bestow
   Th' Heathen, and as thy conquest to be sway'd
Earth's utmost bounds: them shalt thou bring full low
20   With Iron Sceptre bruis'd, and them disperse
   Like to a potter's vessel shiver'd so.
And now be wise at length, ye Kings averse,
   Be taught, ye Judges of the earth; with fear
   Jehovah serve, and let your joy converse
With trembling; kiss the Son lest he appear
   In anger and ye perish in the way
   If once his wrath take fire like fuel sere.
Happy all those who have in him their stay.   (8 August 1653)

Milton's 'kiss the Son' in l. 25 was anticipated by Coverdale, but for obvious reasons has been resented by Jews since the time of St Jerome. It is now acknowledged to be a blatant mistranslation, and has been expurgated from, for instance, David Frost's version in *The Liturgical Psalter*.

Psalm 3 *When he fled from Absalom*

Lord, how many are my foes!
   How many those
  That in arms against me rise!
   Many are they
  That of my life distrustfully thus say,
No help for him in God there lies.
But thou, Lord, art my shield, my glory,
   Thee through my story

The exalter of my head I count;
10   Aloud I cried
    Unto Jehovah, he full soon replied,
And heard me from his holy mount.

I lay and slept, I waked again;
    For my sustain
    Was the Lord. Of many millions
        The populous rout
    I fear not though encamping round about
They pitch against me their pavilions.
Rise, Lord, save me, my God, for thou
20   Hast smote ere now
    On the cheek-bone all my foes,
        Of men abhorred
    Hast broke the teeth. This help was from the Lord;
Thy blessing on thy people flows.   (9 August 1653)

Psalm 4

Answer me when I call,
God of my righteousness.
In straits and in distress
Thou didst me disenthral
And set at large; now spare,
    Now pity me, and hear my earnest prayer.

Great ones, how long will ye
My glory have in scorn,
How long be thus forborne
10 Still to have vanity,
    To love, to seek, to prize
        Things false and vain, and nothing else but lies?

Yet know the Lord hath chose,
Chose to himself apart,
The good and meek of heart
(For whom to choose he knows);
Jehovah from on high
    Will hear my voice what time to him I cry.

Be awed, and do not sin,
20 Speak to your hearts alone,
Upon your beds, each one,
And be at peace within.
Offer the offerings just
    Of righteousness, and in Jehovah trust.

Many there be that say:
Who yet will show us good?
Talking like this world's brood.
But, lord, thus let me pray:
On us lift up the light,
30   Lift up the favour of thy countenance bright.

Into my heart more joy
And gladness thou hast put,
That when a year of glut
Their stores doth over-cloy,
And from their plenteous grounds
    With vast increase their corn and wine abounds,

In peace at once will I
Both lay me down and sleep,
For thou alone dost keep
40 Me safe where'er I lie;
As in a rocky cell
    Thou, Lord, alone in safety mak'st me dwell.

(10 August 1653)

Psalm 5

Jehovah, to my words give ear,
    My meditation weigh;
  The voice of my complaining hear,
My King and God; for unto thee I pray.
    Jehovah, thou my early voice
      Shalt in the morning hear,
  I' the morning I to thee with choice
Will rank my prayers, and watch till thou appear.
    For thou art not a God that takes
10   In wickedness delight
    Evil with thee no biding makes,
Fools or mad men stand not within thy sight.
    All workers of iniquity
      Thou hat'st; and them unblest
    Thou wilt detest that speak a lie;
The bloody and guileful man God doth detest.
    But I will in thy mercies dear,
      Thy numerous mercies, go
    Into thy house; I in thy fear
20 Will towards thy holy temple worship low.
    Lord, lead me in thy righteousness,
      Lead me because of those
    That do observe if I transgress;
Set thy ways right before, where my step goes.
    For in his faltering mouth unstable
      No word is firm or sooth;
    Their inside, troubles miserable;
An open grave their throat, their tongue they smooth.
    God, find them guilty, let them fall
30   By their own counsels quelled;
    Push them in their rebellions all
Still on; for against thee they have rebelled.
    Then all who trust in thee shall bring

Their joy; while thou from blame
　　Defend'st them, they shall ever sing
　　Pity me, Lord, for I am much deject,
And shall triumph in thee, who love thy name.
　　For thou, Jehovah, wilt be found
　　　　To bless the just man still;
　　As with a shield thou wilt surround
40　Him with thy lasting favour and good will.　(12 August 1653)

Psalm 6

Lord, in thine anger do not reprehend me,
　　Nor in thy hot displeasure me correct;
　　Pity me, Lord, for I am much deject,
Am very weak and faint; heal and amend me.
For all my bones, that even with anguish ache,
　　Are troubled, yea my soul is troubled sore,
　　And thou, O Lord, how long? turn, Lord, restore
My soul; oh, save me for thy goodness sake.
For in death no remembrance is of thee;
10　Who in the grave can celebrate thy praise?
　　Wearied I am with sighing out my days,
Nightly my couch I make a kind of sea;
My bed I water with my tears; mine eye
　　Through grief consumes, is waxen old and dark
　　I' the midst of all mine enemies that mark.
Depart all ye that work iniquity,
Depart from me; for the voice of my weeping
　　The Lord hath heard, the Lord hath heard my prayer,
　　My supplication with acceptance fair
20　The Lord will own, and have me in his keeping.
Mine enemies shall all be blank and dashed
　　With much confusion; then grown red with shame
　　They shall return in haste the way they came,
And in a moment shall be quite abashed.　　(13 August 1653)

Psalm 7 *Upon the words of Chush the Benjamite against him*

Lord, my God, to thee I fly;
Save me and secure me under
Thy protection while I cry,
Lest as a lion (and no wonder)
He haste to tear my soul asunder,
Tearing and no rescue nigh.

Lord, my God, if I have thought
Or done this; if wickedness
Be in my hands, if I have wrought
10   Ill to him that meant me peace,
Or to him have rendered less,
And not freed my foe for nought;

Let the enemy pursue my soul
And overtake it; let him tread
My life down to the earth, and roll
In the dust my glory dead,
In the dust; and, there outspread,
Lodge it with dishonour foul.

Rise, Jehovah, in thine ire,
20   Rouse thyself amidst the rage
Of my foes that urge like fire;
And wake for me, their fury assuage;
Judgment here thou didst engage
And command, which I desire.

So the assemblies of each nation
Will surround thee, seeking right,
Thence to thy glorious habitation

Return on high, and in their sight.
Jehovah judgeth most upright
30 All people from the world's foundation.

Judge me, Lord, be judge in this
According to my righteousness,
And the innocence which is
Upon me: cause at length to cease
Of evil men the wickedness
And their power that do amiss.

But the just establish fast,
Since thou art the just God that tries
Hearts and reins. On God is cast
40 My defence, and in him lies,
In him who, both just and wise,
Saves the upright of heart at last.

God is a just judge and severe,
And God is every day offended;
If the unjust will not forbear,
His sword he whets, his bow hath bended
Already, and for him intended
The tools of death that waits him near.

(His arrows purposely made he
50 For them that persecute.) Behold
He travels big with vanity,
Trouble he hath conceived of old
As in a womb, and from that mould
Hath at length brought forth a lie.

He digged a pit, and delved it deep,
And fell into the pit he made;
His mischief that due course doth keep,

Turns on his head, and his ill trade
Of violence will, undelayed,
60   Fall on his crown with ruin steep.

Then will I Jehovah's praise
According to his justice raise,
And sing the Name and Deity
Of Jehovah the most high.   (14 August 1653)

Oesterley remarks: 'This psalm must be described as one of the less inspiring in the Psalter. It gives a vivid picture of the hatred engendered by religious strife, a hatred which is mutual.' Very true, no doubt; but there is other evidence that this hatred was by no means foreign to Milton's temperament. And, however we judge the ethics of the matter, there can be no doubt that *poetically* Milton's heart was in it when we consider stanza 8, beginning starkly with 'God is a just judge and severe, /And God is every day offended', mounting to the daringly violent and poetically vindicated enjambment, the run-over of sense, from the fourth line into the fifth. Oesterley cannot identify 'Chush the Benjamite', though he hides somewhere in 2 Samuel; Oesterley finds other reasons for thinking the Hebrew text corrupt.

Psalm 8

O Jehovah our Lord, how wondrous great
    And glorious is thy name through all the earth!
So as above the heavens thy praise to set
    Out of the tender mouths of latest birth.

Out of the mouths of babes and sucklings thou
    Hast founded strength because of all thy foes,
To stint the enemy, and slack the avenger's brow,
    That bends his rage thy providence to oppose.

When I behold thy heavens, thy fingers' art,
10　　The moon and stars which thou so bright hast set
In the pure firmament, then saith my heart,
　　Oh, what is man that thou rememberest yet,

And think'st upon him; or of man begot,
　　That him thou visit'st, and of him art found?
Scarce to be less than gods, thou mad'st his lot,
　　With honour and with state thou hast him crowned.

O'er the works of thy hand thou mad'st him lord,
　　Thou hast put all under his lordly feet,
All flocks, and herds, by thy commanding word,
20　　All beasts that in the field or forest meet,

Fowl of the heavens, and fish that through the wet
　　Sea paths in shoals do slide, and know no dearth.
O Jehovah our Lord, how wondrous great
　　And glorious is thy name through all the earth!

(14 August 1653)

Psalm 81

To God our strength sing loud, and clear,
　　Sing loud to God our King,
To Jacob's God, that all may hear,
　　Loud acclamations ring.

Prepare a hymn, prepare a song,
　　The timbrel hither bring,
The cheerful psaltery bring along,
　　And harp with pleasant string.

Blow, as is wont, in the new moon
10   With trumpets' lofty sound,
The appointed time, the day whereon
    Our solemn feast comes round.

This was a statute given of old
    For Israel to observe,
A law of Jacob's God, to hold,
    From whence they might not swerve.

This he a testimony ordained
    In Joseph, not to change,
Whenas he passed through Egypt land;
20   The tongue I heard was strange:

'From burden, and from slavish toil
    I set his shoulder free;
His hands from pots, and miry soil
    Delivered were by me.

When trouble did thee sore assail,
    On me then didst thou call,
And I to free thee did not fail,
    And led thee out of thrall.

I answered thee in thunder deep
30   With clouds encompassed round,
I tried thee at the water steep
    Of Meribah renowned.

Hear, O my people, hearken well,
    I testify to thee,
Thou ancient stock of Israel,
    If thou wilt list to me,

Throughout the land of thy abode
   No alien god shall be,
Nor shalt thou to a foreign god
40   In honour bend thy knee.

I am the Lord thy God, which brought
   Thee out of Egypt land;
Ask large enough, and I, besought,
   Will grant thy full demand.

And yet my people would not hear,
   Nor hearken to my voice;
And Israel, whom I loved so dear,
   Misliked me for his choice.

Then did I leave them to their will,
50   And to their wandering mind;
Their own conceits they followed still,
   Their own devices blind.

Oh, that my people would be wise,
   To serve me all their days!
And oh, that Israel would advise
   To walk my righteous ways!

Then would I soon bring down their foes,
   That now so proudly rise,
And turn my hand against all those
60   That are their enemies.'

Who hate the Lord should then be fain
   To bow to him and bend;
But they, his people, should remain,
   Their time should have no end.

And he would feed them from the shock
    With flour of finest wheat,
And satisfy them from the rock
    With honey for their meat.   (1648)

Though it must always seem presumptuous to cavil at Milton, this version seems verbose, in particular *adjectival*. Isaac Watts took just six quatrains, where Milton needed sixteen. However, when Milton in 1673 published his versions of Psalms 80–88 he took care to admit to local elaborations on the biblical model, and to italicize such elaborations.

Psalm 87

Among the holy mountains high
    Is his foundation fast,
There seated is his sanctuary,
    His temple there is placed.
Sion's fair gates the Lord loves more
    Than all the dwellings fair
Of Jacob's land, though there be store,
    And all within his care.
City of God, most glorious things
10   Of thee abroad are spoke;
I mention Egypt, where proud kings
    Did our forefathers yoke;
I mention Babel to my friends,
    Philistia full of scorn,
And Tyre with Ethiop's utmost ends –
    Lo this man there was born.
But twice that praise shall in our ear
    Be said of Sion last;
This and this man was born in her,
20   High God shall fix her fast.

> The Lord shall write it in a scroll,
>   That ne'er shall be out-worn,
> When he the nations doth enrol,
>   That *this man there was born.*
> Both they who sing, and they who dance,
>   With sacred songs are there;
> In thee fresh brooks, and soft streams glance,
>   And all my fountains clear.   (1648)

This psalm as Milton handles it must be one of the least lyrical in the Psalter, as 'lyrical' is nowadays understood and over-esteemed. The lyrical activities of song and dance, and the lyrical properties (in biblical terms) of brooks and streams and fountains, are invoked at the end, but as seen from afar; they are spoken of, but not as anything mimed in the sort of speaking that is the body of the poem. 'I mention Egypt . . . to my friends' quite startlingly sustains the conversational tone; and with 'Lo this man there was born' we seem to see the speaker genially singling out some individual in his audience or congregation. And yet Oesterley finds in this very sentence, meaningfully repeated as it is, that peculiarly lyrical feature: a *refrain*. I am persuaded so far that I have ventured to italicize the three places in Milton's version where this refrain occurs. (Oesterley concedes that in the Hebrew it occurs only twice but, confidently reconstructing as is his habit, he contrives a version where it is uttered *four* times.) It is not unknown for modern writers, for instance frequently Robert Frost, to make a locution, in itself flat and prosaic, take on poetic poignancy by being used as a refrain; but the manoeuvre was rare in the sixteenth and seventeenth centuries. No other version known to me allows for a refrain, as Milton's does; still less a refrain couched in blankly declarative form. The psalm of course is much cherished because it is universal-ist, looking forward (like Deutero-Isaiah among the prophets) to a time when the God of the Jews will be worshipped also by Gentiles – hence the roll-call of Gentile cities like Babylon and Tyre.

Psalm 136

Let us, with a gladsome mind,
Praise the Lord, for he is kind:
   For his mercies aye endure,
   Ever faithful, ever sure.

Let us blaze his name abroad,
For of gods he is the God:
   For his &c.

Oh, let us his praises tell,
10 Who doth the wrathful tyrants quell:
   For his &c.

Who with his miracles doth make
Amazèd Heaven and earth to shake:
   For his &c.

Who by his wisdom did create
The painted heavens so full of state:
   For his &c.
20

Who did the solid earth ordain
To rise above the watery plain.
   For his &c.

Who, by his all commanding might,
Did fill the new-made world with light:
   For his &c.

And caused the golden tressèd sun
30 All the day long his course to run:
   For his &c.

The hornèd moon to shine by night,
Amongst her spangled sisters bright:
   For his &c.

He, with his thunder-clasping hand,
Smote the first-born of Egypt land:
   For his &c.

40

And in despite of Pharaoh fell,
He brought from thence his Israel:
   For his &c.

The ruddy waves he cleft in twain
Of the Erythraean main:
   For his &c.

The floods stood still like walls of glass,
50   While the Hebrew bands did pass:
   For his &c.

But full soon they did devour
The tawny king with all his power:
   For his &c.

His chosen people he did bless
In the wasteful wilderness:
   For his &c.

60   In bloody battle he brought down
Kings of prowess and renown:
   For his &c.

He foiled both Seon and his host,
That ruled the Amorrean coast:
   For his &c.

And large-limbed Og he did subdue,
With all his over-hardy crew:
70   For his *&c.*

And to his servant Israel
He gave their land therein to dwell:
     For his *&c.*

He hath, with a piteous eye,
Beheld us in our misery:
     For his *&c.*

80   And freed us from the slavery
Of the invading enemy:
     For his *&c.*

All living creatures he doth feed,
And with full hand supplies their need:
     For his *&c.*

Let us therefore warble forth
His mighty majesty and worth:
90   For his *&c.*

That his mansion hath on high
Above the reach of mortal eye:
     For his mercies aye endure,
     Ever faithful, ever sure.

Some few of these twenty-four stanzas, with the recurrent refrain, figure in virtually every hymn-book. Sung to a rousing tune (Monkland, arranged by J. B. Wilkes (1785–1869)), the version is so familiar to even infrequent worshippers across the Anglophone world that the verses elude or transcend criticism – which, however, they can well sustain. If Milton's biographers are right to claim the piece was composed when the poet was fifteen, and a pupil at St Paul's School, it reveals him as a precocious prodigy. It first appeared in *Poems in English and Latin* (1645).

RICHARD CRASHAW (1613?–1649)

Psalm 23

Happy me! O happy sheep!
Whom my God vouchsafes to keep;
Even my God, even he it is
That points me to these ways of bliss;
On whose pastures cheerful Spring
All the year doth sit and sing,
And rejoicing smiles to see
Their green backs wear his livery:
Pleasure sings my soul to rest,
10   Plenty wears me at her breast,
Whose sweet temper teaches me
Nor wanton nor in want to be.
At my feet the blubb'ring Mountain
Weeping melts into a Fountain,
Whose soft silver-sweating streams
Make high noon forget his beams:
When my wayward breath is flying
He calls home my soul from dying,
Strokes and tames my rabid grief,
20   And dost woo me into life:
When my simple weakness strays
(Tangled in forbidden ways)
He (my shepherd) is my guide,
He's before me, on my side,
And behind me, he beguiles
Craft in all her knotty wiles:

He expounds the giddy wonder
Of my weary steps, and under
Spreads a Path as clear as Day,
30 Where no churlish rub says nay
To my joy-conducted feet,
Whilst they gladly go to meet
Grace and Peace, to meet new lays
Tun'd to my great Shepherd's praise.
Come now, all ye terrors, sally,
Muster forth into the valley
Where triumphant darkness hovers
With a sable wing that covers
Brooding horror. Come thou, Death,
40 Let the damps of thy dull Breath
Overshadow even the shade
And make darkness self-afraid;
There my feet, even there, shall find
Way for a resolvèd mind.
Still my Shepherd, still my God
Thou art with me, still thy Rod
And thy staff, whose influence
Gives direction, gives defence.
At the whisper of thy word
50 Crown'd abundance spreads my board;
While I feast, my foes do feed
Their rank malice, not their need,
So that with the self-same bread
They are starv'd and I am fed.
How my head in ointment swims!
How my cup o'erlooks her brims!
So, even so, still may I move
By the Line of thy dear love;
Still may thy sweet mercy spread
60 A shady arm above my head
About my Paths, so shall I find
The fair centre of my mind

Thy Temple, and those lovely walls
Bright ever with a beam that falls
Fresh from the pure glance of thine eye,
Lighting to eternity.
There I'll dwell, for ever there
Will I find a purer air
To feed my life with, there I'll sup
70 Balm and Nectar in my cup,
And thence my ripe soul will I breathe
Warm into the Arms of Death.

(1648)

Crashaw is widely taken to be the most respectable poetic voice in English of the Counter-Reformation. But in this piece we see English metrical psalms almost at their worst; diffuseness, fuelled by the need to find a couplet rhyme, is the least of its defects. It is astonishing that the same poet should have written *Charitas Nimia* (see *post*).

The text is from *Steps to the Temple, Delights of the Muses, & Other Poems*, ed. A. R. Waller (Cambridge, 1904).

Psalm 137

On the proud banks of great *Euphrates'* flood,
    There we sat, and there we wept:
Our harps that now no music understood,
    Nodding on the willows slept,
        While unhappy captiv'd we
        Lovely *Sion* thought on thee.
They, they that snatch'd us from our country's breast
    Would have a song carv'd to their ears
In *Hebrew* numbers, then (oh cruel jest!)
10   When Harps and Hearts were drown'd in tears:
        Come, they cried, come sing and play
        One of *Sion*'s Songs today.
Sing? Play? To whom (ah) shall we sing or play
    If not *Jerusalem* to thee?

Ah thee *Jerusalem*! ah sooner may
   This hand forget the mastery
      Of Music's dainty touch, than I
      The Music of thy memory,
Which when I lose, oh may at once my tongue
20   Lose this same busy speaking art,
Unperch'd, her vocal Arteries unstrung,
   No more acquainted with my heart,
      On my dry palate's roof to rest
      A wither'd leaf, an idle guest.
No, no, thy good, *Sion*, alone must crown
   The head of all my hope-nurs'd joys.
But *Edom* cruel thou! thou criedst Down, down
   Sink, *Sion*, down and never rise.
      Her falling thou didst urge, and thrust,
30   And haste to dash her into dust.
Dost laugh, proud *Babel*'s daughter? Do, laugh on,
   Till thy ruin teach thee tears,
Even such as these; laugh, till a venging throng
   Of woes too late do rouse thy fears.
      Laugh till thy children's bleeding bones
      Weep precious tears upon the stones.   (1648)

Psalm 8, v. 4 *Charitas Nimia*, or *The Dear Bargain*

   Lord, what is man? Why should he cost thee
So dear? What had his ruin lost thee?
Lord, what is man, that thou hast overbought
   So much a thing of nought?

Love is too kind, I see, and can
Make but a simple merchant man.
'Twas for such sorry merchandise
Bold painters have put out his eyes.

Alas, sweet Lord, what were't to thee
10   If there were no such worms as we?
Heav'n ne'er the less still heav'n would be,
     Should mankind dwell
     In the deep hell.
What have his woes to do with thee?

     Let him go weep
      O'er his own wounds;
   Seraphims will not sleep,
Nor spheres let fall their faithful rounds.

     Still would the youthful spirits sing,
20   And still thy spacious palace ring.
Still would those beauteous ministers of light
     Burn all as bright,

     And bow their flaming heads before thee;
Still thrones and dominations would adore thee;
Still would those ever-wakeful sons of fire
     Keep warm thy praise
     Both nights and days,
And teach thy lov'd name to their noble lyre.

     Let froward dust, then, do its kind,
30   And give itself for sport to the proud wind.
Why should a piece of peevish clay plead shares
In the eternity of thy old cares?
Why shouldst thou bow thy awful breast to see
What mine own madnesses have done with me?

Should not the king still keep his throne,
Because some desperate fool's undone?
Or will the world's illustrious eyes
Weep for every worm that dies?

      Will the gallant sun
40   E'er the less glorious run?
Will he hang down his golden head
Or e'er the sooner seek his western bed,
      Because some foolish fly
      Grows wanton, and will die?

If I were lost in misery,
What was it to thy heav'n and thee?
What was it to thy precious blood
If my foul heart call'd for a flood?

50 What if my faithless soul and I
      Would needs fall in
     With guilt and sin:
What did the lamb, that he should die?
What did the lamb, that he should need,
When the wolf sins, himself to bleed?

     If my base lust
Bargain'd with death and well-beseeming dust,
     Why should the white
     Lamb's bosom write
     The purple name
60   Of my sin's shame?

Why should his unstained breast make good
My blushes with his own heart-blood?

O my saviour, make me see
How dearly thou hast paid for me;
That, lost again, my life may prove,
As then in death, so now in love.   (1652)

HENRY VAUGHAN (1622–1695)

Vaughan's *Silex Scintillans*, a collection of sacred poems, appeared in two parts (1650 and 1655). Vaughan was a physician ('of the Hermetic variety') who seldom stirred out of his native country, around the Usk valley in South Wales. Though he acknowledged a debt to George Herbert, Vaughan's devout Anglicanism strikes notes not found in Herbert nor in other seventeenth century Christians. 'Celtic' and 'mystical' are words that have been used to define this difference; neither seems to me illuminating.

Psalm 65

Sion's true, glorious God! on thee
Praise waits in all humility.
All flesh shall unto thee repair,
To thee, O thou that hearest prayer!
But sinful words and works still spread
And over-run my heart and head;
Transgressions make me foul each day,
O purge them, purge them all away!
    Happy is he, whom thou wilt choose
10 To serve thee in thy blessed house;
Who in thy holy Temple dwells
And, fill'd with joy, thy goodness tells.
King of Salvation! by strange things
And terrible, Thy Justice brings
Man to his duty. Thou alone
Art the world's hope, and but thee, none.
Sailors that float on flowing seas
Stand firm by thee, and have sure peace.
Thou still'st the loud waves, when most wild,
20 And mak'st the raging people mild.
Thy arm did first the mountains lay

And girds their rocky heads this day.
The most remote, who know not thee,
At thy great works astonish'd be.

The outgoings of the Even and Dawn,
In Antiphons sing to thy Name.
Thou visit'st the low earth, and then
Water'st it for the sons of men.
The upper river, which abounds
30   With fertile streams, makes rich all grounds,
And by thy mercies still supplied
The sower doth his bread provide.
Thou water'st every ridge of land
And settlest with thy secret hand
The furrows of it; then thy warm
And opening showers (restrain'd from harm)
Soften the mould, while all unseen
The blade grows up alive and green.
The year is with thy goodness crown'd
40   And all thy paths drop fatness round,
They drop upon the wilderness,
For thou dost even the deserts bless,
And hills full of springing pride
Wear fresh adornments on each side.
The fruitful flocks fill every Dale,
And purling Corn doth clothe the Vale;
They shout for joy, and jointly sing,
Glory to the Eternal King!   (1655)

Psalm 104

Up, O my soul, and bless the Lord. O God,
   My God, how great, how very great art thou!
Honour and majesty have their abode
     With thee, and crown thy brow.

Thou cloth'st thyself with light, as with a robe,
   And the high, glorious heav'ns thy mighty hand
Doth spread like curtains round about this globe
     Of Air, and Sea, and Land.

The beams of thy bright Chambers thou dost lay
10   In the deep waters, which no eye can find;
The clouds thy chariots are, and thy path-way
     The wings of the swift wind.

In thy celestial, gladsome messages
   Dispatch'd to holy souls, sick with desire
And love of thee, each willing Angel is
     Thy minister in fire.

Thy arm unmoveable for ever laid
   And founded the firm earth; then with the deep
As with a veil thou hidst it, thy floods played
20   Above the mountains steep.

At thy rebuke they fled, at the known voice
   Of their Lord's thunder they retir'd apace;
Some up the mountains passed by secret ways,
     Some downwards to their place.

For thou to them a bound hast set, a bound
   Which (though but sand) keeps in and curbs whole seas;
There all their fury, foam and hideous sound
     Must languish and decrease.

And as thy care bounds these, so thy rich love
30   Doth broach the earth, and lesser brooks lets forth,
Which run from hills to valleys, and improve
     Their pleasure and their worth.

These to the beasts of every field give drink:
 There the wild asses swallow the cool spring;
And birds amongst the branches on their brink
  Their dwellings have and sing.

Thou from thy upper Springs above, from those
 Chambers of rain, where Heav'n's large bottles lie,
Dost water the parch'd hills, whose breaches close,
40 Heal'd by the showers from high.

Grass for the cattle, and herbs for man's use
 Thou mak'st to grow; these (blest by thee) the earth
Brings forth, with wine, oil, bread: all which infuse
  To man's heart strength and mirth.

Thou giv'st the trees their greenness, ev'n to those
 Cedars in *Lebanon*, in whose thick boughs
The birds their nests build; though the Stork doth choose
  The fir-trees for her house.

To the wild goats the high hills serve for folds,
50 The rocks give Conies a retiring place:
Above them the cool Moon her known course holds,
  And the Sun runs his race.

Thou makest darkness, and then comes the night;
 In whose thick shades and silence each wild beast
Creeps forth and, pinch'd for food, with scent and sight
  Hunts in an eager quest.

The Lion's whelps impatient of delay
 Roar in the covert of the woods, and seek
Their meat from thee, who dost appoint the prey
60 And feed'st them all the week.

This past, the Sun shines on the earth, and they
   Retire into their dens; Man goes abroad
Unto his work, and at the close of day
    Returns home with his load.

O Lord my God, how many and how rare
   Are thy great works! In wisdom hast thou made
Them all, and this the earth, and every blade
    Of grass we tread, declare.

So doth the deep and wide sea, wherein are
70   Innumerable creeping things both small
And great; there ships go, and the shipmen's fear,
    The comely spacious Whale.

These all upon thee wait, that thou may'st feed
   Them in due season: what thou giv'st, they take;
Thy bounteous open hand helps them at need,
    And plenteous meals they make.

When thou dost hide thy face (thy face which keeps
   All things in being) they consume and mourn;
When thou withdraw'st their breath, their vigour sleeps,
80   And they to dust return.

Thou send'st thy spirit forth, and they revive,
   The frozen earth's dead face thou dost renew.
Thus thou thy glory through the world dost drive,
    And to thy works art true.

Thine eyes behold the earth, and the whole stage
   Is mov'd and trembles, the hills melt & smoke
With thy least touch; lightnings and winds that rage
    At thy rebuke are broke.

> Therefore as long as thou wilt give me breath
90   I will in songs to thy great name employ
> That gift of thine, and to my day of death
>   Thou shalt be all my joy.

> I'll *spice* my thoughts with thee, and from thy word
>   Gather true comforts; but the wicked liver
> Shall be consum'd. O my soul, bless thy Lord!
>   Yea, bless thou him for ever!   (1655)

The seemingly quaint expression at l. 38, 'Heav'n's large bottles', can be validated by the precedent of *AV* at Job 38.37: 'Who can number the clouds in wisdom? or who can stay the bottles of heaven?' Vaughan's version of Psalm 104 may be the grandest in English. Particularly notable is how Vaughan uses the enjambment, the run-over of sense at the end of a line, no longer as a permissible expedient merely but as an expressive and melodious resource. In this he had been consistently anticipated only by Milton.

It should be clear that Vaughan's and the Psalmist's explanation of purpose in God's providing prey for his ravenous creatures is quite incompatible with any Darwinian explanation, in which indeed 'purpose' has no meaning though it is customarily invoked.

Psalm 104 *The Authorized Version*

1. Bless the Lord, O my soul. O Lord my God, thou art very great; thou art clothed with honour and majesty.

2. Who coverest thyself with light as with a garment: who stretchest out the heavens like a curtain:

3. Who layeth the beams of his chambers in the waters: who maketh the clouds his chariot: who walketh upon the wings of the wind:

4. Who maketh his angels spirits; his ministers a flaming fire:

5. Who laid the foundations of the earth, that it should not be removed for ever.

6. Thou coveredst it with the deep as with a garment: the waters stood above the mountains.

7. At thy rebuke they fled; at the voice of thy thunder they hasted away.

8. They go up by the mountains; they go down by the valleys unto the place which thou hast founded for them.

9. Thou hast set a bound that they may not pass over; that they turn not again to cover the earth.

10. He sendeth the springs into the valleys, which run among the hills.

11. They give drink to every beast of the field: the wild asses quench their thirst.

12. By them shall the fowls of the heaven have their habitation, which sing among the branches.

13. He watereth the hills from his chambers: the earth is satisfied with the fruit of thy works.

14. He causeth the grass to grow for the cattle, and herb for the service of man: that he may bring forth food out of the earth;

15. And wine that maketh glad the heart of man, and oil to make his face to shine, and bread which strengthenest man's heart.

16. The trees of the Lord are full of sap; the cedars of Lebanon, which he hath planted;

17. Where the birds make their nests: as for the stork, the fir trees are her house.

18. The high hills are a refuge for the wild goats; and the rocks for the conies.

19. He appointed the moon for seasons: the sun knoweth his going down.

20. Thou makest darkness, and it is night: wherein all the beasts of the forests do creep forth.

21. The young lions roar after their prey, and seek their meat from God.

22. The sun ariseth, they gather themselves together, and lay them down in their dens.

23. Man goeth forth unto his work and to his labour until the evening.

24. O Lord, how manifold are thy works! in wisdom hast thou made them all: the earth is full of thy riches.

25. So is this great and wide sea, wherein are things creeping innumerable, both small and great beasts.

26. There go the ships: there is that leviathan, whom thou hast made to play therein.

27. These wait all upon thee; that thou mayest give them their meat in due season.

28. That thou givest them they gather: thou openest thine hand, they are filled with good.

29. Thou hidest thy face, they are troubled: thou takest away their breath, they die, and return to their dust.

30. Thou sendest forth thy spirit, they are created: and thou renewest the face of the earth.

31. The glory of the Lord shall endure for ever: the Lord shall rejoice in his works.

32. He looketh on the earth, and it trembleth: he toucheth the hills, and they smoke.

33. I will sing unto the Lord as long as I live: I will sing praise to my God while I have my being.

34. My meditation of him shall be sweet: I will be glad in the Lord.

35. Let the sinners be consumed out of the earth, and let the wicked be no more. Bless thou the Lord, O my soul. Praise ye the Lord.

The wobbling between second and third persons ('Thou' and 'He'), also the unreasonable punctuation (particularly as regards colon and semicolon), illustrate the difficulties that Vaughan had to surmount on the way to his masterly version.

Psalm 121

Up to those bright and gladsome hills
    Whence flows my weal, and mirth,
I look and sigh for him who fills
    (Unseen) both heaven and earth.

He is alone my help, and hope
    That I shall not be moved.
His watchful Eye is ever ope
    And guardeth his beloved.

The glorious God is my sole stay;
10   He is my Sun and shade;
The cold by night, the heat by day,
    Neither shall me invade.

He keeps me from the spite of foes,
    Doth all their plots control,
And is a shield (not reckoning those)
      Unto my very soul.

Whether abroad, amidst the Crowd,
    Or else within my door,
He is my Pillar and my Cloud
20   Now, and for evermore.   (1655)

Psalm 121   *The Authorized Version*

    1. I will lift up mine eyes unto the hills, from whence cometh my help.

    2. My help cometh from the Lord which made heaven and earth.

    3. He will not suffer thy foot to be moved: he that keepeth thee will not slumber.

    4. Behold, he that keepeth Israel shall neither slumber nor sleep.

5. The Lord is thy keeper: the Lord is thy shade upon thy right hand.

6. The sun shall not smite thee by day, nor the moon by night.

7. The Lord shall preserve thee from all evil: he shall preserve thy soul.

8. The Lord shall preserve thy going out, and thy coming in, from this time forth, and even for evermore.

JOHN OLDHAM (1653–1683)

Paraphrase upon the 137th Psalm

1.

Far from our pleasant native Palestine,
Where great Euphrates with a mighty current flows,
And does in wat'ry limits Babylon confine,
Curst Babylon! the cause and author of our Woes;
    There on the River's side
    Sat wretched captive We,
  And in sad Tears bewail'd our Misery,
  Tears whose vast Store increas'd the neighb'ring Tide.
  We wept, and straight our Grief before us brought
10 A thousand distant Objects to our Thought;
  As oft as we survey'd the gliding Stream,
  Lov'd Jordan did our sad Remembrance claim;
  As oft as we th' adjoining City view'd,
  Dear Sion's razèd Walls our Grief renew'd.
We thought on all the Pleasures of our happy Land,
  Late ravish'd by a cruel Conqu'ror's hand;
We thought on every piteous, every mournful Thing
That might Access to our enlargèd Sorrows bring.
  Deep silence told the greatness of our Grief,
20   Of Grief too great by Vent to find relief.

Our Harps, as mute and dumb as we,
   Hung useless and neglected by,
And now and then a broken String would lend a Sigh,
   As if with us they felt a Sympathy,
   And mourn'd their own and our Captivity.
The gentle River too, as if compassionate grown
   As 'twould its Natives' Cruelty atone,
   As it pass'd by, in murmurs gave a pitying Groan.

2.

There the proud Conquerors, who gave us Chains,
30   Who all our Suff'rings and Misfortunes gave,
   Did with rude Insolence our Sorrows brave,
And with insulting Raillery thus mock'd our Pains.
   Play us (said they) some brisk and airy strain,
   Such as your Ancestors were wont to hear
     On Shilo's pleasant Plain
Where all the Virgins met in Dances once a year;
     Or one of those
   Which your illustrious David did compose
   Whilst he fill'd Israel's happy Throne,
40 Great Soldier, Poet, and Musician all in one.
   Oft (have we heard) he went with Harp in hand,
   Captain of all th' harmonious Band,
And vanquish'd all the Quire with 's single Skill alone.
Forbid it Heav'n! forbid thou great thrice-hallow'd Name!
   We should thy sacred Hymns defame,
   Or them with impious Ears profane.
   No, no, Inhuman Slaves, is this a time?
   (Oh cruel and preposterous Demand!)
   When every Joy and every Smile's a crime,
50 A Treason to our poor unhappy native Land?
   Is this a time for sprightly Airs
   When every Look the Badge of Sorrow wears

And Livery of our Miseries,
Sad miseries, that call for all our Breath in sighs
And all the Tribute of our Eyes
And moisture of our veins, our very Blood in Tears?
When nought can claim our Thoughts, Jerusalem, but Thou,
Nought, but thy sad Destruction, Fall, and Overthrow?

3.

Oh dearest City! late our Nation's justest Pride!
60 Envy of all the wond'ring World beside!
Oh sacred Temple! once th' Almighty's blest Abode!
Now quite forsaken by our angry God!
  Shall ever distant Time or Place
Your firm Ideas from my Soul deface?
  Shall they not still take up my Breast,
As long as that, and Life, and I shall last?
Grant Heav'n (nor shall my Pray'rs the Curse withstand)
  That this my learnèd skilful Hand
(Which now o'er all the tuneful Strings can boast Command,
70 Which does as quick, as ready and unerring prove
As Nature, when it would its Joints or Fingers move)
  Grant it forget its Art and Feeling too,
When I forget to think, to wish, and pray for You.
   For ever tied with Dumbness be my Tongue,
When it speaks aught that shall not to your Praise belong,
If that be not the constant Subject of my Muse and Song.

4.

Remember, Heav'n, remember Edom on that day,
  And with like Sufferings their Spite repay,
Who made our Miseries their cruel Mirth and Scorn,
80   Who laugh'd to see our flaming City burn,
   And wish'd it might to Ashes turn.

Raze, raze it (was their cursèd Cry)
Raze all its stately Structures down,
And lay its Palaces and Temple level with the Ground,
Till Sion buried in its dismal Ruins lie,
Forgot alike its Place, its Name, and Memory.
And thou, proud Babylon! just Object of our Hate,
Thou too shalt feel the sad Reverse of Fate,
Tho' thou art now exalted high
And with thy lofty Head o'ertopst the Sky
90 As if thou wouldst the Pow'rs above defy;
Thou (if those Pow'rs (and sure they will) prove just
If my prophetic Grief can aught foresee
Ere long shalt lay that lofty Head in dust,
And Blush in Blood for all thy present Cruelty.
How loudly then shall we retort these bitter Taunts!
How gladly to the Music of thy Fetters dance!

5.

A day will come (oh might I see't) ere long
That shall revenge our mighty Wrong.
100 Then blest, for ever blest be he,
Whoever shall return't on thee,
And grave it deep, and pay't with bloody Usury.
May neither Aged Groans, nor Infant-Cries
Nor piteous Mother's Tears, nor ravish'd Virgin's Sighs
Soften thy unrelenting Enemies.
Let them, as thou to us, inexorable prove,
Nor Age nor Sex their deaf Compassion move.
Rapes, Murders, Slaughters, Funerals,
And all thou durst attempt within our Sion's Walls,
110 Mayst thou endure and more, till joyful we
Confess thyself outdone in artful Cruelty.
Blest, yea thrice-blessed be that barbarous Hand
(Oh Grief! that I such dire Revenge commend)

> Who tears out Infants from their Mother's Womb,
> And hurls 'em yet unborn unto their Tomb.
> Blest he, who plucks 'em from their Parents' Arms,
> That Sanctuary from all common Harms;
> Who with their Skulls and Bones shall pave thy Streets all
>   o'er
> And fill thy glutted Channels with their scatter'd Brains &
>   Gore.   (1676)

This, the most horrible of psalm-versions into English, and among the most risible, is the work of a poet famously commended by Dryden; his reputation as a poet is still considerable (and not unearned). Isaac Watts was already nine years old when Oldham died. Those who find Watts's versions threadbare should consider that this tumid style, unfeeling and profoundly *unimaginative*, is what he set out to purge – successfully, too, as later history shows. After Watts, 'paraphrase' could not mean what Oldham plainly took it to mean: expansion and ornamentation.

See *The Poems of John Oldham*, ed. Harold F. Brooks and Raman Selden (Oxford, 1987).

EDMUND WALLER (1606–1687)

Waller is remembered quite justly by the anthologists as the author of 'Go, lovely rose' and other secular lyrics not much less graceful. His *Sacred Poems*, published in his old age, have gone unregarded because their distinction is prosaic sobriety; as here, '*His will be done*. In fact 'tis always done . . .'

Some Reflections of his Upon the Several Petitions in the Lord's Prayer

1.

His sacred name with reverence profound
Should mentioned be, and trembling at the sound.
It was Jehovah; 'tis Our Father now;
So low to us does Heaven vouchsafe to bow!
He brought it down, that taught us how to pray
And did so dearly for our ransom pay.

2.

His kingdom come. For this we pray in vain,
Unless he does in our affections reign.
Absurd it were to wish for such a King,
10   And not obedience to his sceptre bring,
Whose yoke is easy, and his burthen light,
His service freedom, and his judgments right.

3.

His will be done. In fact 'tis always done;
But, as in Heaven, it must be made our own.
His will should all our inclinations sway,
Whom Nature, and the universe, obey.
Happy the man! whose wishes are confined
To what has been eternally designed;
Referring all to his paternal care,
20   To whom more dear than to ourselves we are.

4.

It is not what our avarice hoards up;
'Tis he that feeds us, and that fills our cup;

Like new-born babes depending on the breast,
From day to day we on his bounty feast;
Nor should the soul expect above a day
To dwell in her frail tenement of clay;
The setting sun should seem to bound our race,
And the new day a gift of special grace.

5.

That he should all our trespasses forgive,
30   While we in hatred with our neighbours live;
Though so to pray may seem an easy task,
We curse ourselves when thus inclined we ask.
This prayer to use, we ought with equal care
Our souls as to the sacrament prepare.
The noblest worship of the Power above
Is to extol, and imitate, his love;
Not to forgive our enemies alone,
But use our bounty that they may be won.

6.

Guard us from all temptations of the foe,
40   And those we may in several stations know:
The rich and poor in slippery places stand.
Give us enough! but with a sparing hand!
Not ill-persuading want, nor wanton wealth,
But what proportioned is to life and health.
For not the dead, but living, sing thy praise,
Exalt thy kingdom, and thy glory raise.   (1685)

Early editions invoke against the fourth line (presumably with
the poet's authority) Psalm 18, v. 3. But an unprejudiced reader
is more likely to see, behind the four verses beginning 'Happy
the man' (i.e. *Beatus vir*, as in the Vulgate) the first two verses of
Psalm 1:

Blessed is the man that hath not walked in the counsel of the ungodly, nor stood in the way of sinners: and hath not sat in the seat of the scornful.

But his delight is in the law of the Lord: and in his law will he exercise himself day and night.

SIR JOHN DENHAM (1615–1669)

Denham's reputation with posterity was determined when Pope in his 'Essay on Criticism' invited us to 'Praise the easy vigour of a line/Where Denham's strength and Waller's sweetness join.' In fact he is a more interesting poet than that time-honoured twinning with Waller suggests. He is now commonly remembered only for the topographical poem 'Cooper's Hill' (1642), which inaugurated a new and influential genre. But in the lifetime of Isaac Watts, who measured himself against Denham (see *post, The Hebrew Poet*), Denham's psalm-versions were greatly esteemed; it is telling, and yet unsurprising, that these pieces are customarily left out of modern editions of Denham's poetry. An unsuccessful Royalist commander in the Civil War, Denham paraphrased resourcefully a part of Virgil's *Aeneid*. See *post*, under Anon., Psalm 124.

Psalm 47

O Clap your Hands with one Accord!
Praise with melodious Notes the Lord!
With Terror he the World commands:
   He only gives us Victory,
   Under our Feet the Nations lie,
And *Israel* shall divide their Lands.

Jacob he loves, and will advance,
And set out his Inheritance;

Ascending, he in Triumph sits:
10   With Trumpets to our King rejoice,
       With Understanding raise your Voice;
To his Commands the World submits.

Exalted on his sacred Throne,
He o'er the Heathen reigns alone:
And now the People's Leaders yield,
     With those of *Abram*'s God to join;
     Whose Glory rais'd on high does shine,
And guards the World as with a Shield.   (1668)

Denham deals with 'inheritance' (l. 8) more neatly and also more
lucidly than either Coverdale, who glosses it 'even the worship of
Jacob, whom he loved', or *The Liturgical Psalter* that has 'that was
the pride of Jacob, whom he loved'. It's hard to make sense of
either 'worship' or 'pride' in this place, unless of course Jacob is
a keen gardener whose plot of land is his 'pride and joy'! The
Hebraists behind David Frost, by denying us 'shield' at the end, deny
us the ringing closure that we get from both Coverdale and Denham.
   Denham's psalm-versions were not printed until 1714.

Psalm 92

'Tis good, our Thanks to God to bring,
And Praises to his Name to sing.
His Love the Morning shall recite,
His Faithfulness the fearful Night.

All Arts which Musick can invent,
Harp, Psaltery, ten-string'd Instrument,
His solemn Praises shall resound;
Whose Works with Joy my Head have crown'd.

How great the Works which God has wrought!
10 And how profound his secret Thought!
Fools to this Knowledge can't ascend,
Nor Brutish Man this comprehend.

When Sin like Grass grows strong and high,
'Tis certain then the Harvest's nigh.
God ever sits on high, and all
His wicked Foes disperst shall fall.

Anointed with fresh Oil, my Horn
Is strong, like that o' th' Unicorn.
My foes shall fall before my Eyes,
20 My Ear shall hear their dying Cries.

The Righteous like a Palm are grown,
Like Cedars spread on *Lebanon*;
Whom God in his own Courts does plant,
They neither Fruit nor Blossoms want.

Thus is our God for ever just,
Firm as a Rock, when him we trust. (1668)

The 'strength' of Denham – applauded by Pope and Johnson, both
meaning by it compactness and rapidity of phrasing – is apparent in:

When Sin like Grass grows strong and high,
'Tis certain then the Harvest's nigh.

This sounds proverbial; and that is high praise.

Psalm 97

The Lord does reign, let Earth advance
His Praise, let all the Islands dance!
    A cloudy Mantle him surrounds:

With Righteousness and Light divine
His Throne and high Pavilion shine,
   Fore-running Fire his Foes confounds.

His Lightnings to the World gave Light,
Earth saw, and trembled at the Sight:
   Hills melt like Wax, like Snow they thaw.
10 When God's bright Presence gilds the Air,
   The Skies his Righteousness declare;
And all the Earth his Glory saw.

Confounded may they be who call
On Idols, or before them fall;
   All Gods on Earth before him bow.
Judah rejoic'd when God was heard,
And *Sion* leap'd when he appear'd,
   For they his righteous Judgments know.

Above the Earth are his Abodes,
20 Rais'd above all created Gods.
   Who love his Name, all Sins reject;
Their Souls in Glory shall appear,
And he their Lives and Fortunes here
   Shall from the wicked Hand protect.

His Light is for the Righteous sown,
Gladness the upright Heart shall crown.
   Bring your Thank-Offerings to the Lord,
Your Joy in chearful Songs express,
His everlasting Holiness
30 Still in your Memory record.   (1668)

Psalm 139

Lord, thou my Ways hast searcht and known,
My Rising up, my Sitting down;
To thee are my Conceptions brought,
E'er they are form'd into a Thought.

My idle Words thou dost condemn,
Before my Lips have fashion'd them;
On ev'ry Part thy Hand's impos'd;
Behind, before, has me enclos'd.

Such Knowledge is for me too high;
10   From thee O whither shall I fly?
If up to Heav'n, thou there dost dwell;
And if my Bed I lay in Hell,

I shou'd not scape thy piercing Eye.
If on the Morning's Wings I fly,
Or th' Ocean's untrac'd Paths shou'd tread,
With thy Right hand I shou'd be led.

If I my Head in Night involve,
Thy Light the Darkness wou'd dissolve;
Ev'n Day and Night are but one Name,
20   For both to thee appear the same.

Nor Reins nor Heart cou'd thee escape,
Thou in the Womb my Form didst shape;
So marvellously I was made,
E'en of my self I stand afraid.

For this my Soul, which knows so well
Thy wondrous Works, thy Praise shall tell.
My Substance was by thee survey'd,
When it was first in secret made.

Thy Hand did free, with curious Art,
30   From Imperfection every Part;
And ev'ry Member, which had yet
No being, in thy Book was writ.

At last, to shew whose Hand it was,
GOD stampt HIS image on the Mass.
O how thy Thoughts my Soul delight!
The sum of them is infinite.

When I to number them wou'd try,
I find they all Accounts outvie;
I sooner might the Sands explore
40   That lie upon the Ocean's Shore;

Yet they my early Thoughts employ.
Lord, thou the Wicked wilt destroy:
Such as blaspheme, and thirst for Blood,
And those whose Counsels thine withstood.

I hated to the last Degree
All those, O God, who hated thee.
Search all my Thoughts, and if they stray
From thee, be thou their Guide and Way.   (1668)

This is the only version of this psalm which I would match up
against the Countess of Pembroke's, which I extol in the Introduc-
tion. (And I am not thinking only of versions *in verse*.) One respect
in which Denham scores heavily against the Countess is, as might
be expected of him, in conciseness – he gets into forty-eight verse-

lines what cost the Countess ninety-one. In him as in her the achievement as poetry is not to be distinguished from its achievement as devotion.

Psalm 145

O Lord, my God, my Songs to thee
Shall, like thy self, immortal be!
For ever I'll thy Praise express,
And ev'ry Day thy Name will bless.

Great is the Lord, his Praise no Bounds
Confine, no Line his Greatness sounds.
That Generation which succeeds
Shall learn from this thy mighty Deeds.

The Honour of thy Majesty
10   I'll sing, how wonderful! how high!
The Measures of thy Grace who know?
Thy Mercy's swift, thy Anger slow.

O'er all, God's Guardian Mercy stands,
His Bounty falls from equal Hands:
His wondrous Pow'r his Works proclaim,
For which the Saints shall bless his Name.

Part II

God's Majesty, his Pow'r, the State
Of his Dominion, Saints relate;
So large, so lasting, so renown'd
20   As neither Place nor Time shall bound.

Thy Hand supports the drooping Head:
Has rais'd the Low, the Hungry fed.
The whole Creation, Men and beasts,
Attending thee, thy Bounty feasts.

Justice and Truth thy Ways secure,
And, like thy self, thy Works are pure.
To them that pray, the Lord is near,
To all who pray, and are sincere.

Their Suits he grants, their Wants supplies,
30 And saves them when he hears their Cries.
All this the righteous Man enjoys,
But the ungodly, God destroys.
My Lips his Praises shall proclaim,
And all who live shall bless his Name.   (1668)

NAHUM TATE (1652–1715) and
NICHOLAS BRADY (1632–1726)

The 'New Version' of the Psalter (1698), designed to supersede the
Elizabethan 'Old Version' of Sternhold and Hopkins, was approved
by William III for congregational use through the kingdom. Nicho-
las Brady, who outlived his collaborator, is a shadowy figure; and
the praise or blame heaped on the New Version is commonly fixed
on Tate, who had the misfortune of being pilloried by Pope in *The
Dunciad*. Appointed Poet Laureate in 1692, Tate had talents which
both Dryden and Henry Purcell were glad to press into service.
Recognizing him as the author of 'While shepherds watched their
flocks by night', we may well suspect that Tate, a graduate of
Trinity College Dublin, has been shabbily treated by posterity.

Psalm 34

Through all the changing scenes of life,
   In trouble and in joy,
The praises of my God shall still
   My heart and tongue employ.

Of his deliverance I will boast,
   Till all that are distressed
From my example comfort take,
   And charm their griefs to rest.

O magnify the Lord with me,
10   With me exalt His name;
When in distress to Him I called,
   He to my rescue came.

The hosts of God encamp around
   The dwellings of the just;
Deliverance He affords to all
   Who on His succour trust.

O make but trial of His love;
   Experience will decide
How blest they are, and only they,
20   Who in His truth confide.

Fear Him, ye saints, and you will then
   Have nothing else to fear;
Make you His service your delight.
   He'll make your wants His care.   (1698)

No. 427 in *The Methodist Hymn-Book*. No. 490 in *Hymns Ancient and Modern* is different. In neither case does the hymn account for more than the first half of the psalm.

Psalm 42

As pants the hart for cooling streams,
     When heated in the chase,
So longs my soul, O God, for Thee,
     And Thy refreshing grace.

For Thee, my God, the living God,
     My thirsty soul doth pine;
O when shall I behold Thy face,
     Thou Majesty divine!

God of my strength, how long shall I,
10   Like one forgotten, mourn?
Forlorn, forsaken, and exposed
     To my oppressor's scorn.

Why restless, why cast down, my soul?
     Hope still, and thou shalt sing
The praise of Him who is thy God,
     Thy health's eternal spring.   (1698)

No. 455 in *The Methodist Hymn-Book.* No. 238 in *Hymns Ancient and Modern* is different. In either case a drastic abbreviation leaves out or mutes some of the most affecting and famous images. See the *AV* version, following.

Psalm 42 *The Authorized Version*

1. As the hart panteth after the water brooks, so panteth my soul after thee, O God.

2. My soul thirsteth for God, for the living God: when shall I come and appear before God?

3. My tears have been my meat day and night, while they continually say unto me, Where is thy God?

4. When I remember these things, I pour out my soul in me: for I had gone with the multitude. I went with them to the house of God, with the voice of joy and praise, with a multitude that kept holyday.

5. Why art thou cast down, O my soul? and why art thou disquieted in me? hope thou in God: for I shall yet praise him for the help of his countenance.

6. O my God, my soul is cast down within me: therefore will I remember thee from the land of Jordan, and of the Hermonites, from the hill Mizar.

7. Deep calleth unto deep at the noise of thy waterspouts: all thy waves and thy billows are gone over me.

8. Yet the Lord will command his lovingkindness in the daytime, and in the night his song shall be with me, and my prayer unto the God of my life.

9. I will say unto God my rock, Why hast thou forgotten me? why go I mourning because of the oppression of the enemy?

10. As with a sword in my bones, mine enemies reproach me: while they say daily unto me, Where is thy God?

11. Why art thou cast down, O my soul? and why art thou disquieted within me? hope thou in God: for I shall yet praise him, who is the health of my countenance, and my God.

At the risk of flogging a dead horse, we may look at *NOAB*, which translates the first verse so as to give no reason *why* the hunted deer looks for a stream, beyond apparently a preference for running water over still. At v. 7, which has brought into the language the idiom (now cliché) 'deep calleth unto deep', Coverdale has: 'because of the noise of the water-pipes' – which suggests defective plumbing; *NOAB* has 'at the thunder of thy cataracts' – which suggests a park or ornamental garden, at all events a freshwater phenomenon, at odds with 'thy waves and thy billows'. It needs no Hebrew, only a knowledge of the behaviour of the Mediterranean, to see that the *AV* 'waterspouts' is the likeliest solution.

From Psalm 102

When I pour out my Soul in Pray'r,
    Do thou, O Lord, attend:
To thy Eternal Throne of Grace
    Let my sad Cry ascend.

O hide not thou thy glorious Face
    In times of deep Distress,
Incline thine Ear, and when I call
    My Sorrows soon redress.

Each cloudy Portion of my Life
10   Like scatter'd Smoke expires;
My shriv'led Bones are like a Hearth
    That's parch'd with constant Fires.

My Heart, like Grass that feels the Blast
    Of some infectious Wind,
Is wither'd so with Grief, that scarce
    My needful Food I mind.

By reason of my sad Estate
    I spend my Breath in Groans;
My Flesh is worn away, my Skin
20   Scarce hides my starting Bones.

I'm like a Pelican become,
    That does in Deserts mourn;
Or like an Owl that sits all day
    On barren Trees forlorn.

In Watchings or in restless Dreams
   I spend the tedious Night;
Like Sparrows, that on Houses' tops
   To sit alone delight.

All day by railing Foes I'm made
30   The Object of their Scorn;
Who all, inspir'd with furious Rage,
   Have my Destruction sworn.

In dust I lie, and all my Bread
   With ashes mixed appears;
When e'er I quench my burning Thirst,
   My Drink is dash'd with Tears.

Because on me with Double weight
   Thy heavy Wrath does lie;
For thou to make my Fall more great
40   Didst lift me up on high.

My Days are like the Ev'ning Shade
   That hastily declines.
My Beauty too, like wither'd Grass,
   With faded Lustre pines:

But thy eternal State, O Lord,
   No length of Time shall waste,
The mem'ry of thy wond'rous Works
   From Age to Age shall last.   (1698)

ANON.

Psalm 124

Had not the Lord (may *Israel* say)
    Been pleas'd to interpose;
Had he not then espous'd our cause
    When Men against us rose;
Their Wrath had swallow'd us alive,
    And rag'd without Controul;
Their Spite and Pride's united Floods
    Had quite o'erwhelm'd our Soul.

But prais'd be our eternal Lord,
10   Who rescu'd us that Day,
Nor to their savage Jaws gave up
    Our threaten'd Lives a Prey.
Our Soul is like a Bird escap'd
    From out the Fowler's Net;
The Snare is broke, their Hopes are crost,
    And we at Freedom set.

Secure is his Almighty Name,
    Our Confidence remains,
Who as he made both Heav'n and Earth,
20   Of both sole Monarch reigns.   (*c.* 1690?)

In Edward Harley's *Essay for Composing a Harmony between the Psalms, and other Parts of the Scripture* (1724), where I found this piece, it is not declared to be by an unknown hand; and it is printed among versions by Denham. Yet the style seems to me not to be Denham's. The version is close to Isaac Watts's version of this psalm, yet is clearly superior.

JOSEPH ADDISON (1672–1719)

Addison's career is a glittering success-story, bringing together political and diplomatic skills in the Whig interest, pioneering journalism (with Richard Steele on the *Tatler*, the *Guardian* and the *Spectator*), and poetry for the stage (*Cato*, 1713).

Psalm 19

The spacious firmament on high
With all the blue ethereal sky,
And spangled heavens, a shining frame,
Their great Original proclaim:
The unwearied sun, from day to day,
Does his Creator's power display,
And publishes to every land
The work of an almighty hand.

Soon as the evening shades prevail,
10   The moon takes up the wondrous tale,
And nightly to the listening earth
Repeats the story of her birth:
Whilst all the stars that round her burn,
And all the planets in their turn,
Confirm the tidings as they roll,
And spread the truth from pole to pole.

What though, in solemn silence, all
Move round the dark, terrestrial ball?
What though nor real voice nor sound
20   Amid their radiant orbs be found?

In reason's ear they all rejoice,
And utter forth a glorious voice,
For ever singing, as they shine,
'The hand that made us is divine'.   (1712)

This version, which appeared first in the *Spectator* in 1712, constitutes
a famous crux in intellectual history, in so far as it shows Christian
orthodoxy trying to come to terms with the sceptical epistemology
of John Locke (1632–1704). The 'reason's ear' that Addison appeals
to is chiefly, perhaps exclusively, the ear of a mathematician. See
my discussion in *The Eighteenth-Century Hymn in England* (1993),
pp. 23–4.

THOMAS PARNELL (1679–1718)

Parnell, Dublin-born and educated at Trinity College Dublin,
became Archdeacon of Clogher and a friend of Swift and Pope.
    See his *Collected Poems*, ed. Rawson and Lock (1989).

Psalm 51

Look mercifully down, O Lord,
    And wash us from our sin.
Cleanse us from wicked deeds without,
    From wicked thoughts within.
Lord, I confess my many sins
    That I against thee do.
Each minute they're before my face
    And wound my soul anew.
So great, my god, my ills have been
10   'Gainst thee and only thee,
Thy Justice, though I were condemned,
    Would good and righteous be.

For at my birth I wickedness
  Did with my breath suck in;
But thou shalt teach me in thy ways,
  And keep me pure from sin.
Thou'lt me with hyssop purge, who am
  All over soils and stains;
Thou with thy sanctifying grace
20 Shalt wash and make me clean.
Thou'lt bless my days with peace, no sound
  But Joy shall reach mine ear;
That where thy Justice, wounded Lord,
  There Gladness may appear.
Blot from thy thoughts past faults, and from
  The present turn thy face.
O make my spirit right and good,
  Confirm my heart with grace:
Thy Presence and thy mercy let
30 Me ever, Lord, possess.
Me with the comfort of thy help
  And with thy love still bless;
Then shall the wicked know thy pow'r
  And turn them from their ways.
Deliver me from blood, my god,
  And I will sing thy praise.
Unseal my lips, and to the bad
  I will thy mercy show,
For since thou lovest not sacrifice,
40 'Tis all that I can do.
A heart that is with sorrow pierc'd,
  My God, thou wilt receive;
This is the sweetest offering
  That we to thee can give.
On Sion graciously look down:
  Preserve us still, we pray,
And hearts upon thine altars, Lord,
  Instead of beasts, we'll lay.

(c. 1696)

Psalm 67

Have mercy, mercy, Lord, on us
    And grant thy blessed grace;
Direct us in the way of life
    By the sunshine of thy face.

So all the nations on the earth
    Shall praise my god and king,
And when they see thy saving health
    Shall in a chorus sing.

Let all thy people praise thy name
10   And lift their voice on high,
Let them extol it so with shouts
    That heav'n may ring with Joy.

Rejoice, O earth, thy god's thy Judge:
    Be glad who righteous are.
He'll rule the world with equity
    And govern it with fear.

Let all thy people praise thy name
    And lift their voice on high,
Let them extol it so with shouts
20   That heav'n may ring with Joy.

Then God shall open heaven's gates
    And pour down all his store;
He shall you bless with great increase
    And you shall him adore.   (*c.* 1696)

ISAAC WATTS (1674–1748)

The Hebrew Poet

This Ode represents the Difficulty of a just Translation of the Psalms of David, in all their Hebrew Glory; with an Apology for the Imitation of them in Christian Language.

(*The first Hint borrowed from* CASIMIRE, *Jessaea quisquis, &c.* Book 4. Od. 7.)

I

Shew me the Man that dares and sings
Great *David*'s Verse to *British* Strings:
Sublime Attempt! but bold and vain
As building *Babel*'s Tower again.

II

The bard that climb'd to *Cooper's-Hill*,
Reaching at *Zion*, sham'd his Skill,
And bids the Sons of *Albion* own,
That *Judah*'s Psalmist reigns alone.

III

Blest Poet! now like gentle *Thames*
10 He sooths our Ears with Silver Streams:
Like his own *Jordan* now he rolls,
And sweeps away our captive Souls.

IV

Softly the tuneful Shepherd leads
The *Hebrew* Flocks to flowry Meads!
He marks their Path with Notes divine,
While Fountains spring with Oil and Wine.

V

Rivers of Peace attend his Song,
And draw their Milky Train along:
He Jars; and Lo, the Flints are broke,
20 But Honey issues from the Rock.

VI

When kindling with victorious Fire
He shakes his Lance across the Lyre;
The Lyre resounds unknown Alarms,
And sets the Thunderer in Arms,

VII

Behold the GOD! th' Almighty King,
Rides on a Tempest's glorious Wing;
His Ensigns lighten round the Sky,
And moving Legions sound on high.

VIII

Ten thousand Cherubs wait his Course,
30 Chariots of Fire and flaming Horse:
Earth trembles; and her Mountains flow,
At his Approach, like melting Snow.

IX

But who those Frowns of Wrath can draw,
That strike Heaven, Earth, and Hell, with Awe?
Red Lightning from his Eye-lids broke;
His Voice was Thunder, Hail, and Smoke.

X

He spake; the cleaving Waters fled,
And Stars beheld the Ocean's Bed:
While the great Master strikes his Lyre,
40 You see the frighted Floods retire:

XI

In Heaps the frighted Billows stand,
Waiting the Changes of his Hand:
He leads his *Israel* thro' the Sea,
And watry Mountains guard their Way.

XII

Turning his Hand with Sovereign Sweep,
He drowns all *Egypt* in the Deep:
Then guides the Tribes, a glorious Band,
Thro' Deserts to the promis'd Land.

XIII

Here Camps with wide embattled Force,
50 Here Gates and Bulwarks, stop their Course:
He storms the Mounds, the Bulwark falls,
The Harp lies strow'd with ruin'd Walls.

XIV

See his broad Sword flies o'er the Strings,
And mows down Nations with their Kings:
From every Chord his Bolts are hurl'd,
And Vengeance smites the rebel World.

XV

Lo, the great Poet shifts the Scene,
And shews the Face of GOD Serene:
Truth, Meekness, Peace, Salvation ride,
60 With Guards of Justice, at his Side.

XVI

No meaner Muse could weave the Light,
To form his Robes divinely bright,
Or frame a Crown of Stars to shine
With Beams of Majesty divine.

XVII

Now in prophetick Light he sees
Ages to come, and dark Degrees:
He brings the Prince of Glory down,
Stript of his Robe and starry Crown.

XVIII

See how the Heathen Nations rage,
70 See, their combining Powers engage
Against th' *Anointed* of the Lord,
The Man whom Angels late ador'd,

XIX

God's only Son: Behold, he dies:
Surprizing Grief! The Groans arise,
The Lyre complains on every String,
And mourns the Murther of her King.

XX

But Heaven's *Anointed* must not dwell
In Death: The vanquish'd Powers of Hell
Yield to the Harp's Diviner Lay;
80   The Grave resigns th' illustrious Prey.

XXI

Messiah lives, *Messiah* reigns:
The Song surmounts the Airy Plains,
T' attend her Lord with Joys unknown,
And bear the Victor to his Throne.

XXII

Rejoice, ye shining Worlds on high,
Behold the Lord of Glory nigh:
Eternal Doors, your Leaves display,
To make the Lord of Glory Way.

XXIII

What mortal Bard has Skill or Force
90   To paint these Scenes, to tread this Course,
Or furnish thro' th' Ethereal Road
A triumph for a rising GOD?

XXIV

Astonish'd at so vast a Flight
Thro' flaming Worlds and Floods of Light,
My Muse her awful Distance keeps,
Still following, but with trembling Steps.

XXV

She bids her humble Verse explain
The *Hebrew* Harp's sublimer Strain;
Points to her Saviour still, and shows
100   What Course the Sun of Glory goes.

XXVI

Here he ascends behind a Cloud
Of Incense, there he sets in Blood;
She reads his Labours and his Names
In spicy Smoke, and Bleeding Lambs.

XXVII

Rich are the Graces which she draws
From Types, and Shades, and *Jewish* Laws;
With thousand Glories long foretold
To turn the future Age to Gold.

XXVIII

Grace is her Theme, and Joy, and Love:
110   Descend, ye Blessings, from above,
And crown my Song. Eternal GOD,
Forgive the Muse that dreads thy Rod.

XXIX

Silent, she hears thy Vengeance roll,
That crushes Mortals to the Soul,
Nor dares assume the Bolt, nor sheds
Th' immortal Curses on their Heads.

XXX

Yet since her GOD is still the same,
And *David*'s Son is all her Theme,
She begs some humble Place to sing
120   In Consort with *Judea*'s King.   (1734)

On its first appearance in *Reliquiae Juveniles* (1734), the poem
glossed the second quatrain: 'Sir John Denham, who gain'd great
Reputation by his Poem, call'd Cooper's-Hill, fail'd in his Transla-
tion of the Psalms of David.'

Matthew Casimire Sarbiewski (1595–1640), called 'the Christian
Horace', a Pole writing verse in Latin, was admired and studied in
the London of the 1690s. He was most recently brought back to the
attention of English-speakers in 1980, in Czeslaw Milosz's speech on
accepting the Nobel Prize for Literature.

To DORIO. The first Lyrick Hour

There's a Line or two that seem to carry in them I know not
what Softness and Beauty in the beginning of that Ode of
Casimire, where he describes his first Attempts of the Harp,
and his commencing a Lyrick Poet.

Albis dormiit in Rosis,
Libisque jacens & violis Dies,
    Primae cui potui vigil
Somnum Pieria rumpere Barbito,

> *Curae dum vacuus Puer*
> *Formosi legerem Littora Narviae,*
> *Ex illo mihi posteri*
> *Florent sale dies,* &c.

I have tried to imitate these Lines, but I cannot form them into *English Lyricks*: I have releas'd myself from the Fetters of Rhyme, yet I cannot gain my own Approbation. I have given my Thoughts a further Loose, and spread the Sense abroad, but I fear there is something of the Spirit evaporates; and tho' the elegant Idea perhaps does not entirely escape, yet I could wish for a happier Expression of it. Such as it is, *Dorio*, with your usual Candour, correct the Deficiencies, and restore the Elegance of the *Polish* Poet, to those six or seven Lines wherein I have attempted an Imitation.

'Twas an unclouded Sky: the Day-star sat
On highest Noon: No Breezes fann'd the Grove,
Nor the Musicians of the Air pursu'd
Their artless Warblings; while the sultry Day
Lay all diffus'd and slumbring on the Bosom
Of the white Lily, the perfum'd Jonquil,
And lovely blushing Rose. Then first my Harp
Labouring with Childish Innocence and Joy
Brake Silence, and awoke the smiling Hour
10 With infant Notes, saluting the fair Skies
(Heaven's highest Work), the fair enamell'd Meads,
And tall green Shades along the winding Banks
Of *Avon* gently flowing. Thence my Days
Commenc'd harmonious; there began my Skill
To vanquish Care by the sweet-sounding String.

Hail happy Hour, O blest Remembrance, Hail!
And banish Woes for ever. Harps were made
For Heaven's Beatitudes; There *Jesse*'s Son
Tunes his bold Lyre with Majesty of Sound,
20 To the Creative and All-ruling Power

Not unattentive: While ten thousand Tongues
Of Hymning Seraphs and disbodied Saints
Echo the Joys and Graces round the Hills
Of Paradise, and spread *Messiah*'s Name.
Transporting Bliss! Make haste, ye rolling Spheres,
Ye circling Suns, ye wingèd Minutes haste,
Fulfil my destin'd Period here, and raise
The meanest Son of Harmony to join
In that Celestial Consort.   (*Reliquiae Juveniles*, 1734)

A Loyal Wish on her Majesty's Birthday, March 1, commonly called St David's-Day

Borrowed from Psalm cxxxii, 10, 11

I

     Silence, ye Nations; *Israel*, hear:
     Thus hath the Lord to *David* sworn,
      'Train up thy Sons to learn my Fear,
And *Judah*'s Crown shall all thy Race adorn;
Theirs be the Royal Honours thou hast won,
Long as the starry Wheels of Nature run;
Nature, be thou my Pledge; my Witness be the Sun.'

II

     Now, *Britain*, let thy Vows arise,
     'May *George* the Royal Saint assume!'
10   Then ask Permission of the Skies,
To put the favourite Name in *David*'s Room:
Fair *Carolina*, join thy pious Cares
To train in Virtue's Path your Royal Heirs,
And be the *British* Crown with endless Honour theirs.   (1705)

Psalm 132, vv. 10, 11, reads in *BCP*:

> For thy servant David's sake: turn not away the presence of
>   thine Anointed.
> The Lord hath made a faithful oath unto David: and he shall not
>   shrink from it; . . .

Watts, it will be noticed, contrives to conflate David the Psalmist
with the patron saint of Wales.

Watts as a Nonconformist was vowed to secure and maintain the
Protestant Succession, in a way that made him vehemently pro-
Whig, anti-Tory. Because Queen Anne's marriage to George of
Denmark produced no heirs, the Protestant Succession seemed, a
few years after this poem was written, endangered. Accordingly in
1721 Watts published a vicious 'Palinodia', reproaching Anne for
having let in the Tories ten years before. The spirituality of Watts's
hymns and psalms should not blind us to the fact that at all times he
was playing a political role in a highly charged political arena.

Psalm 51

O God of mercy, hear my call,
  My load of guilt remove:
Break down this separating wall
  That bars me from thy love.

Give me the presence of thy grace;
  Then my rejoicing tongue
Shall speak aloud thy righteousness
  And make thy praise my song.

No blood of goats, nor heifer slain,
10   For sin could e'er atone;
The death of Christ shall still remain
  Sufficient and alone.

A soul oppress'd with sin's desert
  My God will ne'er despise;
A humble groan, a broken heart,
  Is our best sacrifice.   (1719)

Psalm 72

Jesus shall reign where'er the sun
Does his successive journeys run;
His kingdom stretch from shore to shore,
'Till moons shall wax and wane no more.

Behold the islands, with their kings,
And Europe her best tribute brings;
From North to South the princes meet,
To pay their homage at his feet.

There Persia, glorious to behold –
10 There India shines in eastern gold;
And barbarous nations, at his word,
Submit, and bow, and own their Lord.

For him shall endless prayer be made,
And praises throng to crown his head;
His name, like sweet perfume shall rise
With ev'ry morning sacrifice.

People and realms, of every tongue,
Dwell on his love with sweetest song;
And infant voices shall proclaim
20 Their early blessings on his name.

Blessings abound where'er he reigns;
The pris'ner leaps to loose his chains;
The weary find eternal rest,
And all the sons of want are blest.

Where he displays his healing power,
Death and the curse are known no more;
In him the tribes of Adam boast
More blessings than their father lost.

Let ev'ry creature rise – and bring
30   Peculiar honours to their King:
Angels descend with songs again,
And earth repeat the long AMEN.   (1719)

Lines 5–12, cf. *AV* v. 10: 'The kings of Tarshish and of the isles
shall bring presents: the kings of Sheba and Seba shall offer gifts.'

Watts expands on this to the extent of two whole quatrains; but
contrast Psalm 98, where the nine verses of the Hebrew are con-
tracted into four lean quatrains.

Psalm 74

Will God for ever cast us off?
    His wrath for ever smoke –
Against the people of his love,
    His little chosen flock?

Think of the tribes, so dearly bought
    With their redeemer's blood;
Nor let thy Zion be forgot,
    Where once thy glory stood.

Lift up thy feet, and march in haste;
10   Aloud our ruin calls;
See what a wide and fearful waste
    Is made within thy walls.

Where once thy churches pray'd and sang,
    Thy foes profanely roar:

Over thy gates their ensigns hang,
   Sad tokens of their power.

How are the seats of worship broke!
   They tear thy buildings down;
And he who deals the heaviest stroke
20   Procures the chief renown.

With flames they threaten to destroy
   Thy children in their nest:
'Come, let us burn at once', they cry,
   'The temple and the priest.'

And still, to heighten our distress,
   Thy presence is withdrawn;
Thy wonted signs of power and grace,
   Thy power and grace are gone.

No prophet speaks to calm our woes,
30   But all the seers mourn;
There's not a soul amongst us knows
   The time of thy return.

How long, eternal God, how long
   Shall men of pride blaspheme!
Shall saints be made their endless song,
   And bear immortal shame?

Canst thou for ever sit and hear
   Thy holy name profan'd?
And still thy jealousy forbear,
40   And still withhold thy hand?

What strange deliv'rance hast thou shown,
   In ages long before?

– And now, no other God we own,
    No other God adore.

Thou didst divide the raging sea
    By thy resistless might,
To make thy tribes a wondrous way;
    And then secure their flight.

Is not the world of nature thine –
50   The darkness and the day?
Didst thou not bid the morning shine,
    And mark the sun his way?

Hath not thy power form'd every coast,
    And set the earth its bounds,
With summer's heat and winter's frost
    In their perpetual bounds?

And shall the sons of earth and dust
    That sacred power blaspheme?
Will not that hand which form'd them first
60   Avenge thine injur'd name?

Think on the cov'nant thou hast made,
    And all thy words of love;
Nor let the birds of prey invade,
    And vex thy mourning dove.

Our foes would triumph in our blood,
    And make our hope their jest:
Plead thine own cause, almighty God,
    And give thy children rest.   (1719)

For a painstaking comparison of this version with Christopher Smart's (*post*), see my 'Psalmody as Translation', in *The Eighteenth-Century Hymn in England* (Cambridge, 1993).

Psalm 87

God, in his earthly temple, lays
Foundations for his heavenly praise:
He likes the tents of Jacob well;
But still in Zion loves to dwell.

His mercy visits ev'ry house
That pay their night and morning vows;
But makes a more delightful stay
Where churches meet to praise and pray.

What glories were describ'd of old –
10   What wonders are of Zion told!
Thou city of our God below,
Thy fame shall Tyre and Egypt know.

Egypt and Tyre, and Greek and Jew,
Shall there begin their lives anew:
Angels and men shall join to sing
The Hill where living waters spring.

When God makes up his last account
Of natives in his holy mount,
'Twill be an honour to appear,
20   As one new-born or nourish'd there!   (1719)

Cf. Milton's version (*ante*). In my view Watts more than holds up
under the Miltonic comparison.

Psalm 90

Our God, our help in ages past,
    Our hope for years to come;
Our shelter from the stormy blast,
    And our eternal home:

Under the shadow of thy throne,
    Thy saints have dwelt secure;
Sufficient is thine arm alone,
    And our defence is sure.

Before the hills in order stood,
10   Or earth receiv'd her frame;
From everlasting thou art God;
    To endless years the same.

Thy word commands our flesh to dust,
    'Return, ye sons of men';
All nations rose from earth at first,
    And turn to earth again.

A thousand ages, in thy sight,
    Are like an evening gone;
Short as the watch that ends the night,
20   Before the rising sun.

The busy tribes of flesh and blood,
    With all their lives and cares,
Are carry'd downwards by the flood,
    And lost in following years.

Time, like an ever-rolling stream,
   Bears all its sons away;
They fly, forgotten, as a dream
   Dies at the opening day.

Like flowery fields the nations stand,
30   Pleas'd with the morning light:
The flowers, beneath the mower's hand
   Lie with'ring, ere 'tis night.

– Our God, our help in ages past,
   Our hope for years to come,
Be thou our guard while troubles last,
   And our eternal home.   (1719)

Psalm 98

Joy to the world – the Lord is come!
   Let earth receive her King:
Let every heart prepare him room,
   And heaven and nature sing.

– Joy to the earth – the Saviour reigns!
   Let men their songs employ;
While fields and floods, rocks, hills and plains,
   Repeat the sounding joy.

No more let sins and sorrows grow,
10   Nor thorns infest the ground;
He comes to make his blessings flow,
   Far as the curse is found.

He rules the world with truth and grace;
   And makes the nations prove
The glories of his righteousness,
   And wonders of his love.   (1719)

Psalm 98   *The Authorized Version*

1. O sing unto the Lord a new song; for he hath done marvellous things: his right hand, and his holy arm, hath gotten him the victory.

2. The Lord hath made known his salvation: his righteousness hath he openly shewed in the sight of the heathen.

3. He hath remembered his mercy and his truth toward the house of Israel: all the ends of the earth have seen the salvation of our God.

4. Make a joyful noise unto the Lord, all the earth: make a loud noise, and rejoice, and sing praise.

5. Sing unto the Lord with the harp; with the harp, and the voice of a psalm.

6. With trumpets and sound of cornet make a joyful noise before the Lord, the King.

7. Let the sea roar, and the fulness thereof; the world, and they that dwell therein.

8. Let the floods clap their hands: let the hills be joyful together

9. Before the Lord; for he cometh to judge the earth: with righteousness shall he judge the world, and the people with equity.

(Note the surely unacceptable semblance of enjambment from the penultimate verse to the last.)

From Psalm 102

It is the Lord our Saviour's hand,
Weakens our strength amidst the race.
Disease and death, at his command,
Arrest us, and cut short our days.

Spare us, O Lord, aloud we pray,
Nor let our sun go down at noon:
Thy years are one eternal day,
And must thy children die so soon!

Yet, in the midst of death and grief,
10 This thought our sorrow shall assuage:
'Our Father and our Saviour live;
Christ is the same through ev'ry age'.

'Twas He this earth's foundation laid;
Heaven is the building of his hand:
This earth grows old, these heavens shall fade,
And all be chang'd at his command.

The starry curtains of the sky,
Like garments, shall be laid aside;
But still thy throne stands firm and high;
20 Thy church for ever must abide.

Before thy face thy church shall live,
And on thy throne thy children reign:
This dying world shall they survive,
And the dead saints be rais'd again. (1719)

Psalm 126

When God restor'd our captive state,
Joy was our song, and grace our theme;
The grace, beyond our hope so great,
That joy appear'd a painted dream.

The scoffer owns thy hand, and pays
Unwilling honours to thy name;
While we, with pleasure, shout thy praise –
With cheerful notes thy love proclaim.

When we review our dismal fears,
10 'Twas hard to think they'd vanish so:
With God we left our flowing tears;
He makes our joys like rivers flow.

The man that in his furrow'd field
His scatter'd seed with sadness leaves
Will shout to see the harvest yield
A welcome load of joyful sheaves.   (1719)

Psalm 129

Up from my youth, may Israel say,
    Have I been nurs'd in tears;
My griefs were constant as the day,
    As tedious as the years.

Up from my youth, I bore the rage
    Of all the sons of strife;
Oft they assail'd my riper age,
    But not destroy'd my life.

Their cruel plough hath torn my flesh,
10 With furrows long and deep;
Hourly they vex'd my wounds afresh;
    Nor let my sorrows sleep.

The Lord grew angry on his throne
    And, with impartial eye,
Measur'd the mischiefs they had done
    And let his arrows fly.

How was their insolence surpris'd
    To hear his thunders roll!
And all the foes of Zion seiz'd
20   With horror to the soul.

Thus shall the men who hate the saints
    Be blasted from the sky;
Their glory fades, their courage faints,
    And all their projects die.

What though they flourish tall and fair,
    They have no root beneath:
Their growth shall perish in despair,
    And lie despis'd in death.

So corn that on the house-top stands
30   No hope of harvest gives;
The reaper ne'er shall fill his hands,
    Nor binder fold the sheaves.

It springs and withers on the place:
    No traveller bestows
A word of blessing on the grass,
    Nor minds it as he goes.   (1719)

Psalm 131

Is there ambition in my heart?
    Search, gracious God, and see;
Or do I act a haughty part?
    Lord, I appeal to thee.

I charge my thoughts, be humble still,
    And all my carriage mild;
Content, my Father, with thy will,
    And quiet as a child.

The patient soul, the lowly mind,
10   Shall have a large reward;
Let saints in sorrow lie resign'd,
    And trust a faithful Lord.   (1719)

Psalm 133

Lo, what an entertaining sight
    Are brethren who agree!
Brethren, whose cheerful hearts unite
    In bands of piety!

When streams of love, from Christ the spring,
    Descend to ev'ry soul,
And heavenly peace, with balmy wing,
    Shades and bedews the whole:

'Tis like the oil, divinely sweet,
10   On Aaron's rev'rend head;
The trickling drops perfum'd his feet,
    And o'er his garments spread.

'Tis pleasant as the morning dews,
    That fall on Zion's hill;
Where God his mildest glory shews,
    And makes his grace distil.   (1719)

Psalm 137

I

When by the flowing Brooks we sat,
　　The Brooks of *Babylon* the Proud;
We thought on *Zion*'s mournful State,
　　And wept her Woes, and wail'd aloud.

II

Thoughtless of every chearful Air
　　(For Grief had all our Harps unstrung),
Our Harps neglected in Despair
　　And silent on the Willows hung.

III

Our Foes who made our Land their Spoil,
10　　Our barbarous Lords, with haughty Tongues,
Bid us forget our Groans awhile
　　And give a Taste of *Zion*'s Songs.

IV

How shall we sing in *Heathen* Lands
　　Our holy Songs to Ears profane?
Lord, shall our Lips at their Commands
　　Pronounce thy dreadful Name in vain?

V

Forbid it heaven! O vile Abuse!
　　Zion in Dust forbids it too:
Shall Hymns inspir'd for sacred Use
20　　Be sung to please a scoffing Crew?

VI

O let my Tongue grow dry, and cleave
   Fast to my Mouth in Silence still,
Let some avenging Power bereave
   My Fingers of their tuneful Skill,

VII

If I thy sacred Rites profane,
   O *Salem*, or thy Dust despise;
If I indulge one chearful Strain,
   Till I shall see thy Towers arise.

VIII

'Twas Edom bid the conquering Foe,
30   *Down with thy Tow'rs, and raze thy Walls:*
Requite her, Lord: But *Babel*, know
   Thy Guilt for fiercer Vengeance calls.

IX

As thou hast spar'd nor Sex nor Age,
   Deaf to our Infants' dying Groans,
May some bless'd Hand, inspir'd with Rage,
   Dash thy young Babes, and tinge the Stones.   (1734)

When this translation first appeared, in Watts's *Reliquiae Juveniles* (1734), it was introduced as follows:

  Had *Horace* or *Pindar* written this Ode, it would have been the endless Admiration of the Critick, and the perpetual Labour of Rival Translators; but 'tis found in the Scripture, and that gives a sort of Disgust to an Age which verges too much toward Infidelity. I could wish the Muse of Mr *Pope* would chuse out some few of these Pieces of sacred *Psalmody*, which carry in them the more sprightly Beauties of Poetry, and let the *English* nation know what a Divine Poet sat on the Throne of *Israel*. He has taken *Homer*'s Rhapsodies, and turned them into fine Verse and agreeable Entertainment; and his admirable Imitation of the *Hebrew* Prophets, in his Poem called *The Messiah*, convinces us abundantly, how capable he is of such a Service. This particular *Psalm* could not well be converted into *Christianity*, and accordingly it appears here in its *Jewish* Form: The Vengeance denounced against *Babylon*, in the Close of it, shall be executed (said a great Divine) upon *Anti-christian Rome*; but he was persuaded the *Turks* must do it, for *Protestant* Hearts, said he, have too much Compassion in them to embrue their Hands in such a bloody and terrible Execution.

JAMES THOMSON (1700–1748)

Thomson, who achieved international and long-lasting fame with *The Seasons* and *The Castle of Indolence*, was a humbly-born Scot who lived and wrote and was acclaimed in England.

From *A Paraphrase of Psalm CIV*

To praise thy Author, Soul, do not forget;
Canst thou, in gratitude, deny the debt?
Lord, thou art great, how great we cannot know;
Honour and majesty do round thee flow.
The purest rays of primogenial light
Compose thy robes, and make them dazzling bright;
The heavens and all the wide-spread orbs on high
Thou like a curtain stretched of curious dye;
On the devouring flood thy chambers are
10   Establishèd; a lofty cloud's thy car,
Which quick through the etherial road doth fly
On swift-winged winds that shake the troubled sky.

The changing moon he clad with silver light,
To check the black dominion of the night:
High through the skies in silent state she rides,
And by her rounds the fleeting time divides.
The circling sun doth in due time decline,
And unto shades the murmuring world resign.
Dark night thou mak'st succeed the cheerful day,
20 Which forest beasts from their lone caves survey:
They rouse themselves, creep out, and search their prey.
Young hungry lions from their dens come out
And, mad on blood, stalk fearfully about;
They break night's silence with their hideous roar,
And from kind heaven their nightly prey implore.
Just as the lark begins to stretch her wing
And, flickering on her nest, makes short essays to sing,
And the sweet dawn, with a faint glimmering light,
Unveils the face of nature to the sight,
30 To their dark dens they take their hasty flight.   (c. 1724)

ROBERT LOWTH (1710–1787)

Bishop Lowth, the great Hebraist (see Introduction), in his youth
wrote *The Genealogy of Christ*.

From *The Genealogy of Christ*

And lo! the Glories of th' illustrious Line
At their first Dawn with ripen'd Splendour shine,
In DAVID all exprest, the Good, the Great,
The King, the Hero, and the Man compleat.

Serene he sits, and sweeps the golden Lyre,
And blends the Prophet's with the Poet's Fire.
See! with what Art he strikes the vocal Strings,
The God, his Theme, inspiring what he sings!
Hark – or our Ears delude us – from his Tongue
10 Sweet flows, or seems to flow, some Heav'nly Song.
O! could thine Art arrest the fleeting Sound,
And paint the Voice in magick Numbers bound;
Could the warm Sun, as erst when *Memnon* play'd,
Wake with his rising Beam the vocal Shade;
Then might *He* draw th' attentive Angels down,
Bending to hear the Lay, so sweet, so like their own.   (1729)

CHARLES WESLEY (1707–1788)

Psalm 51

O for a heart to praise my God
    A heart from sin set free,
A heart that's sprinkled with the Blood
    So freely shed for me!

A heart resigned, submissive, meek,
    My great Redeemer's throne;
Where only CHRIST is heard to speak,
    Where JESUS reigns alone.

A humble, lowly contrite heart,
10   Believing, true, and clean!
Which neither life nor death can part
    From Him that dwells within.

A heart in every thought renewed,
   And full of Love Divine,
Perfect, and right, and pure, and good,
   A copy, LORD, of Thine.

Thy nature, gracious LORD, impart:
   Come quickly from above;
Write Thy new Name upon my heart,
20   Thy new best Name of Love.   (1742)

Though Wesley seems to have worked with the Prayer-book open before him, he failed to notice what (see the Introduction) we recognize as Coverdale's distinction. Where Coverdale used three epithets – 'troubled', 'broken' and 'contrite' – Wesley used six: 'humble', 'lowly', 'contrite', 'believing', 'true', 'clean'. Submerged in that pell-mell sequence, 'contrite' is drained of the force that it has in Coverdale. And in this after all quite short piece, there are other adjectival runs: 'resigned, submissive, meek'; 'Perfect, and right, and pure, and good'. Though Methodists may understandably deny it, such self-defeating overkill, 'going over the top', is common in Wesley, and it relegates him from the first rank. One may perceive a similar slackness in the ease with which Wesley describes God as one 'that dwells within'. To this interiorizing, which comes perilously close to conceiving of God as 'our own best self', we can and probably should oppose *The Invading Gospel*, title of a book by another contributor to this anthology, Jack Clemo. In Clemo's experience, as I think in the Psalmist's, God *invades* – that is, He comes from outside.

Psalm 129

Many a time, may *Israel* say,
   My foes have furiously assail'd,
And vexed me from my natal day,
   But never, never yet prevail'd;

Nor could the gates of hell o'erthrow
The church on Jesus built below.

The ploughers plough'd upon my back
   Till all my body was one wound,
Nor could they the foundation shake;
10   A seed, a remnant, still was found,
Preserved by their almighty Lord,
Kept by His everlasting word.

The Lord, the righteous Lord and true,
   Turn'd our captivity again,
The cords of wickedness broke through,
   And burst the dire oppressors' chain:
And still who *Sion* hate shall fly,
And stumble, and forever die.

As grass on the house-top decays,
20   Nor ever fills the mower's breast,
But withers in a moment's space,
   And perishes unreap'd, unbless'd,
So shall the foes of *Sion* fade,
And vanish as a fleeting shade.   (1742)

To compare this with the corresponding piece by Watts prompts
questions of what Wesley does with the extra liberty he allows
himself by departing from Watts's quatrains (for instance, is it the
function of 'gates' to 'o'erthrow'?); but more flagrantly it highlights
how Wesley has simply suppressed the last verse of his original: in
the *AV*, 'Neither do those which go by say, The blessing of the
Lord be upon thee: we bless you in the name of the Lord.' In the
words of Arthur Golding in 1571: 'Neither have the goers-by said,/
The blessing of the Lord be upon you,/we bless you in the name of
the Lord.' The Hebrew poem seems to end on a note of pathos,
even of reluctant compassion; and Wesley rules this out. A poet so
gifted and magisterial as Wesley must obviously be allowed to take

liberties; but in this case (and there are others like it) he seems to have ironed out a play of conflicting sentiments into simple and driving dogmatism.

Psalm 150

Praise the Lord who reigns above
   And keeps his court below;
Praise the holy God of love,
   And all his greatness show;
Praise him for his noble deeds,
Praise him for his matchless pow'r;
Him from whom all good proceeds
   Let earth and heav'n adore.

Celebrate th'eternal God
10   With harp and psaltery,
Timbrels soft and cymbals loud
   In his high praise agree;
Praise him ev'ry tuneful string;
All the reach of heav'nly art,
All the pow'rs of music bring,
   The music of the heart.

Him, in whom they move and live,
   Let ev'ry creature sing,
Glory to their Maker give,
20   And homage to their King.
Hallowed be his name beneath,
As in heav'n on earth adored;
Praise the Lord in ev'ry breath,
   Let all things praise the Lord.
               (1743)

This is No. 23 in the *Baptist Hymnal* (Nashville, 1975).

THOMAS CRADOCK (*fl.* 1756)

The Reverend Thomas Cradock was Rector of St Thomas's, Baltimore County, Maryland. His *New Version of the Psalms of David* was published in Annapolis in 1756.

Psalm 15

Who in thy glorious temple, Lord, shall dwell,
And who shall rest upon thy holy hill?
E'en he, who holds simplicity of heart,
And from thy righteous judgments dreads to part;
Whose faithful tongue, indignant of a lie,
Wounds not his neighbour's peace with calumny;
Whose thoughts no mischief 'gainst a foe intend;
Who vents no killing slander 'gainst a friend:
Who shuns the wicked, and detests their ways;
10   But honours him that heav'n's high will obeys;
Who'll to the indigent his help afford,
And lose his int'rest, ere he'll break his word;
Who with a modest income is content,
Nor takes reward against the innocent;
By acts like these, who can his duty prove,
Shall live for ever with his God above.   (1756)

Psalm 17

Do thou, just God, a just man's pray'r attend;
O listen to the cry that comes unfeign'd;
At thy tribunal *David* asks redress,
With pitying eye behold his sad distress.
'Oft hast thou prov'd me in the silent night,
And found the purpose of my heart was right;

Oft view'd my secret soul, and found, in nought
My tongue e'er differ'd from my inmost thought.
Thy word my rule, and govern'd by thy fear,
10 I from the works of impious men kept clear.
O still preserve me in the path I've trod;
O let me firmly tread, all-gracious God.
Thee have I oft invok'd, for thou wilt hear,
And, while I plead, incline thy gracious ear:
Shew me thy mercy, thou, whose potent arm
Defends the soul, that trusts in thee, from harm.
Thy wings protectful o'er my steps extend;
Me, as the apple of the eye, defend
From that abandon'd crew, my peace that wound;
20 From those my foes, that compass me around;
Who, with their wealth elate, forget their God,
And in their guilt are insolently proud.
In ev'ry secret place they lay the snare;
And 'gainst my life their wily schemes prepare:
Like to the lion, that expects his prey,
Or like his whelp, they keep my soul at bay.
Arise, O Lord; confound their villainy;
From their destructive toils thy servant free.
Thy sword they are; thy wisdom lets them reign;
30 Thou giv'st them here a wide, a large domain,
In wealth they flow and, when they breathe no more,
Their num'rous sons possess their shining store.
For me, by innocence of heart I'll strive
Still in thy favour, in thy light, to live;
Enough, O gracious God, enough for me
To view in bliss thy glorious majesty.'

(1756)

Cradock goes along with Coverdale in *BCP*, in declaring that the
worldly success of the unrighteous is all part of God's plan; they are
His instruments – 'Thy sword they are'. The Hebraists who advised
David Frost on his modern *Liturgical Psalter*, by persuading him to
reserve all the worldly benefits to the righteous, removed all tension

from the last verses as well as flying in the face of common experience. The unrighteous *do* prosper; Coverdale and Cradock have the Psalmist acknowledging this, and coming to terms with it; a reading that eliminates this leaves us with a poem of no interest at all, because at odds with common experience.

Psalm 20

When troubles hem thee round, when foes distress,
And thou to heav'n thy fervent pray'r address,
To thee a list'ning ear th' almighty lend,
Thee by his name may *Jacob*'s God defend:
From his resplendent throne assistance give,
From *Sion*'s sacred temple bid thee live;
Thy victims at his altar not forget,
And thy oblations graciously accept;
Grant to thy heart's desire the ask'd success,
10 Dispel thy woes, and all thy counsels bless.
And when th' almighty God has given his aid,
And crown'd with conquest thy anointed head,
We'll join thy triumphs with according voice,
And in thy great deliv'rer we'll rejoice.
For well we know thou art th' eternal's care,
That from his lofty throne thy suit he'll hear;
That not in vain thou'lt on his pow'r rely;
His strong right-hand will give thee victory.
Let the proud *heathen* in their cars confide,
20 And on their harness'd steeds exulting ride;
Be they their empty boast – more wisely we
Depend, O God, on thy great name and thee.
Their harness'd steeds, their falchion'd chariots fail,
Nor in the day of deep distress prevail;
See, low they fall, while in thy pow'r we rise
And snatch the conquest from our enemies.
Save us and hear – on thee we call, O Lord;

While thou thy strong protection wilt afford,
We dare the menac'd battle of the foe;
30   Fruitless, he darts the spear, and bends the bow.   (1756)

Psalm 43

My great avenger thou, O Lord, to thee
Make I appeal against my enemy;
Against the fraudful, the deceitful man
Do thou, just God, my righteous cause maintain.
Thou art my surest hope, my strong defence;
Why have I not my wonted confidence?
Why do I fruitless mourn my sad distress?
Why with such fury do my foes oppress?
Beam forth thy light, thy kind assistance lend,
10   And 'gainst their fierce assaults my soul defend.
O lead me, lead me to thy holy hill
Where downy peace, where heav'nly comforts dwell.
Then to thy altar I'll with transport go,
My heart with strongest gratitude shall glow;
My voice in hymns of harmony I'll raise,
And strike my lyre, to celebrate thy praise.
Why then, my soul, so dreadfully dismay'd?
Why thee such sad distracting griefs invade?
Dismiss thy fears, and on thy God rely;
20   E'en yet he'll crown thy brows with victory;
Yet with his pow'r thy cause will he support;
Thou still shalt praise him in his sacred court.   (1756)

Psalm 61

All-clement God, attend my earnest cry:
In distant lands tho' roam, an exile, I,
Thee in my heart's distress will I invoke,

Thee will I make my strength, my shield, my rock.
A shelter most secure in thee I've found,
A firm support, when cruel foes surround.
Therefore beneath thy wings, assur'd, I'll rest,
And seek the temple with thy presence blest.
For thou my faithful vows hast constant heard;
10   For me a noble heritage prepar'd;
To rule the nations who thy laws obey;
To make them happy by my gentle sway.
Thou to the king a length of days will give,
Thou to a good old age shalt bid him live.
Long in thy house that he may suppliant stand,
Reach forth thy blessings with a lib'ral hand.
Then free from danger, and devoid of fear,
My grateful tongue thy mercies shall declare;
To thee continual anthems I will sing,
20   And hail the glorious God that guards the king.   (1756)

One way to read this psalm is as if uttered by David, who speaks of himself and his kingship in the third person as well as in the first. This seems to have been Cradock's understanding of it. If it seems strange to have an American voice avowing monarchy as Cradock does in his ringing and exuberantly alliterative last line, such a sentiment was of course entirely possible for a pre-Revolution Marylander.

Psalm 99

Reigns great *Jehovah*; let the people fear;
Bright cherubs guard his throne; thou earth, revere:
Nor yet to *Sion* is his pow'r confin'd;
Worlds feel the influence of *almighty mind*.
His great tremendous name they therefore praise,
The god with mercy and with truth, who sways;
Whose mercy strikes with love, whose pow'r with awe,

Who gives his favour'd tribes his perfect law:
Let all his dread omnipotence extol,
10 And 'fore his footstool reverently fall.
When *Moses* and the holy *Aaron* pray'd,
When faithful *Samuel*, he lent his aid,
His wond'rous goodness to them, gracious, shew'd,
And pointed to immortal bliss the road:
From out the cloudy pillar spoke benign
(O blest result of clemency divine!)
'Cause, faithful, they his sov'reign will obey'd,
Nor from the sacred law he gave them, stray'd.
Yes; thou, benignant father, deign'dst to hear,
20 And, to the obdurate sinner tho' severe,
Indulgent still thine answers didst thou give,
And bad'st the faithful in thy light to live.
For this, ye righteous souls, with joint accord,
Shout forth the praises of your mighty Lord
And, 'cause his glory there delights to dwell,
Fall prostrate 'fore him on his holy hill.   (1756)

Only in the eighteenth century could Coverdale's 'The Lord is great in Sion: and high above all people' be made to yield 'Worlds feel the influence of *almighty mind*'. The eighteenth-century expansion, though certainly audacious, is not necessarily wrong.

Psalm 128

He's trebly blest, who dreads th' omniscient God,
And in his perfect way with fear has trod.
Himself and his – kind providence's care;
The produce of his hands he long shall share.
His wife, chaste object of his faithful loves,
Fills all his wishes, and his joys improves;
Like beauteous olives in a fruitful soil,
His children croud his board, and crown his toil.

Thus blest he lives – his God will still bestow;
10   Still from his God incessant bounties flow;
And, more t'enhance his happiness, he sees
His country blest with opulence and peace;
He sees his own and country's welfare join'd,
While fond parental transports fill his mind;
He sees his race of ev'ry good possest,
Thanks his kind God, and dies supremely blest.   (1756)

CHRISTOPHER SMART (1722–1771)

On the Goodness of the Supreme Being

Orpheus, for so the Gentiles call'd thy name,
Israel's sweet psalmist, who alone could wake
Th' inanimate to motion; who alone
The joyful hillocks, the applauding rocks,
And floods with musical persuasion drew;
Thou, who to hail and snow gav'st voice and sound,
And mad'st the mute melodious! – greater yet
Was thy divinest skill, and rul'd o'er more
Than art or nature; for thy tuneful touch
10   Drove trembling Satan from the heart of Saul,
And quell'd the evil Angel: – in this breast
Some portion of thy genuine spirit breathe,
And lift me from myself; each thought impure
Banish; each low idea raise, refine,
Enlarge, and sanctify; – so shall the muse
Above the stars aspire, and aim to praise
Her God on earth, as he is prais'd in heaven.

    Immense Creator! whose all-pow'rful hand
Fram'd universal Being, and whose Eye
20   Saw like thyself, that all things form'd were good;

Where shall the tim'rous bard thy praise begin,
Where end the purest sacrifice of song,
And just thanksgiving? – The thought-kindling light,
Thy prime production, darts upon my mind
Its vivifying beams, my heart illumines,
And fills my soul with gratitude and Thee.
Hail to the chearful rays of ruddy morn,
That paint that streaky East, and blithsome rouse
The birds, the cattle, and mankind from rest!
30 Hail to the freshness of the early breeze,
And Iris dancing on the new-fall'n dew!
Without the aid of yonder golden globe
Lost were the garnet's lustre, lost the lilly,
The tulip and auricula's spotted pride;
Lost were the peacock's plumage, to the sight
So pleasing in its pomp and glossy glow.
O thrice-illustrious! were it not for thee
Those pansies that, reclining from the bank,
View through th' immaculate, pellucid stream
40 Their portraiture in the inverted heaven,
Might as well change their triple boast, the white,
The purple, and the gold, that far outvie
The Eastern monarch's garb, ev'n with the dock,
Ev'n with the baneful hemlock's irksome green.
Without thy aid, without thy gladsome beams
The tribes of woodland warblers wou'd remain
Mute on the bending branches, nor recite
The praise of him, who, e'er he form'd their lord,
Their voices tun'd to transport, wing'd their flight,
50 And bade them call for nurture, and receive;
And lo! they call; the blackbird and the thrush,
The woodlark, and the redbreast jointly call;
He hears and feeds their father'd families,
He feeds his sweet musicians, – nor neglects
Th' invoking ravens in the greenwood wide;
And though their throats coarse ruttling hurt the ear,

They mean it all for music, thanks and praise
They mean, and leave ingratitude to man, –
But not to all, – for hark the organs blow
60 Their swelling notes round the cathedral's dome,
And grace th' harmonious choir, celestial feast
To pious ears, and med'cine of the mind;
The thrilling trebles and the manly base
Join in accordance meet, and with one voice
All to the sacred subject suit their song.
While in each breast sweet melancholy reigns
Angelically pensive, till the joy
Improves and purifies; – the solemn scene
The Sun through storied panes surveys with awe,
70 And bashfully with-holds each bolder beam.
Here, as her home, from morn to eve frequents
The cherub Gratitude: – behold her eyes!
With love and gladness weepingly they shed
Extatic smiles; the incense, that her hands
Uprear, is sweeter than the breath of May
Caught from the nectarine's blossom, and her voice
Is more than voice can tell; to him she sings,
To him who feeds, who clothes and who adorns,
Who made and who preserves, whatever dwells
80 In air, in steadfast earth, or fickle sea.
O he is good, he is immensely good!
Who all things form'd, and form'd them all for man;
Who mark'd the climates, varied every zone,
Dispensing all his blessings for the best
In order and in beauty: – raise, attend,
Attest, and praise, ye quarters of the world!
Bow down, ye elephants, submissive bow
To him, who made the mite; though Asia's pride,
Ye carry armies on your tow'r-crowned backs
90 And grace the turban'd tyrants, bow to him
Who is as great, as perfect and as good
In his less-striking wonders, till at length

The eye's at fault and seeks the assisting glass.
Approach and bring from Araby the blest
The fragrant cassia, frankincense and myrrh,
And meekly kneeling at the altar's foot
Lay all the tributary incense down.
Stoop, sable Africa, with rev'rence stoop,
And from thy brow take off the painted plume;
100 With golden ingots all thy camels load
T' adorn his temples, hasten with thy spear
Reverted, and thy trusty bow unstrung,
While unpursu'd thy lions roam and roar,
And ruin'd tow'rs, rude rocks and caverns wide
Remurmur to the glorious, surly sound.
And thou, fair India, whose immense domain
To counterpoise the Hemisphere extends,
Haste from the West, and with thy fruits and flow'rs;
Thy mines and med'cines, wealthy maid, attend.
110 More than the plenteousness so fam'd to flow
By fabling bards from Amalthea's horn
Is thine; thine therefore be a portion due
Of thanks and praise: come with thy brilliant crown
And vest of furr, and from thy fragrant lap
Pomegranates and the rich ananas pour.
But chiefly thou, Europa, seat of grace
And Christian excellence, his goodness own,
Forth from ten thousand temples pour his praise;
Clad in the armour of the living God
120 Approach, unsheath the spirit's flaming sword;
Faith's shield, Salvation's glory-compass'd helm
With fortitude assume, and o'er your heart
Fair truth's invulnerable breast-plate spread;
Then join the general chorus of all worlds,
And let the song of charity begin
In strains seraphic, and melodious pray'r.
'O all-sufficient, all beneficent,
Thou God of goodness and of glory, hear!

Thou, who to lowliest minds dost condescend,
130 Assuming passions to enforce thy laws,
Adopting jealousy to prove thy love:
Thou, who resign'd humility uphold,
Ev'n as the florist props the drooping rose,
But quell tyrannic pride with peerless pow'r
Ev'n as the tempest rives the stubborn oak.
O all-sufficient, all-beneficent,
Thou God of goodness and of glory, Hear!
Bless all mankind, and bring them in the end
To Heav'n, to immortality, and THEE!'   (1756)

From *A Song to David*

O DAVID, highest in the list
Of worthies, on God's ways insist,
   The genuine word repeat:
Vain are the documents of men,
And vain the flourish of the pen
   That keeps the fool's conceit.

Praise above all – for praise prevails;
Heap up the measure, load the scales,
   And good to goodness add:
10 The generous soul her saviour aids,
But peevish obloquy degrades;
   The Lord is great and glad.

For ADORATION all the ranks
Of angels yield eternal thanks,
   And DAVID in the midst;
With God's good poor which, last and least
In man's esteem, thou to thy feast,
   O blessed bridegroom, bidst.

For ADORATION seasons change,
20   And order, truth, and beauty range,
      Adjust, attract, and fill:
   The grass the polyanthus cheques;
   And polish'd porphyry reflects
      By the descending rill.

   Rich almonds colour to the prime
   For ADORATION; tendrils climb,
      And fruit-trees pledge their gems;
   And Ivis, with her gorgeous vest,
   Builds for her eggs her cunning nest,
30   And bell-flowers bow their stems.

   With vinous syrup cedars sprout;
   From rocks pure honey gushing out
      For ADORATION springs:
   All scenes of painting crowd the map
   Of nature; to the mermaid's pap
      The scalèd infant clings.

   The spotted ounce and playsome cubs
   Run rustling 'mongst the flow'ring shrubs,
      And lizards feed the moss;
40   For ADORATION beasts embark,
   While waves upholding halcyon's ark
      No longer roar and toss.

   While Israel sits beneath his fig,
   With coral root and amber sprig
      The wean'd advent'rer sports;
   Where to the palm the jasmin cleaves,
   For ADORATION 'mongst the leaves
      The gale his peace reports.

Increasing days their reign exalt,
50   Nor in the pink and mottled vault
      The opposing spirits tilt;
And, by the coasting reader spied,
The silverlings and crusions glide
      For ADORATION gilt.

For ADORATION rip'ning canes
And cocoa's purest milk detains
      The western pilgrim's staff;
Where rain in clasping boughs inclos'd
And vines with oranges dispos'd
60   Embow'r the social laugh.

Now labour his reward receives,
For ADORATION counts his sheaves
      To peace, her bounteous prince;
The nectarine his strong tint imbibes,
And apples of ten thousand tribes,
      And quick peculiar quince.

The wealthy crops of whit'ning rice
'Mongst thyine woods and groves of spice
      For ADORATION grow;
70   And, marshall'd in the fencèd land,
The peaches and pomegranates stand
      Where wild carnations blow.

The laurels with the winter strive;
The crocus burnishes alive
      Upon the snow-clad earth:
For ADORATION myrtles stay
To keep the garden from dismay,
      And bless the sight from dearth.

The pheasant shows his pompous neck;
80 And ermine, jealous of a speck,
    With fear eludes offence:
The sable, with his glossy pride,
For ADORATION is descried
    Where frosts the wave condense.

The chearful holly, pensive yew,
And holy thorn, their trim renew;
    The squirrel hoards his nuts:
All creatures batten o'er their stores,
And careful nature all her doors
90   For ADORATION shuts.

For ADORATION, David's psalms
Lift up the heart to deeds of alms;
    And he, who kneels and chants,
Prevails his passions to control,
Finds meat and med'cine to the soul
    Which for translation pants.   (1763)

Psalm 22

O my God, my God, receive me,
    Why am I no more thy care,
Why dost thou recede to leave me
    In a state of pain and pray'r?

Lord, thou hearest not, thro' illness
    As I weep upon my knees;
All the day, and in the stillness
    Of the night I have no ease.

But there is no diminution
10   Of thy holiness and grace,
Through all change and revolution,
    O thou praise of Jacob's race.

Faithful were our sires, and steady
    To the hope they built in thee;
And thy gracious hand was ready
    To support and set them free.

By thine angel they were aided
    As they call'd upon thy name,
And of thy good truth persuaded,
20   They escap'd disgrace and shame.

But thy servant is neglected
    Like a worm upon the turf;
Scarce a man, and disrespected
    By the very scum and scurf,

All with smiles of scorn exploding,
    As with taunts their spite is fed,
And with ignominy loading,
    Shoot their lips and shake their head.

'On the Lord for help he waited.
30   Let the help attend his call,
If a wretch so vile and hated
    Be of any price at all.'

But thy pow'rful love embrac'd me
    Soon as from the womb I sprung;
And in thy remembrance plac'd me
    When upon the breasts I hung.

I have walk'd by thy direction
    Ever since my natal hour;
Thou the God of my protection,
40   From my mother's womb, in pow'r.

Keep not mercy at a distance
    Now when trouble presses hard;
For I fail of all assistance,
    If the Lord will not regard.

Youthful insolence confounds me,
    Striplings of the hostile seed,
And maturer strength surrounds me,
    Pride of Bashan's brawny breed.

Stalking to the gates of Zion
50   They my face with wrath behold,
Like the ramping roaring lion,
    When he came upon my fold.

Loose, as to a fluid turning,
    Are my bones, my joints relax,
And my heart, within me burning,
    Is become like melting wax.

Like the fragments of a potter,
    All my strength is dried and broke,
Parch'd my organs, and I totter,
60   As thou gave the final stroke.

For with mows of malediction
    Crowds against my peace consent,
And with dark disguise and fiction
    Artful traitors circumvent.

For my death their cross erecting,
    Both my hands and feet they wound;
I can tell my bones projecting
    To the staring crowd around.

As a spoil my garment's taken,
70   Into shares their band divide,
For my vest their lots are shaken
    Their contention to decide.

But, O Lord, by long secession,
    Leave me not with woe to waste;
Thou my helper in oppression,
    Quick to my deliv'rance haste.

From the weapons of the cruel,
    Take my soul to life and light;
Mine inestimable jewel
80   From the carping pow'rs of spite.

From the tyrants that arraign me,
    Speed me to thy righteous throne,
Thou that didst by grace sustain me
    In the wilderness alone.

Jesus in my private station,
    With my brethren will I praise;
And before the convocation
    Will his peerless marvels blaze.

Praise the Lord all ye that fear him,
90   And exalt him voice and mind;
You of Jacob's seed revere him,
    And in Abr'ham all mankind.

For the friendless and unable
   He disdains not to supply,
Nor rejects them from his table,
   But attends whene'er they cry,

With communicants assembling
   To thy church, my praise is thine;
And my vows with fear and trembling
100   To their pray'rs I will subjoin.

God shall give the poor in spirit
   Bread with everlasting peace;
Faith and praise shall realms inherit,
   Where their pow'rs shall never cease.

Christ, by farthest earth asserted,
   Shall remind them of their end;
All mankind shall be converted,
   And the Christian Church attend.

For to Jesus is dominion,
110   Him all tongues and climes obey;
Wanton will and vague opinion
   To the truth in Christ give way.

Such as in the world have flourish'd,
   Whom true worth and fame reward,
Have been in the spirit nourish'd
   By the nurture of the Lord.

Every saint that serves his Maker
   Unto death, he shall restore
With his Son to be partaker
120   Of a life to die no more.

As for me and my descendants,
   We will reverence his laws;
Reckon'd as the chief dependants
   On his honour, house and cause.

My posterity shall glory,
   As the heavens declare his reign,
Preaching his stupendous story
   To the souls he shall regain.   (1765)

Smart Christianizes very strenuously indeed, giving such latitude to christology and typology that in the end his trochaics refer more to the New Testament than the Old. This is remarkable in that the original, dating from the fourth or third centuries B.C., affords no toe-hold for such interpretations.

Psalm 39

With severest circumspection
   I will guard my ways, I said,
Lest at any time objection
   To my converse should be made.

And my mouth as with a bridle
   I will carefully restrain,
While the reprobate and idle
   In my wearied sight remain.

With such rigour of suppression
10   Was I mute, that I forbore
Ev'n from words of good discretion,
   But I was afflicted sore.

As I ponder'd with vexation,
    My sad heart within me burn'd
Till it caused an inflammation
    When my wonted speech return'd.

Lord, by thy divine monition
    Let me calculate my days,
That their length and their condition
20   May have influence on my ways.

Lo! a span is the dimension
    Of my life, and all my reign
Is not worthy thine attention –
    Surely every man is vain.

For in vain himself aggrieving
    'Tis a shadow man pursues,
Gathering riches, nor conceiving
    Who the hoarded heap shall use.

Where is therefore my affiance,
30   To what shelter shall I flee?
    Truly, Lord, my sole reliance
And my hope is placed in Thee.

With thy hand of mercy lenient
    Heal me, where my conscience wounds;
Stop the jesting inconvenient,
    Which from thence the scoffer grounds.

I was of my speech divested,
    And no more my lips could move,
For thy pow'r is uncontested
40   When thou wouldst our patience prove.

Cease the stripes of thy displeasure,
    Which I can no longer stand,
I am wasted out of measure
    By thy strict afflicting hand.

The severe compunction goading,
    All our beauties fade and wane,
As the wool by moths, corroding:
    Surely every man is vain.

Hear my prayer, O Lord, as falling
50   On my face to thee I cry,
Let thine ears attend my calling,
    And to these my tears reply.

For with Thee I am a stranger,
    And a pilgrim's lot I share;
Train'd in hardship and in danger,
    Ev'n as all my fathers were.

For a little space O spare me,
    And my strength a while restore,
Ere thy final sentence bear me
60   To be seen on earth no more.   (1765)

Smart's performance as a psalmodist is extremely uneven, and it
seems only fair to show him at his worst, as here. The hilarious
disaster of 'Till it caused an inflammation' is not just a casualty of
semantic change since the eighteenth century; nor is 'falling/On my
face', in the antepenultimate quatrain. Smart's temperament, along
with the procedures it had led him to perfect, equips him splendidly
for rendering the many psalms that are triumphant, but disqualifies
him from coping with psalms like this one, of which the tone is not
triumphant at all.

Psalm 68

Arouse – and let thy foes disperse,
Thou master of the universe,
    Arise thee from on high;
Take up the trumpet and alarm,
And at the terror of thine arm
    Let those that hate thee fly.

Like as afflicting smoke's dispelled,
Let them be driv'n away and quell'd,
    As wax before the fire;
10 Let fraud at thine effulgence fail,
And let the multitudes in mail
    Before my God retire.

But let the men of righteous seed,
Accepted in their father's deed,
    Rejoice before the shrine;
Yea, let them shout till heav'n resounds,
There is no need of end or bounds
    To joyfulness divine.

Give praise – with songs your praises blend,
20 And as your thoughts to heav'n ascend,
    And leave the world beneath,
Extol his universal name,
Who rides on the celestial flame,
    In IAH, which all things breathe.

The father of the friendless child,
To keep the damsel undefil'd
    And judge the widow's cause,
Is God upon his righteous throne,
Whence he the hands to rapine prone
30   O'ersees and overawes.

Thy Lord domestic peace creates,
And those his Mercy congregates,
   Who solitary dwell;
The slave delivers from his chain,
But rebels in dry wastes remain,
   And where no waters dwell.

When thou Jehovah led the way
Before thy people in array
   From Egypt's barb'rous coast;
40   Thro' boundless wilds exposed and parch'd,
In pillar'd majesty thou march'd
   The captain of the host.

The earth in ecstasy gave place,
With vast vibrations on her base
   The present God she found;
Ev'n Israel's God – the heav'ns dissolv'd,
And Sinai's mount in clouds involv'd
   Felt all his rocks rebound.

O God, thou bad'st the heav'ns dispense
50   The bread of thy benevolence,
   Down with the daily dew;
And fixt the people of thy pow'r,
Amidst their doubtings, by a show'r
   Miraculous and new.

Therein thy congregation dwelt,
E'en midst the manna, which thou dealt
   So plentiful and pure;
Thy goodness to confirm the weak,
Thy charity to bless and break,
60   The largess for the poor.

God, in stupendous glory deck'd,
His gracious covenant direct
    Came down from heav'n to teach;
Great was the trembling and the fear
Of crowds that rush'd that word to hear
    They were enjoin'd to preach.

Each talking tyrant at the head
Of thousands and ten thousands fled,
    They fled with all their might;
70 And all Judea's blooming pride,
The spouse, the damsel and the bride,
    Dispos'd the spoil at night.

Though ye the bitter bondage wept,
And midst Rhamnesian tripods slept,
    Hereafter is your own;
Ye shall as turtle-doves unfold
The silver plumage wing'd with gold,
    And make melodious moan.

When kings were scatter'd for our sake,
80 And God alarm'd his host to take
    His vengeance on the foe,
On Israel's countenance benign
He made his radiant grace to shine
    As bright as Salmon's snow.

Jehovah's hill's a noble heap,
And ev'n as Bashan's spiry steep
    From which the cedars nod;
And Zion's mount herself sublimes,
And swells her goodly crest and climbs
90   To meet descending God.

Ye haughty hills that leap so high,
What is th' exertion that ye try?
    This is God's hallow'd mount,
On whose blest top the glories play,
And where the Lord desires to stay
    While we his praise recount.

The chariots of the Lord are made
Of angels in a cavalcade
    Ev'n twenty thousand strong;
100 Those thousands of the first degree
O'er Sinai – in the midst is HE,
    And bears the pomp along.

God is gone up from whence he rose.
With gifts accepted for his foes
    His loaded altars smoke;
Captivity, from chains repriev'd,
Is made his captive, and receiv'd
    To thy most blessed yoke.

God is our help from every ill,
110 And gives to every want its fill
    For us and all our race;
By him we're every hour review'd,
To him the daily pray'r's renew'd
    For daily bread and grace.

God, that great God whom we profess,
Is all–benevolent to bless,
    Omnipotent to save;
In God alone is our escape
From death and all the gulfs that gape,
120   From terror and the grave.

God shall not send his blessing down
To rest upon the hoary crown
   Of those which grace resist;
But shall afflict the heads of all
That after his repeated call
   To penitence, persist.

From Bashan, which they pass'd of yore,
Said God, I will my tribes restore,
   And bring them back again;
130 Where Abr'ham worshipp'd and was bless'd,
Of Canaan they shall be possess'd,
   Emerging from the main.

That thy baptizèd foot may tread
Where proud blasphemers laid their head,
   By judgments unreclaim'd;
And that thy shepherd's dogs may chase
Thy flocks into their pleasant place
   Who made the earth asham'd.

They've seen their errors to disprove
140 My God in blest procession move,
   The pomp of God my king;
Accordant to the train below,
The dances rise, the streamers flow,
   And holy flow'rs they fling.

The goodly shew the singers lead,
The minstrels next in place proceed,
   With music sweet and loud;
The damsels, that with wild delight
The brisk-resounding timbrels smite,
150   Are in the mid-most crowd.

O thou Jeshurun, yield thy thanks,
All ages, sexes, tribes and ranks,
    In congregated bands;
To God united thanks restore,
Brought from the heart its inmost core,
    And with protesting hands.

There Benjamin in triumph goes,
Least but in love the Lord of those
    That dwell in tents and bow'rs;
160   And Judah next to the most high,
With Zebulon and Naphtali
    Their princedoms and their pow'rs.

God to the sires of all the tribes
Some great peculiar gift ascribes,
    To each his talent's told;
The loan with such long-suff'ring lent,
Do thou establish and augment
    Ten thousand thousand fold.

From this thy temple which we lay,
170   To thee the homage they shall pay,
    To thee the praise impute;
Kings shall their annual gifts renew,
And give Melchisedec his due,
    The glory and the fruit.

Rebuke the spearmen with thy word,
Those calves and bulls of Bashan's herd,
    Which from our ways abhor;
Let them pay toll, and hew the wood,
Which are at enmity with good
180   And love the voice of war.

The nobles from the sons of Ham
Shall bring the bullock and the ram,
   Idolatrous no more;
The Morians soon shall offer alms,
And bow their heads, and spread their palms,
   God's mercy to implore.

Ye blessed angels of the Lord,
Of nations and of kings the ward,
   That further thanks and pray'r,
190   To Jesus Christ your praise resound,
Collected from the regions round
   Your tutelary care.

In other days before the sev'n,
Upon that ante-mundane heav'n,
   In glorious pomp he rode –
He sends a voice, which voice is might,
In inconceivable delight
   Th' acknowledg'd word of God.

Ye heroes foremost in the field
200   That couch the spear, or bear the shield,
   Bless God that ye prevail;
His splendour is on Israel's brow,
He stands all-pow'rful on the prow
   'Midst all the clouds that sail.

O God, all miracle thou art,
Ev'n thou the God of Israel's heart
   Within thy holy shrine,
Thou shalt with strength and pow'r protect
Thy people in the Lord elect.
210   Praise, endless praise be thine.   (1765)

Smart made direct application of the Psalmist's text to the public
life of his own Great Britain. Thus the stanzas enumerating the

twelve tribes of Israel, and the gifts they bring (outrageously amplified by Smart from a single verse of the Hebrew – see *AV*), is paralleled with a difference among the murky splendours of *Jubilate Agno* (*Rejoice in the Lamb*):

1. For there be twelve cardinal virtues the gifts of the twelve sons of Jacob.

2. For Reuben is Great. God be gracious to Lord Falmouth.

3. For Simeon is Valiant. God be gracious to the Duke of Somerset.

4. For Levi is Pious. God be gracious to the Bishop of London.

5. For Judah is Good. God be gracious to Lord Granville.

6. For Dan is clean – neat, dextrous, apt, active, compact. God be gracious to Draper.

7. For Naphtali is sublime – God be gracious to Chesterfield.

8. For Gad is Contemplative – God be gracious to Lord Northampton.

9. For Ashur is Happy – God be gracious to George Bowes.

10. For Issachar is strong – God be gracious to the Duke of Dorsett.

11. For Zabulon is Constant – God be gracious to Lord Bath.

12. For Joseph is Pleasant – God be gracious to Lord Bolingbroke.

13. For Benjamin is Wise – God be gracious to Honeywood.

Psalm 74

Lord Jesus, why dost thou retard
   The grace thou lov'st to send,
And all thy pastoral regard
   In kindling wrath suspend?

O think upon thy chosen seed,
   Reproach'd and disesteem'd,
Which, as thy holy word decreed,
   Thy precious blood redeem'd.

O think upon Jehudah's race,
10   The tribe so much thine own,
And on fair Zion's special place,
    Where thou hast fixt thy throne.

Prepare thy blessed feet, and come
    With peace angelic shod,
And purge away the dross and scum
    That stain the house of God.

Thy foes display their flags and boast
    That they thy battles fight,
And schismatics maintain their post
20   Amongst the sons of light.

The servile hand that hewed the wood
    From out the stately trees
Was, in his place, ordain'd to good,
    And shap'd his work to please.

But now these artizans untune
    The musick that they made,
The carvers break each fair festoon,
    And counteract their trade.

Nay more, they've carried force and fire
30   Against each shrine around;
And levell'd, in their godless ire,
    Thy temple with the ground.

Yea, in their wishes they combine
    That not a church should stand,
And thus incendiaries mine
    The faith of all the land.

No signs the wonted grace attest –
    The services unsung;
And few to prophesy the best,
40   And learn each sacred tongue.

O God, how long shall traitors sting,
    And hiss with spite and guile,
And with th' established church and king
    Their Saviour Christ revile?

Why dost thou our defence withdraw
    At this so great alarm,
Nor keepest Antichrist in awe
    By thine almighty arm?

For Christ, my king from long ago,
50   Is with me to this hour;
All hope above, and help below,
    Are solely from his pow'r.

That pow'r astonished floods avow'd,
    Dividing heap from heap;
Thou smote the dragons as they plough'd
    The waters of the deep.

The huge Leviathan was stunn'd
    At that stupendous roar
Of billows, breaking to refund
60   The fishes on the shore.

The living springs and streams profuse
    Thy people to supply,
Thy mandate could from rocks educe,
    And made the river dry.

The day is subject to thy rule,
    The night to thy decree,
The blessed sunshine and the cool
    Are made and chang'd by thee.

Thou by thy wisdom hast ordain'd
70   The borders of the world,
And summer's genial heat maintain'd,
    And wintry winds unfurl'd.

Consider, Lord, how men blaspheme
    The honour of thy name,
And fools, in their ambitious dream,
    Have lost the sense of shame.

Let not thy turtle-dove be sold
    To crowds and ruffian rage,
Nor from the prostrate poor withhold
80   Thy love for such an age!

Thy gracious covenant review,
    For in this earth beneath
The worldlings dark designs pursue,
    And fell revenge they breathe.

Let not the simple man depart
    Abash'd at fruitless pray'r;
But give the poor a joyful heart
    Thy glory to declare.

Arise, O God, thy cause support,
90   Thine own eternal cause,
Reclaim the folly that in sport
    Contemns thy name and laws.

O let thy words of comfort drown
   The voice of rank excess,
And bring their gross presumption down
   To worship and to bless.   (1765)

In my 'Psalmody as Translation', in *The Eighteenth-Century Hymn in England* (Cambridge, 1993), I have compared this version with Isaac Watts's (see *ante*), finally giving the palm to Smart.

Psalm 127

If the work be not direct,
   And the Lord the fabric build,
All the plans that man project
   Are but labour idly spill'd.

If the Lord be not the guard,
   And the forts and tow'rs sustain,
All the city gates are barr'd,
   And the watchman wakes in vain.

Vainly for the bread of care
10   Late and early hours ye keep,
For 'tis thus by fervent pray'r
   That he lays the blest asleep.

Lo! thy children are not thine,
   Nor the fruits of female love,
But an heritage divine,
   And a blessing from above.

Like as arrows in the grasp
   Of a valiant man of might,
Are the children that you clasp
20   In some future hour of fight.

Blest! who in his quiver stows
    Darts like these, a goodly freight,
Nor shall blush when with his foes
    He shall parley in the gate.   (1765)

Psalm 127 *The Authorized Version*

1. Except the Lord build the house, they labour in vain that build it: except the Lord keep the city, the watchman waketh but in vain.

2. It is vain for you to rise up early, to sit up late, to eat the bread of sorrows: for so he giveth his beloved sleep.

3. Lo, children are an heritage of the Lord: and the fruit of the womb is his reward.

4. As arrows are in the hand of a mighty man; so are children of the youth.

5. Happy is the man that hath his quiver full of them: they shall not be ashamed, but they shall speak with the enemies in the gate.

Psalm 134

Attend to the musick divine
    Ye people of God with the priest,
At once your Hosanna combine
    As meekly ye bow to the east.

Ye servants that look to the lights
    Which blaze in the house of the Lord,
And keep up the watch of the nights
    To bless each apartment and ward,

The holy of holies review,
10   And lift up your hands with your voice,
And there sing your anthem anew,
    In praise to Jehova rejoice.

The Lord that made heav'n and earth,
 Which rules o'er the night and the day,
His blessing bestow on your mirth,
 And hear you whenever ye pray.   (1765)

Psalm 144

The glory to the Lord I yield,
 Whose hands new strength impart
To brave the ensanguin'd field
 And top the warrior's art.

My hope, my Saviour, and my helm,
 My castle and my fort,
By whom my subject realm
 Themselves in peace comport.

Lord, what is man, that thou should leave
10 For his concerns thy rest,
A sinful son of Eve
 So cherish'd and so blest?

Man is a thing of little worth,
 Thro' folly and misdeeds
Resembling from his birth
 The shadow that recedes.

Bow down the heav'ns, O Lord, in pray'r
 As I thy name invoke;
Upon the mountains bear,
20 And incense they shall smoke.

Cast forth thy lightnings, and disperse
 Ungodliness and gloom,
Thine arrows fiery-fierce
 Shall Satan's works consume.

O send and save me with that hand
    Which all attempt controls
From adverse floods that land
    The foreigners in shoals:

From every loud vainglorious fool
30   With tongue by truth unaw'd,
Whose right hand is a tool
    Of violence and fraud.

O Lord, I will an anthem choose
    Of novelty divine,
And with thy holy muse
    The ten-string'd bass shall join.

The royal arms have peace thro' thee,
    By victory restor'd;
And David now is free
40   From hostile fire and sword.

Save me from tongues of foreign stile
    And of thy grace bereft,
Whose right hand is of guile,
    A hand of blood and theft;

So that our sons like plants may grow,
    Our polish'd daughters shine
Like cherubs in a row,
    Carv'd in the holy shrine;

So that our garners be profuse
50   With much and various stores,
And that our sheep produce
    Ten thousand at our doors;

So that our oxen may be strong,
    As toil disease defeats;
That murmurs, rapes and wrong
    No more infest our streets.

Blest is the people which have got
    Such treasure in their coasts;
Yea, blessed is their lot
60   Who serve the Lord of hosts.   (1765)

Psalm 147

HOSANNA – musick is divine
When in the praise the psalmists join,
    And each good heart is warm;
Yea, joy is sweetest so renew'd,
And all the rites of gratitude
    Are rapture to perform.

The Lord fair Salem shall replace,
And set upon his ancient base
    Hananiel's goodly tow'r;
10 Make captives free, the barren big,
And under his own vine and fig
    All Jacob re-embow'r.

He shall the broken heart repair,
And for all sickness and despair
    A cure in Christ provide;
And heal the wounded and the bruis'd,
His oil into their sores infus'd,
    And soothing balm applied.

Tho' their bright swarms the sand surpass,
20   Of every magnitude and class
      He knows th' etherial flames;
The numb'rer of their host is He,
And to his summons 'Here we be',
      They answer by their names.

For God is magnitude immense,
His prowess is omnipotence
      That knows no date or end;
His wisdom infinitely great,
And all duration, depth and height,
30   His mysteries transcend.

The Lord with approbation sees
The meek, and from his faithful knees
      He lifts him up on high;
But spurns the sinner and unjust,
And leaves low luxury and lust
      To worms that never die.

Sing praises all degrees and ranks,
As in the pray'r of general thanks
      The holy church commune;
40   As to the touch the harp revives,
Sing praises with your lips and lives
      To Christ the word and tune.

He the blue heav'n in beauty shrouds,
And balances the plumy clouds
      Which for the rain he wrings;
He causes the mild dew to drop,
And grass upon the mountain top
      In tufted verdure springs.

For every thing that moves and lives,
50   Foot, fin, or feather meat he gives,
     He deals the beasts their food
Both in the wilderness and stall,
And hears the raven's urgent call,
     And stills her clam'rous brood.

And yet his maker has no need
Of the train'd ox, or prancing steed,
     Tho' thunder cloath his chest;
And man that manages the rein
Is but a creature brief and vain
60   With such proportion blest.

But God is pleas'd with duteous fear,
Men with clean hands and conscience clear,
     Which at thy mercy-gate
With ceaseless application knock,
And patient on him as their rock
     For sure redemption wait.

O Sion, praise the Lord, and thou,
Fair Salem, to his praises bow
     Thine olives and thy palms;
70   Are there afflicted? Let them pray,
But mirth shall dedicate her day
     To hymns and festive psalms.

For by his might the Lord supports
Thy mounds, and fortifies thy forts,
     Thy brazen bars he nails;
Thy sportive children fill the streets,
Thy foe without the wall retreats,
     Nor want within prevails.

He sheathes the sword and blunts the spears,
80   And thy redoubtable frontiers
     Barbarian inroads scorn;
That thou may'st in thy peace possess
The blessings of a social mess,
     And flour of choicest corn.

He sends his word upon the earth
To call conception into birth,
     And kind with kind to match;
And to sustain all human race,
The blessed angels of his grace
90   Make infinite dispatch.

His snow upon the ground he teems,
Like bleaching wool beside the streams,
     To warm the tender blade;
Like ashes from the furnace cast,
His frost comes with the northern blast
     To pinch and to pervade.

Like vitreous fragments o'er the field,
In ice the waters are congeal'd,
     Their liquid swiftness lost;
100 The breath steams on the sharpen'd air,
And who so hardy as to bear
     The quickness of his frost!

He sends the word of his command
To melt and loosen all the land,
     And let the floods at large;
He blows, and with the genial breeze
The fount and river by degrees
     Their usual tale discharge.

His word to Jacob he disclos'd
110 When he upon the stones repos'd
And worship'd in a trance;
And laws to Israel enjoin'd
When o'er the nations of mankind
He bade his tribes advance.

Such wond'rous love has not been shown,
But to the patriarch's seed alone
His duty to requite;
And judgments on the rest impend,
Till Jesus make them comprehend
120 His ways, his truth and light. (1765)

JOHN NEWTON (1725–1807)

Olney Hymns: Hymn XLVI
Psalm 73.25 *None upon earth I desire besides thee*

How tedious and tasteless the hours
When Jesus no longer I see;
Sweet prospects, sweet birds, and sweet flowers
Have lost all their sweetness with me;
The midsummer sun shines but dim,
The fields strive in vain to look gay;
But when I am happy in him,
December's as pleasant as May.

His name yields the richest perfume,
10 And sweeter than music his voice;
His presence disperses my gloom,
And makes all within me rejoice.

I should, were he always thus nigh,
    Have nothing to wish or to fear;
No mortal so happy as I,
    My summer would last all the year.

Content with beholding his face,
    My all to his pleasure resign'd,
No changes of season or place
20   Would make any change in my mind:
While bless'd with a sense of his love,
    A palace a toy would appear;
And prisons would palaces prove,
    If Jesus would dwell with me there.

Dear Lord, if indeed I am thine,
    If thou art my sun and my song;
Say why do I languish and pine,
    And why are my winters so long?
O drive these dark clouds from my sky,
30   Thy soul-cheering presence restore;
Or take me unto thee on high,
    Where winter and clouds are no more.   (1779)

For John Newton, see 'The author of "Amazing Grace"', in *The
Eighteenth-Century Hymn in England* (Cambridge, 1993).

Olney Hymns: Hymn XLIX
Psalm 107.7 *He led them by a right way*

When Israel was from Egypt freed,
    The Lord, who brought them out,
Help'd them in ev'ry time of need,
    But led them round about.

To enter Canaan soon they hop'd,
 But quickly chang'd their mind
When the Red Sea their passage stopp'd,
 And Pharoah march'd behind.

The desert fill'd them with alarms,
10 For water and for food;
And Amalek, by force of arms,
 To check their progress stood.

They often murmur'd by the way,
 Because they judg'd by sight;
But were at length constrain'd to say
 The Lord had led them right.

In the Red Sea, that stopp'd them first,
 Their enemies were drown'd;
The rocks gave water for their thirst,
20 And manna spread the ground.

By fire and cloud their way was shown
 Across the pathless sands;
And Amalek was overthrown
 By Moses' lifted hands.

The way was right their hearts to prove,
 To make God's glory known;
And shew his wisdom, power, and love,
 Engag'd to save his own.

Just so, the true believer's path
30 Through many dangers lies;
Though dark to sense, 'tis right to faith,
 And leads us to the skies.   (1779)

ROBERT BURNS (1759–1796)

The First Six Verses of the Ninetieth Psalm

O Thou, the first, the greatest friend
    Of all the human race!
Whose strong right hand has ever been
    Their stay and dwelling-place!

Before the mountains heav'd their heads
    Beneath Thy forming hand,
Before this ponderous globe itself
    Arose at Thy command;

That pow'r which rais'd and still upholds
10   This universal frame,
From countless unbeginning time
    Was ever still the same.

Those mighty periods of years
    Which seem to us so vast,
Appear no more before Thy sight
    Than yesterday that's past.

Thou giv'st the word; Thy creature, man,
    Is to existence brought;
Again Thou say'st, 'Ye sons of men,
20   Return ye into nought!'

Thou layest them, with all their cares,
    In everlasting sleep;
As with a flood thou tak'st them off
    With overwhelming sweep.

They flourish like the morning flow'r,
   In beauty's pride array'd;
But long ere night cut down it lies
   All wither'd and decay'd.   (1781)

ANON.

Psalm 148

Praise the Lord! ye heavens, adore him;
   Praise him, angels in the height;
Sun and moon, rejoice before him;
   Praise him, all ye stars and light.
Praise the Lord, for he hath spoken;
   Worlds his mighty voice obeyed;
Laws, which never shall be broken,
   For their guidance hath he made.

Praise the Lord, for he is glorious;
10   Never shall his promise fail;
God hath made his saints victorious;
   Sin and death shall not prevail.
Praise the God of our salvation;
   Hosts on high, his power proclaim;
Heaven and earth and all creation,
   Laud and magnify his name.   (1796)

The hymn was for a collection of hymns used at the Foundling
Hospital, London. See Erik Routley, *Hymns and the Faith* (Green-
wich, Connecticut, 1956): 'Foundling Hospitals, Orphanages,
Magdalen Hospitals and similar institutions were one of the con-
sequences of the Evangelical Revival in our great cities, pre-eminently

London, and their childrens' choirs became famous for their music-
making ... It was written, moreover, to carry the tune *Austria*,
recently composed by Haydn ...'

HENRY KIRKE WHITE (1785–1806)

Kirke White, once famous as 'the Evangelical Chatterton', was dead
at the age of twenty-one.

Psalm 22

My God, my God, oh, why dost thou forsake me?
    Why art thou distant in the hour of fear?
To thee, my wonted help, I still betake me,
    To thee I clamor, but thou dost not hear.

The beam of morning witnesses my sighing,
    The lonely night-hour views me weep in vain,
Yet thou art holy, and, on thee relying,
    Our fathers were released from grief and pain.

To thee they cried, and thou didst hear their wailing,
10   On thee they trusted, and their trust was sure;
But I, poor, lost, and wretched son of failing,
    I, without hope, must scorn and hate endure.

Me they revile; with many ills molested,
    They bid me seek of thee, O Lord, redress:
On God, they say, his hope and trust he rested,
    Let God relieve him in his deep distress.

To me, Almighty! in thy mercy shining,
    Life's dark and dangerous portals thou didst ope;

And softly on my mother's lap reclining,
20   Breathed through my breast the lively soul of hope.

Even from the womb, thou art my God, my Father!
    Aid me, now trouble weighs me to the ground:
Me heavy ills have worn, and, faint and feeble,
    The bulls of Bashan have beset me round.

My heart is melted and my soul is weary,
    The wicked ones have pierced my hands and feet!
Lord, let thy influence cheer my bosom dreary:
    My help! my strength! let me thy presence greet.

Save me! oh, save me! from the sword dividing,
30   Give me my darling from the jaws of death!
Thee will I praise, and, in thy name confiding,
    Proclaim thy mercies with my latest breath.   (1805?)

JAMES MONTGOMERY
(1771–1854)

Psalm 4

How long, ye sons of men, will ye
    The servant of the Lord despise,
Delight yourselves with vanity,
    And trust in refuges of lies?

Know that the Lord hath set apart
    The godly man in every age:
He loves a meek and lowly heart;
    His people are his heritage.

Then stand in awe, nor dare to sin;
10   Commune with your own heart; be still;
The Lord requireth truth within,
     The sacrifice of mind and will.   (1822–41)

Gordon Jackson has remarked to me, of the word 'heritage' in l. 8,
that Montgomery's usage 'gives it a fuller value than it ever had
before'.

   Montgomery was born and raised in the Moravian church. Texts
are from Montgomery's *Poetical Works* (1860).

Psalm 24

Lift up your heads, ye gates of brass,
     Ye bars of iron, yield,
And let the King of Glory pass;
     The Cross is in the field.

Ye armies of the living God,
     His sacramental host,
Where hallowed footstep never trod
     Take your appointed post.

Though few and small and weak your bands,
10   Strong in your Captain's strength
Go to the conquest of all lands;
     All must be His at length.

O fear not, faint not, halt not now;
     Quit you like men, be strong;
To Christ shall every nation bow,
     And sing with you this song:

> 'Uplifted are the gates of brass;
>   The bars of iron yield;
> Behold the King of Glory pass!
> 20   The Cross hath won the field.'   (1822–41)

The Methodist Hymn-Book, No. 265; *Hymns Ancient and Modern*, No.
586 is sufficiently different to be quoted in full:

> Lift up your heads, ye gates of brass;
> Ye bars of iron, yield
> And let the King of Glory pass:
> The Cross is in the field.
>
> That banner, brighter than the star
> That leads the train of night,
> Shines on the march, and guides from far
> His servants to the fight.
>
> A holy war those servants wage;
> 10 In that mysterious strife,
> The powers of Heav'n and hell engage
> For more than death or life.
>
> Ye armies of the living GOD,
> Sworn warriors of CHRIST's host,
> Where hallow'd footsteps never trod,
> Take your appointed post.
>
> Though few and small and weak your bands,
> Strong in your Captain's strength,
> Go to the conquest of all lands;
> 20 All must be His at length.
>
> The spoils at His victorious Feet
> You shall rejoice to lay,
> And lay yourselves as trophies meet,
> In His great judgment day.
>
> Then fear not, faint not, halt not now;
> In JESUS' Name be strong!

To Him shall all the nations bow,
And sing the triumph song: –

Uplifted are the gates of brass,
30   The bars of iron yield;
Behold the King of Glory pass;
The Cross hath won the field.

The Anglican version is fuller, and richer in so far as it carries through in more detail the military analogy. Yet the Methodist version may be thought, precisely by its terseness, to be more militant and more triumphal; to *be* in fact that 'triumph song' to which the Anglican version only exhorts us. We must in any case be disconcerted to discover that neither version, both of them credited to Montgomery, accounts for more than three verses of the original. See the *BCP* version, which follows.

Psalm 24 *The Authorized Version*

1. The earth is the Lord's, and all that therein is: the compass of the world, and they that dwell therein.

2. For he hath founded it upon the seas: and prepared it upon the floods.

3. Who shall ascend into the hill of the Lord: or who shall rise up in his holy place?

4. Even he that hath clean hands, and a pure heart: and that hath not lift up his mind unto vanity, nor sworn to deceive his neighbour.

5. He shall receive the blessing from the Lord: and righteousness from the God of his salvation.

6. This is the generation of them that seek him: even of them that seek thy face, O Jacob.

7. Lift up your heads, O ye gates, and be ye lift up, ye everlasting doors: and the King of glory shall come in.

8. Who is the King of glory: it is the Lord strong and mighty, even the Lord mighty in battle.

9. Lift up your heads, O ye gates, and be ye lift up, ye everlasting doors: and the King of glory shall come in.

10. Who is the King of glory: even the Lord of hosts, he is the
King of glory.

Psalm 29

Give glory to God in the highest! give praise,
　　Ye noble, ye mighty, with joyful accord;
All-wise are his counsels, all-perfect his ways;
　　In the beauty of holiness worship the Lord!

The voice of the Lord on the ocean is known,
　　The God of eternity thundereth abroad;
The voice of the Lord, from the depth of his throne,
　　In terror and power; – all nature is awed.

At the voice of the Lord the cedars are bow'd,
10　　And towers from their base into ruin are hurl'd;
The voice of the Lord, from the dark-bosom'd cloud
　　Dissevers the lightning in flames o'er the world.

See Lebanon bound, like the kid on his rocks,
　　And wild as the unicorn Sirion appear:
The wilderness quakes with the resonant shocks;
　　The hinds cast their young in the travail of fear.

The voice of the Lord through the calm of the wood,
　　Awakens its echoes, strikes light through its caves;
The Lord sitteth King on the turbulent flood;
20　　The winds are his servants, his servants the waves.

The Lord is the strength of his people; the Lord
　　Gives health to his people, and peace evermore;
Then throng to his temple, his glory record,
　　But, O! when He speaketh, in silence adore.　　(1822–41)

This psalm is thought to be certainly one of the earliest in the Psalter. Montgomery's anapaests strike me as manifestly superior to, for instance, Philip Sidney's version.

Psalm 39

Lord! let me know mine end,
    My days, how brief their date,
That I may timely comprehend
    How frail my best estate.

My life is but a span,
    Mine age as nought with Thee;
Man, in his highest honour, man
    Is dust and vanity.

A shadow even in health,
10   Disquieted with pride
Or rack'd with care, he heaps up wealth
    Which unknown heirs divide.

What seek I now, O Lord?
    My hope is in thy name;
Blot out my sins from thy record,
    Nor give me up to shame.

Dumb at thy feet I lie,
    For thou hast brought me low:
Remove thy judgments, lest I die;
20   I faint beneath thy blow.

At thy rebuke, the bloom
    Of man's vain beauty flies;
And grief shall, like a moth, consume
    All that delights our eyes.

Have pity on my fears,
    Hearken to my request,
Turn not in silence from my tears,
    But give the mourner rest.

A stranger, Lord! with Thee
30   I walk on pilgrimage,
Where all my fathers once, like me,
    Sojourned from age to age.

O spare me yet, I pray!
    Awhile my strength restore,
Ere I am summon'd hence away,
    And seen on earth no more.   (1822–41)

The psalm dates from the third century B.C. The transgression for
which the speaker has paid with sickness is moved by Montgomery
to the head of the psalm. It is the unseemly and as everyone knows
impossible request to 'know mine end'. Since Smart's rendering has
already been taken as an example of how not to do it, Montgomery's
version is offered as a counter-example. He is obviously a less gifted
poet than Smart, but he modestly and reverently knows what he is
about.

Psalm 72

Hail to the Lord's Anointed;
    Great David's greater Son!
Hail, in the time appointed,
    His reign on earth begun!
He comes to break oppression,
    To set the captive free,
To take away transgression,
    And rule in equity.

He comes with succour speedy
10   To those who suffer wrong;
To help the poor and needy,
    And bid the weak be strong:
To give them songs for sighing,
    Their darkness turn to light,
Whose souls, condemned and dying,
    Were precious in His sight.

He shall come down like showers
    Upon the fruitful earth:
Love, joy, and hope, like flowers,
20   Spring in His path to birth:
Before Him, on the mountains,
    Shall peace the herald go;
And righteousness in fountains
    From hill to valley flow.

Kings shall fall down before Him,
    And gold and incense bring;
All nations shall adore Him,
    His praise all people sing;
To Him shall prayer unceasing
30   And daily vows ascend;
His kingdom still increasing,
    A kingdom without end.

O'er every foe victorious,
    He on His throne shall rest;
From age to age more glorious,
    All-blessing and all-blest.
The tide of time shall never
    His covenant remove;
His name shall stand for ever,
40   His changeless name of Love.   (1822–41)

This is Isaac Watts's 'Jesus shall reign where'er the sun' (see *ante*). But there isn't in Watts the note of resentment on behalf of the lower ranks of society, which is clear in Montgomery's second stanza – omitted, perhaps significantly, from the version in *Hymns Ancient and Modern* (No. 219). Montgomery, who had been a radical journalist, makes much of it; but he has warrant – see the *BCP* version. This may seem to sit oddly with W. O. E. Oesterley's insistence that the psalm is the work of 'a court-poet' hailing a secular sovereign; and that it 'was never intended for liturgical worship, and was never used in the worship of the Synagogue'. But Oesterley means only to concede that the focus is socio-political rather than directly religious.

Psalm 122

Glad was my heart to hear
    My old companions say:
Come, in the house of God appear,
    For 'tis a holy day.

Our willing feet shall stand
    Within the temple door,
While young and old, in many a band,
    Shall throng the sacred floor.

Thither the tribes repair
10   Where all are wont to meet,
And joyful in the house of prayer
    Bend at the mercy-seat.

Pray for Jerusalem,
    The city of our God;
The Lord from heaven be kind to them
    That love the dear abode!

Within these walls may peace
And harmony be found;
Zion, in all thy palaces
20   Prosperity abound!

For friends and brethren dear
Our prayer shall never cease;
Oft as they meet for worship here,
God send His people peace!   (1822–41)

FITZ-GREENE HALLECK
(1790–1867)

Halleck was a principal ornament of New York City's literary life in the 1820s. He figures in that role, fleetingly, in Gore Vidal's historical novel, *Burr*. Ezra Pound in 1964 thought that Halleck's novel-in-verse, *Fanny* (1821), could stand comparison with Byron. Thirty or fifty years later, Pound thought, American verse-writing could no longer hold its own with British performances.

Psalm 137 'By the rivers of Babylon'

We sat us down and wept,
Where Babel's waters slept,
And we thought of home and Zion as a long-gone, happy
    dream;
We hung our harps in air
On the willow-boughs, which there,
Gloomy as round a sepulchre, were drooping o'er the stream.
The foes whose chain we wore
Were with us on that shore,

Exulting in our tears that told the bitterness of woe.
10   'Sing us', they cried aloud,
         'Ye once so high and proud,
The songs ye sang in Zion ere we laid her glory low.'

And shall the harp of heaven
To Judah's monarch given
Be touched by captive fingers, or grace a fettered hand?
   No! sooner be my tongue
   Mute, powerless, and unstrung,
Than its words of holy music make glad a stranger land.

May this right hand, whose skill
20   Can wake the harp at will,
And bid the listener's joys or griefs in light or darkness come
   Forget its godlike power
   If for one brief, dark hour,
My heart forgets Jerusalem, fallen city of my home!

Daughter of Babylon!
Blessed be that chosen one
Whom God shall send to smite thee when there is none to
         save:
   He from the mother's breast
   Shall pluck the babe at rest,
30   And lay it in the sleep of death beside its father's
         grave.   (1825?)

ROBERT GRANT (1779–1838)

Psalm 104

O worship the King,
    All glorious above;
O gratefully sing
    His power and His love:
Our shield and defender,
    The ancient of days,
Pavilioned in splendour,
    And girded with praise.

O tell of His might,
10   O sing of His grace,
Whose robe is the light,
    Whose canopy space;
His chariots of wrath
    The deep thunder-clouds form,
And dark is His path
    On the wings of the storm.

The earth with its store
    Of wonders untold,
Almighty! Thy power
20   Hath founded of old,
Hath stablished it fast
    By a changeless decree,
And round it hath cast,
    Like a mantle, the sea.

Thy bountiful care
    What tongue can recite?
It breathes in the air,
    It shines in the light,

It streams from the hills,
30   It descends to the plain,
And sweetly distils
   In the dew and the rain.

Frail children of dust,
   And feeble as frail,
In Thee do we trust,
   Nor find Thee to fail;
Thy mercies how tender,
   How firm to the end,
Our Maker, Defender,
40   Redeemer, and Friend!

O measureless Might!
   Ineffable Love!
While angels delight
   To hymn Thee above,
The humbler creation,
   Though feeble their lays,
With true adoration
   Shall lisp to Thy praise.   (1833)

'Sir Robert Grant was . . . a distinguished public servant – as judge advocate-general he supported and helped to push through the Jewish Emancipation resolution – who was also a modest but not negligible religious poet.' Thus Margaret A. Doody, in *The State of the Language*, ed. Ricks and Michaels (Berkeley, Los Angeles, 1990). Ms Doody, who places Grant as poetically a follower of Cowper, protests at how the English of Grant's version of Psalm 104 has been emasculated in *Inclusive Language Hymns*, emanating from the First Congregational Church, Amherst, Massachusetts. 'O worship the King' becomes in this politically correct, republican version: 'We worship thee, God'. (And isn't that nice of us?) Assaults launched on the English of sacred poetry, in the interests of 'inclusive language', are to be noticed elsewhere than in the United States.

JOHN KEBLE (1792–1866)

Psalm 58

Will ye maintain indeed
    The scorn'd and smother'd right?
At your award, ye mortal seed,
    Shall equity have might?

Nay, but in heart ye frame
    All evil: in all lands
Ye weigh, and measure out, and aim
    The rapine of your hands.

As aliens from the womb
10   Th' ungodly start aside;
E'en from their mothers' breasts they roam,
    Their false hearts wandering wide.

A loathsome gall they yield,
    As gall of aspic fell;
Like the deaf adder, who hath seal'd
    His ear against the spell;

Whom whisperers ne'er might take,
    Nor wily sorcerer win
With deepest lore. – Almighty, break
20   Their teeth, their lips within.

Come shiver with strong arm
    The lion's jaws, O Lord!
This way and that, to shame and harm
    As water they are pour'd.

Each arrow they would shoot
Falls shiver'd from the bow;
They pass like melting snail, or fruit
Of some untimely throe.

They ne'er saw morning ray: –
30   Yes – ere your cauldrons know
The thorn, His winds shall sweep away
Green wood and brands that glow.

The just in joyful mood
Th' avenging storm will view,
And wash his footsteps in the blood
Of yon rebellious crew;

Till man on earth shall cry,
'The righteous soul hath yet
His meed: O yet a God on high
40   To judge the world is set.'   (1839)

From Keble's *The Psalter: or Psalms of David: in English Verse*
(Oxford, 1839). Keble the hymnist is a lot better than Keble the
psalmodist. Compare the Countess of Pembroke. Who would recog-
nize a miscarried human embryo in Keble's 'fruit/Of some untimely
throe'? And what that early Victorians had done would they
recognize as to 'aim/The rapine of your hands'? The difference
between the Countess and Keble is the difference between vocabular-
ies that can, and cannot, seize on actualities.

HENRY FRANCIS LYTE
(1793–1847)

Lyte, educated at Trinity College Dublin, ministered in Ireland and then at Marazion in Cornwall, where in 1818 he experienced by his own account a great spiritual change. He composed the hymn 'Abide with me, fast falls the eventide'.

Psalm 84

Pleasant are Thy courts above,
In the land of light and love;
Pleasant are Thy courts below,
In this land of sin and woe.
O my spirit longs and faints
For the converse of Thy saints,
For the brightness of Thy face,
For Thy fullness, God of grace!

Happy birds that sing and fly
10   Round Thy altars, O Most High!
Happier souls that find a rest
In a heavenly Father's breast!
Like the wandering dove that found
No repose on earth around,
They can to their ark repair,
And enjoy it ever there.

Happy souls! Their praises flow
In this vale of sin and woe;
Waters in the desert rise,
20   Manna feeds them from the skies.
On they go from strength to strength,

Till they reach Thy throne at length;
At Thy feet adoring fall,
Who hast led them safe through all.

Lord, be mine this prize to win:
Guide me through a world of sin;
Keep me by Thy saving grace;
Give me at Thy side a place.
Sun and shield alike Thou art;
30   Guide and guard my erring heart:
Grace and glory flow from Thee;
Shower, O shower them, Lord, on me!   (1834)

Psalm 84 utters the sentiments of pilgrims approaching the entirely
earthly courts of Jerusalem: it says nothing of any afterlife.

Psalm 103

Praise, my soul, the King of heaven,
    To His feet thy tribute bring;
Ransomed, healed, restored, forgiven,
    Who like thee His praise should sing?
        Praise Him! Praise Him!
    Praise the everlasting King.

Praise Him for his grace and favour
    To our fathers in distress;
Praise Him, still the same for ever,
10   Slow to chide and swift to bless:
        Praise Him! Praise Him!
    Glorious in His faithfulness.

Father-like He tends and spares us;
    Well our feeble frame He knows;
In His hands he gently bears us,

Rescues us from all our foes:
    Praise Him! Praise Him!
Widely as His mercy flows.

Angels in the height, adore Him;
20   Ye behold Him face to face;
Sun and moon, bow down before Him;
    Dwellers all in time and space,
        Praise Him! Praise Him!
Praise with us the God of grace.   (1834)

JOHN CLARE (1793–1864)

Psalm 102

Lord, hear my prayer when trouble glooms,
Let sorrow find a way,
And when the day of trouble comes,
Turn not thy face away:
My bones like hearthstones burn away,
My life like vapoury smoke decays.

My heart is smitten like the grass,
That withered lies and dead,
And I, so lost to what I was,
10 Forget to eat my bread.
My voice is groaning all the day,
My bones prick through this skin of clay.

The wilderness's pelican,
The desert's lonely owl –
I am their like, a desert man
In ways as lone and foul.

As sparrows on the cottage top
I wait till I with fainting drop.

I hear my enemies reproach,
20   All silently I mourn;
They on my private peace encroach,
Against me they are sworn.
Ashes as bread my trouble shares,
And mix my food with weeping cares.

Yet not for them is sorrow's toil,
I fear no mortal's frowns –
But thou hast held me up awhile
And thou hast cast me down.
My days like shadows waste from view,
30   I mourn like withered grass in dew.

But thou, Lord, shalt endure for ever,
All generations through;
Thou shalt to Zion be the giver
Of joy and mercy too.
Her very stones are in thy trust,
Thy servants reverence her dust.

Heathens shall hear and fear thy name,
All kings of earth thy glory know
When thou shalt build up Zion's fame
40   And live in glory there below.
He'll not despise their prayers, though mute,
But still regard the destitute.

(1841)

The recovery for the canon of the Northamptonshire peasant-poet Clare is one of the few modern achievements of criticism and literary scholarship in English. The recovery is not yet assured, as witness *The New Oxford Book of Romantic Period Poetry* (1993).

THOMAS CARLYLE (1795–1881)

Psalm 91 *(by way of Martin Luther)*

A safe stronghold our God is still,
    A trusty shield and weapon;
He'll help us clear from all the ill
    That hath us now o'ertaken.
        The ancient prince of hell
        Hath risen with purpose fell;
        Strong mail of craft and power
        He weareth in this hour;
On earth is not his fellow.

10 With force of arms we nothing can,
    Full soon were we down-ridden;
But for us fights the proper Man,
    Whom God Himself hath bidden.
        Ask ye: Who is this same?
        Christ Jesus is His name,
        The Lord Sabaoth's Son;
        He, and no other one,
Shall conquer in the battle.

And were this world all devils o'er,
20   And watching to devour us,
We lay it not to heart so sore;
    Not they can overpower us.
        And let the prince of ill
        Look grim as e'er he will,
        He harms us not a whit:
        For why? His doom is writ;
A word shall quickly slay him.

God's word, for all their craft and force
  One moment will not linger,
30 But, spite of hell, shall have its course;
    'Tis written by His finger.
      And though they take our life,
      Goods, honour, children, wife,
      Yet is their profit small:
      These things shall vanish all;
The city of God remaineth.   (1831)

Carlyle's version of Luther's *Ein feste Burg ist unser Gott* appears thus
as No. 494 in *The Methodist Hymn-Book*. It appeared originally in
Carlyle's essay, 'Luther's Psalm', in *Fraser's Magazine* (1831).

EDWARD CHURTON (1800–1874)

Psalm 67

God of grace, O let thy light
Bless our dim and blinded sight;
Like the day-spring on the night
  Bid Thy grace to shine.

To the nations led astray
Thine eternal love display:
Let Thy truth direct their way
  Till the world be Thine.

Praise to Thee, the faithful Lord:
10 Let all tongues in glad accord
Learn the good thanksgiving word,
    Ever praising Thee.

Let them moved to gladness sing,
Owning Thee their Judge and King;
Righteous truth shall bloom and spring
   Where Thy rule shall be.

Praise to Thee, all faithful Lord;
Let all tongues in glad accord
Speak the good thanksgiving word,
20   Heart-rejoicing praise.

So the fruitful earth's increase,
Bounty of the God of peace,
Never in its course shall cease
   Through the length of days.

While His grace our life shall cheer,
Furthest lands shall own His fear,
Brought to Him in worship near,
   Taught His mercy's ways.   (1854)

This is No. 364 in *Hymns Ancient and Modern.*

Psalm 96

Raise the psalm: let earth adoring,
   Through each kindred, tribe and tongue,
To her God His praise restoring,
   Raise the new accordant song.
Bless His name, each farthest nation:
   Sing His praise, His truth display:
Tell anew His high salvation
   With each new return of day.

    Tell it out beneath the heaven
10   To each kindred, tribe and tongue.
    Tell it out from morn till even
      In your unexhausted song:
    Tell that God for ever reigneth,
      He, who set the world so fast,
    He, who still its state sustaineth
      Till the day of doom to last.

    Tell them that the doom is coming
      When that righteous doom shall be:
    Then shall heaven new joys illumine,
20   Gladness shine o'er earth and sea.
    Yea, the far-resounding ocean
      Shall its thousand voices raise,
    All its waves in glad commotion
      Chant the fullness of His praise.

    And earth's fields, with herbs and flowers,
      Shall put on their choice array,
    And in all their leafy bowers
      Shall the woods keep holy-day:
    When the Judge, to earth descending,
30   Righteous judgment shall ordain,
    Fraud and wrong shall then have ending,
      Truth, immortal truth, shall reign.   (1854)

Archdeacon Churton, in *The Cleveland Psalter* (1854), claimed to
have incorporated ideas and lines from Wyatt, Sidney, Sandys and
others, also from the ancient Anglo-Saxon version which he attrib-
uted to Aldhelm of Sherborne (*ob.* A.D. 709).

HENRY WADSWORTH LONGFELLOW (1807–1882)

A Psalm of Life *What the Heart of the Young Man said to the Psalmist*

Tell me not, in mournful numbers,
    Life is but an empty dream!
For the soul is dead that slumbers,
    And things are not what they seem.

Life is real! Life is earnest!
    And the grave is not its goal;
Dust thou art, to dust returnest,
    Was not spoken of the soul.

Not enjoyment, and not sorrow,
10   Is our destined end or way;
But to act, that each tomorrow
    Find us farther than to-day.

Art is long, and Time is fleeting,
    And our hearts, though stout and brave,
Still, like muffled drums, are beating
    Funeral marches to the grave.

In the world's broad field of battle,
    In the bivouac of Life,
Be not like dumb, driven cattle!
20   Be a hero in the strife!

Trust no Future, howe'er pleasant!
    Let the dead Past bury its dead!
Act – act in the living Present!
    Heart within, and God o'erhead!

Lives of great men all remind us
   We can make our lives sublime,
And, departing, leave behind us
   Footprints on the sands of time; –

Footprints, that perhaps another,
30   Sailing o'er life's solemn main,
A forlorn and shipwrecked brother,
   Seeing, shall take heart again.

Let us, then, be up and doing,
   With a heart for any fate;
Still achieving, still pursuing,
   Learn to labour and to wait.   (1839)

Longfellow's 'Psalm of Life' first appeared in *Voices of the Night* (1839). Some of the verses are very familiar to English-speakers, few of whom, however, take note of the jeering sub-title, which exposes how incompatible is the Americanism that Longfellow espoused with the tragic vision of the Psalmist. Nevertheless, Longfellow would go on to translate Dante's *Divine Comedy* in 1867.

HENRY WILLIAMS BAKER
(1821–1877)

Psalm 23

The King of love my shepherd is,
   Whose goodness faileth never;
I nothing lack if I am his
   And he is mine for ever.

Where streams of living water flow
   My ransomed soul he leadeth,
And where the verdant pastures grow
   With food celestial feedeth.

Perverse and foolish oft I strayed,
10   But yet in love he sought me,
And on his shoulder gently laid,
   And home, rejoicing, brought me.

In death's dark vale I fear no ill
   With thee, dear Lord, beside me;
Thy rod and staff my comfort still,
   Thy cross before to guide me.

Thou spread'st a table in my sight;
   Thy unction grace bestoweth;
And oh, what transport of delight
20   From thy pure chalice floweth!

And so through all the length of days
   Thy goodness faileth never;
Good Shepherd, may I sing thy praise
   Within thy house for ever.   (1868)

Erik Routley pointed out that, with 'unction' and 'chalice', Baker notably (and quite legitimately) fashioned this psalm, so often translated before, to serve the purposes of 'a distinguished high-Church Anglican, influenced by the new eucharistic teaching of the Oxford Movement'.

GERARD MANLEY HOPKINS
(1844–1889)

'Thou art indeed just' (Psalm 119, vv. 137–60)

Thou art indeed just, Lord, if I contend
With thee; but, sir, so what I plead is just.
Why do sinners' ways prosper? and why must
Disappointment all I endeavour end?
    Wert thou my enemy, O thou my friend,
How wouldst thou worse, I wonder, than thou dost
Defeat, thwart me? Oh, the sots and thralls of lust
Do in spare hours more thrive than I that spend,
Sir, life upon thy cause. See, banks and brakes
10 Now, leavèd how thick! lacèd they are again
With fretty chervil, look, and fresh wind shakes
Them; birds build – but not I build; no, but strain,
Time's eunuch, and not breed one work that wakes.
Mine, O thou lord of life, send my roots rain.   (1880?)

The justly famous lines about 'fretty chervil' are an entirely legit-
imate – indeed, inspired – gloss upon 'quicken' in Coverdale's
vv. 154, 156, 159.

  Hopkins's collected poems did not appear until 1918.

THOMAS HARDY (1840–1928)

In Tenebris

I

Percussus sicut foenum, et aruit cor meum – Ps. CI

   Wintertime nighs;
But my bereavement-pain
It cannot bring again:
   Twice no one dies.

   Flower-petals flee;
But, since it once hath been,
No more that severing scene
   Can harrow me.

   Birds faint in dread:
10   I shall not lose old strength
In the lone frost's black length:
   Strength long since fled!

   Leaves freeze to dun;
But friends can not turn cold
This season as of old
   For him with none.

   Tempests may scathe;
But love can not make smart
Again this year his heart
20   Who no heart hath.

Black is night's cope;
But death will not appal
One who, past doubtings all,
    Waits in unhope.

II

*Considerabam ad dexteram et videbam; et non erat qui cognosceret me
. . . non est qui requirat animam meam* – Ps. CXLI

When the clouds' swoln bosoms echo back the shouts of the
    many and strong
That things are all as they best may be, save a few to be right
    ere long,
And my eyes have not the vision in them to discern what to
    these is so clear,
The blot seems straightway in me alone; one better he were
    not here.

The stout upstanders say, All's well with us: ruers have
    nought to rue!
30 And what the potent say so oft, can it fail to be somewhat
    true?
Breezily go they, breezily come; their dust smokes around
    their career,
Till I think I am one born out of due time, who has no
    calling here.

Their dawns bring lusty joys, it seems; their evenings all that
    is sweet;
Our times are blessed times, they cry: Life shapes it as is most
    meet,
And nothing is much the matter; there are many smiles to a
    tear;
Then what is the matter is I, I say. Why should such an one
    be here? . . .

Let him in whose ears the low-voiced Best is killed by the
    clash of the First,
Who holds that if way to the Better there be, it exacts a full
    look at the Worst,
Who feels that delight is a delicate growth cramped by
    crookedness, custom, and fear,
40 Get him up and be gone as one shaped awry; he disturbs the
    order here.   (1895–6)

III

*Heu mihi, quia incolatus meus prolongatus est! Habitavi cum
habitantibus Cedar. Multum incola fuit anima mea* – Ps. CXIX

There have been times when I well might have passed and
    the ending have come –
Points in my path when the dark might have stolen on me,
    artless, unrueing –
Ere I had learnt that the world was a welter of futile doing:
Such had been times when I well might have passed, and the
    ending have come!

Say, on the noon when the half-sunny hours told that April
    was nigh,
And I upgathered and cast forth the snow from the crocus-
    border,
Fashioned and furbished the soil into a summer-seeming
    order,
Glowing in gladsome faith that I quickened the year thereby.

Or on that loneliest of eves when afar and benighted we
    stood,
50 She who upheld me and I, in the midmost of Egdon
    together,

Confident I in her watching and ward through the blackening
heather,
Deeming her matchless in might and with measureless scope
endued.

Or on that winter-wild night when, reclined by the
chimney-nook quoin,
Slowly a drowse overgat me, the smallest and feeblest of folk
there,
Weak from my baptism of pain; when at times and anon I
awoke there –
Heard of a world wheeling on, with no listing or longing to
join.

Even then! while unweeting that vision could vex or that
knowledge could numb,
That sweets to the mouth in the belly are bitter, and tart, and
untoward,
Then, on some dim-coloured scene should my briefly raised
curtain have lowered,
60   Then might the Voice that is law have said 'Cease!' and the
ending have come.   (1896)

Because the Vulgate that Hardy was working from is in its number-
ing one awry from *BCP*, the Latin epigraphs correspond, in Cover-
dale's version, to (I) Psalm 102.4, 'My heart is smitten down, and
withered like grass'; (II) Psalm 142.4, 'I looked also upon my right
hand: and saw there was no man that would know me'; and (III)
Psalm 120.4–5, 'Woe is me, that I am constrained to dwell with
Mesech: and to have my habitation among the tents of Kedar./My
soul hath long dwelt among them . . .'

Hardy had formally 'lost his faith' twenty years before; it's the
more remarkable that at the crisis of his career, when *Jude the
Obscure* failed with the public and with it failed his first marriage, he
should have turned to the psalms to articulate his desperation.

On the Tune Called the Old-Hundred-and-Fourth

We never sang together
   Ravenscroft's terse old tune
On Sundays or on weekdays,
In sharp or summer weather,
   At night-time or at noon.

Why did we never sing it,
   Why never so incline
On Sundays or on weekdays,
Even when soft wafts would wing it
10   From your far floor to mine?

Shall we that tune, then, never
   Stand voicing side by side
On Sundays or on weekdays? . . .
Or shall we, when for ever
   In Sheol we abide,

Sing it in desolation,
   As we might long have done
On Sundays or on weekdays
With love and exultation
20   Before our sands had run?   (1922)

---

2 Thomas Ravenscroft (1590?–1633?) published a famous book of metrical psalm tunes.

ISAAC ROSENBERG (1890–1918)

Rosenberg, a Jew, was born in Bristol, but raised and educated in Stepney. Aspiring to be a painter, he was enabled by benefactors to enrol at the Slade School. He published at his own expense three pamphlets of poems. In 1915 he returned from safety in South Africa, and enlisted. He was killed in action in France on 1 April 1918.

Ode to David's Harp

Awake, ye joyful strains! awake,
In silence sleep no more;
Disperse the gloom that ever lies
O'er Judah's barren shore.
Where are the hands that strung thee
With tender touch and true?
Those hands are silenced, too.

The harp that faster caused to beat
The heart that throbbed for war,
10   The harp that melancholy calmed,
Lies mute on Judah's shore.
One chord awake – one strain prolong
To wake the zeal in Israel's breast;
Oh sacred lyre, once more, how long?
'Tis vain, alas! in silence rest.

Many a minstrel fame's elated
Envies thee thy harp of fame,
Harp of David – monarch minstrel,
Bravely – bravely, keep thy name.
20   Ay! ev'ry ear that listen'd,
Was charmed – was thrilled – was bound.
Every eye with moisture glisten'd
Thrilling to the harp's sweet sound.

Hark! the harp is pouring
Notes of burning fire,
And each soul o'erpowering,
Melts the rousing ire.
Fiercer – shriller – wilder far
Than the iron notes of war,
30 Accents sweet and echoes sweeter,
Minstrel – minstrel, steeds fly fleeter
Spurred on by thy magic strains.

Tell me not the harp lies sleeping,
Set not thus my heart aweeping,
In the muses' fairy dwelling
There thy magic notes are swelling.
But for list'ning mortals' ear
Vainly wait, ye will not hear.
So clearly sweet – so plaintive sad
40 More tender tone no harper had.
O! when again shall Israel see
A harp so toned with melody?   (1905)

See Rosenberg's *Poems*, ed. Gordon Bottomley (1922), and *Collected Poems*, ed. Gordon Bottomley and D. W. Harding (1949).

EDMUND BLUNDEN (1896–1974)

Report on Experience (Psalm 37, v. 25)

I have been young, and now am not too old;
And I have seen the righteous forsaken,
His health, his honour and his quality taken.
  This is not what we were formerly told.

I have seen a green country, useful to the race,
Knocked silly with guns and mines, its villages vanished,
Even the last rat and last kestrel banished –
  God bless us all, this was peculiar grace.

I knew Seraphina; Nature gave her hue,
Glance, sympathy, note, like one from Eden.
I saw her smile warp, heard her lyric deaden;
  She turned to harlotry; – this I took to be new.

Say what you will, our God sees how they run.
These disillusions are his curious proving
That he loves humanity and will go on loving;
  Over there are faith, life, virtue in the sun.   (1929)

From *Collected Poems* (1972).

Blunden's archaisms are exceptionally learned and exact (see 'quality' in the first stanza, and 'note' in the third). This is what gives special mordancy to what is – in Blunden, a survivor of trench warfare in 1914–18 – undoubtedly a repudiation of the Christian promise, as of the promise of the psalm that he alludes to.

RUDYARD KIPLING (1865–1936)

Non nobis Domine! (Psalm 115)

Non nobis Domine! –
  Not unto us, O Lord!
The Praise or Glory be
  Of any deed or word;
For in Thy Judgment lies
  To crown or bring to nought
All knowledge or device
  That Man has reached or wrought.

And we confess our blame –
10 How all too high we hold
That noise which men call Fame,
  That dross which men call Gold.
For these we undergo
  Our hot and godless days,
But in our hearts we know
  Not unto us the Praise.

O Power by Whom we live –
  Creator, Judge, and Friend,
Upholdingly forgive
20 Nor fail us at the end:
But grant us well to see
  In all our piteous ways –
Non nobis Domine! –
  Not unto us the Praise!   (1934)

EZRA POUND (1885–1972)

From *Canto 29* (Psalm 42.7)

Past the house of the three retired clergymen
Who were too cultured to keep their jobs.
Languor has cried unto languor
  about the marshmallow-roast
(Let us speak of the osmosis of persons)
The wail of the phonograph has penetrated their marrow
             (1930)

Cf. *AV*: 'Deep calleth unto deep at the noise of thy waterspouts: all
thy waves and thy billows are gone over me.'

From *Canto 83* (after Psalm 104, probably
via Robert Grant, see *ante*)

With clouds over Taishan – Chocorua
   when the blackberry ripens
and now the new moon faces Taishan
one must count by the dawn star
   Dryad, thy peace is like water
There is September sun on the pools

Plura diafana
   heliads lift the mist from the young willows
there is no base seen under Taishan
10   but the brightness of ὕδωρ
the poplar tips float in brightness
only the stockade posts stand

And now the ants seem to stagger
   as the dawn sun has trapped their shadows,
this breath wholly covers the mountains
   it shines and divides
it nourishes by its rectitude
does no injury
overstanding the earth it fills the nine fields to heaven

20 Boon companion to equity
   it joins with the process
      lacking it, there is inanition

                                    (1949)

Cf. Psalm 104 (Coverdale): 'When thou lettest thy breath go forth
they shall be made: and thou shalt renew the face of the earth'; also
Grant, op. cit: 'It breathes in the air,/It shines in the light,/It streams
from the hills,/It descends to the plain,/And sweetly distils/In the
dew and the rain.' This brilliant conjecture originated with Peter
Makin, in his *Pound's Cantos* (1985).

CARL RAKOSI (b. 1903)

Carl Rakosi, Jewish, was born in Berlin in 1903, but was raised in Hungary. He was taken to the United States in 1910, and was educated in the Universities of Chicago and Wisconsin. He was enrolled by Louis Zukofsky in *The Objectivist Anthology* (1931); it is a classification – 'objectivist' – that Rakosi has never been happy with. See *Carl Rakosi: Man and Poet*, ed. Michael Heller (Orono, Maine, 1993).

From *Exercises in Scriptural Writing*

1.

The king shall understand
that Yahweh is
Lord of four kingdoms.
There is the kingdom of fire
that is the compend of His word.
And the kingdom of the earth
of which men say that it was Eden
(now but merchants).
And the kingdom of the air
10   where birds make offering to our Lord
for His benevolent attitude.
And finally there is the kingdom of water,
history of many winds
and sailors in their salty coffins.
                              Certainly
our Lord is like the apex in the south
and like the sceptre of the north.

2.

Sandalwood comes to my mind
when I think of you
and the triumph of your shoulders.
20 Greek chorus girls came to me
in the course of the day
and from a distance
Celtic vestals too,
but you bring me the Holy Land
and the sound of deep themes
in the inner chamber.

I give you praise
in the language
of wells and vineyards.

30 Your hand recalls
the salty heat of barbarism.
Your mouth is a pouch
for the accents of queens.
Your eyes flow over
with a gentle psalm
like the fawn eyes
of the woodland.

Your black hair
plucks my strings.

40 In the foggy wilderness
is not your heart
a hermit thrush?

You are timeless
as the mirrors,
Jewess of the palm country,
isolate as the frost
on the queen of swans.

Now that I have seen
the royal stones and fountains
50   and the tetrarch's lovely swans,
I am satisfied that you are
a mindful of white birds
in the folly of an old Jew.

Because of the coral
of your two breasts
are the prophets angry
but I have my lips upon them
and the song shall go on.   (1925–39)

ALLEN CURNOW (b. 1911)

From *Not in Narrow Seas* (Psalm 122)

III

Strut on the beach loos'd nervous limbs
And they praised God with bad hymns,
Quavering in a huge volcanic crack
With the iron water at their back.

Doubtless their liturgy had prayer
For establishing truth and virtue there,
For the wind clipping the reverent scalps
Howled the joke to the high Alps:

'We shall not blacken this land O Lord,
10   Thou hast given us without sword;
Our weapon and our lust lie at home
And in peace for peace we are come.'

IV

Escape in seeming from smoke and iron,
The hammered street and the hot wheels,
Clanging conquest of the deep-rich hills.

Left behind the known germ and poison
Breeding and soaking in decrepit soils.

Jerusalem is built as a city
That is at unity in itself,
20   Built with liturgy and adequate capital
Dwelling of the elect, the selected immigrants.   (1939)

Curnow, a New Zealander, celebrates (ambiguously) the establishment in 1850 of the South Island province of Canterbury as the wished-for terminus of, in the words of his prose gloss, 'a pilgrimage under the blessing of the Church of England, more definitely religious in its professions, perhaps, than any since the *Mayflower*'. The allusion in the last lines is to Psalm 122: 'Jerusalem is builded as a city that is compact together' (*AV*).

JACK CLEMO (b. 1916)

Growing in Grace (Psalm 81)

My native clay
Symbols grow unreal.
Blunt clanging tools
Corroded rock
Kiln-scorching . . .
O Shepherd
Of green pastures!

Purgation's landscape
Fails to purge,
10   Makes us afraid.
Slap of hose-jets
Blinding
Deafening blast
Rattle on bleared dunes
Scoops and sirens'
Howl over stagnant mud.

Waters of Meribah,
I proved thee at the . . .
I proved thee.
20   Baptized into the death . . .
O Shepherd
Of green pastures!   (1976)

Psalm 81 names 'Meribah' (in *AV* but not *BCP*): 'I answered thee
in the secret place of thunder: I proved thee at the waters of
Meribah.' It is God speaking; and 'proved' means 'put to the proof
and found wanting'. It is thus in Exodus: 'And he called the name of
the place Massah and Meribah, because of the chiding of the
children of Israel, and because they tempted the Lord, saying, Is the

Lord among us or not?' *Massah* is from the Hebrew verb 'test', and *Meribah* from the verb 'find fault' (*NOAB*, which comments: 'names which became memorials of Israel's faithlessness'). Clemo's poem thus seems to say that we should praise God *because we have failed him*. How this can be appears if we attend to the title, *Growing in Grace*. By ourselves we can do nothing but betray and fall short; only God's grace can save us. But before it can do so we have to be convinced of our inadequacy. Only then can grace descend upon us. The fractured syntax is like that in T. S. Eliot's *Ash-Wednesday* – which is out of the way of Clemo's usual style.

DAVID L. FROST (b. 1939)

Psalm 11

1. In the Lord I have found my refuge:
     how then can you say to me
         'Flee like a bird to the mountains;

2. 'Look how the wicked bend their bows,
         and notch the arrow upon the string:
     to shoot from the darkness at the true of heart;

3. 'If the foundations are destroyed:
     what can the just man do?'

4. The Lord is in his holy place,
         the Lord is enthroned in heaven:
     his eyes search out,
         his glance tries the children of men.

5. He tries the righteous and the wicked:
   and him that delights in violence his soul abhors.

6. He will rain down coals of fire and brimstone
      upon the wicked:
   a scorching wind shall be their cup to drink.

7. For the Lord is righteous and loves righteous acts:
   the upright shall see his face.   (1977)

Francis William Newman wrote in 1847 (*A History of the Hebrew Monarchy*), 'it is credible that David composed the 11th psalm', and if so it 'seems to be his earliest extant composition'. But this depends on Newman's unsupported supposition that it refers to an episode early in David's career, when he was warned, first by his wife Michal and then by Jonathan, not to obey a seemingly friendly summons by Saul to Saul's court.

Psalm 33

1. Rejoice in the Lord, you righteous:
   for it befits the just to praise him.

2. Give the Lord thanks upon the harp:
   and sing his praise to the lute of ten strings.

3. O sing him a new song:
   make sweetest melody, with shouts of praise.

4. For the word of the Lord is true:
   and all his works are faithful.

5. He loves righteousness and justice:
   the earth is filled with the loving-kindness of the Lord.

6. By the word of the Lord were the heavens made:
   and their numberless stars by the breath of his mouth.

7. He gathered the waters of the sea as in a water-skin:
   and laid up the deep in his treasuries.

8. Let the whole earth fear the Lord:
   and let all the inhabitants of the world stand in awe of
   him.

9. For he spoke, and it was done:
   he commanded, and it stood fast.

10. The Lord frustrates the counsels of the nations:
    he brings to nothing the devices of the peoples.

11. But the counsels of the Lord shall endure for ever:
    the purposes of his heart from generation to generation.

12. Blessed is that nation whose God is the Lord:
    the people he chose to be his own possession.

13. The Lord looks down from heaven
    and surveys all the children of men:
    he considers from his dwelling-place
    all the inhabitants of the earth;

14. He who fashioned the hearts of them all:
    and comprehends all that they do.

15. A king is not saved by a mighty army:
    nor is a warrior delivered by much strength;

16. A horse is a vain hope to save a man:
    nor can he rescue any by his great power.

17. But the eye of the Lord is on those that fear him:
     on those that trust in his unfailing love,

18. To deliver them from death:
     and to feed them in the time of dearth.

19. We have waited eagerly for the Lord:
     for he is our help and our shield.

20. Surely our hearts shall rejoice in him:
     for we have trusted in his holy name.

21. Let your merciful kindness be upon us, O Lord:
     even as our hope is in you.   (1977)

Psalm 40

1. I waited patiently for the Lord:
    and he inclined to me and heard my cry.

2. He brought me up from the pit of roaring waters,
        out of the mire and clay:
    and set my feet upon a rock, and made firm my foothold.

3. And he has put a new song in my mouth:
    even a song of thanksgiving to our God.

4. Many shall see it and fear:
    and shall put their trust in the Lord.

5. Blessed is the man who has made the Lord his hope:
    who has not turned to the proud,
        or to those who wander in deceit.

6. O Lord my God,
   great are the wonderful things which you have done,
      and your thoughts which are towards us:
   there is none to be compared with you;

7. Were I to declare them and speak of them:
   they are more than I am able to express.

8. Sacrifice and offering you do not desire:
   but my ears you have marked for obedience;

9. Burnt-offering and sin-offering you have not required;
   then said I, Lo, I come.

10. In the scroll of the book it is written of me,
    that I should do your will:
    O my God, I long to do it, your law delights my heart.

11. I have declared your righteousness
    in the great congregation:
    I have not restrained my lips, O Lord,
    and that you know.

12. I have not hidden your righteousness in my heart:
    I have spoken of your faithfulness and of your salvation.

13. I have not kept back your loving-kindness and your
    truth:
    from the great congregation.

14. O Lord, do not withhold your mercy from me:
    let your loving-kindness and your truth ever preserve me.

15. For innumerable troubles have come upon me:
    my sins have overtaken me, and I cannot see.

16. They are more in number than the hairs of my head:
    therefore my heart fails me.

17. Be pleased, O Lord, to deliver me:
    Lord, make haste to help me.

18. Let those who seek my life to take it away:
    be put to shame and confounded altogether.

19. Let them be turned back and disgraced who wish me evil:
    let them be aghast for shame who say to me 'Aha, aha!'

20. Let all who seek you be joyful and glad because of you:
    let those who love your salvation say always
       'The Lord is great.'

21. As for me, I am poor and needy:
    but the Lord will care for me.

22. You are my helper and my deliverer:
    make no long delay, O Lord my God.   (1977)

Psalm 49

1. O hear this, all you peoples:
   give ear, all you inhabitants of the world,

2. All children of men and sons of Adam:
   both rich and poor alike.

3. For my mouth shall speak wisdom:
   and the thoughts of my heart
      shall be full of understanding.

4. I will incline my ear to a riddle:
    and unfold the mystery to the sounds of the harp.

5. Why should I fear in the evil days:
    when the wickedness of my deceivers surrounds me,

6. Though they trust to their great wealth:
    and boast of the abundance of their riches?

7. No man may ransom his brother:
    or give God a price for him,

8. So that he may live for ever:
    and never see the grave;

9. For to ransom men's lives is so costly:
    that he must abandon it for ever.

10. For we see that wise men die:
    and perish with the foolish and the ignorant,
        leaving their wealth to others.

11. The tomb is their home for ever,
        their dwelling-place throughout all generations:
    though they called estates after their own names.

12. A rich man without understanding:
    is like the beasts that perish.

13. This is the lot of the foolish:
    the end of those who are pleased with their own words.

14. They are driven like sheep into the grave,
        and death is their shepherd:
    they slip down easily into the tomb.

15. Their bright forms shall wear away in the grave:
and lose their former glory.

16. But God will ransom my life:
he will take me from the power of the grave.

17. Do not fear when a man grows rich:
when the wealth of his household increases,

18. For he will take nothing away when he dies:
nor will his wealth go down after him.

19. Though he counts himself happy while he lives:
and praises you also when you prosper,

20. He will go to the company of his fathers:
who will never see the light.

21. A rich man without understanding:
is like the beasts that perish.   (1977)

Psalm 56

1. Be merciful to me, O God, for men are treading me
down:
all day long my adversary presses upon me.

2. My enemies tread me down all the day:
for there are many that arrogantly fight against me.

3. In the hour of fear:
I will put my trust in you.

4. In God, whose word I praise, in God I trust and fear not:
   what can flesh do to me?

5. All day long they afflict me with their words:
   and every thought is how to do me evil.

6. They stir up hatred and conceal themselves:
   they watch my steps, while they lie in wait for my life.

7. Let there be no escape for them:
   bring down the peoples in your wrath, O God.

8. You have counted my anxious tossings;
      put my tears in your bottle:
   are not these things noted in your book?

9. In the day that I call to you, my enemies shall turn back:
   this I know, for God is with me.

10. In God, whose word I praise, in God I trust and fear not:
    what can man do to me?

11. To you, O God, must I perform my vows:
    I will pay the thank-offering that is due.

12. For you will deliver my soul from death,
       and my feet from falling:
    that I may walk before God in the light of the living. (1977)

Psalm 62

1. My soul waits in silence for God:
   for from him comes my salvation:

2. He only is my rock and my salvation:
　　my strong tower, so that I shall never be moved.

3. How long will you all plot against a man to destroy him:
　　as though he were a leaning fence or a buckling wall?

4. Their design is to thrust him from his height,
　　　and their delight is in lies:
　　they bless with their lips, but inwardly they curse.

5. Nevertheless, my soul, wait in silence for God:
　　for from him comes my hope.

6. He only is my rock and my salvation:
　　my strong tower, so that I shall not be moved.

7. In God is my deliverance and my glory:
　　God is my strong rock and my shelter.

8. Trust in him at all times, O my people:
　　pour out your hearts before him, for God is our refuge.

9. The children of men are but breath,
　　　the children of men are a lie:
　　place them in the scales and they fly upward,
　　　they are as light as air.

10. Put no trust in extortion,
　　　do not grow worthless by robbery:
　　if riches increase, set not your heart upon them.

11. God has spoken once, twice have I heard him say:
　　that power belongs to God,

12. That to the Lord belongs a constant goodness:
    for you reward a man according to his works.   (1977)

The superiority of this modern version to others is particularly clear at v. 3, where 'as though he were a leaning fence or a buckling wall' corresponds to (Golding), 'as a leaning mud wall, or as a stone wall that is shaken'; to (*BCP*), 'yea, as a tottering wall shall ye be, and like a broken hedge'; to (*AV*), 'as a bowing wall shall ye be, and as a tottering fence'. Not only is Frost the most concise, but in 'buckling' he finds the word that the older translators had looked for in vain – to distinguish what happens to an unsound wall, from what happens to a fence or a hedge. Moreover he's plainly right to take fence and wall alike as similitudes for the man plotted against, not for the plotters.

Frost is vindicated again if we look at v. 9, which he rejuvenates by going back to the *literal* sense of the Hebrew for 'breath' (rather than other versions' 'vanity'), and for 'lie' (rather than 'deception').

Psalm 71

1. To you, Lord, have I come for shelter:
   let me never be put to shame.

2. In your righteousness rescue and deliver me:
   incline your ear to me and save me.

3. Be for me a rock of refuge, a fortress to defend me:
   for you are my high rock, and my stronghold.

4. Rescue me, O my God, from the hand of the wicked:
   from the grasp of the pitiless and unjust.

5. For you, Lord, are my hope:
    you are my confidence, O God, from my youth upward.

6. On you have I leaned since my birth:
    you are he that brought me out of my mother's womb,
        and my praise is of you continually.

7. I have become as a fearful warning to many:
    but you are my strength and my refuge.

8. My mouth shall be filled with your praises:
    I shall sing of your glory all the day long.

9. Cast me not away in the time of old age:
    nor forsake me when my strength fails.

10. For my enemies speak against me:
    and those that watch for my life
        conspire together, saying,

11. 'God has forsaken him:
    pursue him, take him, for there is none to save him.'

12. Be not far from me, O God:
    my God, make haste to help me.

13. Let my adversaries be confounded and put to shame:
    let those who seek my hurt
        be covered with scorn and disgrace.

14. As for me, I will wait in hope continually:
    and I will praise you more and more.

15. My mouth shall speak of your righteousness all the day:
    and tell of your salvation, though it exceeds my telling.

16. I will begin with the mighty acts of the Lord my God:
    and declare your righteous dealing – yours alone.

17. O God, you have taught me from my youth upward:
    and to this day, I proclaim your marvellous works.

18. Forsake me not, O God, in my old age,
        when I am grey-headed:
    till I have shown the strength of your arm
        to future generations, and your might
        to those that come after.

19. Your righteousness, O God, reaches to the heavens:
    great are the things that you have done;
        O God, who is like you?

20. You have burdened me with many and bitter troubles,
        O turn and renew me:
    and raise me up again from the depths of the earth.

21. Bless me beyond my former greatness:
    O turn to me again, and comfort me.

22. Then will I praise you upon the lute
        for your faithfulness, O my God:
    and sing your praises to the harp, O Holy One of
        Israel.

23. My lips shall rejoice in my singing:
    and my soul also, for you have ransomed me.

24. My tongue shall speak of your righteous dealing
        all the day long:
    for they shall be put to shame and disgraced
        that seek to do me evil.   (1977)

Psalm 76

1. In Judah God is known:
   his name is great in Israel.

2. At Salem is his tabernacle:
   and his dwelling is in Zion.

3. There he broke in pieces the flashing arrows of the bow:
   the shield, the sword and the weapons of battle.

4. Radiant in light are you:
   greater in majesty than the eternal hills.

5. The valiant were dumbfounded, they sleep their sleep:
   and all the men of war have lost their strength.

6. At the blast of your voice, O God of Jacob:
   both horse and chariot were cast asleep.

7. Terrible are you, Lord God:
   and who may stand before you when you are angry?

8. You caused your sentence to be heard from heaven:
   the earth feared and was still,

9. When God arose to judgment:
   to save all the meek of the earth.

10. For you crushed the wrath of man:
    you bridled the remnant of the wrathful.

11. O make vows to the Lord your God, and keep them:
    let all around him bring gifts
       to him that is worthy to be feared.

12. For he cuts down the fury of princes:
and he is terrible to the kings of the earth.   (1977)

Psalm 82

1. God has stood up in the council of heaven:
in the midst of the gods he gives judgment.

2. 'How long will you judge unjustly:
and favour the cause of the wicked?

3. 'Judge for the poor and fatherless:
vindicate the afflicted and oppressed.

4. 'Rescue the poor and needy:
and save them from the hands of the wicked.

5. 'They do not know, they do not understand,
they walk about in darkness:
all the foundations of the earth are shaken.

6. 'Therefore I say, "Though you are gods:
and all of you sons of the Most High,

7. ' "Nevertheless you shall die like man:
and fall like one of the princes." '

8. Arise, O God, and judge the earth:
for you shall take all nations as your possession.   (1977)

This short psalm is very important, because it reveals traces of
polytheism. Psalm 58 is the only other that speaks of a plurality of
gods. *AV* fudges the issue: 'God standeth in the congregation of the
mighty; he judgeth among the gods.' So too Coverdale in *BCP*:
'God standeth in the congregation of princes: he is a Judge among

gods.' Frost, however, is in the right, for the Hebrew is quite unequivocal – 'gods' it is who sit in the council, no mention of 'the mighty' or of 'princes'. And Coverdale plainly falls into contradiction; for if the beings in question are in v. 1 already 'princes', how can princedom be in v. 7 the condition they are demoted to?

We should not try to be hard-and-fast: we speak of Lucifer as Prince of Darkness, and in Job, Satan is one of Yahweh's emissaries, doing his bidding. Obviously, and not unexpectedly, Jewish thought passed through stages on its way to monotheism; at one such stage there were more gods than one, though one reigned supreme among them. We should, however, expect this psalm to be 'primitive', certainly pre-exilic; and it is disconcerting to learn from Oesterley that the psalm cannot be dated even approximately on these grounds, since thought along these lines persisted into the second century B.C.

Psalm 93

1. The Lord is King, and has put on robes of glory:
   the Lord has put on his glory,
       he has girded himself with strength.

2. He has made the world so firm:
   that it cannot be moved.

3. Your throne is established from of old:
   you are from everlasting.

4. The floods have lifted up, O Lord,
       the floods have lifted up their voice:
   the floods lift up their pounding.

5. But mightier than the sounds of many waters,
       than the mighty waters or the breakers of the sea:
   the Lord on high is mighty.

6. Your decrees are very sure:
   and holiness, O Lord, adorns your house for ever.   (1977)

Psalm 105

1. O give thanks to the Lord and call upon his name:
   tell among the peoples what things he has done.

2. Sing to him, O sing praises:
   and be telling of all his marvellous works.

3. Exult in his holy name:
   and let those that seek the Lord be joyful in heart.

4. Seek the Lord and his strength:
   O seek his face continually.

5. Call to mind what wonders he has done:
   his marvellous acts, and the judgements of his mouth,

6. O seed of Abraham his servant:
   O children of Jacob his chosen one.

7. For he is the Lord our God:
   and his judgements are in all the earth.

8. He has remembered his covenant for ever:
   the word that he ordained for a thousand generations,

9. The covenant that he made with Abraham:
   the oath that he swore to Isaac,

10. And confirmed it to Jacob as a statute:
    to Israel as an everlasting covenant,

11. Saying 'I will give you the land of Canaan:
    to be the portion of your inheritance',

12. And that when they were but few:
    little in number and aliens in the land.

13. They wandered from nation to nation:
    from one people and kingdom to another.

14. He suffered no man to do them wrong:
    but reproved even kings for their sake,

15. Saying 'Touch not my anointed:
    and do my prophets no harm.'

16. Then he called down a famine on the land:
    and destroyed the bread that was their stay.

17. But he had sent a man ahead of them:
    Joseph who was sold into slavery,

18. Whose feet they fastened with fetters:
    and thrust his neck into a hoop of iron.

19. Till the time that his words proved true:
    he was tested by the Lord's command.

20. Then the king sent and loosed him:
    the ruler of nations set him free;

21. He made him master of his household:
    and ruler over all his possessions,

22. To rebuke his officers at will:
    and to teach his counsellors wisdom.

23. Then Israel came into Egypt:
    and Jacob dwelt in the land of Ham.

24. There the Lord made his people fruitful:
    too numerous for their enemies,

25. Whose hearts he turned to hate his people:
    and to deal deceitfully with his servants.

26. Then he sent Moses his servant:
    and Aaron whom he had chosen.

27. Through them he manifested his signs:
    and his wonders in the land of Ham.

28. He sent darkness, and it was dark:
    yet they would not obey his commands.

29. He turned their waters into blood:
    and slew the fish therein.

30. Their country swarmed with frogs:
    even the inner chambers of their kings.

31. He spoke the word, and there came great swarms of flies:
    and gnats within all their borders.

32. He sent them storms of hail:
    and darts of fire into their land.

33. He struck their vines and their fig-trees:
    and shattered the trees within their borders.

34. He commanded, and there came grasshoppers:
    and young locusts without number.

35. They ate up every green thing in the land:
    and devoured the fruit of the soil.

36. He smote all the first-born in their land:
    the first-fruits of all their manhood.

37. He brought Israel out with silver and with gold:
    and not one among their tribes was seen to stumble.

38. Egypt was glad at their going:
    for dread of Israel had fallen upon them.

39. He spread out a cloud for a covering:
    and fire to lighten the night.

40. The people asked, and he brought them quails:
    and satisfied them with the bread from heaven.

41. He opened a rock, so that the waters gushed:
    and ran in the parched land like a river.

42. For he had remembered his holy word:
    . that he gave to Abraham his servant.

43. So he led out his people with rejoicing:
    his chosen ones with shouts of joy;

44. He gave them the land of the nations:
    and they took possession of the fruit of other men's toil.

45. So that they might keep his statutes:
    and faithfully obey his laws. O praise the Lord.   (1977)

Psalm 141

1. O Lord, I call to you, make haste to help me:
   and hear my voice when I cry.

2. Let my prayer be as incense before you:
   and the lifting up of my hands as the evening sacrifice.

3. Set a guard, O Lord, on my mouth:
   and keep the door of my lips.

4. Let not my heart incline to evil speech,
       to join in wickedness with wrongdoers:
   Let me not taste the pleasures of their table.

5. But let the righteous man chastise me:
   and the faithful man rebuke me.

6. Let not the oil of the wicked anoint my head:
   for I pray to you still against their wickedness.

7. They shall be cast down
       by that Mighty One who is their judge:
   and how pleasing shall my words be to them then!

8. As when a farmer breaks the ground:
   so shall their bones lie scattered at the mouth of Sheol.

9. But my eyes look to you, O Lord my God:
   to you I come for refuge, do not pour out my life.

10. Keep me from the snare that they have laid for me:
       and from the traps of the evildoers.

11. Let the wicked fall together into their own nets:
    whilst I pass safely by.   (1977)

Frost's versions for *The Liturgical Psalter* are professedly and in practice very conservative. It is the more extraordinary to find in him here a brilliant audacity: 'and how pleasing shall my words be to them then!' How the taunting tone of this (it is not far short of 'Yah-boo') can be conveyed in liturgical song or chant, I cannot imagine. But in so far as Frost's versions are a *literary* exploit (as they unavoidably are), it represents an imaginative solution to a problem that has defeated all other translators and commentators. Unfortunately the psalm in the Hebrew was certainly for liturgical use.

Smart's handling of the crucially corrupt vv. 5–7 is too memorable not to be taken note of:

> No, let the righteous rather thwart
>   And friendly smite my cheek,
> I would not then retort,
>   But be resign'd and meek.
>
> But let not what they give for balm
>   Increase my raging smart;
> Nay, I will pray my psalm
>   Against their hand and heart.
>
> Let such false judges as commend
>   Their harsh precarious prose,
> To this my song attend,
>   Which in sweet measure flows.

'Harsh precarious prose' – so much for commentators!

Frost's 'the pleasures of their table' is surely excellent for the *AV*'s 'their dainties'.

Psalm 149

1. O praise the Lord, and sing to the Lord a new song:
   O praise him in the assembly of the faithful.

2. Let Israel rejoice in him that made him:
   let the children of Zion be joyful in their king.

3. Let them praise him in the dance:
   let them sing his praise with timbrel and with harp.

4. For the Lord takes delight in his people:
   he adorns the meek with his salvation.

5. Let his faithful ones exult in his glory:
   let them sing for joy upon their beds.

6. Let the high praise of God be in their mouths:
   and a two-edged sword in their hands,

7. To execute vengeance on the nations:
   and chastisement upon the peoples,

8. To bind their kings in chains:
   and their nobles with fetters of iron,

9. To visit upon them the judgment that is decreed:
   such honour belongs
       to all his faithful servants. Praise the Lord.   (1977)

DONALD DAVIE (1922–1995)

The Thirty-ninth Psalm, Adapted

I said to myself: 'That's enough.
Your life-style is no model.
Keep quiet about it, and while
you're about it, be less overt.'

I held my tongue, I said nothing;
no, not comfortable words.
'Writing-block', it's called;
very discomfiting.

Not that I had no feelings.
10   I was in a fever.
And while I seethed,
abruptly I found myself speaking:

'Lord, let me know my end,
and how long I have to live;
let me be sure
how long I have to live.

One-finger you poured me;
what does it matter to you
to know my age last birthday?
20   Nobody's life has purpose.

Something is casting a shadow
on everything we do;
and in that shadow nothing,
nothing at all, comes true.

(We make a million, maybe;
and who, not nobody but
who, gets to enjoy it?)

Now, what's left to be hoped for?
Hope has to be fixed on you.
30   Excuse me my comforting words
in a tabloid column for crazies.

I held my tongue, and also
I discontinued my journals.
(They accumulated; who
in any event would read them?)

Now give me a chance. I am
burned up enough at your pleasure.
It is all very well, we deserve it.
But shelved, not even with mothballs?

40   Hear my prayer, O Lord,
and please to consider my calling:
it commits me to squawking
and running off at the mouth.'   (1988)

GORDON JACKSON (b. 1938)

Psalm 1

Oh how well off he will be
       whose nose has not been led by know-alls,
       whose feet have not been swept along with the crowd,
       who has not joined in the laughter of those who belittle
                    whatever is decent.

His pleasure is more on the mind of God;
> it is fixed on him in all seasons.
He is sound as a tree that grows beside running water,
> whose autumn will be full of fruit;
His leaves will never lack green;
10 > his labours will all pay off.
The ones that abandon God will not be so lucky;
> the wind will carry them off like chaff;
In a just society they will have no place;
> on Judgement Day they will not have a leg to stand on.
The ones that seek the Lord, the Lord is already with them;
> but those that get their own way will live to regret it.

> (1992)

Gordon Jackson, introducing his *Asgill Psalter* (which includes this psalm-version), explains: 'Without departing from the awesome authority of Coverdale, I have tried, by shifts of register, to repersonalise the matter, and by giving greater sway to the metaphors, and unity to the rhythm, to recover a feel of their essentially poetic character. I do this in all ignorance of Hebrew, and in great astonishment that no one seems to have done it before.' Accordingly his versions from *The Asgill Psalter* are here interleaved with Coverdale's versions from *BCP*.

Psalm 1   (*Miles Coverdale*)

1. Blessed is the man that hath not walked in the counsel of the ungodly, nor stood in the way of sinners: and hath not sat in the seat of the scornful.

2. But his delight is in the law of the Lord: and in his law will he exercise himself day and night.

3. And he shall be like a tree planted by the waterside: that will bring forth his fruit in due season.

4. His leaf also shall not wither; and look, whatsoever he doeth, it shall prosper.

5. As for the ungodly, it is not so with them: but they are like the chaff, which the wind scattereth away from the face of the earth.

6. Therefore the ungodly shall not be able to stand in the judgement: neither the sinners in the congregation of the righteous.

7. But the Lord knoweth the way of the righteous: and the way of the ungodly shall perish.

Psalm 2

Why are the nations up in arms, and men drawn into insane
    dreams?
The world's rulers are in accord – against God, and the
    Lord's Anointed:
'Old God's authority is at an end – long live the Revolution!'
The Lord in heaven is laughing; to him their threats are a
    joke.
But one day his top will blow, and his fury flow like lava.
Here on my holy mountain, behold the man, the Anointed
I say what I heard the Lord speak –
               You are my Son; this day have I begotten you;
The nations are yours for the asking, the ends of the earth your
    estate:
10   *With a sceptre of iron judge them; smash them to smithereens.*
Learn wisdom smartly, O Captains, and Rulers, remember
    your place:
Bow to the Lord in fear, and rejoice in him with trembling:
Kiss the Son, stay his displeasure, and beware his infolded
    fire;
Once it erupts it will engulf all but the blessed he
    shelters.   (1992)

Psalm 2   (*Miles Coverdale*)

1. Why do the heathen so furiously rage together: and why do the people imagine a vain thing?

2. The kings of the earth stand up, and the rulers take counsel together: against the Lord, and against his Anointed.

3. Let us break their bonds asunder: and cast away their cords from us.

4. He that dwelleth in heaven shall laugh them to scorn: the Lord shall have them in derision.

5. Then shall he speak unto them in his wrath: and vex them in his sore displeasure.

6. Yet have I set my King: upon my holy hill of Sion.

7. I will preach the law, whereof the Lord hath said unto me: Thou art my Son, this day have I begotten thee.

8. Desire of me, and I shall give thee the heathen for thine inheritance: and the utmost parts of the earth for thy possession.

9. Thou shalt bruise them with a rod of iron: and break them in pieces like a potter's vessel.

10. Be wise now therefore, O ye kings: be learned, ye that are judges of the earth.

11. Serve the Lord in fear: and rejoice unto him with reverence.

12. Kiss the Son, lest he be angry, and so ye perish from the right way: if his wrath be kindled, (yea, but a little,) blessed are all they that put their trust in him.

Psalm 8

O LORD OUR GOD, over ALL THE EARTH
  how FULL OF GLORY is YOUR NAME
    you have written it in stars across the heavens:
    to the shame and silence of your enemies
    it speaks in the mouths of sucklings and of babies
    leaving the wisdom of this world confounded;
    under the mighty vast of heaven's vault
    tricked out with the delicate stars your fingers set there
    what is mere man that you respect him so,
10   the kin of Adam that you care about him?
    you created him just two inches short of a god,
    gave him a glorious crown and did him honour;
    you put a sceptre of power into his hands

and all his fellow creatures under his feet;
all sheep and livestock, all the feral beasts,
fowls of the air and fishes of the flood,
all that wander the pathways of the waters.
O LORD OUR GOD, over ALL THE EARTH
how FULL OF GLORY is YOUR NAME.   (1992)

Psalm 8   (*Miles Coverdale*)

1. O Lord our Governor, how excellent is thy Name in all the world: thou that hast set thy glory above the heavens!

2. Out of the mouth of very babes and sucklings hast thou ordained strength, because of thine enemies: that thou mightest still the enemy, and the avenger.

3. For I will consider thy heavens, even the works of thy fingers: the moon and the stars, which thou hast ordained.

4. What is man, that thou art mindful of him: and the son of man, that thou visitest him?

5. Thou madest him lower than the angels: to crown him with glory and worship.

6. Thou makest him to have dominion of the works of thy hands: and thou hast put all things in subjection under his feet;

7. All sheep and oxen: yea, and the beasts of the field;

8. The fowls of the air, and the fishes of the sea: and whatsoever walketh through the paths of the seas.

9. O Lord our Governor: how excellent is thy Name in all the world!

Psalm 27

God is my sun and my destiny; what should I be afraid of?
　　　My strength, my protector; what have I got to fear?
The threats of enemies that prowl about me, that try to trip me,
　　　they are nothing, they are the ones that will stumble.
If a regiment came against me I wouldn't care;

if a whole army came they wouldn't disturb me.
I have asked just one thing of God, I want nothing more;
    to live with him, every day, in my house or his,
    to enjoy him, and all the beauty he gives rise to.
10 In his company, under his roof, how can misfortune touch me?
    he will hide me, he will cradle me in his arms;
He will set me up on a pinnacle, with walls about me;
    the enemies way down below are no cause to fear.
But I have cause to praise him, to sing for joy,
    to lavish thanks on him for all he has done.

Hear the prayer, Lord, that my heart addresses;
    hear, and have mercy; let it touch your heart.
You told me always to look you in the eye;
    now I am looking, don't turn away, I beg you;
20 Even if you are angry, I am still your child.
    I am still your friend, I am still devoted to you.
You have always been my support, don't take it away,
    don't let me down now when I need you most;
My father may let me down, and even my mother,
    but not you, Lord: not you.
Show me how to proceed and what to do;
    don't let the envious get the better of me;
Let us walk together straight through their ambushes,
    let us confound their lies, make them stick in their
      throats.
30 But whatever befall, I know this for sure:
    I shall see the goodness of the Lord in the land of the living.
So wait on the Lord;
    be strong, be courageous, be stubborn;
    but wait on the Lord.   (1993)

Psalm 29

Give the Lord his due, you who are his sons,
Give him his due, worship and honour and thanks;

Put on your smartest dress, and kneel before him.
The voice of the Lord that stirs the mighty waters,
The voice of the Lord that bellows in thunder,
The voice of the Lord that screams in the teeming rain,
The voice of the Lord is power, and majesty,
The voice of the Lord that breaks the hearts of cedars,
The voice of the Lord that flattens the forests of Lebanon,
10   Sirion skips like an ox to hear it, Lebanon like a calf,
The voice of the Lord that explodes the mountains of fire,
The voice of the Lord that causes the desert's contractions,
That makes the desert of Kadesh writhe in labour,
The voice of the Lord that speaks in the pains of labour,
That tears the leaf from the tree, the tree from the ground.
To God in his Temple everything gives glory, glory for ever,
Who gives his strength to his people, who gives his people
          peace.   (1993)

Psalm 33

Enjoy the Lord, you who love what is good;
          if you are just, it will be your pleasure to praise him.
Tell your thanks on the harp and on the fiddle;
          tell it on the ten-stringed rotta.
Sing something avant garde;
          something not done before, something brilliant;
Something you can sing your heart out in;
          something as true as the word of the Lord is true;
Something enduring like that;
10   something he might be proud of.
The Lord loves true art and true justice,
          and his earth is made with a love that never runs out.
One word from him and the heavens came into being,
          and out of his breath the orders of angels filled them.
He held in his hand the seven seas in a bottle,

and blessed the earth with the treasures of the deep.
The earth and everything in it should fear the Lord,
    all creatures be in awe of his wit and power.
He spoke, and it happened;
20   he commanded, and things were made.
He brings to nothing the policies of nations,
    he overturns the peoples' plans and pronouncements;
But the Lord's designs can never be frustrated,
    and his mind shall be known in every generation.
The land whose God is the Lord can count itself lucky,
    its people he has chosen to call his own.
From heaven the Lord looks down on the race of Adam;
    over all the earth there isn't a thing he misses;
He sees whatever we do, but more than that
30   he knows the heart from which any action springs.
No army is big enough to defend a king;
    no strength is great enough to preserve a hero;
No horse has strength or stamina enough
    to help his getaway from the weight of God.
But those who fear the Lord have God for a lookout,
    those who count on his love that never runs out,
He will look after them and be
    their food in famine, deliverance in death.
We have waited on the Lord, we have banked on him;
40   He alone is our hope and our only help.
We trust in one who will not let us down;
    that's why our hearts have good reason to be glad:
And as much as we trust you, Lord, as much as we hope,
    may the love that never runs out be our reward.

(1993)

Psalm 36

Sin speaks to the inmost heart of the man without principle;
    he has no fear of God and is proud of it;
In his own eyes he is highly intelligent;

if he is found out, he reckons he'll get away with it.
He has learnt to be convinced by his own lies;
    he has lost all contact with judgement, all sense of
        good.
Even his dreams are dark with machinations;
    there's nothing too evil for him to contemplate.
But your love that never runs out, Lord, reaches to heaven;
10   your goodness is more expansive than the sky;
Your judgement is sound and strong as the Himalayas;
    your wisdom deeper than the deepest sea.
O God, whose care extends to man and beast,
    how wonderful is your love that never runs out!
Under the shade of your mighty motherly wings
    all creatures of the good earth find sanctuary;
The house of plenty you made shall supply their needs;
    they shall drink of the pleasures you created for them.
All life looks back to you as its source;
20   all light goes back to your brightness.
May those who are yours have love that never runs out;
    may honest men rejoice in the God of the just.
But preserve me from the fate of the proudfoot tyrant,
    and the reward of red-handed violent men;
They grovel about where they fell, gritting their teeth;
    their legs are as broken clay, they are down forever.

(1993)

Psalm 37

Are you incensed because the wicked do so well?
    Do you envy them their success? Forget it.
    They may flourish like leaves, but remember autumn
        is coming.
Be wise; do good, and trust the Lord;
    Mind your own business, leave others to theirs;
    Set your heart on God, and he will look after you.

Confide in the Lord, commit all your dealings to him;
   With him as your backer how can you fail to prosper?
   The good of your name will shine like the sun in the
    sky.
10 Don't be upset by others that prosper dishonestly;
   They get their way, yes, but at what a cost;
   Don't worry; God's mercy is more than money.
Envy will do you no good, neither will anger;
   You know the dishonest will get their just deserts;
   But those who rely on God have a fortune in him.
For a little time the wicked may rule the roost;
   A little time, and no more; others supplant them;
   But in the end the land will revert to the humble.
Green with envy, the wicked detest the honest;
20   They feel derided; God derides them indeed;
   He knows the ending of their curious plans.
Hatred of weakness, of good, excites them to action;
   They are armed with sword and bow and pocket-
    book;
   Weapons they lived by but yet will be their undoing.
Innocents have a power unknown to the wicked;
   The power of arms, of armies, of allies will fail;
   Yet the Lord, unseen, will preserve his own forever.
Justice demands that the Lord will provide for the just;
   Misfortune, oppression, will never distress them long;
30   They will come, with him, through famine, and
    war, and flood.
Kings of the castle may think themselves secure
   But they will fall as sure as autumn leaves;
   They will burn as rubbish, and even their smoke
    will vanish.
Loans to the wicked rarely get paid back,
   But the Lord will repay the good and the bad in his
    time;
   The good are generous givers, and so is our God.
Men with a mind to be upright sons shall be so;

The Lord will hold them steady on their feet;
 From time to time they may stumble, but won't fall
  down.
40 Never have I seen a good man begging his bread,
 Not from when I was young to my old age now;
 He always has something to spare, for friends, for
  the needy.
Order your days; do good; make peace where you can;
 God who loves justice will always favour the just;
 His law will deal with the lawless and their kind.
Possession of lands will pass to those who deserve them;
 Peace follows justice; with peace comes prosperity;
 Who will remember the names of past grasping
  landlords?
Reason and rhyme will season a good man's language;
50 A level head is matched with a witty heart;
 Workman's words that hit the nail on the head.
Stealth is the wicked man's trade, and seeming important;
 Getting the weak in their clutches is their profession;
 But the Lord will not let them keep the fruits of
  their labour.
Trust in the Lord; he will keep you out of their hands;
 You will yet live to see the land you love rejoicing;
 You will see those that ruined it come down
  themselves to ruin.
Up to all sorts of tricks, the unworthy will rise;
 I have seen them dining in their successful villas;
60 I have passed again, and seen them gone and forgotten.
Virtue and honesty leave good things behind them
 Worthy to carry on a good man's name;
 But they try to conceal their names, the disgraced
  ones' children.
When trouble comes to the good, the Lord is their lawyer;
 He will take their case, he will use the law to save
  them;
 Because they were innocent: because they trusted in
  him.
            (1993)

Psalm 41

How well-off is the man who looks after the poor;
        the Lord will do the same for him when he needs it;
The Lord will preserve him, the Lord will prosper him,
        the Lord will protect him from his enemies' spite;
The Lord will nurse him on his sick-bed,
        the Lord will bring him back to health and strength.
Lord, have mercy on me, that is my prayer,
        restore my blemished soul that has sinned against you.
My enemies are gloating over me;
10   He won't last long, they say; his line is finished;
My visitors all come with empty greetings,
        eager for bad news, and keen to pass it on;
My enemies have put their heads together,
        whispering, smiling, waiting for the worst;
He is under a curse, they say,
        confined to his bed, he will never leave it again;
And even the friend I trusted, who ate at my table,
        consents to put the boot in now I am down.
But you can restore me, Lord, you can raise me up,
20   and that will show them;
By that I shall know you delight in me, you forgive me;
        so take the untimely triumph out of their mouths;
And raise me, Lord, and be my health and strength,
        and keep me always under your careful eye;
And blessed be the good Lord, God of Israel,
        as long as time shall last. Amen. Amen.   (1993)

Psalm 44

Our fathers have told us the tale, O Lord,
        and our ears were eager to hear it
Of amazing deeds you did in their days
        and your works in the world before them;

You drove the occupiers from the land to plant your people
        in it;
You dispossessed the settled peoples to give your folk a
        home;
The land was won for our fathers not by their swords,
        not by their strength or courage such as it was,
But by your arm alone, by your right hand,
10   by your face that shone like the sun and favoured us.
You are my God and King, you are the strength of Jacob;
        your name is enough to disperse our enemies.
I do not trust in my bow, or my sword to save me;
        only in you who will put them all to flight.
Our pride is in our God;
        him we will praise as long as suns rise and set.
But today, Lord, why today do you humble us,
        why are we fighting on our own without you?
We turn our backs, we run in all directions;
20   foreigners fill their knapsacks with our treasures;
You have left us to the kind mercy of the butcher;
        we must hide in foreign countries as we can;
You have sold your people and got nothing for us,
        just thrown us away;
You have made us the laughing-stock of neighbour nations;
        they spit on us and laugh;
You have made our name a joke, a word of contempt;
        even the lowest now look down on us;
Look where I will disgrace is always in front of me,
30   I am ashamed even to own my name;
It's become a word of abuse on foreigners' lips
        and dogs me viciously wherever I go.
Though all this has come to pass, you are still our God;
        we still stand by our faith in you;
We have not looked to some other protector;
        we have not turned our hearts elsewhere;
Even when monsters of hell have turned their spite on us;
        when dragon-smoke covered our heads and filled
        our lungs.

If we had set aside the name of our God,
40   if we had prayed and sacrificed to some other,
You would know about it, you would have seen it,
          you who see even the secrets of the heart.
But it's with your name in our hearts we are done to death;
          we are your sheep, slaughtered and offered to foreign
               ·   gods.
So wake up, Lord. What's keeping you?
          Get up, don't let us down till it's all too late.
Why so shy? Do our sufferings embarrass you?
          We are down as low as we can be. We are in the pits.
Get up, while there's still just time to save us;
50   save us, if only for your own self's sake.   (1993)

Psalm 46

God is our refuge, God is our relief,
          an ever-ready help in trouble;
When the earth quakes we shall not be afraid;
          when mountains slide into the sea,
When tidal waves sweep over the land,
          when mountains shake with fire and thunderclaps.
God is our refuge,
          and his city is graced with healing streams;
He lives there himself,
10   it will never be overthrown;
He comes with the break of day
          to protect and provide for it.
Nations shall come to blows,
          powers will rise and fall,
The earth itself will crumble and cower
          when his voice speaks.
But the Lord of Legions fights with us,
          the God of Jacob is our castle wall.
Come and inspect the plans and works of the Lord;

20   look at the ruins he has engineered.
    Over every foot of earth he has stamped out war,
              he has made all armaments redundant;
    The bow is broken, the spear is snapped in two,
              the submarine is gone to scrap.

    Shush! I am God, you know.
              The nations are under my thumb,
                        everything on earth is.

    The Lord of Legions fights with us,
              the God of Jacob is our castle wall.   (1993)

Psalm 49

Now hear this, it concerns you;
          this is a lesson for all to hear,
                    rich man, poor man, beggarman, thief;
Let the wise value wisdom,
          let the discerning take my words to heart,
                    let them weigh the truth of prophecy.
Why should I worry in times when evil prospers,
          When I am hounded and despised,
                    when those who have made it wallow in their
                    power?
10 Can a man worm his way into God's favour?
          Can he plead the importance of his place?
                    Can he buy off his destiny with his wealth?
He can't. He could never afford it.
          And if he could he'd be shelling out for ever,
                    he would never consent to face the fact of death.
Even the wisest die, that's true,
          but the stupid, do they come off any better?
                    Do they keep their gains? Are their graves more
                    comfortable?

Yet they carry on as if there is no tomorrow,
20   as if their businesses will keep them in business,
            as if their names on labels and lands
                will keep them from being 'late'.
But man is no better than livestock in the main:
       one day, as is usual, he is fed and watered;
          the next day, like it or not, he's led
             and slaughtered.
That's the lot of the man who doesn't think,
       of him and all his hangers-on;
          and those who walk in his shoes will find the
          same.
30 Like sheep they are herded into hell
       by Death who is their shepherd
          and the dogs that gladly and loudly do his
          bidding.
No one remembers them on earth
       and under it their bodies stink and rot;
          where just men rule, their souls are only
          shadows.
My life, though, is in the hands of God;
       death has no power over it, nor hell,
          except by his allowance.
So never envy a man his wealth or power,
40   his person, his importance, his prestige;
          he must leave every scrap of it behind.
He must leave all his flatterers and friends,
       his power to purchase what he would, or whom,
          his precious chattels other people fancied,
And go where all the wealthy went before,
       all his important, titled predecessors,
          into a place where no one knows his name.
For man is no better than livestock in the main:
       one day, as is usual, he is fed and watered,
50   *the next day, like it or not, he's led*
          and slaughtered.

Psalm 50

The Lord God, the only God, has sent word
  and the whole world has to come to his summons
    from the sun's first rising to when it sets for good.
Here comes the shekinah, out of regal Sion;
  he comes with a purpose, his mouth is about to
    open.
He is dressed in a robe of fire;
  it wreathes and it rages about him;
    it burns everything in his path.
He orders the heavens above and the lowly earth,
10 he orders everything that he has made
    to witness the judging of his people.
Gather the ones who are mine,
  who bound themselves to me,
    who sealed themselves to me with sacrifices.
It is God himself who sits in the judgement seat
  and all the heavens look to see justice done.

Listen to me, my dear ones,
  I have this to say against you.
    I am God, the one who made you.
20 *It isn't your churchgoing I find fault with,*
  your prayers and offerings regular as clockwork.
I don't exactly need your sacrifices
  or your animals: I'm not a pauper.
You'll find my brand on every one of your cattle,
  my mark on every sheep on a thousand hills;
I don't need rings to tell me which pigeon is which,
  I own the wild rabbits that nobody else lays claim to.
If I am hungry I don't have to turn to you,
  I own the whole supermarket of the world.
30 *Do you think your overdone steak is my delight?*
  Do you think my favourite tipple is billy-goats' blood?

No, give me your private selves,
    your most inward selves,
        and whatever you give your word on, see you do it.
Turn to me frankly in your need and I'll help you;
    The time to give me thanks is when you mean it.

God's message to his enemies is this:

What right have you to open your mouths
    against the very one
40   *who gave you mouths to open?*
You who won't be told,
    no, not even for your own good;
        who turn your backs on me while I'm speaking to you.
You find out a man's a thief, you ask for a lesson;
    your neighbour commits adultery, you say 'So what?'
Your mouths are full of smut and swearing;
    if slander come your way you're eager to spread it.
No one is in your good books, not even your brother;
    not even your mother's son escapes your smearing.
50 *All of these things you've done, and because I was silent*
    you reckoned I was like you at heart, a scoundrel.
But every word you've ever said
    and every deed you've ever done
        I'm going to face you with them.
Think about this, you who put God out of mind,
    think on;
A day will come when they will come for you,
    and nothing on earth will help.

He who only thanks me for what I have done
60   *has done what is proper,*
        and that's all I ask for;
And he who is wise enough to let me guide him
    shall have a God to help him
        and a friend.

            (1993)

Psalm 53

The idiot has persuaded himself
       THERE IS NO GOD.
Men are, in the main, vile; disgusting; depraved;
       as for doing good, none of them tries it,
From high in heaven God inspected the children of Adam,
       to find just one, perhaps, who kept him in mind.
But no, not one; they were infidels to a man;
       and as for doing good, no one was trying it.
They have swallowed up my people as if they were bread,
10   and did anyone think to say grace?
Now look at them, fleeing from shadows,
       wet with fear where there's nothing for them to fear.
Now look again, where they camp against my people;
       their tents are gone, but their bones are left behind
         them.
And in that way shall Israel be delivered,
       when God shall come from Sion to save his people;
Then you'll hear rejoicing out of Jacob;
       then there'll be all-night singing in Israel.   (1993)

Psalm 67

God is good to us, he is blessing us,
The face of God is shining down on us,
His way is shown in every place,
His healing touch has come to every people.
       So let the nations thank the Lord our God
       And all his people praise his holy name.
Let all the nations be glad in their own way,
Let them rejoice that he will judge with justice,
Let them cheer to have so good a government.
10   So let the nations thank the Lord our God

And all his people praise his holy name.
The earth is ripening into harvest
And God, as good as his word, is blessing us.

He is blessing us
He is always blessing us
And end to end of the earth ought to give him thanks.   (1993)

Psalm 68

When God comes up, his enemies turn shadows;
   like mists they are dispersed in his presence;
   melted like wax before a fire;
   blown away like smoke in a wild wind.
So shall the wicked encounter the face of God;
   the true-hearted, though, will greet him as day,
They will crow their good fortune,
   they will laugh for very joy.

Sing for God's sake, make his name an opera,
   who rides on horseback on the desert storm;
Whose very name is Being;
   sing to him from the heart;
Who is father to those that have lost their fathers;
   those that have lost their husbands depend on him;
Whose home is open to all;
   the homeless in him find shelter;
Those that are bound in prison
   in him have freedom that cannot be taken away:
But those that have turned against him
   have made a waterless desert for themselves.

O God, in the days when you walked before your people,
   when you strode yourself across the wilderness,
The earth quaked underfoot,

and the very heavens trembled
In face of the God of Sinai,
      in face of the God of Israel;
Your goodness then was providence for your followers,
      rain to refresh them, even the desert bloomed;
For those that put their trust in you,
30   that dwell in deserts for your sake,
You give them your own country for their own,
      wells in their hearts and in their prayers manna.

The word is out
      and all the women telling the tale,
The Kings have taken to their heels
      and all their armies with them;
Leaving their precious plunder behind
      the old women are helping themselves to;
One has a dove with silver wings,
40   *its feathers tipped with the finest gold,*
Look how it sits on the mantelpiece
      of the cattle-shed she lives in.
Meanwhile the Kings are scattered and blown
      like snowflakes over Mount Zalmon.

The mountains of Bashan tower like gods
      with their many pinnacles and peaks;
Yet, Bashan, looking down from your many peaks
      why do you envy the hill that the Lord prefers,
The hill he is fond of,
50   the hill he calls his home?
Look at his entourage of chariots,
      thousands after thousands,
and all the regiments of angels
      bringing him there from Sinai,
In victory, in triumph,
      all his defeated acknowledge;
All his new neighbours shall yield to him,
      whether or not they like it.

All day and every day
60   the name of the Lord is a blessing,
Who is our daily providence,
        who is our daily protector,
Who keeps death from us,
        who keeps our enemies in check,
Who brings down their pride,
        who makes nothing of their vanity.
I will fetch my people home, says the Lord,
        from the realms of the Dragon, from the depths of
            the sea;
Your feet shall be red with your enemies' blood
70   and dogs shall rejoice at their refuse.

See, the great coming of the Lord
        into his sanctuary, into his holy place;
First comes the choir, then the band,
        and next the dancing-girls with tambourines;
All Israel in this great Festival
        bless the Name of the Lord our God and King;
The little tribe of Benjamin takes the lead
        then all the mighty names of Judah,
Scores out of Zebulon,
80   legions from Naphtali.

Our power is all in God,
        and in that power we shall do mighty things;
To honour your Temple in Jerusalem
        magi and kings shall bring great gifts to you;.
Break the backs that bow down to the Savage Bull,
        and those that suck up to the Golden Calf;
Those that delight in war, break them and their standards;
        let them melt down their gods to pay you tribute;
Let them come on their knees from opulent Egypt,
90   let them come from proud Cush with cap in hand.

Sing to the Lord, all nations of mankind,
      sing songs that revel in him,
Who rode on the heavens before time was,
      before the foundations of the earth were laid;
His voice, when he speaks forth,
      is the mighty thunder;
All power in heaven and earth is his,
      all Israel's strength is his;
Nothing can strike more terror into a heart
100   than his face seen outside of grace;
He is the keeper of Israel;
      he gives his saints their strength and comeliness.

The name of the Lord is a blessing.   (1993)

Psalm 69

Come to my rescue, Lord; the waters are up to my neck;
      I am standing on mud, on quicksand;
The water is rising, it will soon be over me;
      I have shouted till I lost my voice;
My throat is parched, I can't see a thing,
      and, Lord, I can't hold on much longer.
So many hate me, more than the hairs on my head;
      so many, and for no good reason;
There's no appeasing them,
10   not even by giving back things I never took;
You know the truth of it, Lord, what a fool I am,
      you know the sins that I've managed to keep from
         others;
O mighty God, don't let any that trust in you
      be put to shame for anything I have done;
O God of Israel, don't let any that trust in you
      be put to shame for any fault of mine.
For your sake, Lord, I have put up with insults,

I don't dare show my face in public now;
I have to keep away from my kith and kin;
20   my brothers never mention me.
I was your champion, now I'm paying for it;
          they get at me as a way of getting at you.
I fasted, and they called me hypocrite;
          I put on sackcloth, and they called me a show-off;
Important people sneer at me in their speeches;
          in the pubs and clubs there are endless jokes about me.
But I, Lord, while there is still time left to me,
          pray to you.
I know you hear me, I know you will help me,
30   I know you will keep faith and be good to me;
Lift me out of the mire, don't let me sink;
          don't let it all come over my head;
Don't let the waters get me;
          don't let the well be closed, and its cover sealed.
Give me your answer, Lord, now;
          show me once more your love that never runs out;
Don't turn your back on me, Lord,
          not on a servant who loves you as much as I do.
Come to my help, Lord; quickly, if you've a mind to;
40   you know my enemies' strength, and how much I
                    need you.
You know what I've had to put up with,
          you've seen me praying when my heart was broken;
You've seen me humbled over and over again;
          you've seen my patience and my perseverance;
You've seen me struggling without a crumb of comfort;
          I've eaten humble pie; I was given vinegar for my
                    thirst.
And their own tables groaned with a thousand feasts;
          I hope they dig their graves with their knives and
                    forks;
I hope what their eyes popped out at makes them blind;
50   I hope that 'what ached for love' will ache for ever.

Let them be troubled with your indignation;
      let them be scalded with your tears of anger;
Empty their palaces, rip up their tents,
      for setting on the one you were chastising,
For adding vicious blows and vulgar insults
      to him you had already injured.
Let their injustice have its due reward,
      and when they look for justice let them have it;
In the Book of Life where you write the names of the just
60   if you come across theirs be sure to rub them out.
But lift me, Lord, by the hands that love to do good,
      out of this present pain, out of this horror,
And I will use what breath of life remains to me
      singing your praises, tiring your ears with thanks;
You'll like that better than any amount of bulls,
      any amount of hooves and horns and leather.
Let those who are poor take note,
      and those take heart who want to come closer to God:
He hears the poor,
70   and those who honour him he will never let down.
Let the sky praise him, and the earth, and the sea,
      and everything in all three that has power to move;
God will uphold his Sion, he will rebuild Judah;
      and those who love him, those who uphold his name,
They and their children will inherit them,
      they and their children will call those places home.

          (1993)

Psalm 73

God loves his Israel, he loves the open-hearted;
      yet my tongue came close to slipping, and my feet
        as well.
And why? Because of envy, and indignation,
      at how the unscrupulous prosper, and brag about it.

They never go short, they don't know what it means to
                scrape;
      they enjoy good health and get the best of attention;
The problems and sufferings of others pass them by;
      misfortune always seems to leave them alone.
Their pride sits on them like a chain of office,
      and cruel indifference like a cloak of ermine.
Their eyes are spoilt with success;
      mad as their schemes may be they get their own way.
Their mouths are full of mockery and malice;
      no one, not even God, can share majesty with them.
They cheapen everything they talk about;
      whoever listens to them is corrupted.
Why do my people follow them?
      Can't they see them for what they are?
Or don't they care? Do they say
      'If these get away with it, why shouldn't I as well?'
Well, that seems the way of the world;
      'If you can't beat 'em, join 'em.'
In that case I was a fool all my life to be honest,
      to tell the truth, to keep my hands clean.
I've never got anything out of it, that's a fact,
      and it's cost me more than my fair share of trouble.
Yet had I allowed myself to talk like this
      I would have been betraying all decent people;
So I tried to work it out in my head,
      but, hard as I tried, I couldn't get on top of it;
Not till I ventured into the house of God:
      that's where I realized what these men would come
        to.
They think they are standing on firm ground
      but you have made it slippery;
One moment they are so full of themselves,
      the next they are down, with death in close
        attendance;
Lost like a dream that a man forgets when waking,

like images of sleep lost in broad daylight.
When my heart was full of bitterness over it
40   and I was green inside with envy,
Oh what a fool I was, what a silly ass!
          Lord, you must have taken me for a dodo!
Yet I am always with you, you hold my hand,
          you guide me, advise me, someday you'll bring me
             to glory.
You are all that I look for in heaven;
          having you is all that I value on earth;
My heart and my body will fail me someday
          but God I will always possess.
They are lost indeed who have lost you, Lord;
50   you abandon those who have given you up:
But my greatest good and my joy is being near you;
          you are mine, dear God, for ever and ever. Amen.

                                        (1993)

Psalm 79

Look, Lord, at the foreign powers that enter your city,
          that desecrate the sanctuary, that make Jerusalem a
             ruin.
Watch them throw out the corpses of those that served you
          for carrion birds and beasts to do what they will
             with.
See their blood clogging all the drains of Jerusalem;
          there is no one to do them the rite of burial.
Look at the headlines of our neighbour nations,
          let their gibes and their jew-baiting ring in your ears.
How long, O Lord, does it take to get your anger up?
10   You tell us your jealousy is like a fire!
Well, now's a good time to show it to those who oppose you,
          to nations that make nothing of you and yours;

See how they have emptied the homes of Jacob
     and left them smoking stones.
Please don't hold the sins of the past against us;
       look at us now, distraught, and have pity on us.
Save us, O God our Saviour, for your own name's honour;
       erase our sins from your heart, for your own name's
         honour;
The heathen are asking *Where is their god now?*
20   show them, let them see your anger in action.
Have ears for the cries of prisoners in the death-camps;
       in your might and in your mercy set them free.
And remember the words our neighbours used against you;
       make them repent, seven times for every word.
And we, your own folk, the flock you call your own,
       will all our days forever give you thanks
And praise your name through all our generations.   (1993)

Psalm 89

Lord, I shall go on singing for ever and ever
       to celebrate your favours and loving-kindness;
Your goodness is surer than the earth we stand on,
       your promises are like stars, for all to see:
I have made an eternal covenant with my elect,
       sworn to my servant David with an oath;
Your line shall continue to the end of time,
       your throne preside over all generations.
The heavens themselves, O Lord, declare your praises
10   like any congregation of your saints;
Who else who walks on the skies is like the Lord?
       Where is his like in all the court of heaven?
In all the holy assembly who is more awesome,
       who stands head and shoulders above the rest?
Who can compare with you, Lord God of Hosts,
       burning with power and shining with faithfulness?

You curb the boisterous arrogance of the oceans;
　　　　you keep the seas in check, and the waves obey you.
With a single blow you crushed the head of Egypt;
20　　　　with a single arm you scattered your enemies.
You are maker of heavens, you are author of the earth;
　　　　you founded the world, and all that it contains.
The north wind and the south rise at your bidding;
　　　　Tabor and Hermon wear the style of your seasons.
Your arm is strength, your hand is cunning,
　　　　your right hand is commandment.
On truth and justice is your throne established;
　　　　mercy and peace precede you wherever you go.
How lucky are those with the sense to worship you,
30　　　　they are enlightened by you in everything;
They rejoice all day in your name for it is their comfort;
　　　　it will sustain them in every trial they come to;
Your glory is their glory, your strength their strength;
　　　　that's what our pride is, that's what keeps our heads
　　　　　up,
That God himself is our shield,
　　　　that our true king is the Holy One of Israel.
You gave this prophecy some time ago
　　　　to those you trusted:
I picked you out from the crowd and set you above them,
40　　　　*I honoured you with the crown of a warrior-king;*
I set my seal on my servant David;
　　　　with holy oil he became my anointed one.
My hand shall protect him, my arm shall be his courage;
　　　　no enemy will trick him, no adversary get the better of him;
I will defeat their malice myself,
　　　　I will put paid to their mischief.
My faithfulness and mercy shall go with him
　　　　and through my name he shall win his victories.
I will stretch out the strength of his dominion
50　　　　*from the Euphrates to the sea.*
He will call me 'My Father and my God,

my Rock and my Salvation';
I will acknowledge him my first-born son,
            king above all the kings of the earth.
I will maintain my favour to him for ever
            and the covenant I made him will never be broken;
His throne shall stand as long as the heavens stand
            and his line shall never cease;
Should his sons forget my law and his children forsake my
                        judgements,
60   *should they lay my statutes by and ignore my*
                        commandments,
I will bring their folly to book, I will punish them roundly,
            but never deprive them of the love I have sworn to,
            and never forget the word I am bound to honour;
My covenant is firm and my promise fixed;
            To David I swore it on my holiness, and I will not let
                him down.
His line shall run to the end of time,
            his throne prevail like the sun;
It shall continue as long as the moon returns,
            as long as the stars continue in the sky.

70 In spite of that, you reject your anointed one now,
            your face is turned against him, your foot is against
                him;
You have put the promise you made him out of mind,
            and knocked the crown off his head into the dirt;
You have broken down his walls, made his strongholds ruins;
            he is easy plunder; a laughing-stock to all.
You have given comfort and power to his enemies;
            you have broken his sword in battle and left him
                helpless;
His kingdom has come to an end, his throne is toppled;
            his strength and vigour are turned to cowering
                shame.
80 How long, O Lord, will you keep yourself to yourself?
            How long will you keep up your anger?

Remember I am but a man, that my days are numbered,
        that all of us come to the grave and what lies
            beyond it.
And remember your acts of love, Lord, your former mercies,
        and the oath you made yourself to your servant
            David.
Remember the taunts I have had to hear, O Lord,
        the slanders I've had to endure from all and sundry;
Insults to you as well, Lord, not just me,
        all of the line of the king that you anointed.

90   May the Lord's name be praised for ever
        Amen. Amen.   (1993)

Psalm 94

O Lord, the God of retribution,
        O God of vindication, rise and be seen.
Arise and judge the earth
        and give the vile and the arrogant what they deserve.
How long will they enjoy, O Lord,
        how long will the wicked enjoy their spoils?
How long continue effing and blinding,
        how long keep up their swaggering and bragging?
Lord, your own people they beat up in the streets;
10   they enact iniquitous laws against your children;
Widows they murder, and even foreign lodgers;
        they have the stomach to strangle helpless babies;
They reason, *If the God of Jacob has eyes,*
        it's clear he doesn't give a damn about them.
Most brutal of all mankind, take heed to yourselves;
        you think there's a future in folly?
You think the one who invented the ear is deaf?
        you think the inventor of the eye needs glasses?
You think the schoolmaster of nations

20   is wanting the means to correct them?
The Lord knows the thoughts of a man even while he is
                    thinking,
              and knows for the most part they are only empty
              balloons.

But the man who has you, Lord, to teach him,
              I call him lucky;
Sure you lay down the law, but you keep him as well out of
                    trouble,
              while the victors are digging his death-pit.
The Lord will not forsake his own folk,
              he will never abandon his people;
And justice will follow the man who is just
30   and the true of heart stand in the heart of truth.
Who will stand and be counted with me against the corrupt?
              Who will support me against the workers of evil?
Had the Lord not been my backer
              I would by now be shut up and in my grave;
When I felt my feet go from under me
              I was standing on air, Lord; your love was holding
              me up.
Yes, like anyone else I have practised how to worry,
              but your presence sooner or later puts all things right.
Could you ever, under title of law, be a party to crime?
40   Could you lend your support to any perversion of
              justice?
They will drag the innocent before their tribunals,
              and condemn the blood of the righteous to be shed;
But the Lord himself is my safety,
              my rock and my refuge is God.
Who will vindicate the just, and guarantee
              their retribution to the promoters of wrong;
The Vindicator will bring their schemes to nothing;
              the Lord our God will stop their mouths for good.
                                                (1993)

Psalm 104

Honour the Lord, my soul;
            for you, Lord, are my God and you are magnificent;
Your majesty is splendid as the sun's;
            you are the very essence of light;
You set up the heavens as if they were a tent;
            their stable footings stand upon the waters;
The terrible storm-clouds are your chariot
            that rides on the hurricane's wings;
The winds post with your messages
10   and angels quick as lightning do your bidding;
You laid the earth on its firm foundation stone,
            now nothing will ever shift it;
Not even the deep that covered it once like a cloak
            and hid the tops of the mountains;
At your command they cowered, they ran away,
            they shrank back to their station in the valleys;
You set a bourn for them and a boundary stone
            that they dare not pass to cover the earth again;
You pierce the mountainsides with pleasant springs
20   and they fill the hills with the sounds of running water;
The beasts of the field are glad of them,
            the wild asses drink their fill;
The birds of the air are grateful for their greenery;
            their song comes out of the leaves;
You look down on your mountains and water them
            so that all of your fields are the richer;
Your livestock thrives on the grass you grow for them
            and man on your table of greens;
He gets his bread out of the dirt of the earth
30   and wine that gladdens his heart;
The oil that brings a shine to his face
            and the meat that keeps up his strength;
You give the trees of the forest rains for their thirst,

cedars of Lebanon that were green shoots once
The Lord himself had planted – see them now,
    a paradise of birds, a tenement of untidy storks;
You give the mountain-goat on the hills his living
    among the boulders that house the whistling marmot;
Your moon and its phases tells us the time;
40   your sun keeps pace with the seasons;
As soon as it sets the night comes on,
    with darkness, and those the night hides;
They come out, the lions, the creatures of the dark,
    they bay to the Lord for their food;
And when your day dawns they slink back
    to take their rest in the shadows;
But man then goes off to his work
    and his shift will last till the evening.
What you have created, O Lord,
50   how many, how varied, how amazing!
The Milky Way and the molecules,
    who can tell us how you have done it?
Your sea is a thing unfathomable
    with its own strange population,
Numberless under our trafficking ships,
    that Leviathan has for a playpool.
And all of us look to you, Lord,
    when the hunger-pangs remind us;
As soon as you give we guzzle,
60   we trust you at feeding-time;
When you hide your face we are troubled;
    when you hold back your hand we bite the dust;
Breathe life into us, we revive,
    and the earth comes to life again.
All glory is God's, and for ever,
    and his joy is in all of his works.
He has only to look at the earth and it quakes;
    one touch, and the hills are on fire.
As long as I live I will love the Lord,

70   all day I will sing my God lovesongs.
May what I sing him please him,
        may he take delight in my thoughts.
And let those that deny him be nothing,
        be as if they had never been made.

And you, my soul, praise the Lord.

Do honour to him who made you.   (1993)

Psalm 108

My heart is firm, O Lord, it is centred on you;
        it is tuned and taut as a string, and ready for music;
I will dawn with the day, with the birds that wake up
        singing,
        and lift my spirit to you in a fulsome psalm;
I will fill the air with thanks, and the ears of all people;
        my voice will carry your praise to the ends of the
        earth;
Your love that never runs out outstretches the heavens;
        your truth looks down on altitudes of sky.
Let us see your face, O God, high over the heavens,
10   your glory shining down all over the earth;
And deliver all in need who are dear to you;
        hear us, O Lord; save us with your right hand.

This is the holy word the Lord has sent us:
        I will arise and carve up Shechem into pieces;
I will measure the vale of Succoth and parcel it out;
        Manasseh is mine, and so is Gilead;
Mount Ephraim will guard my head, Judah will house my
        lawcourts;
        Edom will be my footstool, Moab my lavatory;
My battle-cry will terrify Philistia.

20   Such was the prophecy of old;
    But who will lead us into Edom now?
              who will make the strong-walled city surrender,
    If you, Lord, have abandoned us,
              if you don't lead our armies out against them?
    Lord, in our trouble be our help,
              because no human help is any good;
    But with your assistance we shall all be heroes
              because we shall have some share in your victory.

                                                              (1993)

Part 1 of this psalm is the same as Psalm 57; part 2 the same as
Psalm 60.

Psalm 109

O God that I take pleasure in praising,
          why are you quiet when others have plenty to say?
They lie through their teeth about me, they lie to my face;
          they hedge me around till I have no one to turn to.
They reward the help I gave them with an attack,
          with accusations that make me out some monster;
For the good I did they pay me out with evil,
          and in return for love all I get is their spite.
Those that have good reason to pray for me
10   give me this curse instead:
Give him a master who knows how to undermine him;
          a right-hand man to store up accusations;
Let him come out of the court with guilt stamped on him;
          let his pleading with God fall on deaf ears;
Let the remainder of his days be few;
          let him see someone he hates take over his office;
Let his children want a father;
          let his wife want a husband;
Let his children beg in the streets,
20   *friendless and homeless;*

Let all his goods come to the pawnbroker,
       let strangers bid for them in public auctions;
Let not a soul stick by him;
       let none take pity on his orphaned children;
Let his line be brought to a close,
       let his name be discontinued beyond the present;
Let the sins of all his fathers be visited on him;
       and let all his mothers' sins be openly broadcast;
Let them remain in the record-books of the Lord,
30   *and let him wipe out their names from the earth instead.*
Such as will pray like this shall never know
       what friendship is, or loyalty;
He is a hunter of the down-and-out,
       a hound who has got the scent of the broken-hearted;
For his love of cursing, let him reap the curse he has sown;
       may he have all the blessings he ever wished on
          others;
He revelled in cursing as a king in his robes;
       may it cover him like a rash, and eat into his bones;
Let it be a skin to him,
40   a tight-fitting costume that he can never take off.
So may the Lord treat all who falsely accuse me,
       all who seek to destroy me with perjury.
But you deal with me, Lord, as honour requires;
       deliver me by your love that never runs out;
You see how down I am, how broken in spirit;
       I am only a shadow, faint, and as light as a cricket;
With fasting and prayer I can't stand straight on my knees;
       I am fainting for want of food;
The sight of me has become a joke,
50   it cheers them up to see me.
Help me, Lord, and save me,
       by your goodness that never runs out;
And let all men know this is your doing,
       that the honour is yours alone.
They will curse, but you will give blessing;

they will come in the end to shame, but we shall
            have joy;
My accusers shall wear their dishonour
        and their shame for all to see;
And I will open my mouth to the Lord
60   to give thanks before all, and to praise him,
For standing beside the poor and the honest,
        standing up against all satans for them.   (1993)

Psalm 111

Hallelujah!

All that I am I offer in praise of the Lord,
Being in the band of the blessed, all good men and true.
Can we give adequate, accurate praise for his works?
Dearer and dearer he is to us, as we consider them.
Exalt him as much as we may he is always more worthy
For the meters of mortals are useless to measure his good
    with.
Great is his name, and yet he deserves a far greater;
Heaven's his nickname, and Holiness, Mercy, Truth, Grace.
10 If those who fear him hunger, see how he feeds them!
Keeping his word for his own honour's sake;
Look how he gave his people the lands of others,
Making them gifts of cities by his own strength.
Nothing he does that is not done deeply with justice;
On stone his laws are written, and they will not adjust;
People and fashions will change, but not his wisdom;
Right is right with him, and truth is truth.
Saving his people again and again he is faithful
To a promise his people have broken again and again.
20 Unworthy as we are, his holy name honours us;
Vital wisdom it is that we trust him and fear him,
Wanting his teaching, enjoying our own understanding,
Yielding our wisdom to his, and gaining by giving.   (1993)

Psalm 112

Hallelujah!

A man who bows himself to the Lord is in clover,
Blest with the joy he finds in divine directives;
Celebrated far and wide for his children's accomplishments,
Delighting in their integrity most of all.
Every good thing shall have place within his house,
For his own heart is a just and intelligent measure;
Good is his beacon in all things, even in darkness,
Honest men find him a great encouragement;
10   In generosity nobody will outdo him,
Just in his dealings, jealous of his good name;
Let things go against him, he'll never bend or buckle;
Men will long remember his name with respect.
News of disaster will not dismay him
Or ever unsettle the trust he puts in the Lord;
Patience and perseverance are his watchwords,
Quiet in spirit as enemies triumph, and fail.
Rich is the man who freely gives to the needy,
Sustained by the Lord who so freely gives to his own;
20   Trusting and true, he may hold his head up high.
Ungodly souls shall be aggrieved to see it,
Violent hatred and envy shall tear them in two,
While all their evil hopes are disappointed.   (1993)

Psalm 113

Hallelujah!

Praise the Lord, you that delight to serve him,
        praise the High Name of God.
Bless the Lord's Holy Name,

bless him today and for ever.
When the sun comes up may the Lord be praised
non-stop till the time of its setting.   (1993)

Psalm 115

Not ours, Lord, no, not ours,
        the glory is yours alone,
The honours belong to your name
        for keeping faith with us, for your love that never
            wearies.
Why do the godless ask
        Where is their God in hiding?
He hides in his heaven as clear as the day
        and he does whatever he pleases.
They have their statues made out of gold and silver,
10   gods that workmen have moulded;
Mouths they have, but you never hear them speak,
        eyes that can't make anything out;
Fitted with ears but they never hear a thing,
        and nostrils they can't smell with;
Hands they can't feel with, feet they can't walk on,
        and throats they can't get a sound from.
Those who made them will come to be like them,
        and those who put their faith in them as well.
But Israel, you have the Lord to trust in,
20   to be your helper and to be your shield;
House of Aaron, you have the Lord to trust in,
        to be your helper and your shield;
God-fearing men, you have the Lord to trust in,
        to be your helper and your shield;
The Lord always keeps us in mind;
        he is always ready to bless us;
He will bless the race of Israel,
        he will bless the house of Aaron;

He will bless every one that respects him,
30   no matter how poor, or how rich.
Let the Lord be your prosperity,
         you and your children after you;
Live in the joy of his blessing
         who has made both heaven and earth;
The heavens are his, and his people's,
         and the earth that he shares with mankind.
The dead, Lord, offer no praises,
         nor those that are quiet as the grave.   (1993)

From *See Me Through: a version of Psalm 119*

Give a mind to your word on which
    your servant builds his hopes;
Gratitude for it makes light of
    all the afflictions that pinch me.
Gentlemen knowingly sneer at
    the way I cling to your word;
Good you have been in the past
    and the memory heartens me now.
Gainsaying your say is the fashion;
10   blasphemous words make me cringe.
Gibberish jangles about me, yet
    within is the PSALM of your law.
Gloom gathers round us, grim ogre;
    I hold on to the hand of the LORD:
Grant me no more than this
    that I never let go and get lost.

Hear this: what I own is the
    LORD – to obey, to observe, to adore;
Hasn't my heart besieged him with
20   'O LORD, make haste to help us'?
Having weighed all in the balance

I turn to your music's measure,
Happy to keep to the rhythm
    your law excites within me.
Heretics hustle and heckle, but
    I hold to the whole of your word;
Hour by hour I praise you –
    you are just in every season.
How I embrace them that love you,
30   that have their joy in your word.
Hilarity hallows the earth, O LORD,
    as your homilies hallow me.

In fulfilment of your word,
    O LORD, you have been good to me.
Instruct me in reason and knowledge;
    all learning is love of your law.
I was wrong when I thought I
    had wisdom, but you taught
    me my lesson – in love.
40 Intense is your goodness, inerrant;
    just teach me, and I will learn.
Insolent wit of the clever I
    forget when I mind your mind;
Ignoring your ignorant mockers,
    my pride is in knowing your will.
It is good to be schooled in affliction
    if it gains me knowledge of you.
Isn't one word of your mouth worth
    mountains of silver and gold?

50 Just as you made me, as truly
    PERFECT my understanding.
Jovial faces surround me
    of others revering your word.
Judgements, O LORD, of your
    mouth – they only are just,

though they hurt me.
Joy of your kindness I cherish;
    you promised – be kind to me now.
Jubilance follows your justice;
60   have mercy on my condition.
Justly the crestfallen liars
    submit to the law that I love;
Joined to all those that respect
    you, we many – UNITED – rejoice.
Jewels of lore my adornment,
    and I jealously guard them all.

Keeping watch for the word of
    your coming – my soul is
    worn out YET IT HOPES.
70   Keen was the lookout I kept; oh
    when will it come to restore me?
Kitchen smoke kippers a wineskin;
    I am shrivelled as much, yet I trust.
Kept in suspense, my time passes;
    your answer must surely come soon.
Killers prepare me an ambush;
    they take no account of your law;
Knives in their hands at the ready,
    make speed to save me, O LORD.
80   Knocked senseless, kicked and nigh
    dead, but still I wait on your word.
King of all kindness, O save me
    let me prosper IN YOUR HELP.

LORD, your word is inscribed
    indelibly in the heavens;
Laws that you laid the earth by
    keep faith with our generations;
Lasting and life-giving logic
    that loyally follows your will.

90 Lost I would be through affliction
        if love had not bound you to me.
    Life is the lot you supplied me,
        a lesson I tell your love by.
    Learning your will is my study:
        as I am your own, oh save me.
    Liers in wait look to trap me,
        but I lie in wait in your will.
    Limits curb even the best things
        but not the regime of your
100   GOODNESS.

    Meditating the meaning of law
        moves me to love you extremely;
    Makes me wiser than all detractors
        when my mind paces its maze.
    More than my teachers I master
        when I set my heart on your mind;
    More than doctors of divinity when
        I keep your directions in awe.
    Mindful of your commandments
110   I consider each step with care;
    Measured against your meaning,
        moving as if you moved me.
    Meat to my hunger your mysteries,
        music to marry my feet to.
    Manifest through your mandata
        the sly double-dealing of SIN.

    Newel for all my steps is your will,
        your word is a torch for my way.
    Never to flout your just decree
120   I give you my oath, and will keep it.
    Now quicken up my life, O LORD,
        send word to the heavy-hearted;
    News from heaven makes merry,

let me have word from you soon.
Narrow escapes I am used to, the
   ways of your will are well-known.
Need of your mercies each morning
   shall keep me close to your voice;
Nurtured upon your own promise
130   that I shall inherit in time –
Nothing shall keep me from it,
   nothing, from claiming MY OWN.   (1986)

Contrast with the penultimate section here, the exercise on the initial 'M', what *NOAB* makes of it:

Oh, how I love thy law!
   It is my meditation all the day.
Thy commandment makes me wiser than my enemies,
   for it is ever with me.
I have more understanding than all my teachers,
   for thy testimonies are my meditation.
I understand more than the aged,
   for I keep thy precepts.
I hold back my feet from every evil way,
   in order to keep thy word.
I do not turn aside from thy ordinances,
   for thou hast taught me.
How sweet are thy words to my taste,
   sweeter than honey to my mouth!
Through thy precepts I get understanding;
   therefore I hate every false way.

Verse by verse Jackson can be seen to cleave to the *AV* version as faithfully as *NOAB* does, but to have re-experienced the experiences of the Hebrew poet, not just followed the run of the Hebrew words. This saves him from the exclamatory, priggish or stroppy voice that comes through the *NOAB* version. One might from this comparison take off into an examination of modernizing Scripture generally: no doubt at all, such modernizing is 'legitimate' – as much in the twentieth century as in the seventeenth; but only on the understanding that the modernizer is learned in, and alert to, the semantic and other history of English over the centuries to the present day. And such persons are far harder to find than anyone wants to acknowledge. Even when one of them like Gordon Jackson is found, his talent is not harnessed by co-opting him on to a committee where his 'input' is taken note of. Reliable, not to speak of memorable, translations are just not arrived at in this way. Jackson's ingenious approximation to the abecedarian acrostic structure of the Hebrew is from this point of view the least of his virtues.

Psalm 123

I lift my eyes up to heaven
   for it's said that's where you live.
As a slave's eye is fixed on his master's hand,
   and the slave-girl watches her mistress,
So are our eyes on the Lord our God
   as we await his mercy.
Show us your mercy, O Lord, show us your love,
   we have had so much to put up with;
I don't think we can take it much more,
10   the rich man's ridicule,
     the pride of the man of power.   (1993)

Psalm 124

Had the Lord not been with us, Israel can say,
   had the Lord not been with us when they attacked,
When their temper was up against us,
   they would have eaten us alive;
The floods would have swept us away,
   the waves overwhelmed us,
And wallowing in the waters we would have drowned.

But the Lord be praised, who preserved us from their teeth.
We had a narrow escape
10   like a bird from a fowler's trap;
The trap just broke,
            and so we got away.
It was the name of the Lord that came to our help,
            the manufacturer of earth and heaven.   (1993)

Psalm 135

Hallelujah!

Praise the name of the Lord;
            you who desire to serve him,
Who delight to be in his house,
            who come each day to his courts, praise him.
Praise the Lord, it is good to;
            honour his name with psalms, it will gladden your
                  hearts.
The Lord has chosen out Jacob for himself
            and Israel for his favour.
10 The Lord is great beyond reckoning,
            the Lord is above all gods.
The Lord does what he pleases,
            in heaven and earth, and in the depths of the seas;
He raises clouds from the ends of the earth,
            he unleashes their rains with lightning,
And he calls forth winds and forth they come
            from the places where they were hidden.
All the firstborn in Egypt, both man and beast,
            he struck them down.
20 He showed his power to Egypt in signs and wonders,
            to Pharaoh and all his subjects.
He undid the might of the nations,
            he did for their kings,

Sihon king of the Amorites, Og of Bashan,
     and all the potentates of Canaan,
Giving their lands to Israel
     to be his people's possession.
Your name will live forever, O Lord,
     all generations shall praise you,
30   Who will see that justice shall be done
     and compassion shall grace your people.
The gods of the heathen are silver and gold
     that the hands of men have moulded;
They are made with mouths that cannot speak
     and eyes unable to see;
They are given ears that do not hear
     and noses that cannot breathe:
Those who fashion them make themselves the same,
     as do all who try to trust them.
40   But sons of Israel, you will bless the Lord;
     sons of Aaron, you will bless the Lord;
Sons of Levi, you will bless the Lord;
     and all who respect the Lord will bless the Lord.
In Sion forever shall the Lord be blessed,
     and in Jerusalem his city.

Hallelujah!   (1993)

Psalm 142

I cry to the Lord, loudly I call upon him;
     I pour all my troubles out to him in abandon.
When my courage is come to an end
     you are here beside me.
You know the way I should go,
     you know where their traps are.
At my right hand I have no friend to count on,
     and no escape in sight, no rescue to hope for.

So I cry to you, Lord,
10   I tell you 'You are my refuge;
You're all that I have
        in this life and any other.
Hear what I ask, as I ask it in desperation:
        save me from those who are hunting me, Oh so
            many!
Just get me out of this hole
        and I'll praise you for ever,
With all who are loyal as well
        giving thanks for your favour.'   (1993)

Psalm 143

Lord, hear my prayer, as you are faithful hear me,
        as you love justice listen to my plea;
But not as a judge armed with rigour of law,
        since in that case there's not a man living could face
            you.
You know my oppressor hounds me, has ground me down,
        has darkened things so much I wish I were dead;
You know how depressed I am,
        I try to pick myself up but it doesn't work.
I dwell on the past, the prayers you answered,
10   I call to mind the wonders your hands have done.
I lift my open hands to you, to fill them;
        I am a waste land that pleads with you for water.
Hear me, Lord, before it's too late;
        don't turn away and leave me to sink or swim;
Let me see your love again with the light of the morning,
        as much as I have put my trust in you.
I have made my heart an empty sheet before you
        for you to write on; tell me what to do.
Save me from them, Lord;
20   I am counting on you.
As you alone are my God, let me know your pleasure;

let your spirit light up the road you have set before me.
For your own name's sake, Lord, save me;
    save those who honour you, who turn to you for
        justice.
And as you love me, spare me my enemies' triumph;
    and as I serve you, deal with your servant's
        tormentors.   (1993)

Psalm 145

Allworthy God, I honour you as my king,
    and as long as I have breath it will praise your name;
Be my days many or few, each one will bless you
    each one be a holy day as I give it to you;
Can anyone overpraise the Lord,
    can anyone exaggerate his greatness?
Don't his miracles simply astonish us,
    don't witnesses find it hard to make others believe in
        them?
Essentially my theme is one and the same,
10   your glory that is hidden in private knowledge;
For all that your public displays of saving power
    fill men with awe and profitable fear,
Grateful and humble hearts keep their gladness close
    and treasure the infinite goodness you graced them
        with.
He is gracious, they know, he is considerate,
    he is patient, he is kind beyond compare;
Isn't he everyone's God, and his love
    available to all his beloved creatures?
Justly, O Lord, your creatures who know you praise you,
20   rightly they find in you a blessing each day;
Let them enlarge their language to talk of your glory,
    let them tell their own tale,
Making no bones about what they know of you,
    you and your Majesty, you and your dearest Mercy;

Not to diminish with anger, not to decline with age,
>no, your goodness is faultless, and your mercy is
>>perfect.
Oh how true to his word he is, how reliable;
>once he has given a promise then count it fulfilled;
Perhaps you will trip, maybe fall, he will help you up;
30 >perhaps be depressed, he will help you get out of it.
Quail they do not who look to you, Lord, in hope,
>and sure enough you stead them in your season,
Ready and bountiful and providential
>you give your living creatures what they need.
See if he isn't just in all his ways,
>see if he isn't true to his every word;
Try him and see, come close as you dare to him,
>and if you are straight with him he will show you
>>his love.
Up to your eyes in worry, just ask for his help;
40 >be honest with him, be frank, and he will respect you.
Vicious and oily souls have good cause to fear him,
>but those who respect him he will account his own.
Which is why I have good reason to praise the Lord,
>and why we should all bless his name for ever and
>>ever.   (1993)

This is another acrostic psalm (the last of these in the Psalter); and
Jackson, dutifully but inventively, goes through the alphabet from
A to W, missing K, for the initial letter of every other line.

Psalm 146

Hallelujah!

Praise the Lord, my soul,
>praise him as long as breath remains,
Praise God with psalms as long as your being lasts.

It's useless to trust in ministers, or any man;
      they have no power to help;
They too when their time comes will surrender their breath;
      they will come to dust, and what can they do for
        you then?
But he whose helper and friend is the God of Jacob
10   is really in luck; whose hope is in the Lord,
The one who has to his credit the whole creation,
      heavens and earth and seas and everything else;
Who is true to his promises,
      who guarantees his justice to the just,
Who is bread to the hungry,
      who is freedom to the enchained;
Who is sight to the blind,
      who bears the cross of the burdened,
Who is ever the friend of innocence,
20   who is the foreigner's protector;
Who is the champion of orphan and widow,
      who brings the double-dealer to final audit.
He is the Lord and his reign shall last for ever;
      he is your God, O Sion, and always will be.

Hallelujah!   (1993)

Psalm 150

Hallelujah!

O praise God: in the holy chancel of his love
      in the mighty nave of his creation.
O praise God: for all his intricate artefacts,
      for all his grandeur of design.
O praise God: sound his name with brass,
      pick it out on harpstrings.
O praise God: write it with dancing in the dust,

sign it with flutenotes on wind.
10 O praise God: on cymbals wake the dead with it;
        transmit it through all outer space;
every drawn breath speaks his honour.

Hallelujah!   (1993)

JEREMY HOOKER (b. 1941)

At the Statue of Isaac Watts

1.

Image set
Among sticky buds:

Dated, the marble
Establishes a prodigal
Home for good.

Clear through traffic,
Trains and horns
The Civic Centre chimes
'Our God, our help . . .'

2.

10 The measured tide
Moves congregations;
Its undertow sways
Outside the walls.

Across the narrow sea
From Western Shore
(Refinery hazy
Under the Forest)
An impure land delights.

Against sluggard wit
20　And muddy spirit,
Dr Watts stands proof.

At his granite base,
Place tributary strands
Of living wrack.　　　　　　　　　　(From *Solent Shore*, 1978)

CLIVE WILMER (b. 1945)

The Earth Rising

The men who first set foot on the bleached waste
That is the moon saw rising near in space
A planetary oasis that surpassed
The homesick longings of their voyaging race:

Emerald and ultramarine through a white haze
Like a torn veil – as if no sand or dust
Or stain of spilt blood or invading rust
Corrupted it with reds, browns, yellows, greys.

So visionaries have seen it: to design
10　Transparent, luminous and, as if new-made,
Cut from surrounding darkness. Praise the Lord,
For *Heaven and earth* (the psalmist sang) *are thine*;
The foundation of the round world thou hast laid,
And all that therein is. And plague and sword.
　　　　　　　　　　　　　　(From *Of Earthly Paradise*, 1992)

Psalm 137

Here the waters converge and in their fork
    we sit on the ground and weep.
        So this is exile.

Their currents flow by me. Why should they heed
    a man in love with the past
        of his own country,

lost to him now, elsewhere? Our home river,
    gone underground, flows counter.
        And when our masters –

10   half in mockery, yet half curious
    to hear such foreign lore –
        call for an old song,

I hang my harp high on a willow bough
    leaning across the flood.
        Jerusalem,

let the hand that writes these verses wither and die
    if I forget you now
        in this ill time;

Let my tongue stick in my throat if I sell short
20   the source of all my words,
        fail to remember

where my joys began. In the mean time,
    Daughter of Babylon, you
        have humbled us:

you may publish us to the world, you may ignore us.
    But we have time. In time
        we will be revenged.   (1992)

When first published, this piece was headed, simply, 'Psalm'. And it is true that it can be given a secular meaning, having to do with the poet, his responsibility, and his audience.

TABLE OF PSALMS IN TRANSLATION